WARRIORS OF WIND AND ASH

MERCILESS DRAGONS BOOK TWO

REBECCA F. KENNEY

This book is a work of fiction. Names, characters, places, and incidents are the product of the author's imagination or are used fictitiously. Any resemblance to actual events, locales, or persons, living or dead, is coincidental.
Copyright © 2024 by Rebecca F. Kenney
All rights reserved. In accordance with the U.S. Copyright Act of 1976, the scanning, uploading, and electronic sharing of any part of this book without the permission of the publisher is unlawful piracy and theft of the author's intellectual property. If you would like to use material from the book (other than for review purposes), prior written permission must be obtained by contacting the publisher at rfkenney@gmail.com. Thank you for your support of the author's rights.

First Edition: September 2024

Kenney, Rebecca F.
WARRIORS OF WIND AND ASH / by Rebecca F. Kenney—First edition.
Cover art by Ann Fleur

Playlist

AIN'T NO MOUNTAIN HIGH ENOUGH (Epic Version)—Joseph William Morgan, Shadow Royale
BELLS IN SANTA FE—Halsey
DRAGON RIDER—Two Steps from Hell
CARRY ON WAYWARD SON—Neoni
WHAT A WONDERFUL WORLD—Joey Ramone
EYE OF THE UNTOLD HER—Lindsey Stirling
FALL INTO ME—Forest Blakk
THE OPEN—Becky Shaheen
WONDERWALL (Epic Trailer Version)—J2, Miranda Dianne
COUNTING STARS (2023 Version)—OneRepublic
QUEEN—Loren Gray
WE GO DOWN TOGETHER—Dove Cameron, Khalid
WONDERWALL—Alex Goot
STICK WITH YOU—Highasakite
THE OTHER SIDE—Stephen Sanchez
POWER OVER ME—Dermot Kennedy
DOWN BAD—Taylor Swift

VOHRAIN

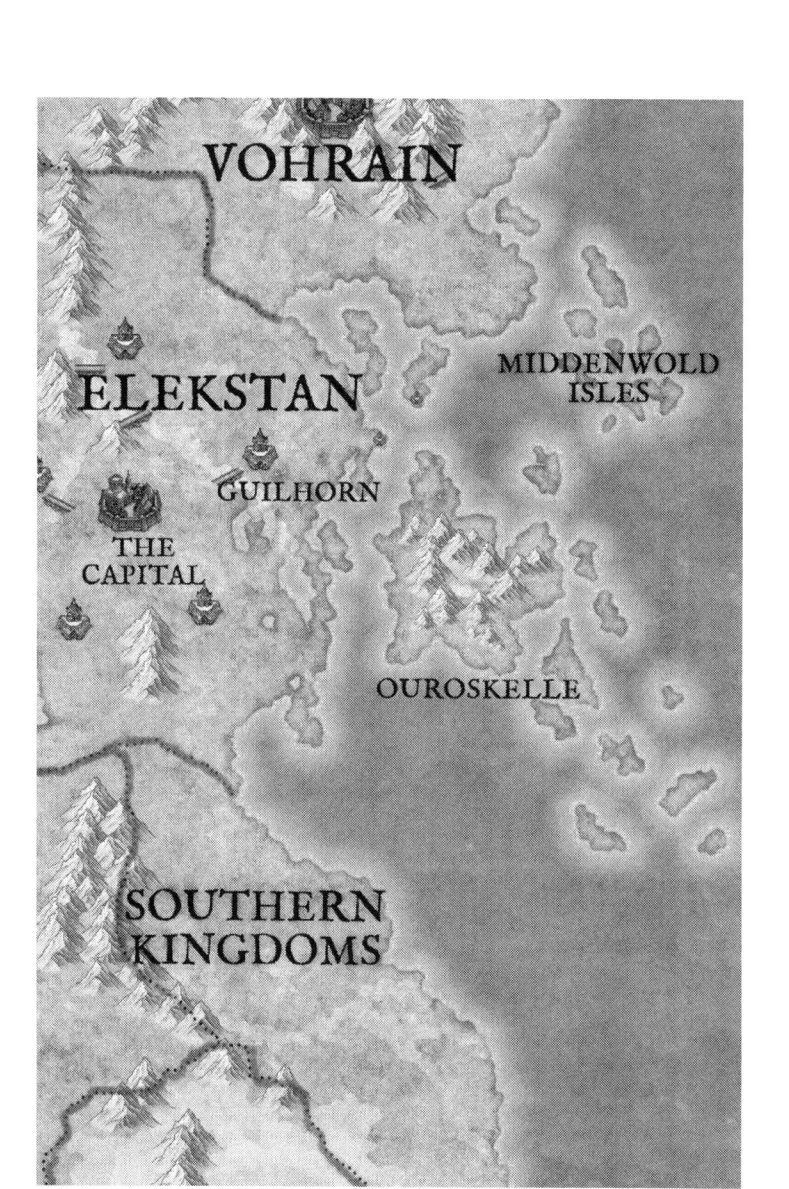

ELEKSTAN

GUILHORN

THE
CAPITAL

MIDDENWOLD
ISLES

OUROSKELLE

SOUTHERN
KINGDOMS

Reading Guidance

Murder, war, death, violence
Gaslighting
Mental and physical abuse by a captor
Threat of rape
Spit, gore, nausea/vomit
Non-consensual touch/kissing (by the villain and his guests)

PRONUNCIATION GUIDE

Kyreagan: kai-REE-gahn, ("Ky" rhymes with "sky")
Serylla: seh-RILL-ah
Hinarax: HIN-ar-ax
Meridian: Muh-RID-ee-ahn
Rahzien: RAH-zee-ehn
Ouroskelle: oo-ruh-SKEL
Varex: VAIR-ex
Vylar: rhymes with Skylar
Vohrain: Vore-AIN
Ashvelon: ASH-vell-on

1

Kyreagan

I perch on a sun-soaked peak, letting my scales drink the warm light while I survey the island of Ouroskelle, the domain I rule alongside my brother Varex.

I've been flying from cliffs to caves, from mountains to meadows, calculating the damage done by the Mordvorren, the sentient storm that battered Ouroskelle for days.

Mentally I tally up the losses.

Three deaths—one dragon and two humans, killed in the partial collapse of a cave.

Severe flooding in the low-lying parts of the island.

Heavy damage to the landscape from wind, lightning, and rockfalls. Beaches littered with debris churned up by the storm.

Most of the vegetation is wrecked, inedible. Prey is almost nonexistent.

And yet I have hope. Because during my visits to each member of the clan, I counted eleven eggs. With the two eggs Serylla and I produced, the total from this mating season is thirteen. I saw some women whose bellies are still round, who will soon lay the eggs they carry, and I'm hopeful that more have been bred, though they may not yet show it.

Varex sits on a lower ledge of the same mountain on which I rest, taking in the same view. I was relieved to see him alive, though he bears a ragged wound along his throat. When I saw it, I nearly killed his woman, Jessiva, but Varex took my neck in his jaws and shoved me out of his cave before I could attack.

"She tried to kill you," I snarled at him, but he only said, "That's between me and her." He wouldn't speak about it any further, nor does she seem to be carrying his eggs—though I only caught a brief glimpse of her, so it's difficult to be sure.

Varex stretches his wings and shakes out his long neck and shoulders. He does not relish the sun the same way I do—his preference is star-glow and moonless nights. Still, I can tell he's pleased that the storm has passed. He seems bone-weary, though, even more so than I am.

"Rothkuri and a few of the others who are skilled with fishing have gone to hunt eels, sharks, and whatever else they can find," I tell him. "We all need to eat and regain our strength. Then we can fly to the Middenwold Isles and see how the animals there have fared. If they survived, we will have plenty to feed the hatchlings when the time comes."

"The Mordvorren did not touch the Middenwold Isles," Varex says.

"How do you know?"

A shudder traces through his entire body. "I just know."

I extend my neck and touch his wingtip with my nose. "You're not yourself. Is this about Jessiva, or the ones we lost?"

He shifts away from my touch. "Both."

"And something else, too. You cannot fool me, brother."

"I can't talk about it yet," he hisses. "I don't understand it, and I'd rather not speak of it."

"Very well. Know that I'm here, whenever you decide to share your thoughts."

He chuffs softly in assent.

"Have you gained control of when you change?" I ask.

"More or less. I can only remain in human form for a total of eight hours before I'm forced to transform into a dragon. And if I've been a dragon for sixteen consecutive hours, I'm forced into human shape. But within those parameters I can manage it, parcel out the time, and plan when I want to be in each form."

"I've learned the same thing." A twinge of restlessness flickers through my heart. I've been surveying the island and checking on my people for a long while. It's high time I found some food and returned to the nest where my Princess and my eggs await me.

My mental attention shifts to the wisp of awareness between me and Serylla—my instinctive sense of her location.

I should be able to find that thread easily... but no matter how hard I concentrate, it's not there.

Ice runs through my veins, and I lift my head, extending my neck to its full height.

My connection with Serylla has vanished.

"What is it?" asks Varex.

Whipping out my wings, I plunge down from the peak, angling for the fastest wind channel to gain maximum speed.

Varex follows me. "Kyreagan, what's wrong?"

"Serylla. I can't sense her. I've been so distracted—I can't remember when I last felt her presence. Shortly after I left the cave, I think. Fuck..."

Varex doesn't reply. Perhaps he and Jessiva do not share the same link that Serylla and I do. Our bond is new, untested... perhaps I shouldn't be so frantic about its absence. But I can't shake the dread crawling along my bones, the suspicion that something is very wrong.

With Varex at my side, I soar toward the entrance of my cave and land hastily on the ledge.

"Serylla!" I hate how desperate I sound. Her scent is everywhere, but it's not fresh. It has faded over a number of hours.

With a wondering light in his eyes, Varex crawls toward the nest where the two eggs sit side by side. "Your little ones."

"Serylla!" I call again. I return to the brink of the ledge, peering down at the ground far below. Maybe she fell, maybe she jumped… but she wouldn't. She *wouldn't*. Not after I promised to take her back to the mainland and set her free.

I shouldn't have stayed out so long. I told myself it was my responsibility to speak with every member of the clan, as well as each captive. But maybe I was also putting off the conversation Serylla and I planned to have—our discussion of her departure. She said we would talk about it when I returned. Maybe my dread of that talk twined with my need to care for my clan, and delayed my return. This is all my fault. I should have come back sooner.

"Where is she?" My claws grate into the rock, carving deep grooves. "Where is she, Varex? I don't see a body. She didn't fall. She's not here."

"Perhaps another dragon came by and gave her a ride somewhere."

"Where?" I snarl. "Where could—"

The peaks of my brother's wings stiffen and his nostrils flare suddenly. "Be still a moment. Don't move, don't breathe." He lowers his snout to the floor of my cave and prowls along, sniffing deeply.

I'm able to detect a fellow dragon's scent when they're nearby, or if they've spent a significant amount of time in a certain space, and I can smell a human from some distance away. But Varex can pick up faint traces of an odor hours after its carrier has left the spot.

"Who is it?" I snarl. "Who do you smell?"

He raises his head, alarm in his eyes. "Fortunix."

Fiery liquid churns in my stomach. While Varex and I surveyed the island today, I told him my suspicions—how I believe Fortunix was behind the plague that ravaged our islands and killed most of our prey. The plague he instigated drove us close to starvation and forced our clan to ally with Vohrain.

"You're sure it's him?" I grit out the words between clamped jaws.

"My nose is better than yours, you know that. Fortunix was here, briefly, some hours ago."

"He took Serylla."

"He wasn't at the gathering of the clan, where we chose our partners," Varex muses. "Several dragons commented on his absence. Maybe he sheltered somewhere alone, and he has been driven mad with the need to mate. Maybe he's going to—"

"No!" I snarl. "That's not it. Think, Varex. Who wanted the Princess of Elekstan? Who was willing to pay for her?"

My brother's eyes widen. "The King of Vohrain. Fortunix is taking her to Rahzien."

The fiery bile that has been lurching in my gut finally surges onto my tongue. I explode from the mouth of the cave into the sky, spewing streams of orange flame into the rain-washed air.

"Traitor!" I roar through the flames, the loudest cry I've ever voiced, immense as a peal of the Mordvorren's thunder. My voice echoes from cliff to cliff, all through the mountains.

I climb higher, raking my fire across the sky, screaming my fury until my chest aches. Dragons streak from their caves and fly at a cautious distance, hovering anxiously, sharing in my grief and rage even though they don't yet understand what I've lost. Some of the dragons carry human women on their backs, and the sight is like a voratrice's acid burning through my scales, because my woman is lost. My partner is missing.

"Give us a few moments," Varex calls to the other dragons. "Then we will gather in the Conch Valley and explain what has happened. Bring any food you have left, so we may all share it."

The others disperse, except for Varex, Hinarax, and Ashvelon, who carries the enchantress Thelise on his back.

"I can't stay for a meeting," I tell them. "I'm leaving now. I have to find her. Varex, you were there, you heard what Rahzien said. You know what he plans to do to Serylla."

"Explain, Prince," says Thelise, her brown eyes holding mine. "I'm a friend to your Princess, and if something has happened to her, I may be able to help."

In broken phrases I choke out the truth of Fortunix's treachery and his kidnapping of Serylla.

"I'm not surprised he's a bad seed," Thelise says dryly. "I never liked that one. Varex, how old was Fortunix's scent? How long ago did he visit Kyreagan's cave?"

"A few hours, maybe," he replies.

I swallow the liquid fire creeping up the back of my throat. "He must have arrived not long after I left."

"A few hours…" Thelise muses. "So Fortunix has already reached the mainland with the Princess. By the time you make it to the coastline, Serylla will already be in the hands of the King of Vohrain. Rahzien knows you did not want to give her up. He'll be hiding her somewhere, just in case you come after her. Vohrain's army is much better armored and has stronger weapons than Elekstan, and now that your alliance with them is over, they pose a greater threat. You'll have to be careful. Besides, you can't charge into a newly occupied city, burning citizens and smashing buildings as you hunt for her. You need a plan."

"She's right, my Prince," comments Ashvelon. "The Vohrainians have hand cannons that shoot armor-piercing projectiles. We've all seen them in action against Elekstan's armies. It won't take much for our former allies to turn those weapons on us."

"They're called *guns*," offers Hinarax, a dragon with coppery scales. He's been hovering nearby, listening. "A new kind of weapon, not very reliable or accurate, but dragons are large targets. The Vohrainian army didn't have many guns at the start of the war, but the soldiers I spoke with told me their king is obsessed with such weapons, and is having new designs developed, along with better ammunition."

"Guns, yes," continues Ashvelon, with a sidelong look at Hinarax. "As I was saying… stealth and caution are required here."

"I prefer the charging, smashing, and hunting idea," I growl.

"You'll end up hurting Serylla or getting yourself killed," Thelise points out.

Varex moves a wingbeat closer to me. "She's right, brother. Besides, we can't risk angering Vohrain and jeopardizing our ownership of the Middenwold Isles."

"Rahzien signed those islands over to us," I say. "He can't go back on his word."

"Still, this will take delicate handling, unless you want another war," Varex replies. "We can't survive an all-out conflict with Vohrain. Whatever you do must be in the best interest of our clan—both dragons and humans."

I bare my teeth at him, but I know he speaks the truth. In my urge to save Serylla, I must not forget my duty to my own kind.

Thelise taps her chin. "I'm having a thought."

"Shit, we're in trouble now," mutters Ashvelon.

"Hush, you." She smacks his neck, an affectionate rebuke. "The King of Vohrain may not know that dragons can take human form now. Fortunix might not have passed along that bit of information. And whether Rahzien knows about it or not, he won't recognize you in human form. That's your angle. Your human face is the perfect disguise. With it, you can stroll right into the Elekstan capital… or approach the King's fortress in Vohrain, depending on where Fortunix took the Princess. You said he wants to use her to subdue the people, right? So I'm guessing he'll keep her in Elekstan. He might try to impregnate her quickly, to legitimize his claim on the kingdom."

My reaction to Thelise's last statement is visceral, uncontrollable. A possessive fury explodes through my body, and I roar another burst of flame in the enchantress's general direction. Ashvelon darts quickly aside so I don't burn his precious life-mate.

"Avoid that topic," Varex tells her sharply.

"Right." Thelise looks somewhat paler. She extracts a tiny flask from a pocket in her clothing and takes a swig.

I toss my head, groaning as I fight to suppress another gush of fire. When I have myself mostly under control, I say tightly, "You're forgetting one thing. I have horns, claws, and a forked tongue when I'm in human form. Won't they give me away?"

Thelise arches a brow. "Your horns stay with you when you change? Interesting. There have been a few such vagaries among the others, too. I suppose even the best-planned spells can go slightly awry. While I can't alter the spell itself, I can add a charm that allows you to dispel your horns and modify your tongue and claws when you're in human form."

Hinarax moves closer, inserting himself into the conversation again. He's young, twenty-five like Varex and I, and a bit of a trouble-maker. During our alliance with Vohrain, I had to chastise him a few times for disobeying my orders and wandering off to chat with Vohrainian soldiers. He's obsessed with humans and their technology, though he deeply distrusts their magic.

"My Prince," Hinarax ventures. "Forgive me, but I don't think this plan will work. You'd have to pass yourself off as human—not just human-*shaped*, but human-*born*, with all their knowledge and habits. If you plan to infiltrate the Elekstan palace or a Vohrainian fortress, you'll have to dress convincingly, in the right clothes. You'll have to know their protocols, their idioms, their honorifics. You'll have to eat the way they do."

By the Bone-Builder... he's right.

"I'll go with you," Hinarax offers. "You know I spent time with the humans—I was punished for it often enough." Unrepentant laughter shines in his eyes. "I can help you fit in, or at least advise you as you learn the humans' ways."

"This scheme sounds like it will take too long," I hiss. "Too much time has passed already. Serylla could be in pain right now. She could be enduring—" I choke on the words, unable to verbalize my fear. "Besides, don't you have a human captive to care for?"

"The girl I captured chose someone else," Hinarax says carelessly. "I prefer male company anyway. Ilbryen, Thytar, and I weathered the storm together and explored some very interesting new ways to mate. I'll tell you about it on the way, if you like."

I don't relish the idea of this bright-eyed, human-obsessed male accompanying me, but he's a decent fighter and he's willing to join me for what will be a dangerous mission. I'd prefer my brother's company, but one of us must stay behind to lead the clan.

"I suppose you can come with me," I tell Hinarax grudgingly. "But I'm in no mood for hearing about your mating habits."

"Understood, my Prince." Hinarax bobs his head.

"Ashvelon and I will fetch the supplies for the charm," says Thelise. "We'll meet you at your cave."

"And my Prince—" Ashvelon's eyes meet mine, sympathy in his gaze. "If this scheme fails, and you need the clan, we will fight for you and the Princess. Love is worth starting a war."

"So dramatic." Thelise smacks his neck again. "Come on, pet."

They wheel around and soar away.

"I'll fetch Jessiva," says Varex. "She and I will watch over your eggs while you're gone."

"No," I snarl. "I don't want that woman anywhere near my offspring. Have Rothkuri and his partner do it. You can check in on them now and then."

Varex looks as if he might argue, but after glowering at me he says, "Very well. I'll address the clan and have food brought to your cave. You should eat something before you go."

"I'll fetch the food," Hinarax offers. He heads off in the direction of Conch Valley, while Varex hovers before me, anxiety furrowing his brow ridges.

"I know you must go after the Princess," he says. "But Kyreagan—be careful. Be wise as Grimmaw, strategic as Vylar, and—"

"Diplomatic as you?"

He chuckles. "Exactly."

"I will think of the clan and do my best to avoid further conflict. But Serylla is..." I struggle for words. Nothing seems to fully express what she means to me.

"I know," he says softly, an ache in his voice. "Trust me, I know."

Without another word, he soars away.

I wish we had more time. I know something is troubling him, and I want to help—but every bone in my body is screaming to leave Ouroskelle and race after Serylla. If I'd known there was the slightest danger of something like this happening, I wouldn't have left her for a moment.

Diving back into my cave, I prowl over to the nest and gently tilt the eggs with my clawed forepaw. An inspection of each egg's entire surface reveals that they are still intact, undamaged. I tip them carefully upright again and scrape some of the grass closer around them.

The blankets which covered Serylla lie discarded in the nest. When I push my nose against one of them, her scent rushes into me, an earthy sweetness that sends shards of pain through my heart.

"I'm going to save your mother," I tell the eggs in Dragonish. "Whether I bring her back with me, or whether she chooses her own path, I want you to know that she is the most beautiful, clever, kind, musical, funny, precious person I've ever known, and you are both lucky to have come from her. I claim the protection of the Bone-Builder over you both. Know that I'm only leaving you because I have to. You will be in excellent hands while I'm gone, and I promise to return as soon as possible. On the bones of Grimmaw and Lorgin, of Arzhaling and Zemua, I swear it."

Despite all the flames I spewed in my rage and sorrow, I feel more liquid fire in my belly, more energy ready to be used. Since the mating frenzy, my powers seem to have amplified. Which will be useful when I get Serylla back—because once I know she is safe, I plan to burn everyone who touched her to the fucking ground.

2

SERYLLA

Wind blasts my cheeks and whips tears from my eyes. I forgot how uncomfortable it is to fly for hours, grasped in the bony claws of a dragon who doesn't care for my well-being. Fortunix said he's supposed to deliver me undamaged, but apparently he doesn't think a few bruises will interfere with him receiving his reward from the King of Vohrain.

We're high up, gliding through wispy clouds as we approach the capital city of Elekstan. Fortunix is angling slightly south. If he continues this trajectory, we'll bypass the city entirely.

"If you're aiming for the palace, you should be heading due west," I call.

"Thank you, Princess," he replies in a dry, grating tone. "If it wasn't for you, I'd be utterly lost, bumbling about with no sense of direction."

"Fine, so we're not heading for the palace. Where are we going?"

"Wait and see."

I sigh gustily and fall silent, watching the landscape roll beneath me. It's familiar and yet foreign, since I'm not used to seeing any of it from this height. When Kyreagan carried me away from my home, I was too frantic to appreciate the view. I'm scared now, too, but it's a different kind of fear, not the raw panic I felt on the day Vohrain conquered my kingdom. Perhaps I've grown more used to danger and unexpected occurrences.

Apart from some debris along the beach, I've seen no damage from the Mordvorren during our flight, for which I'm relieved. My kingdom has suffered enough without bearing the fury of a monstrous storm. According to the tales, the storm tends to choose particular places over which to hover. Targets to torture, I suppose. For some reason it selected Ouroskelle. I'm still curious about why I couldn't see the receding cloud mass when Fortunix and I left Kyreagan's cave. The Mordvorren should have still been visible on the horizon. But it was utterly gone, as if something swallowed it up. Convenient that it disappeared when it did, since we were all on the brink of starvation.

Speaking of which, I'm famished. I'm not sure what sort of reception to expect when I'm brought to the King of Vohrain, but I hope it includes food.

Kyreagan told me Rahzien had offered to buy me. Apparently Rahzien is struggling to secure his control over Elekstan, and if he uses me to produce a rightful heir to the Elekstan throne, it will solidify his claim.

It chafes my soul to know that even in the most civilized kingdoms, war can reduce women to nothing more than empty holes and fertile wombs in the eyes of men. I hate that I'm not physically stronger. I wish I'd trained harder and learned more effective techniques for self-defense—although deep down I know that in this case, none of that would help. Even the most well-trained woman can be subdued by enough men with malicious intentions. And I'm not a warrior like the women in the Elekstan army. I'm not made of sinew and whipcord and steel. I'm too soft, too vulnerable. Easy prey.

My only resources are my mind and my words. Maybe I can strategize an escape, or talk my way out of bedding the King of Vohrain. But what if I can't? What if he forces me?

I'll have to endure whatever comes my way. Fight when I can, submit when I can't, escape as soon as I have the chance. If the King takes my body by force, I'll retreat behind mental defenses until it's over. I have no doubt many an Elekstan woman has had to do the same thing since the Vohrainian occupation.

That thought upsets me more than my own impending violation. Knowing that such atrocities have likely occurred among the palace staff and the people of the capital, imagining all that pain—it makes me shudder so violently that Fortunix notices.

"Be still, human, unless you want me to drop you," he snarls.

"You won't drop me. You need me."

He rumbles in grudging admission. "Listen, when we arrive, keep quiet about the enchantress's spell."

"You don't want the King of Vohrain to know you can turn into a human? Why not?"

"Because I am *ashamed*," he grits out. "Humanity is weakness. I've told the King that Kyreagan's plan to turn women into dragons didn't work. That's all he knows."

I vent a sardonic laugh. "What's to stop me from telling him the truth? You think I'll keep your secret out of the goodness of my heart?"

"Not *my* secret," he says. "But you'll keep Kyreagan's secret."

"What do you mean?"

"How do you think the King of Vohrain will react if he finds out that a powerful race of dragons can now take human form? He's a man with a mind for conquest, a man who sees threats everywhere. A suspicious man who wants to protect what's his while claiming even more. He would find some way to use this knowledge against our clan."

"And you have your clan's best interest at heart," I say dryly.

"The things I've done were necessary to avenge terrible wrongs, but now that my vengeance is complete, all I want is to live out my days quietly, in the midst of my own hoard. The other dragons may hate and revile me, but I wish them no harm."

"You're delusional," I tell him. "You've been the cause of so many deaths—"

"You would rebuke *me* for causing death?" His voice rises, hot with fury. "Your people hunted, killed, and desecrated my loved ones."

I want to protest that the dragon hunts happened forty years ago, before I was born, but I decide against it. When I had similar conversations with Kyreagan, he was willing to listen, to understand my perspective, and to perceive his own mistakes. And he accepted my sincere regret about my own apathy and inaction. Fortunix is not open to such a conversation. He is impervious to any suffering but his own. So I keep silent again, alternating my gaze between the granite underside of the dragon's throat and the bushy tops of the trees below me. We're gliding lower, and soon Fortunix dives into a clearing, landing on his back legs and clumsily folding his wings while still gripping me in his front claws.

He gives a long, droning bellow, like a signal. Then he waits, while I try to adjust my body within the cage of his bony claws. My belly is still swollen and sore from laying the two dragon eggs. I crave a soft bed and a cup of hot tea, preferably turmeric and ginger with honey.

"Put me down," I demand, but the dragon ignores me.

After several long minutes, four soldiers march out of the forest. They wear the smoky blue uniforms of the Vohrainian military, complete with armored vests. Their skull-like helmets all bear the same metallic, skeletal grin beneath twin eye-slits. I've never seen a Vohrainian soldier in person—I've only heard descriptions and seen sketches. Facing those grinning silver helmets in real life is spine-chilling.

One of the soldiers is pushing a small cart with a large wooden chest on it. Judging by the angle of the man's body, the chest is heavy. Probably full of gold—Fortunix's payment for delivering me.

"The Princess of Elekstan, as promised." Fortunix opens his claws and I tumble ungracefully into the grass. Wincing and holding my stomach, I climb to my feet.

The tallest soldier surveys me, his helmet tilting up and down. "She looks more like a waif of the wood. Tell me, girl, are you the Crown Princess?"

"No, sir," I say in a breathy, squeaky voice. "No, I ain't. I'm Maisie Wimple from River's Twist, down yonder. This big beastie snatched me up and told me to pretend I'm a princess, but I don't know how to pretend such things, begging your pardon, sir, seeing as I ain't got much learning and no manners to speak of—"

"It's her all right. The Crown Princess herself. Sly as ever." A shadow emerges from the trees behind the four Vohrainian soldiers.

I know that voice. It belongs to Zevin Harlowe, one of the young lords I used to invite to palace dinners. He has a saucy, sharp sense of humor that sent me into fits of helpless laughter every time he dined with us. We kissed once, but I knew his reputation for gossiping about his trysts in detail afterward, so I refused to indulge him any further. He used to call me "cruel" for denying him—laughingly of course, but I always suspected he truly resented my refusal. Toward the end of the war, he was called up for service—a fate he'd previously been spared due to being one of my favorites. I haven't seen him since then.

He saunters through the dappled sunlight of the clearing, his pale eyes fixed on me.

"Well met, Princess." He gives me a tight, cold smile and sweeps off his hat. Half his skull is bald, wreathed with the dark, knotty scars of frost-fire burns. More burn scars cover his throat and the side of his face.

"You like my new adornments?" He grins wider and pulls open his shirt and doublet. What used to be a smooth, paneled chest worthy of a young god is now a mass of twisting scars and knotted flesh. "I had a shitty healer, you see. She saved my life, but she couldn't fix *this*. And before you ask—yes, it's all over my body. Even my dick. I won't show you that, though—it still works, but it's so grotesque you'd faint."

"I'm sorry," I breathe. "But, Zevin—your beauty was never the best part of you. I liked you because you were smart, and funny—"

"And rich, and well-bred, and noble-born." His upper lip curls. "I served you faithfully, and you threw me away. Tossed me out into the war, where I got fried by the fucking dragons. Now it's your turn to suffer." He nods to the tall soldier. "You have confirmation of her identity. Take her."

Instantly I dart to the left, heading for the trees, but I've only taken a dozen steps when my bare foot impales itself on a sharp branch. I scream and stumble, unable to keep my balance, and as I crash onto my left shoulder, pain explodes through the joint. My abdomen goes into another series of dull, aching cramps, leaving my insides weak and wobbly.

It's too soon after the birth of the eggs. My body is still recovering, nowhere near ready for such physical exertion.

One of the Vohrainians comes forward, yanks my arms together, and clasps manacles around my wrists. He jerks me to my feet and tugs sharply at the chain linked to my wrists. I have no choice but to stagger after him into the trees.

A last look over my shoulder shows Fortunix collecting his chest of treasure and taking to the sky. Much as I hate that dragon, my fear deepens once he's gone, as if some small measure of protection left with him. Perhaps I was hoping he'd change his mind, but there's no chance of that now.

The enemy soldiers hustle me through a narrow belt of trees and up a broad path bordered by crisply-trimmed box hedges, toward the entrance of a stately manor. I've been here before. It's the ancestral home of the Harlowes.

So Zevin is identifying prisoners for the Vohrainians *and* letting them use his family home. Bitterness stings my tongue. This must be how Kyreagan felt when he learned of Fortunix's treachery.

"Your mother once called this house 'quaint.'" Zevin walks beside me, his tone conversational, but with a trace of venom. "It wasn't a compliment, of course. She thought this manor was old, run-down, and inconveniently distant from the bustle of the city center. But my family had reasons for maintaining this residence, in addition to our townhouse within the capital."

"Reasons?" I ask.

"Oh yes. There are certain private activities we enjoy. I've made my own share of life-changing memories here." He gazes up at the building's gabled peaks and narrow dormer windows. Smoke drifts from two of the chimneys, trailing away into the blue sky.

My wounded foot leaves wet, scarlet prints as I'm forced to mount the steps of the house.

"Are your parents home?" I ask. Perhaps Zevin's mother and father would be more loyal to my family than he appears to be.

"Oh no, my parents fled the kingdom. Of course they killed Grandfather and Aunt Dara first, since they were both too old to make the journey. I should be glad they didn't slit my throat as well. Mother and Father left me behind because I'm too noticeable, too grotesque for the new life they plan to begin." Zevin steps aside as we enter the foyer and watches, smiling, while I'm dragged across the marble floor. I hear the clip of his boots as he falls in behind us, following me and my captors down a long corridor and through a thick door reinforced with strips of iron. Steps lead down into lantern-lit gloom.

I've never been down here. Didn't even realize there was a lower level, a dungeon of sorts beneath the manor. My gaze skips from the worn pavers of the subterranean floor to the dark, splattered stains on the stone walls. Those dark splashes tell a tale about Zevin's family that I'd rather not know.

The Vohrainian soldiers shove me into a large room, a cell whose gray stone bears more hideous stains. Metal loops and hooks are bolted to the walls.

The tall soldier attaches the chain of my manacles to one of the hooks and locks it in place. I have barely any leeway for moving my arms, and there's not enough slack for me to sit down. I can only slump wearily against the wall for support.

After the soldiers leave the cell, Zevin Harlowe approaches me. The remaining tufts of his blond hair aren't carefully coiffed like they used to be—they stick out wildly from his head. His eyes hold a glint of mad humor.

"Look at you," he says. "The Crown Princess who always thought she was so *good* because she did a few servants' chores. Fortunix told us you were taken to be a dragon's whore. Did you let a dragon fuck you, Serylla?" He lays a hand on my stomach, which has shrunk somewhat, but is still more distended than usual. "Looks like you've been stretched out by dragon cock. I hope he tore your hole wide open. Spread your legs and let me see."

"Lord Harlowe." The tall soldier stands in the doorway of my cell, one hand on his sword hilt. "The King gave orders that no one was to touch the girl except him."

"It's my fucking house," snaps Zevin.

A low rasp as the soldier slides the sword partway out of its sheath. "This house and everyone in it are subject to the word of the King of Vohrain."

Zevin snarls a few curses, but he stomps out of the cell, past the soldier, and up the stairs. The tall soldier remains in the doorway, his helmet angled toward me.

"I'm in pain," I tell him. "My foot is bleeding, and my stomach hurts. Please… if there's anything you can do…"

The soldier closes the giant wooden door. A key grates and clicks in the lock, and booted feet walk away.

"Well… shit," I whisper.

3

KYREAGAN

"What we're doing—it's called *reconnaissance*," says Hinarax eagerly. "Two or three advance units sneaking in and scoping out an area when you don't want to arouse suspicion with large numbers. It's a human military term."

"That's not just a human term," I tell him flatly.

He does a loop in the air, seemingly oblivious to my reply. "You were right not to bring the human enchantress along. I don't trust her."

"Neither do I, but that isn't why I left her behind. She's too well-known, too recognizable, and our goal is stealth—at least until we find out where the Princess is and how heavily she's being guarded. Then I will determine whether you and I can free her ourselves, or whether we need to summon the power of the entire clan. I hope to avoid that. It would doubtless result in the deaths of more dragons, and we are few in number as it is."

Hinarax dips lower, letting his back claws trail through the sea foam. "I hope one day there can be peace among dragons and humans. No warring kingdoms, no dragon hunts. Prince Varex says humans can teach us how to craft things we haven't been able to make before."

"Perhaps. But don't be too inquisitive on this journey. You and I must keep our true nature a secret while we're in Elekstan."

"That may be difficult. Where will we hide when we revert to dragon form?"

"I haven't thought that far ahead," I admit. "In the woods, or in a large empty building? A cave, perhaps? Surely they have caves. We'll keep our eyes open for potential hiding spots. It will be your job to track the number of hours we've spent in each form, and to determine how much time we have left. In addition to helping me fit in among the humans."

"Right, yes, of course, I can almost certainly, possibly, help you try to do that."

I give him a sidelong glance. "Because you're so knowledgeable about them, as you boasted to us a few hours ago."

He swallows, dips his head a little. "Y-y-es. I'm very knowledgeable."

"Hinarax."

"You can trust me, Prince. I watched the Vohrainian soldiers put on their uniforms and eat together. The fashions and manners of the palace can't be much different, can they?"

"I have no idea."

"It will be fine." He says it firmly, cheerfully, as if by sheer willpower he will make it so.

I release a long sigh and beat my wings, speeding toward a sheltered cove up ahead.

Since Fortunix was on an errand for the King of Vohrain, he would have flown openly, not trying to conceal his presence. Hinarax and I will travel on foot, at least during the day, so Rahzien won't be warned of our approach. Before we begin our journey, we must determine whether Fortunix headed north to

Vohrain or west to the Capital, and to get that information, we'll have to find humans who may have seen a dragon flying overhead recently.

We land in the cove, at the base of a rocky bluff. The instant my claws grate against the pebbled beach, several gulls rise, squawking. I inspect them carefully as they flap and circle overhead.

Rahzien used to have more than two dozen talking birds, but many of them were killed during the war. Their red glowing eyes, a side effect of the magic that enabled them to speak, served as a dead giveaway, and Elekstan's archers would target them on sight. Because they were so noticeable, Rahzien typically used the birds as messengers, not spies. He could not risk them too close to the enemy.

As far as I know, he has only a few talking birds left, with no way to get more since the sorcerer who spelled them died months ago. I doubt he would send his remaining birds to do random surveillance flights, but I should keep watch for them all the same.

"Watching for Rahzien's birds?" Hinarax inquires.

"Just in case."

"During the war, I befriended one of the keepers of the royal birds—a very handsome fellow, as humans go. He told me the phrases Rahzien must use every time he commands his birds—one special phrase to open the bird's mind, and another phrase to confirm the order. Of course the keeper was very drunk that night. Didn't seem to remember anything the next day. I wonder if we'll have a chance to get drunk during this mission? I would love to try wine, and ale, and mead, and rum..."

"Doesn't liquor interfere with one's mental capabilities?" I ask. "If so, we should avoid it. As I recall, Rahzien forbids his soldiers from drinking except on rare occasions."

"True... but many of them drank in secret," Hinarax replies. "Some of them were very amusing to watch, once they'd emptied a few tankards."

"We should keep our minds on the task at hand." I unclasp my left front claw, releasing a bundle of clothing onto the beach. Among other things, I brought with me a pair of boots, two shirts, and two pairs of pants, items Serylla scavenged from Thelise's stash. They fit me well enough, though I'm not sure what sort of human they're meant to clothe, and for which occasions.

Serylla seems to draw a distinction between certain outfits. She tried to explain it to me once, while we were sheltering from the Mordvorren. Some clothes are for sleeping, others for hard work, others for walking or riding, and still others for dinner and visiting. Then there are finer clothes for special occasions, like feasts or balls.

To me, human clothing is divided into two categories—shiny and not shiny. I prefer shiny things. Unfortunately, none of the clothing currently in my possession is shiny. Perhaps at some point I can purchase a more attractive outfit.

Next I inspect my long black claws and focus my thoughts on banishing them, as Thelise instructed. Before we left Ouroskelle, Ashvelon brought the enchantress to my cave, where she performed another charm, one she claimed would affect not only me, but all dragons, enabling them to summon or dispel their horns and claws while in human form. She wrote the words of the spell on a flat stone with ink, then had Ashvelon trace them deeper into the rock with his claw. Once that was done she arranged many polished stones and clumps of herbs around the stone slab, along with a scale from Ashvelon.

During the casting of the spell, her eyes glowed violet, and afterwards she slumped over, conscious but weary. Ashvelon carried her off to rest, shortly before Rothkuri and his companion, Everelle, entered my cave. Everelle seemed thrilled to be one of the guardians for my eggs, and she asked shyly if, when the time came, she could lay her own eggs in the same nest, so that she and Rothkuri could watch over all of them at once. I have never seen a dragon look so overjoyed and proud as Rothkuri did when she made the request, so of course I said yes. Much as I hated leaving my offspring behind, it eases my mind to know they will be well cared for.

Thelise's spell must have worked, because once I harness my thoughts again and focus them on my claws, the pointed black nails transform into rounded, pale ones. I concentrate on my tongue next, feeling its cloven tip merge into one seamless, fleshy curve.

"This is the oddest feeling." I form the words carefully, testing the new shape of my tongue. Pleased to find that my speech is barely affected by the change, I turn my thoughts to the last telltale sign of my nature and will it to vanish. "Are my horns gone, Hinarax?"

He glances over and nods. "Well done! You look perfectly human."

So does he. His human form is skinny and tall, with deep brown skin and a mass of chestnut locs down to his waist, like hundreds of tiny bronze ropes that glitter in the bright sun. He's standing in the shallows of the cove, watching the water swirl around his toes, apparently fascinated by his own feet.

"You should get dressed," I remind him.

"Oh, of course!" He hurries back to the beach, pulls on the second pair of pants, and dons a loose shirt. "Now, put on the boots."

"I'd rather not." I grimace at the tall leather prisons in which I'm supposed to encase my feet. "*You're* going barefoot."

"Because there are no shoes for me. But humans wear shoes all the time, especially boots, so if you want to blend in, get on with it... my Prince," he adds, with an apologetic wince. "Respectfully."

With a muttered curse, I shove my sandy foot into one of the boots. The sensation is horrible—grainy and sticky. I push my other foot into the second boot and attempt to stand.

Hinarax tilts his head. "I think you should switch them. The curved part should be on the inside of each foot."

"Fuck," I snarl, and wrestle the boots off before tugging them on again. "I hate these."

"They can't be that bad if humans wear them all day."

"Why don't *you* wear them, then?"

"Didn't your Princess give them to you?"

"She saved them for me in case I wanted them, which I do not. Please take them."

"Well, if you're offering..." Hinarax beams as I drag the boots off and hand them over. His smile fades once he puts them on, but he doesn't complain.

I pick up the remaining items from the bundle—a selection of my favorite jewelry from my private hoard. I sling several of the gold and silver necklaces around my throat and tuck them under my collar, so they're partly visible through the open neck of my shirt. Then I slip the bracelets and earrings into the pockets of my pants. That's another thing I appreciate about human clothing—pockets, which are small bags sewn right into the garment.

Hinarax has also brought some pieces from his personal collection. Once he has stowed the treasure in his own pockets and lined his fingers with rings, we trudge out of the cove and down the beach, toward a distant cluster of buildings. A fishing village, by the look of it.

During the trek to the village, Hinarax keeps stumbling on the rounded rocks that litter the beach, but he forges on bravely, determined to conquer the boots. We take a sandy path between grassy dunes and encounter our first humans of the day—tiny ones with round cheeks, who are flying paper dragons attached to strings.

"Greetings, small humans," I say loudly.

Hinarax elbows me in the ribs and whispers, "Don't say 'humans' like that."

I nearly correct it to "hatchlings," but I manage to summon the right word. "Greetings, children. Have you seen any dragons flying today?"

They stare at me with round eyes, then look at their paper dragons.

"Real ones," I clarify. "Not those frail imitations."

"I saw a real dragon," pipes up one of the children.

"What color was it?" asks Hinarax.

"Gray. Big. Like a flying stone. And its wings had marks all over them."

He's describing Fortunix. "Which way did the dragon go?" I ask.

The child shrugs.

"That way?" I point north, toward Vohrain. "Or that way?" I swerve my hand west, toward the Capital.

The boy cocks his head, a calculating expression on his chubby face. "What'll you give me?"

I dig into my pocket. A small piece of information deserves a small reward, so I seize the tiniest earring I can find—a bit of gold with a starry white jewel dangling from it. "You can have this."

The boy's eyes widen. He snatches the bauble from my claws and points emphatically to the west. "That way."

"We can tell you things too!" The other children gather around me. "Do you have any more questions?"

I feel small fingers nudging into my pockets, so I bat them away. "Let's head for the Capital," I tell Hinarax.

"But we need supplies first. Food, and other things," he protests. "Surely we have time for a few purchases."

"Oh, very well." I stride through the swarm of little ones, wishing I dared transform and frighten them into giving me space. Accompanied by their pattering feet and eager voices, we enter the village.

Several wooden tables line the main street. Fabric coverings stretched across poles provide shade for the humans and their wares.

"Fresh fish!" bawls a man loudly near my ear.

"Spiced nuts! Currant buns! Meat pies!" squawks a woman from a table across the street. "Two bits for a pie, one for a bun!"

I don't know what a "bit" is, but she's selling food. Food for which I do not need to hunt or forage. Food prepared by someone else, ready for the taking, as long as I exchange something for it. The sheer convenience is astounding.

Intrigued, I head for the woman's table. "I'll take these, and this, and all of these." I gesture to most of the food she has laid out.

She peers at me, methodically chewing a wad of green weed. Her eyes linger on my necklaces. "That'll be two dolems."

I pull a gem-studded bracelet from my pocket. "Will this do?"

She gapes, and the wad of weed nearly tumbles from her mouth. She pokes the lump back into the side of her cheek and scowls. "You shittin' me?"

I glance sideways at Hinarax.

"The soldiers used to say that," he says eagerly. "She doesn't believe you're really offering her the bracelet in exchange for the food."

"I assure you, I mean it," I tell the woman. "This is my offer."

She shakes her head. "That's too much, lad. I ain't got change for a piece like that."

"Just take it, then," I say. "Give us the food."

"Please," adds Hinarax.

By now, several adult humans have drawn closer, lured by the haggling and perhaps by the glitter of gemstones. With a suspicious glance at her fellow villagers, the woman snatches the bracelet from me and tucks it into the front of her brown dress.

"You can have it all," she says. "I'll wrap it up for you. But mind you eat the pies before sunset. Won't be no good later than that."

"Since we apparently overpaid, do you happen to have an extra pair of boots for my friend here?" Hinarax inquires.

"What?" I mutter. "*No*."

"You'll need them, trust me," he whispers.

The woman nods. "Might have an old pair of Wirram's boots somewhere about. Wait here."

She ducks into a weatherbeaten building that looks as if one good nudge from a dragon's wingtip would topple it. After a few moments she returns with a pair of floppy brown boots. "Here you are."

"I'll take those," says Hinarax quickly. "You can have these." He sits down on the street, pulls off the black boots, and puts on the worn brown ones.

"Traitor," I say. "You want those because they look more comfortable."

He grins up at me, and I shake my head with a brief answering grin.

I pull on the black boots while Hinarax fumbles over the laces of his. Finally he pays one of the bystanders a gold ring to tie them for him, while the vendor packs up the food we purchased, half of it in a large basket, and half in a cloth bag. I claim one of the meat pies and bite into it. To my pleasure and astonishment, it tastes similar to the stew Serylla made for me during the Mordvorren.

Perhaps my brother and Hinarax are right. Perhaps taking human form now and then could enrich our lives in ways beyond the pleasures of sex. Food is limited on Ouroskelle, but if we learn how to cultivate crops and cook meals as they do here on the mainland, perhaps I wouldn't have to be so constantly anxious about our food supply. As dragons, we would still need to hunt from time to time, but those hunts could be fewer and farther apart. We could sustain ourselves with smaller meals when in human form, and we'd have a greater variety of edible options.

As Hinarax rises and the woman hands over our food, a shout from down the street catches my attention. A group of armed men and women are striding toward us. One carries an ax, another a thick staff, and the third a crossbow. The leader, a stocky man with a prodigious frown, grips the hilt of the sword at his hip. On his left shoulder gleams a silver medallion emblazoned with a curved pair of leafy branches.

"Ho there!" he calls. "You! Put down your bundles and raise your hands!"

I dislike him at once, and I stare at him coldly, even as his companion lifts the crossbow and readies it.

"Put your things down," repeats the man with the medallion. "By order of the village watch."

"The village watch?" asks Hinarax.

"That's right. You've been flashing around a lot of jewelry, paying a king's ransom for things like directions, meat pies, and—" He glances at the gathered villagers.

"And old beat-up shoes," offers the woman behind the table. I throw her a glare, and she shrugs unrepentantly.

"That's right," continues the man with the medallion in a pompous tone. "As the constable, it is my duty to take into custody all suspicious characters that might otherwise heretofore cause something of an unseemly uproar in this here, our peaceful village, what has just started to recover from the toils of war, and therefore we do not under any circumstances welcome such strangers as yourselves, who must be either fine lords fleeing the new regime, or brigandish thieves of the robberly sort. In which case, in summation and conclusion, the proper course of action is to put you two in a cell and commandeer or requisition such articles of value as you might have upon your persons."

"You're the guards of this village. You don't like the way we barter, so you're taking our treasure and imprisoning us," translates Hinarax pleasantly.

"Not to put too fine a point on it—yes," replies the constable.

Hinarax leans over and whispers to me out of the side of his mouth. "We could transform."

I glance around at the villagers crowding the street, at their fragile homes and their tables of simple wares. Transforming into dragons here would cause too much damage, and word of the incident would travel swiftly to the King of Vohrain. Much as I ache to get to Serylla, it's too early to reveal our true nature.

"We'll go along with them," I mutter to Hinarax.

"Right." He doesn't seem at all perturbed by the idea of being locked up. In fact, he looks rather excited about it as he addresses the constable. "We'll come with you and give you our valuables, as long as you let us keep our food. And the shoes."

The constable looks rather surprised, but he says, "Fair enough."

The armed men close in and escort us along the street to the only stone building in the village. A storm like the Mordvorren would devastate a place like this, where most of the structures are fabricated of wood and bricks. These people are fortunate the Mordvorren decided to hover over Ouroskelle instead of battering the coastline.

What's strange to me is the way the Mordvorren vanished so abruptly, without a trace. When I left my cave, I expected to see it receding into the distance. But the ocean and the sky were clear on all sides. I haven't taken the time to ponder it until now… and within seconds I'm distracted from the mystery as I enter a human building for the first time.

As we step inside, I summon my limited experience with humans during the war, as well as everything I learned from Serylla, and I try to identify as many items as I can. Tables. Chairs. Fireplace. Some black metal rods that stand beside the fireplace... not sure what their function is. Lanterns. Rugs. Maps on the walls. And books, very large books, one of which lies open on a table while a woman hunches over it, writing rows of numbers and phrases in the Eventongue. Some sort of notation, perhaps to do with the business of the village. She looks up at Hinarax and me, and I get the distinct feeling that her sharp eyes are taking in every detail. Something about her reminds me of Jessiva, my brother's keen-eyed, red-haired captive, and the similarity sets me on edge.

We're taken to a small room at the back of the building... "a *prison cell*," Hinarax whispers, with all the delight of a hatchling seeing a waterfall for the first time.

Straw covers the floor of the otherwise empty cell. If we were to transform in here, we would explode right through the stone wall into freedom. Perhaps we'll do that during the night. We could transform long enough to break out, then switch back to human form and run for the woods. Once we put enough distance between us and the village, we could take to the sky and find cloud cover. As long as the people don't see our dragon forms, they'll think we had secret magic or hidden explosives to facilitate our escape.

The constable takes our jewelry, placing it in a small brown satchel which he buckles shut and pats contentedly. "I'll keep this safe until we figure out what's what with you two." He slams an iron gate shut across the doorway of the cell and locks it, a process which Hinarax observes with keen curiosity.

After the constable stumps away, I seat myself onto the straw, propping my back against the wall. "Once it's dark, we're leaving."

"We could have tried to fight them in our human forms," says Hinarax. "I've watched weaponless men battle with their fists and arms. They kick, too. Some of them even bite, though I believe among humans that's considered dishonorable."

"You and I aren't trained to fight in this form," I reply. "This was the only choice if we wanted to maintain our disguise and avoid causing damage. The Bone-Builder knows we've done enough harm in this land already." The ache of my guilt joins the gut-wrenching pain of Serylla's absence, and for a moment I don't know how I'll survive the agony of it all.

Hinarax gathers his locs and sweeps them over one shoulder before sitting down beside me. "The war was inevitable. In your position, any of us would have done the same thing. We followed you into battle, not just because of your bone-oath, or because of your title, but because we could see no other way."

"Perhaps we need to become a bit more innovative, as a species," I reply.

"I won't argue with that. But my Prince, you must not carry the weight of the war alone. We were all there. We all made choices. You were not solely responsible."

I inhale deeply and let the breath out gradually. I think I have been waiting for one of my people to say those very words to me. It does not absolve me for what I have done, but it gives me a little relief.

After a long silence, Hinarax inquires, "What's the plan, my Prince?"

"Wait till dark, explode out of here, run for the woods. Once we get there, we'll transform and fly to the Capital under cover of darkness and clouds. Also, while we are on this mission you may dispense with the honorifics. Call me Kyreagan. Or perhaps Ky is a more human name."

"Ky." He nods, pleased. "I like it. And you can call me Rax… or Hin? Or Arax?"

He keeps trying out various abbreviated forms of his name while I stare at the iron gate and wonder if Serylla's current accommodations are any better than mine. I hope they are. I hope she is comfortable. If not, I'm sure she will make it known, loudly.

I can't help smiling a little, remembering her demands and her whining when I first captured her. My fears for her safety are justified, but I must also remember who she is—a clever actress who can be dreadful, devious, or charming by turns.

My attempt to save her is not going well so far. Perhaps, by the time I make it to the Capital, she will have rescued herself.

4

SERYLLA

I've been in the dark for hours.

The chain linking my manacles to the wall is too short for me to sit down, so I lean against the stone until I'm too exhausted to stand for another second. I try kneeling for a while, but that position tugs at the manacles, making them dig painfully into the backs of my hands. My full bladder is swollen, aching, and my stomach muscles continue cramping occasionally. Pain stabs through my injured foot every few seconds, and my shoulder hurts where I landed on it. Besides which, I'm starving.

The worst part is the need to relieve myself. My bowels are churning a bit from the process of birthing the eggs, and though I've been able to control it so far, I'm rapidly reaching my limit. If no one comes, I'm going to end up letting everything out right here, on the floor.

Things scurry through the pitch darkness occasionally. Now and then, a thin, jointed leg brushes against my bare foot, and I have to bite back a scream.

I can feel my sanity flaking away like shavings from a stick. Time is a merciless blade, carving me thinner and thinner.

Just as I think my bladder will burst, I hear footsteps in the hallway. They're faint, almost inaudible through the thick wood of the cell door.

"Please," I rasp. The act of trying to speak makes me realize how thirsty I am, how thick and dry my tongue is. "Please, I need the privy, or a chamber pot, or a bucket. Anything, please."

Something clinks in the lock, and the cell door opens with a groaning creak.

A burly figure enters and sets down the lantern he's carrying. By its glow I devour his appearance, eager for any clue about who he is and whether I can convince him to help me.

He's not as tall as Kyreagan is in human form, but he's taller than the average man. Black fur cloaks his broad shoulders. Gold jewelry glints in a bushy reddish beard, and thick brows bristle above deep-set eyes. There's a gold ring through his septum, a mark of Vohrainian nobility, and it's set with a single tiny ruby that identifies him as royalty.

This is Rahzien, King of Vohrain. I'm looking at the man who conquered my kingdom, the one who humiliated and executed my mother. The only being in the world whom I could kill without feeling a drop of regret.

"Serylla." His voice is gruff and low. He purposely omits my title and uses no honorifics.

"Rahzien," I reply.

"Master," he says.

"What?"

"You'll call me Master."

"Fuck you," I hiss.

He turns on his heel and heads for the door.

"Wait! I need the privy."

"'I need the privy, *Master*.'"

Is he being serious? I let out a derisive laugh, but he only stands unmoving, waiting. Demanding that I verbally demean myself and acknowledge him as my superior.

I'm a woman with pride and a decent amount of inner strength, but I've never been as proud or steely as my mother. Even when I worked hard alongside the palace servants, I enjoyed my rest and my comforts, too. And what I'm requesting isn't even a comfort—it's a basic need. One I've resisted for so many hours that I'm desperate.

The last thing I want to do is piss and shit all over myself in front of the man who killed my mother.

It's just a word. One word, and then maybe he'll let me visit a privy or at least give me a bucket. "I need the privy... Master."

Immediately Rahzien returns, detaches my manacles from the wall, picks up the lantern, and motions for me to follow him.

A little way down the hall there's a rank-smelling privy, featuring a battered wooden toilet with metal pipes leading into the wall. A few rags lie near the toilet. There's no door.

Rahzien stands in the hall, watching me enter the privy.

"Could you turn around?" I ask.

"Say, 'Turn around please, Master.'"

I grit my teeth, and through them I mutter, "Turn around, please, Master."

He turns his back, and he doesn't look my way until I've finished with everything. It's difficult to clean myself with my hands shackled, but I manage it.

For a second I consider fleeing down the hallway, but before I can make a move, the King grabs the back of my neck in his giant hand, steers me along the corridor, and shoves me back into my cell. He grabs the chain between my wrists and lifts it high, as if he's going to attach it to the wall again.

"Wait, please! Could I be allowed to sit?" I ask. "And may I have some water?"

He waits.

Fuck him, fuck him, *fuck*... He wants me to call him "master" again. What the hell am I doing? Why am I going along with this? I've been in his presence for less than an hour and I'm already caving to his wishes. It's weak, it's shameful. I should be stronger than this.

"You have to let me go." I lift my chin, straighten my spine, and try to look bold, but instead I wince and nearly cry out at the pain twitching through my muscles. I hold back the whimper and force myself to speak as steadily as I can. "I was stolen from the Prince of Dragons. He'll come to fetch me, and he'll make sure you rue the day that you took what's his."

"You think he'll come to fetch you?" Rahzien yanks my arms up and attaches the chain to the wall again. "What makes you believe that?"

"He—" I hesitate, reluctant to reveal Kyreagan's affection for me. "The dragon prince is very possessive. To him I'm a war prize, a valuable object. Part of his hoard. He will view this as the deepest insult." My voice thins and a cough barks through my dry, scratchy throat. "I need water."

"You *are* a war prize. A valuable object."

I frown. "Yes... that's what I said."

"You were his pet, and now you're mine."

"No—"

"You are my pet. You do as you're told. When you do as you're told, you receive good things."

I hate every word he just said, but I bite back a caustic response. Deep inside me resonates a warning, an instinct that being saucy will not have the same effect on Rahzien that it did on Kyreagan. From the day we met, I had a sense of Kyreagan's nobility, his reluctance to hurt me. I sense nothing of the kind from the King of Vohrain. In fact, when he's this close to me, my very bones tighten and my skin breaks into goosebumps, as if my body is silently screaming to get away from him.

"We can avoid further conflict," I say hoarsely. "You once promised to be lenient to my mother and me, if we surrendered. And though she refused to give in, I would have yielded for the sake of my people, if I'd had any authority to do so. We can come to an arrangement that spares you from Kyreagan's wrath and ensures a peaceful transition of power."

A peaceful transition... until I can persuade the Southern Kingdoms to help me overthrow this bastard.

"Interesting." The King stares at me, and another chill rushes along my spine because I've never seen eyes like his. There's a flatness to his stare, an impenetrable cruelty. His voice rises and falls like anyone else's, but it's almost as if he's forcing the cadence, as if beneath his normal human tones there lies a blank monotone—the true timbre of his voice.

"You would yield to me for the sake of your people," he says. "I wonder if they would do the same? Would they obey me, if it meant sparing you pain?"

"I'm not sure what you mean."

"You are beloved among the citizens of Elekstan, in a way your mother never was. Perhaps you are not aware of their affection for you. I personally don't understand it. You seem rather soft and simple to me. You weren't made to rule or to think, only to open your sloppy mouth for cock."

His hand drops to his belt, and I shut my mouth tight.

He notices the clench of my jaws and smiles a little. "I thought you wanted a drink."

I shake my head.

"I'll make you a deal. Repeat these words five times, and you may have some water." He doesn't touch me, just keeps staring into my eyes with that soulless expression. "You are my pet. You do as you're told. When you do as you're told, you receive good things. Say it."

"Kyreagan will find me," I reply faintly, although I'm not quite sure of it. What if Ky thinks I made my own arrangements to leave Ouroskelle? What if he realizes I've been taken but doesn't care about my fate, since I was planning to leave him anyway? What if he cares, but he can't figure out where I am?

"Kyreagan is no longer your master," repeats the King of Vohrain in that steady tone. "You are my pet. You do as you're told. When you do as you're told, you receive good things, like water. *Say it.*"

They're only words. And I'm so thirsty it's becoming difficult to think about anything except sweet, cold, clear liquid running down my throat, rehydrating the parched tissues, renewing my mind, clarifying my speech. I feel as if my brain itself has shriveled up. To have my faculties again—to survive— I must do this. I must yield a little more.

"Say it," urges the King quietly. "Five times. And you'll have all the water you can drink."

Just a few phrases. I don't have to believe them. Saying them doesn't make them true.

I form the mantra with my thirst-thick tongue, hating myself with every word. "I am your pet. I do as I'm told. When I do as I'm told, I receive good things."

I say it five times. After the fifth time, the King leaves the cell for a moment and returns with a pitcher and a ladle. He holds the ladle to my lips while I drink deeply of the fresh water within. When I ask for more, he refills it without demanding that I call him "Master."

With two basic needs taken care of, my body switches focus to the pain in my foot, my stomach, and my shoulder. I haven't been able to rest much since I birthed the eggs, and if I can't lie down soon, I think I might faint.

"Could you unhook me from the wall?" I ask. "I need to sit."

Rahzien pretends not to hear. He pours the remaining water from the pitcher over the floor, where it darkens the stone and pools in the cracks.

"You're a cruel bastard." My voice trembles. "Why are you doing this? Do you enjoy demeaning and humiliating women? I heard what you did to my mother, you heartless beast."

"You call me a beast, and yet you wish to return to one who is truly a beast, in every sense of the word," he says calmly. "What does the Dragon Prince offer that I cannot?"

I chew my lip, unwilling to share my new, tender feelings for Kyreagan with this brutal king. Finally I settle on the simplest of responses. "He was good to me."

"I will be good to you as well. You are my pet. You do as you're told. When you do as you're told, you receive good things."

"Stop saying that." I shiver involuntarily.

"I'm offering you all the comfort and luxury you're accustomed to, as long as you submit. I will give you another lesson to repeat, and if you say it well, I will permit you to lie down."

Instead of refusing him outright, I wait, my good shoulder propped against the wall, my thighs trembling with weariness.

Rahzien sets down the pitcher and steps back, folding his arms. "You will say the following: 'I did not save my people, nor can I save myself. I am worthless. I am foolish. I am alone. I have no value, and no one wants me.'"

The words echo in my head.

I did not save my people, nor can I save myself.
I am worthless. I am foolish. I am alone.
I have no value, and no one wants me.

Each phrase is a frozen dagger, a slim shard of poisoned ice piercing my heart, melting and spreading lethal venom. These words have greater power, because they're doubts I've battled ever since the conquest of Elekstan… and perhaps longer.

"Say it," says the King. "And you may lie down."

My whole frame quakes at his words. Tears slip down my cheeks, but I force myself to say one word. One small defiance. "No."

He takes the lantern and the pitcher. Slams my cell door, locks it.

Something chitters in the inky blackness, and tiny feet scamper near the ceiling. I shudder violently, then sag against the wall, my wrists spiking with pain. Tears flood my eyes, spilling the precious water from my body even as I try to hold them back.

"Kyreagan," I whisper brokenly. "Kyreagan, please."

5

KYREAGAN

The only illumination in our gloomy cell is a distant, watery glow from a lamp in the front room. Hinarax has been pacing for a while, watching as the light from the window at the end of the hall faded. It's dark now. Nearly time for our explosive escape.

Part of me seethes with impatience, aching to break out and fly toward the Capital. But another part of me wonders if I'm already too late. I'm terrified that we'll make it all the way to the palace only to discover that Serylla has been tortured and killed, like her mother.

I don't think Rahzien would kill her, not yet. But he could wound her deeply, injure her in ways I can't bear to imagine. And I have to sit here and *wait*, because if we reveal what we are, and word gets to Rahzien, he will either kill the Princess or hide her where I'll never find her. Or he'll ambush Hinarax and me, and Serylla will be left to the King's mercy—which, judging by my fleeting acquaintance with him, is practically nonexistent.

In moments like this I miss my family more painfully than ever. I miss the sparkle in Grimmaw's eyes, her throaty voice, her words of brusque encouragement. I miss Vylar's intensity, her wholehearted devotion to every task. I miss Mordessa's steadiness, her loyalty, her gentle calm. My Promised was a formidable warrior, but there was never any hint of frenzy about her, not even during the heat of battle.

I miss my father, the Bone-King, though my memory of him is somewhat soured by the terrible oath with which he bound me. And I miss my mother, lost years ago to a voratrice. If only she and Varex hadn't ventured out that night, perhaps she would be here to advise me. Perhaps her wisdom could have redirected my father's purpose, prevented our involvement in the war, guided me to a different future.

And yet… I can't bring myself to truly regret my choices, because each one was necessary to bring Serylla into my life. My soul has wrapped itself together with hers, and I can't imagine an existence without knowing her.

I said the word "love" aloud to her once. It was nearly a confession, one she did not return. I suppose I deserved that. It's justice for my failure to return Mordessa's love when she confessed it to me. I now feel the same pain and uncertainty she must have felt.

Hinarax tosses the slim ropes of his coppery hair over his shoulder and plants himself in front of me. "It's time," he says in an undertone. "Do you want to break the wall or should I?"

"It should be me. If the change doesn't do the trick, I'll be able to focus my fire and explode the stones themselves."

He looks a bit disappointed, but doesn't protest. We both know that his yellow fire isn't as hot as mine.

Wearily I climb to my feet, trying to shed the heaviness of my body and spirit. I'm about to switch to dragon form when Hinarax and I hear two voices. One is a woman's, and the other is lighter, younger, and male.

"Where are they?" asks the male.

"Back there, in a cell. The head watchman locked their goodies in the safe behind the map of Revalor."

"Child's play. I'll have it open in no time."

"Don't tell me about it, just do it," responds the woman dryly.

"Of course, of course! I was never here."

"And I'm heading home, so I can pretend I didn't see you. Watch yourself, now. The prisoners don't seem like fighters, but you never know."

"Sweet Thora, always looking out for me. So may you rise."

"So may we all," she responds.

Footsteps, and then a door creaks and closes.

The last two phrases they exchanged sounded like a password of some kind. Varex, Vylar, and I used to make up such passwords as hatchlings—phrases with responses known only to the three of us.

Hinarax glances at me. "Escape now?" he whispers.

I shake my head. The human male, whoever he is, obviously intends to take our treasure and either kill us or release us. My guess is the former. Perhaps, if I'm patient for a few more minutes, we can discern his intentions and devise a way out of this that doesn't include destroying a large chunk of this building and calling attention to our escape.

The man in the front room is humming, and I'm immediately reminded of Serylla. I wonder if she's singing her annoying song for her new captor. At the thought, my body heats with possessive jealousy. That horrible, repetitive tune is *our* song, and she had better not be sharing it with the King of Vohrain.

When the sound of clinking metal reaches our ears, Hinarax wraps both hands around the barred door of the cell and mutters, "The human is taking our treasure. My jewelry, my coins. I planned to buy more clothes..."

"Our priority is rescuing the Princess," I hiss at him.

"Yes, but... one can rescue people while being well-dressed."

A moment later, footsteps scuff the floor, and the person who's humming comes into view, his right leg dragging slightly as he leans on a gnarled staff. By the light of the lamp in his free hand, he inspects us, and we stare at him.

His voluminous wavy hair is a dark red, like dragon blood. He wears a patch over his right eye, and a crooked scar runs through both lips along the right side of his mouth, giving him a perpetual twisted smirk. Black tattoos of roses and antlers cloak his throat. He's carrying the satchel that contains our treasure.

Without a word, he sets down the lamp, produces two slivers of metal, and pokes them into the keyhole of the lock on our cell. Seconds later, the lock pops open, and the cell door swings wide.

The man with the staff doesn't wait. He simply walks away, moving with surprising speed despite his limp.

Hinarax and I exchange glances, then follow him to a side door of the building. We emerge into the cool blue darkness of night and hurry across the grass to the edge of the nearby forest.

Only when we're deep among the trees, in a clearing dimly lit by starlight, does the man with the eye-patch pause. After propping his staff against a tree, he takes out a thin stem of wood with a tiny bowl at one end. He presses something into the bowl with his thumb, takes a chip of stone from his bag, and produces a spark. Setting the stem to his mouth, he inhales, then blows a puff of fragrant smoke into the air.

"What is that thing?" Hinarax asks.

The man scoffs lightly. "Never seen a pipe before?"

"No," replies Hinarax, with guileless curiosity.

"Well, hang me by the heels and beat my shiny buttocks," says the man. "Thora was right. You two are odd ducks and no mistake. Foolish, too, flaunting gold coins and fine jewelry in a village market, buying information from a child with an earring that could purchase this entire village and everyone in it."

"That's no business of yours," I tell him.

"But it is my business, see. I'm the one they call when oddities like yourselves show up—particularly oddities with money."

"So you're a thief," I say.

He splays a hand over his chest. "I'm deeply insulted. Thieves are common miscreants—I am an *artist*. Besides which I'm fairly sure that the two of you are thieves, which takes us into the realm of the pot calling the kettle black—"

"We did not steal the treasure you took. We scavenged it."

"Scavenged." He takes another puff of his pipe. "*Scavenged*. Oh, I like that as a euphemism for thievery. Are you pirates then? That would explain your attire, and the treasure—although there's still the matter of how you seem to be completely ignorant regarding the true worth of your valuables."

"We're not pirates," Hinarax replies.

"And we don't have time for this." I step forward, pleased to find that I'm much taller than the human. "Give us the treasure, and be on your way. You may keep a few pieces, with our thanks."

"Generous of you," he replies. "But you haven't answered my questions. Where did you come from? What's your purpose in Elekstan? Do you realize we've just been conquered? Is that where you got your loot—from ransacking the manors abandoned by the fleeing families of the nobility?"

This human won't stop asking questions, nor does he seem in a hurry to leave. Now that we're free of the cell and out of the village, I don't want to waste another minute. I'm not sure how to fight without my claws, my teeth, and my fire, but I'm willing to give it a try if it will silence him.

The red-haired man must sense the threat in my stance, because he tucks his pipe between his scarred lips and casually presses his thumb to the side of his walking stick. With a *snick* of metal, spikes emerge from the head of the staff. He hefts the weapon.

"I'd advise you to answer my questions," he says pleasantly. "And speak toward my left ear, if you would. The right one's hard of hearing."

Like Hinarax, I've observed humans brawling before. They generally curl their fingers and use their balled-up hands as weapons to strike their opponent. I frown at my own hand. My fingers look unusually thick and short now that my claws have been charmed away. I could summon my claws with a thought, but that would raise more suspicions in the mind of this inquisitive fellow.

Carefully I curl my fingers, then lunge toward the red-haired man, leading with my fist.

He sidesteps and whacks the side of my wrist with his staff. Pain erupts through my arm.

"Fuck," I snarl.

Hinarax charges in, trying to seize the staff or grapple with the man—I can't tell which. He ends up on the ground, on his hands and knees, while the human lays a swift blow across his backside.

The man is only using the rod of the staff on us, not the spiked head. I hate that he's showing us mercy. I despise how powerless I feel in this form.

"You can't be pirates or brigands, because you're terrible fighters," comments the stranger. "In fact, it's almost as if neither of you has ever thrown a punch." When Hinarax and I grimace at each other, the stranger barks out an incredulous laugh. "Is this your first fight?"

"No." I'm about to try attacking him again when a buzzing sensation quakes through my body. Once glance at Hinarax tells me he's feeling the same thing.

"How long has it been?" I gasp.

"I thought it was seven hours but—shit—it must have been eight," he groans.

I'm not about to lose the only set of clothes I have, so I begin tearing off my shirt and pants, while Hinarax does the same.

The stranger watches us with a shocked expression.

"Gentlemen, I've experienced my share of good times where fighting led to fucking, but I usually prefer to know someone for longer than half an hour before we get naked—"

"Stand back!" The words rip from my chest in a throaty growl.

The stranger's eye widens, and he staggers back just in time as Hinarax explodes into his true form—a sleek dragon with coppery scales and bronze wings. I shift as well and toss my head, shaking off the eddies of the transformative magic before looking down at the human from the height of my long spiked neck.

White-faced, the stranger says, "Well, spank me silly. That answers a few of my questions, and I have a hundred more."

"Your questions will go unanswered," I tell him. "There is someone we must find, and time is short. Give us the satchel."

The man wraps one arm around it protectively. "Not until you agree to talk."

"I can incinerate you quickly and easily," I say.

"But you won't. You two are trying—clumsily—to avoid notice, which means you won't risk using dragon fire so close to the village. The attempted stealth means you don't want your presence reported to the King of Vohrain. If you were here as his allies, you wouldn't mind being seen. Which means you are enemies of his, or at least at odds with him. And since we have a mutual enemy, perhaps we also have grounds for a conversation."

"There is nothing to discuss, and we're out of time. Keep the treasure." I attempt to stretch my wings in the cramped clearing, but Hinarax expands his at the same time and our wingtips collide. We'll have to take turns mounting into the air.

51

"You say you're looking for someone," persists the stranger. "You'll never find them if you keep bumbling about like this. I don't know how you managed to obtain human form, even temporarily, but it's obvious neither of you knows how to behave among humans. You'll be caught before you even come close to locating the person you seek."

"I have knowledge of humans," Hinarax says proudly.

"Do you now?" The stranger smirks. "What's a tinderbox?"

"I... well, it's a... something that you use to... aw, fuck," grumbles Hinarax.

"Exactly. That's something every human would know." The stranger presses his thumb to the same spot on his staff, and the spikes disappear. "Let me instruct you, help you, and guide you. In return, you'll help me."

"How?" asks Hinarax.

"I can think of a few ways, but for now, let's focus on monetary payment. I need this treasure. I came to the coast to see if I could borrow the funds I require, but that didn't work out, nor have I managed to find an abandoned trove in the manor of an absent lord... not for lack of searching. But this—" he pats the satchel. "It's more than enough to sway the people I need to bribe."

I snort. "Humans despise dragons for hoarding treasure, and yet you lust for it yourselves, even more powerfully than we do. You will harm others for it—even kill."

The stranger's face sobers, and his gaze pierces me like a spear of blue steel. "And you dragons kill for land. Do you think we, the people of Elekstan, do not know the price you were paid to slaughter us? You wanted islands that belonged to the King of Vohrain, and he gave them to you. You killed thousands of us, for *land*. Sucked my eye from its socket and ruined my ear, for land. When I say I will help you, it's not because I want to. It's because for some reason I cannot fathom, you have turned against your master. You wish to shed your scales and walk upon two legs. For my part, I wish to drive the Vohrainians out of this region. And I want to kill their king."

A wicked glee sparks in my heart at those words. Vaguely I recall Varex begging me not to start another war... and yet, in this moment, the idea of destroying Rahzien and freeing Elekstan sounds so delectable I cannot resist.

I lower my head until my jaws are level with the stranger's face. My breath glows faintly orange in the night air. "In this, our purposes are aligned."

He grins, darkly triumphant. "Then perhaps we have something to discuss, after all."

The discussion is a long, slow exchange of all the pertinent information, and though I know it's necessary, the delay frays my patience. The roguish stranger, whose name is Meridian, continues to be far too chatty and inquisitive for my taste.

"Humans talk too much," I growl, thrashing my tail. It knocks against a tree, and a squirrel scurries out of a hole with an alarmed squawk and chitters angrily at me. I narrow my eyes and hiss at the creature, blowing superheated orange mist in its direction. With a panicked chirp it scrambles away, leaps to another tree, and disappears into the dark forest.

"What I'm proposing is far more satisfying than terrorizing helpless woodland animals," says our new acquaintance. "It smacks of redemption, reparation, and... and..." He snaps his fingers a few times. "I can't think of a third thing to go with that, but—ah! Rebellion! That's the one! Or revolution. Redemption, reparation, and revolution. Brilliant."

"So you're part of a group that's resisting Vohrain's occupation?" asks Hinarax.

"Not just part of it, mate. I'm the damn organizer—the leader, you might say, if we believed in leaders. When Thora sent me a message about you two, I'd just finished meeting with a gallant band of pirates. They wouldn't loan me gold, but they did promise to partner with us and harass any Vohrainian ships that approach the Elekstan coast. Vohrain hasn't got much of a navy, which is a good thing for us—"

"What the fuck does this have to do with my rescue of the Princess?" I interject.

"Settle your spikes, big guy," says Meridian. "Surely you can see how two enormous dragons could be helpful to the resistance. I'll help you come up with plausible disguises so you can gain access to not only the city, but the palace itself. That way, you can locate your royal belle and sneak her out from under Rahzien's nose. In return, you'll help us kill Rahzien and drive out the Vohrainians so we can set up a new democratic government."

"Democratic." Hinarax mouths the word carefully with his long jaws. "What does that mean?"

"Aren't you adorable." Meridian pats Hinarax's muzzle. "It means no more kings or queens."

"But if you overthrow Rahzien, Serylla should be queen," I interrupt. "It is her birthright. Is that not how it's done among humans?"

"Things can change," Meridian replies. "My band will bow to the wishes of the people. If they want Serylla on the throne, I won't object, though it's not my preferred form of government. In fact my preferred form of government is no government at all. I'll admit anarchy rarely works well in practice, but still... a fellow can dream." He gives Hinarax another pat, on the cheek this time. "What do you say? Will you let me be your guide into the palace?"

"By your own admission, you're a thief and a rogue," I say. "Untrustworthy."

"Thief, pickpocket, highwayman, locksmith, juggler, and yes... I'll answer to *rogue*. Go on."

"How will someone like you gain admission to the palace?"

"Ah, but that's the beauty of it! Remember the pirates I spoke of? They told me that one of the Southern Kingdoms, Zairos, is sending its seventh prince to meet with Rahzien, to officially acknowledge his conquest of Elekstan and recognize him as its new ruler. But the prince's ship was attacked, looted, and sunk by the pirates, and the prince drowned. No one in Elekstan knows this yet, so we have a small window in which to act."

"To act?" I narrow my eyes.

"After the conquest, the Capital was locked down," says Meridian. "Getting inside takes certified permits, which citizens can only obtain from one of Vohrain's census stations, and only if they're a verified resident or tradesperson. We've been harassing Vohrain very effectively throughout the countryside, but our access to the Capital is limited, which means finding the Princess isn't as simple as sending in a few spies. So we have to go bigger."

"How big?" For once, Hinarax sounds apprehensive.

"Diplomatic papers are easier to forge than the official stamped permits the locals have to procure," Meridian explains. "You with the black hair—you look remarkably like the seventh Prince of Zairos—and I know that because one of the pirates snagged the prince's portrait from his royal cabin before they scuttled the vessel. They're using the portrait for dart practice in the galley aboard the pirate ship. Good times."

He sighs with dramatic wistfulness, then continues. "You'll pretend to be the Southern prince, while your friend here acts as your esquire, your most trusted servant. I'll play the part of your attendant and entertainer. A few friends of mine can act as your guards, and together we'll be welcomed into the palace."

"You told us we can barely pass as human, and now you're suggesting we masquerade as foreign dignitaries?" I say coldly. "You're a fool."

"Don't mind him," Hinarax says. "He's been through a lot, and he's suffering because he's in love with the Princess."

My only answer is a threatening snarl.

"How absolutely charming," says Meridian. "A dragon in love with a princess. Rather poetic, that. What about you, handsome?" He surveys Hinarax. "What's your preferred flavor? He? She? They? All?"

Hinarax arches his bronze neck, then slides his slender muzzle past Meridian's cheek, letting his tongue glide along the rogue's jaw.

"So that's how it is." Meridian chuckles, a little breathless.

"Don't mind *him*, either," I comment. "We're at the end of our mating season, and he's still a bit randy."

"Indeed." There's a gleam in the rogue's eye as he touches the place on his jaw where Hinarax licked him. "Well... back to business. If you agree to this plan, we should set off for the Capital at once. My people have a hideout in the mountains north of the city—a network of caves."

"Caves?" My interest perks.

"Indeed. Some of the chambers are quite large, big enough to accommodate a dragon. You say you can remain human for about eight hours at a time?"

"Yes."

"Good. We'll use that time to teach you some courtly manners. Since you're pretending to be from the Southern Kingdoms, they'll overlook a few differences in your speech or behavior, but complete ignorance like the kind you displayed in the market will not be excused."

"Understood." I arch my wings. "If you're coming with us, you'll have to ride Hinarax. The Princess is the only one who rides me."

"I'll bet she does," murmurs the rogue.

I ignore his comment. "The clouds are low tonight. We'll fly above them to escape notice. It will be cold."

"I can endure it," Meridian assures me cheerfully. "This leg of mine wasn't damaged in the war—it's been my companion since childhood. Discomfort is an old friend."

His plucky attitude enhances my opinion of him. As he said, our interests are currently aligned, and it's plain that Hinarax and I need help. The bits of human culture Hinarax gleaned from watching the Vohrainian soldiers was clearly insufficient for this mission. I realize that now.

"Onward, then," I say.

Once Meridian has mounted Hinarax, I extend my wings. It's a struggle to take off in such a small clearing, but I manage it, clumsily. I head straight for the cloud cover, darting through the gray, misty mass and hovering just above it while I wait for Hinarax and his passenger.

The Rib Moon was days ago, and the moon is waxing again, slowly. As its faint light shimmers on my scales, I think of Varex—of the ragged wound in his throat, and his odd behavior. He wasn't himself when I left him in charge of Ouroskelle, yet I abandoned him to deal with a clan of dragons fresh from the mating frenzy, not to mention a bunch of hungry human captives, some of whom were carrying eggs or had recently birthed them. He will have to assign dragons to help with the island cleanup and the disposal of storm debris. He'll grieve with the clan over the three lives lost, and collect bone-tribute from the dragon who drowned with his two women. He'll check on my offspring from time to time, and he'll lead the first hunting party to the Middenwold Isles, without me.

Once again, I've forced him to clean up a mess I left behind, when he has endured as much grief and loss as I have. I rely on him when I can't bear the weight of being a Prince of Ouroskelle... but on whom does *he* rely, when he's weary or troubled? I told him I would listen if he needed to talk—but I'm not there, am I? I left him with his bitch of a partner, that redheaded, murderous devil Jessiva. To think I admired her spirit at first—

Hinarax breaks through the clouds, with Meridian clinging desperately to his back. "Ready to fly?"

In answer, I bank upward, catch the sleek surface of a brisk night wind, and I coast westward, toward the city where my enemies sleep.

6

SERYLLA

My wrists are raw. I didn't realize how quickly skin could be rubbed away.

I alternate between kneeling, which hurts my wrists and knees, and standing, which hurts everything. Twice I start to doze off, but both times, the chittering and scrabbling in my cell grows louder, and I jerk awake, terrified that the creatures will sense my loss of consciousness and come to nibble at me. I have no idea what the crawly things are. The cell is black as a cave, so even when my eyes are open, I can't see anything.

Ever since I drank the water, I've felt vague and muddled—dizzy and drowning in the dark, and thirstier than ever. Maybe the King drugged me. Or perhaps my wounds are becoming infected. Chills keep surging over my skin, followed by painfully intense flashes of heat that slick my body with sweat. I'm parched, practically dying of thirst, and I'm so hungry my stomach feels as if it's stuck to my backbone.

This is true captivity, true cruelty. Even before Kyreagan and I developed a connection, he was reasonable. Any deprivation I experienced with him wasn't malicious—he simply didn't think of everything, or understand what I needed. The bruises he gave me were the result of his inexperience with handling humans. He regretted them as soon as he noticed them, and he never handled me so carelessly again. When he learned more about my needs and wants, he did his best to accommodate them.

But this man, this human king—he has none of Kyreagan's consideration or mercy. He is pitiless.

Still, it's almost a relief when Rahzien enters my cell again. He's wearing different clothes—a simple ivory shirt and a pair of brown leggings that hug his massive thighs.

He sets down his lantern and surveys me, twisting one of the gold beads in his beard. I know he must have bodyguards and servants somewhere—perhaps upstairs, waiting for his call. Not that they would need to remain within earshot for his safety. I'm a limp, trembling mess, the furthest thing from a threat.

He's a busy man, with an army at his command and a conquered nation to subdue, and yet he prefers to come here alone and devote time to breaking my spirit. As if this is the work he truly prefers.

My mother used to enjoy breaking horses. It was one of her few hobbies, and she never indulged in it without a healer close by in case she was injured. The stablemaster would send one of his boys out to the market beyond the city's eastern wall, where horses, cattle, and all kinds of animals were sold and traded. The boy would find the fiercest stallion or the most restive colt and bring it back to the palace for my mother to break in her spare time. She tamed each horse with vicious beatings and the sheer force of her will, and sometimes with deprivation. I could never watch the process for long—it made me furious, and usually resulted in a savage argument between us, after which she would ban me from the stables and gardens for weeks on end.

I understand enough of the process to know what Rahzien is doing, to witness my own slow unwinding into a creature of groveling need. Even as the King surveys me, I'm teetering on the verge of brokenness, balancing on the crumbled edges of my self-worth. My mind is blurred, my body feverish, my eyes swollen, my lips cracked. Strangely, I don't need to pee, which is worrying since I've been like this for hours. At least I think it's been hours. Days?

"Do you still think the Dragon Prince will come to save you?" asks the King.

I frown, trying to conjure Kyreagan's face. My exhausted brain keeps switching between his dragon features and his human ones.

"Yes," I rasp. "He'll come. He'll... kill you."

"I'm not worried," replies Rahzien. "Not about him, or any of the dragons. They'll all be dead soon."

Fear twists inside me, sharp enough to pierce my mental haze for a moment. "Dead? What do you mean?"

The King smiles, and it's like the ruthless grin of a shark. "I heard that the Mordvorren was sighted over Ouroskelle. That's why Fortunix didn't bring you to me sooner. The storm spent several days there, didn't it? Which means the island's natural resources will have been severely depleted."

"The dragons are resilient," I say.

"True." He strokes his beard. "You know those bits of land they wanted? The ones I gave them as their reward for helping me conquer Elekstan? Every animal on those islands has been infused with a magical poison that activates upon contact with a dragon's saliva."

He waits for my reaction, but I can only stare vaguely at him. What he's saying doesn't make sense.

"After the storm, the dragons must have been hungry," Rahzien continues. "By now they'll have hunted and consumed prey from the Middenwold Isles. Those islands are the only remaining source of prey other than the mainland—and the dragons won't hunt here. They're too honorable for that."

"What are you saying?" I falter.

"Within the next day or so, the dragons will fall ill, every single one of them. And by the time they realize why they're sick, it'll be too late. Every dragon will be dead by the end of the week."

Panic spurs my sluggish heartbeat. "You're lying. If this was true, you would have mentioned it last time."

"I choose when to give you information. I am your master."

"No poison like that exists. I don't believe you."

"I may not have any sorcerers with battle skills, but I've got one who creates the most intricate, ingenious poisons—like the one currently flowing through *your* veins. The one that was infused in the water you drank."

I choke on a mirthless, despairing laugh. "Why would you poison me? It makes no sense. You need me as leverage with the people."

"Ah, but this poison doesn't kill you... not exactly. It prevents you from going too far from me. Let's say I was standing in the center of your palace, and you were headed toward the city wall. By the time you got there, you would start feeling sick and faint, and if you persisted, you would eventually collapse, bleeding from the eyes, nose, and ears. If you managed to crawl farther, you would slip into unconsciousness, and if anyone carried you beyond that point, you would die."

"Liar," I whisper. It's the only word that makes sense, the only defense I can muster. "Liar."

"Try to escape, and you'll find out if I'm lying," Rahzien answers. "The proximity poison is somewhat inconvenient for me, I'll confess. I've had to remain nearby to avoid accidentally killing you, which complicates some of my duties. The sooner you submit, the sooner we can both return to your palace and proceed with our new lives. I shall proclaim myself Emperor of Vohrain, Elekstan, and Ouroskelle, while you shall take your place as my first 'Conquered Consort.' I came up with the title myself. What do you think of it?"

"Fuck you," I wheeze.

"Yes, you will." His beard twitches as he smirks. "As for the other thing, the extermination of the dragons—I have long believed that those creatures were far too powerful to be allowed to exist. Our alliance gave me the chance to evaluate the threat they pose, and I've decided there's no place for such monsters in the empire I'm building."

A hideous wave of heat roars through my body, followed by a burst of nausea. I imagine the dragons sickening, spasming, dying, unable to fulfill Kyreagan's promise and set their captives free after mating season. I picture the women stranded in caves, unable to return to the ground, slowly starving. I envision the eggs—my eggs—the pretty violet one and the marbled blue one, hatching alone in the cave, with their father's skeleton as their sole guardian. The little ones will suffer and perish, with no one to bring them food or teach them to fly. They will die, believing themselves unloved and unwanted, when nothing could be farther from the truth. Their father did terrible things to ensure their existence, to provide for them.

"Kyreagan." Fuck, I said his name aloud. The boundary between my thoughts and my voice has grown watery, imagination and reality blending together.

Kyreagan. Is he suffering right now, writhing in agony as the poison does its work? Is he torn by anxiety, worrying about everyone else even as he's dying? Is he already dead, disintegrated by the dawn, a majestic warrior faded into nothing but wind and ash?

No. *No.*

I need him to exist, even if I suffer, even if I die. I need him to keep *being.* "I don't believe it," I gasp. "Any of it."

"I'll find you proof," says the King. "Might take a while, but I'll send some men out to Ouroskelle and have them bring back—what do the dragons call it? Bone-tribute?" He chuckles tonelessly. "I'll have them bring back a bone of Kyreagan's. Maybe I'll carve it into a butt plug for you. That way, when I'm fucking you, he'll be there too."

"You're the worst excuse for a human being to ever walk this earth." I can barely manage the words because the chills are back, and my teeth keep clicking together compulsively.

"I see you have a fever," observes Rahzien. "Probably from that wound in your foot."

I glance down and nearly vomit at the sight of my foot. It's swollen and unrecognizable, mottled in shades of sickly taupe, olive-green, and purple.

"I assume you'd like treatment for that," he says. "Some food and water? A bed?"

"What's the point? I may as well die."

"Because of the dragon?" Rahzien leans closer, his stare oddly intense. "You want to die because he's dead?"

The question rings through me like a bright bell, and for an instant I'm alert, fully cognizant.

To live, knowing that Kyreagan is gone, will hurt, every single day. But I can do it, if somewhere in the future lies a promise of revenge. I can do as I'm told, bear any brutality, suffer any assault, in the interest of one day finding the chance to kill Rahzien with my own hands—or at the very least, look into his eyes while someone else slaughters him at my feet.

If Fortunix can bide his time for so long, and wreak such far-reaching vengeance upon the kingdom who hunted his mates, I can do *this*. I can be the soft, submissive creature Rahzien wants. I can do anything he requires of me.

This is the game, the task, the strategy—my tragic masterpiece. Just as I played the arrogant, demanding princess for Kyreagan, so I will play the defeated, spiritless doll for Rahzien.

Until the day the doll rises up, and stabs him to death with a splinter of her own broken heart.

I let myself sag in my chains. "Yes, I want a bed, and food, and medicine. Please, Master."

"That's a good little fool." He grabs my chin, tilts my face up to his bearded one so I'm forced to stare into his eyes. He's trying to see if I mean it, if he has broken the spirit of the wild horse.

I let my misery, dizziness, weariness, and grief flood my eyes, oceans of hopeless submission surging over my true motives, concealing the black anchor of vengeance buried in the depths of my heart.

Rahzien seems satisfied with what he observes in my gaze. "Repeat after me."

He pronounces the mantra, and I speak it five times for him, in a voice faint and shaking.

"I did not save my people, nor can I save myself. I am worthless. I am foolish. I am alone. I have no value, and no one wants me."

7

Kyreagan

The flight to the rebels' hideout takes longer than I hoped, since we have to travel with the clouds and remain unseen. At one point we're forced to descend and wend our way slowly through a dark forest, whose limbs drag at my wings and scrape my scales, setting my teeth on edge. Then another cloud bank moves in, and we're able to take to the sky again.

In the darkness just before dawn, we arrive at a wide waterfall—a sheet of froth and foam plunging off a cliff and crashing into a pool that Meridian claims is bottomless. There's a narrow path leading to the waterfall—leading *behind* it, according to the rogue.

"Let me go first, along the path, and prepare the others for your arrival," he says. "If two dragons come blasting through the waterfall into our hideout, my friends are liable to perish from terror."

I'm reluctant to let him go, especially since he's still carrying our treasure. What if he disappears into some narrow tunnel where we can't follow? What if we're left stranded here, without the help he promised?

"Do you think we can trust him?" I ask Hinarax over the rushing thunder of the waterfall.

"As a rule, I think he's about as trustworthy as the Mordvorren," replies Hinarax. "But for this particular purpose— yes, we can trust him. He and I talked on the way. He truly hates the King of Vohrain. Hates all kings, in fact. Any sort of authority, really. He likes being able to take what he wants, whenever he wants it."

"Isn't that what human kings do? Perhaps he hates them because he would like to *be* them."

"I hadn't thought of it that way." Hinarax lifts a fore-claw to scratch behind his jaw spikes. "Being human is far more complicated than I expected. And more interesting, too. What do you think a palace looks like, inside?"

"Dainty and gilded, full of breakable things, no doubt. No place for dragons. There will be many objects we don't recognize or understand, but the best thing to do is ignore them, show no surprise or curiosity, and remain focused on our task."

"No curiosity at all?" Hinarax's long tongue traces his jaws.

"Maybe a little curiosity. But only to Meridian, and you must ask him your questions *quietly*, do you understand?"

"Of course." His enthusiasm quivers through his whole frame, and I can't help chuckling. The impulse is a small relief from the constant tension in my body, the ache in my heart.

A second later, Meridian reappears, leaning on his staff and beckoning to us.

"Time to meet some rebels." I spread my wings and mount into the sky, doing a few loops before streaking toward the waterfall. Behind the glittering spray, I can dimly discern the shape and height of the cave entrance.

I've flown through waterfalls before. It can be a dangerous thing for dragons, since the thundering weight of the water can bear us down. Hesitation can result in a dragon floundering at the base of the falls, pinned by the crashing flow. The trick is to build up speed, enter the falls at a slightly higher point than you wish to exit, and zip through as swiftly as possible.

I dart through so fast that I only feel the hammering water for a moment. Human voices shriek faintly at my arrival, but I ignore them until Hinarax is safely inside, flaring his wet wings.

We stand in the mouth of a cavern, a craggy chamber lit by lanterns on chains. We'll have to be careful not to dislodge those lanterns as we move about in dragon form. Other immediate hazards are the wooden crates, makeshift tables, and bedrolls strewn along the edges of the cave. Thankfully there's plenty of open space in the cavern's center, so we can move deeper inside without wrecking our new allies' belongings.

At the fringes of the space, humans are gathered, alone or in small clusters. I count over forty of them, and I suspect more are lurking in deeper chambers of the cave network.

As Hinarax and I pace slowly forward, Meridian moves out in front of us, gesturing expansively. "Here they are! The great dragons Kyreagan and Hinarax!"

"I thought you were telling tales again, Meri." The young woman who speaks is perched atop a large barrel, spinning knives in both hands. She has thick, tightly curled brown hair tied back with a string. A few straggling locks frame an attractive, tawny face with a sullen expression. Her dark eyes are hooded, and she seems utterly unimpressed by us.

A big olive-skinned man steps forward, his face grim beneath a bushy black beard. "And why should we welcome these killers?"

"I never said you have to welcome them, Odrash," says Meridian. "They are temporary allies whose goals are currently aligned with ours. That's all. We're not talking of friendship or eternal loyalty here—this is strictly a bargain of the moment, to serve a mutual end."

"Who's to say they won't burn us all in our beds?" This speaker is a woman as well, much older than the knife-spinning one. She is tall, gaunt, and leathery, with prominent cheekbones and eyes that look as haunted as my heart feels. One of her hands is curled tight, gnarled with scars. She holds it up. "Dragons did this to me. And you expect us to shelter them?"

Guilt drags its claws through my heart. I've never had to see the long-term results of dragon-fire, the lasting damage done to survivors like Meridian and this woman.

"We were wrong to ally with Vohrain." My deep tones reverberate through the cavern. "I could explain why we did it. I could tell you that we were on the verge of starvation and needed the hunting grounds Vohrain could provide. But nothing can excuse the carnage we wrought. I neither deserve your respect nor demand your forgiveness. I only ask to scheme alongside you for the overthrow of the Vohrainian king, whose lust for conquest has already cost so many lives among your people and mine. Let us help you drive Vohrain from your nation. Let me kill Rahzien for you. I swear the only lives I take while I'm here will be Vohrainian."

It's a good speech—diplomatic, disarming, and spoken straight from my heart. If Varex were here, he'd lower his head as a sign of his approval and respect.

Meridian pipes up, "This is the dragon who carried off the Crown Princess. He's madly in love with her now."

Of course the rogue had to ruin my speech with such talk. My spines bristle and I suppress a growl.

"Princess Serylla." The gaunt woman nods, her expression softening. "The Queen was a bitch, but the Princess is decent enough. A sweet girl. Spineless, but sweet."

"The only good royal," concedes Odrash.

"What will you do with the Princess once you have her?" asks the knife-spinning girl. "Will you take her back to your island?"

"I seek to set her free," I reply. "She may go anywhere she wishes, and do anything she likes."

"So you *do* love her, then." The girl nods. "Good enough for me."

"Good enough for *now*," corrects Odrash. "Meridian, do you plan to explain exactly *how* these two are going to kill the King? Two dragons could do a lot of damage to the palace, but they'd be brought down by Vohrainian guns before they ever got near Rahzien."

"Ah, that's the best part." Meridian rubs his hands together. "And you must all keep it a strict secret, understand? These dragons can transform into humans."

A disbelieving silence drops over the rebels.

"I could show you, briefly," offers Hinarax. "But I'll have to revert to my dragon self right away. There's a limit on how long we can remain in each form."

"We can explain the details later," Meridian says, with a wink. "Go on and show us, handsome. I won't say no to seeing that body again."

Hinarax bows his long neck until his snout nearly touches the cave floor—and then, with a burst of purple light, he transforms into his human shape.

The rebels gasp. The knife-wielding girl drops one of her blades and leans forward, her eyes bright with interest.

Hinarax turns in a slow circle, grinning, then switches to dragon form again.

An explosion of excited chatter breaks out among the humans. When Meridian finally manages to calm them down, he explains the plan, then immediately begins issuing orders, like the leader he claims not to be. "Inja, if you and Annu could go into the storage chamber and look for the loot we got when we pulled the Shrifshaw job—fine clothing in the Southern style, shoes with upturned toes, that sort of thing."

Next he turns toward the knife-spinning girl. "Aeris, you should be one of the bodyguards, since you're not from this region—along with Odrash and Kehanal, I think. There's less chance of you three being recognized by anyone in the Capital. We'll have to find you some uniforms. Ask Anzuli—he hails from the border villages and he has visited the South. He'll know what the royal guards of Zairos wear. And Norril, you worked in the palace until the conquest, didn't you? Perhaps you can educate our little acting troupe regarding some of the palace routines and manners."

A blond man steps forward. "I was one of Princess Serylla's bodyguards," he says, holding my gaze. "I could not have served a kinder soul."

"Yes." I can barely grit out the word. "She is kind."

"She does not deserve whatever Rahzien is doing to her."

The room quiets at Norril's words. He says nothing more, but when the conversation resumes among the rebels, it carries a stronger undercurrent of urgency, of purpose. With that single sentence, Norril stoked the entire group to more fervent action on behalf of the Princess.

And I could not be more grateful.

Unfortunately, we cannot soak up a few hours of knowledge and then head for the capital. According to Meridian and Norril, it will take more than a single day to teach two dragons to pull off this ruse. Which makes sense, but the delay infuriates me nonetheless. Serylla needs me.

"I could fly to the palace right now and challenge Rahzien," I tell them. "He *has* to speak to me—we're allies, or we were until he stole what is mine. I'll demand that he return her. I'll offer treasure—"

"He has all the treasures of his own kingdom and whatever remains in Elekstan's coffers," says Meridian. "You have a nice selection of gold and silver, I'll admit, but I'm not sure it would be enough to tempt him."

"We have more," Hinarax says.

Fuck him and his honesty. I swivel my neck around and deliver a glare that makes him shrink.

"How much more?" Avarice lights Meridian's eyes. "Enough."

But Norril shakes his head. "The Princess represents much more to him than money. She's the symbol he needs. The people are angry that their loved ones died in a losing war. They hate Rahzien more bitterly than they hated their former queen. Which means Rahzien won't give up the Princess, not for any sum. Though he might kill her to spite you, or to teach the people a lesson. In the short time he has ruled here, he's proven himself to be merciless and unpredictable."

Norril doesn't elaborate, and I don't ask. I feel as if I might gnaw my own leg off or scorch this entire cavern if I can't do something useful immediately. I've never encountered a situation such as this, where I yearned so deeply for a prize I could not obtain through force or fire. I want to soar from this cave like a thunderous storm and tear the palace down, layer by layer, room by room, until I find Serylla. But in doing so I would harm the servants and staff—people Serylla cares about. And I've sworn not to kill any more citizens of Elekstan.

"We get precious few reports from within the city," Meridian says. "But we've heard no rumor of the Princess being spotted anywhere in the Capital."

"She could still be in the palace, but sequestered out of sight," says Norril. "Or he could be keeping her somewhere else. Somewhere no one would think to look."

Despair weighs my heart as I remember how long I searched for Serylla back on Ouroskelle, after she escaped the enclosure. Humans are small. They can hide in so many places where a dragon cannot venture.

Reluctantly I give up the idea of bribery and return my focus to Meridian's plan. Mad as it seems, I fear it's our only option. With a respectful bow of my head, I settle my scaly bulk down onto the cave floor. "Teach us what we need to know."

"Happily," says Meridian, and for the next several hours he and Norril talk.

And talk.

And talk.

I try to grasp all the facts they're sharing, but everything is so unfamiliar that the topics get jumbled up in my mind—modes of address tangled with dinner courses, maps of the Southern Kingdoms merged with hasty sketches of the palace's layout. Norril is the type to forge ahead with blunt, stark explanations, while Meridian tries to fill in the gaps, defining and describing things Hinarax and I don't know.

At last, weary from the overabundance of new information, we snatch a few hours of sleep, then rouse again and switch to human form, whereupon several of the rebels descend upon us with layers of human clothing, from tight undergarments and leggings to tunics, shirts, and vests. Hinarax and I each have to try on a few different outfits until the humans agree on which ones work best.

"We have enough to pack a small trunk for you," says a woman named Kyteia, as she pins a sort of blanket to my left shoulder and drapes it artfully. "But we should have an explanation for why you don't have more luggage. I'm sure Meri will think of something. Now the boots."

"No boots," I protest.

"Oh, but you must have boots, tall ones with turned-up toes. They're the latest fashion."

"Perhaps the Southern Kingdoms haven't heard of boots," I offer helpfully.

"I'm quite sure they have. Now lift your foot."

Kyteia's gray hair marks her as an elder among humans, and I've been taught to defer to the wisdom of elders, so I grudgingly obey. She covers my feet in something called *socks*, which make the boots a bit less uncomfortable. Still, my feet feel crushed and imprisoned, and I don't like it.

"Try to look a bit less like you're being tortured," says Kyteia pleasantly. "You're doing very well, Hinarax."

He smiles at her, despite being fully encased in suffocating layers of leather and satin, including a puffy thing called a doublet.

"Now then, Kyreagan," says Kyteia, a note of stern encouragement in her tone. "Try walking, would you?"

I walk stiffly forward, trying to shake the fold of heavy cloth off my left arm. "What is the purpose of this blanket on my back?"

"It's a cloak, dear. This one is mostly ornamental, styled after the Southern fashion. The effect is usually rather dashing, but with you…" Her voice trails off and she grimaces as I stalk past her. "Relax your gait. You look as if you have fence-posts for legs."

"Hey now," says Meridian as he passes by, giving her a kiss on the cheek. "Some of my best friends have wooden legs."

"And I'll wager they walk with more grace than his dragon Highness here," says Kyteia. "Perhaps you could try a bit of a swagger, love?"

I stare at her. "Swagger?"

"Care to demonstrate, Meri?"

Meridian flourishes his walking stick and saunters for several steps. His limp is still noticeable, but there's a flair to his gait nonetheless, an undeniable ease with every part of himself.

"It's all in *here*." He spins on his heel and taps his chest. "In the soul. Feel the swagger, and then let it out. Confidence, gentlemen. You're already a prince, Kyreagan, so that's not much of a stretch. But you must imagine that you've been raised in luxury—what *humans* call luxury, which means a wealth of shiny, beautiful things around you, all the most exquisite comforts, and lots of people to boss around. You have several brothers ahead of you, so you'll never touch the throne. Your role is traveling to various kingdoms on diplomatic errands for your father, enjoying the best that each nation has to offer. Maybe one day you'll resent your lack of power, but for now, you're enjoying yourself. And you—" He gestures to Hinarax. "You're the trusted servant of the Prince, his esquire, a highly regarded official. Your duties are many, but you handle them skillfully, and you're pleased to be traveling at the Prince's expense. You're both young, good-looking, ready to be amused."

"Amused?" I quirk an eyebrow at him. "Elekstan is still volatile. The war has barely ended. Isn't it strange for a foreign prince to show up expecting to be entertained?"

"Perhaps," admits Meridian. "But since Rahzien's conquest is so new, he's eager for any acknowledgement from nearby nations. A visit from Zairos' royal family supports his claim to Elekstan. He'll welcome you and do his best to provide suitable entertainment. Tell him you'll stay for—how long do you think, Norril?"

"A week," Norril replies. "Long enough, but not too lengthy an imposition. That will give you time to inquire about the Princess. All the royal guards either fled or died within a few days of the conquest, so I can't direct you to any of my former friends for help, but I can give you the names and descriptions of a few servants to seek out, those with an ear to the ground and an eye for trouble. If the Princess is in the palace, they'll be able to tell you where."

"Enough strategizing for now," Kyteia urges. "The Prince must practice walking with pride and confidence."

I try to feel the *swagger* in my chest and stalk boldly across the cave, lifting my feet high with each step. Somehow the cloak wraps around my boot heel and I stumble, stagger, and manage to right myself with a few muttered *fucks*.

Kyteia cocks her head and purses her lips, deepening the wrinkles around her mouth. "Would it help if you thought of the cloak as a big floppy wing?"

I raise an eyebrow. "No. That would not help at all."

"Right... well perhaps a shorter cloak, then." She unpins it and withdraws to a nearby table. "I'll see what I can do about hemming it."

"Keep practicing the stride and the swagger," Meridian advises. "And while you're doing that, Anzuli will tell you a brief history of Zairos, and then Norril will go over the forms of address again. Won't that be fun?"

"Riveting," I respond.

"Yes, well... I'm off to mastermind dastardly plots against the occupying forces." Meridian gives me one of his lopsided grins. "Can't let operations grind to a halt just because you two beasties are here. I learned a long time ago not to put all my eggs in one basket, you see. And I have a particularly complex and important basket that's been in progress since the Vohrainians took the northern villages, and it needs tending."

He saunters away, and I cross the uneven floor of the cavern again, trying to imitate his gait, trying not to let his comment about *eggs* derail my thoughts from the task at hand. But I can't help picturing two beautiful eggs in a nest—one purple, one blue. My offspring.

For their sake, I will perform any role, endure any ridicule, swallow all the knowledge I can.

A searing certainty thrums through my chest, and I stride forward, flush with purpose, barely feeling the boots for once.

Meridian glances back over his shoulder. Then he turns around, watching me, and he smiles wider. His one blue eye sparkles with approval. "Now *that*, my friend, was the walk of a prince."

8

SERYLLA

Terror grips my limbs, turning my muscles rigid as I lunge upright. With a desperate shriek I thrash, half-believing that the sheets twined around my legs are the barbed tongues of a voratrice, that the edge of the mattress is the brink of a cliff.

My body crashes to the floor and I flail, unable to make sense of my surroundings.

"Your Highness! Your Highness!" The voice is familiar, and so are the hands grasping my wrists, the face floating above mine. "Princess Serylla!"

I stop fighting. "Parma?"

My maid nods, her lower lip trembling. "Princess."

Impulsively I seize her in a desperate hug, pulling her close even as I gasp, "No, you're not supposed to be here, you're supposed to be safe, not in the palace with that monster—"

"Are you referring to me?" booms a male voice.

A burly figure looms behind Parma. For a moment I don't recognize him, because his huge war-beard is gone, and what remains has been trimmed close to his jawline. The thick mane of his reddish-orange hair has also been cut short. Rahzien looks startlingly different—less like a brawling warrior and more like a well-kept king—an effect enhanced by the diamond-studded circlet he's wearing.

My mother's crown.

I want to tear it from his head, or demand that he take it off. Just in time, I remember my resolve to feign submission.

He rewarded me when I yielded to him. I'm in a bedroom, and my fever is gone, which means I was given medicine or treated by a healer, probably the latter. My tongue, while dry, isn't painfully parched anymore.

Slowly I sit up, brushing my tangled hair back from my face. "Master, forgive me. I was dreaming of monsters from the dragons' island."

"Do you remember your lesson?" His eyes are cold, calculating. He didn't buy my excuse. He suspects that I'm not quite broken.

"I think I can remember the lesson," I reply.

"Say it."

I hate repeating the words in front of Parma, letting her see how I've been conquered. But I have no choice. I must convince Rahzien I'm obedient, or I'll end up back in that cell where I nearly died.

"I am your pet. I do as I'm told. When I do as I'm told, I receive good things."

"And the other lesson." Rahzien's voice is low, almost soothing, but there's an undercurrent of dead things in it, like a river choked with murdered souls.

"I did not save my people, nor can I save myself. I am worthless. I am foolish. I am alone. I have no value, and no one wants me."

"Excellent. See that you remember your place, or you'll be back in that hole with the spider-mice. In fact, I think I shall call you *Spider*, as a reminder."

"Whatever pleases you, Master."

"This maid is my gift to you. A gesture of goodwill. I thought perhaps you could use a familiar face. She will prepare you for our first public appearance together." He nudges Parma's rear with the toe of his boot as she kneels beside me. "Get up, maid. The Princess must eat quickly, and then you will put her in the second outfit. The wrap, not the dress."

"My lord." She bows her head in assent.

The King leaves the room, and I realize with poignant shock that it's *my* room, my enormous royal chamber, with its thick rug embroidered with lavender peonies, its gold-fringed drapes, its immense canopy bed, and its array of white furniture, painted with more peonies in various shades of rose and plum. It's an airy, welcoming space, with three wide windows overlooking the garden. An archway leads into my white-marble bathroom with its gold finishes.

Behind the closed doors to my right lies my closet, containing dozens of brilliant gowns and all sorts of pants, from loose, colorful lounge-wear and soft white doeskin to shiny black leather. To my left, behind another door, lies the study, with its bookshelves and piano. The doors across from my bed lead to the sitting room, where I've done everything from receiving stately guests to hosting raucous parties with twenty-something nobles.

But this suite, as beloved and familiar as it is, seems sinister to me now—a precious gift that the King of Vohrain can easily steal away. He can visit me here, anytime he likes. He can corrupt every good memory I have of these rooms.

"Princess?" Parma's lips are wobbling again, and she stares at me with the eyes of a frightened doe. "You must eat something, and then I'm supposed to fix your hair, and dress you for—what the King said."

I nod, looking down at the plain ivory nightdress I'm wearing. "We'd better do as he commands."

She glances over her shoulder toward the open doorway that leads to the sitting room. Two men stand outside the doorway with their backs to us. They're wearing Vohrainian uniforms and helmets. Beyond them, on the far side of the sitting room, there's a door leading into the hallway, but that's only one of three paths out of my suite.

My plan to be the King's subservient doll is still viable, but if there's a chance to escape, I have to take it.

"The study door?" I whisper to Parma.

She shakes her head. "Guarded."

"And the passage through the closet? Did they find it?"

She nods, wincing. "It's been bricked up."

Shit.

One of the guards at the door turns around. "No whispering. Perform the command of the King."

Parma points to a covered tray on my nightstand. Beneath the lid, I find a dish of chicken, peas, and rice seasoned with broth. One of my childhood favorites.

The meal nourishes my heart as well as my body, because I know who crafted this dish for me. I recognize the familiar seasoning. This is the work of the head cook, Myron, a big, jovial fellow, a lover of stories and songs. No one else makes this dish quite the same way. He must have been told the meal was for me, and the flavors are almost as good as one of his bearlike hugs.

After days on the dragon's island and more days in a dungeon, nothing has ever tasted so exquisite. I'm thankful the food is simple, or my half-starved stomach might not be able to manage it.

After eating, I seat myself on the cushioned stool at my dressing table, and my maid performs her usual duties in silence. The sensation of the brush grazing my scalp and her gentle fingers manipulating my hair is a delight I've missed immensely. Both my hair and body feel clean, so I must have been bathed at some point, but I don't remember it, nor can I recall being transported from Zevin's family home to the palace. I must have been delirious or unconscious during the journey.

What if the King took advantage of me during that time? I could be pregnant with his child already and not even know it. Although I'm not sure I'd be fertile again so quickly after carrying Kyreagan's eggs.

I risk one more question. "Do you know if the King touched me while I was asleep?"

"Not to my knowledge, Princess," Parma whispers. "I've been with you since you were brought here. The King's healer tended you, and then Azra and I bathed you and put you to bed."

I fall silent again while she deftly braids my hair into an elaborate design. When she's done, she walks over to the closet, and I lean to the right, eager for a glimpse of all my beautiful clothes.

But when Parma opens the closet, there are no gowns on the hanging bars, no shirts or tunics folded on the shelves, no scarves in the baskets, and no jewelry dripping from the boughs of the sculptural golden tree at the far end. The entire closet is empty, except for two items hanging side by side—a lacy white gown with thin shoulder straps, and a scrap of gauzy black material.

Some people collect rare editions of books, or sets of dishes, or fine paintings. I had a curated selection of tailored clothing, in which each piece represented something of my personality. They weren't just clothes—they were moments, memories. They were *me*. And now, all the clothes I commissioned or collected are simply *gone*.

Tears well up in my eyes. It's a silly, shallow thing to cry about, but I can't help it. The sight of that empty closet is like a knife to my chest. I know my wardrobe isn't important in the grand scheme of things, but its absence is more painful because of everything else I've lost.

Parma returns, carrying the filmy black garment. I swallow hard, blinking back the tears. I refuse to sob over stolen clothes in front of her, when my people have been suffering so much worse.

Slowly, my brain registers the scandalous, gauzy thing in Parma's hands. "This is what I'm supposed to wear for a public appearance?"

She looks as if she might cry again. "I'm sorry, Princess."

"It's not your fault," I reassure her hastily. Then, for the benefit of the guards, I add, "What my Master wants, my Master receives."

After I remove the nightdress, Parma wraps the gauzy garment around me. It's voluminous, almost cape-like. A strip of black satin belts it at my waist, turning it into a sort of dress, but it's so sheer that it barely veils my body—which is no doubt the King's intent. He wants to shame me, as he did my mother. At least he's allowing me some semblance of clothing, while she had to appear naked. Rahzien is sending a message to the people—that even though I'm one of the defeated royals of this land, I have surrendered to him, so I benefit from his mercy.

When I do as I'm told, I receive good things.

I hate that Parma is here, caught in the middle of this. The King knows I care about her, which means he can use her as leverage.

She's leaning close, applying cosmetics to my face, so I risk another whisper, barely audible so the guards outside the door won't hear.

"What about Taren and Huli?" I whisper.

"They fled to her brother's farm," she breathes. "They are safer there."

Relief swamps my bones, turning my muscles liquid. Physically, I don't feel like myself at all—I'm weaker, wearier. What if it's not just because of the deprivation, or the fever, or carrying the dragon eggs? What if Rahzien is right, and something virulent is twining along my nerves, slithering through my veins? Something the healer couldn't cure—the poison that tethers me to the King.

Can I really feel it, or am I merely *imagining* that I can? Maybe I'm losing my mind at last, after the volatility and peril of the past few weeks.

Both Kyreagan and I suffered terrible grief and a massive upheaval of our worlds, far beyond what most people endure. At first, we had little time to process any of it; we were too focused on surviving. And yet, we began to slowly unwrap those bundles of grief and trauma together… laying the pieces out in the open, viewing each other's pain, and healing in the process. We were shockingly good for each other, and I miss him more terribly than I've ever missed anyone.

The sudden flare of pain in my heart triggers a chain of panicked memories, things I had lost temporarily while I was unconscious. The poison Rahzien mentioned, contaminating all the flocks and herds of the Middenwold Isles. A poison triggered by dragon saliva.

Kyreagan isn't dead. *He's not dead, he can't be dead. But he might die soon, and I have to warn him… but I have no way to warn him, and any message I send would be too late, too late… I love him, I love him, and I never told him I love him, oh god I'm spiraling, I'm sinking, and I can't stop…*

"Your Highness." Parma's gaze glimmers with sorrow as she tries to sweep neat black lines beneath my eyes, but I'm crying, and the moisture is making her task impossible.

"I'm sorry," I whisper.

"Don't be sorry." She gives a little sob, sucks in a breath, grits her teeth. She drags her thumb beneath my left eye, wiping away the smeared paint. "The King wants you in full makeup, and I'll keep working until we get there. I don't want that bastard to have any excuse to hurt you."

The insult is barely audible, but it's more defiance than I've ever seen from her. Parma is a timid person. When she first came to work at the palace, she could barely squeak a terrified word. Determined to draw her out, I shone kindness on her like the sun, and I made sure my other servants treated her well, too. She was only just beginning to blossom when Vohrain invaded. Seeing her brief flare of courage makes me proud.

A Vohrainian guard marches into my sitting room and speaks to the two men by the bedroom door. "It's time. She's been summoned."

Parma expertly paints my mouth with a dash of my favorite lip color and steps back. I rise from the stool.

But instead of heading for the sitting room, I walk to the door of my study. My fingers curl around the handle, and I hesitate, scared to look inside.

I'm proud of the library of books within this room. I've always allowed the servants and staff to borrow novels, poetry collections, historical volumes, and anything else they desire, as long as they mark it in the ledger I keep by the door and put it back precisely in its place when they're done.

In addition to books of all genres, I have quite the collection of sheet music, most of it composed by the great musicians of our land. And there are shelves of slim leather-bound volumes filled with my own compositions as well.

"Come, Princess," demands one of the guards.

"One moment." I hold my breath and open the study door.

Bare shelves, some of them smashed.

A torn page lying discarded here and there.

The piano's keys have been crushed by something hard and heavy.

Wretchedness grips my heart in pitiless fingers. Why did I think a conquering nation would leave my possessions alone? Why did I hope that everything might be exactly as I left it?

Maybe because my bedroom looks intact. Even though some items are missing, it appears as it did the morning I left to visit the wounded soldiers.

And yet nothing is the same.

My heartbeat quickens as I turn back into my bedroom, as I rush to one of the dressers and yank open its top drawer, then the next drawer, and the next. All empty. I keep racing around the room, frantically opening drawers and boxes, while Parma and the guards watch me.

My delicate underthings, my hosiery, my keepsakes, my slippers, my ribbons, my jewelry—gone. The loose sheets of paper with partially completed song lyrics scrawled on them—gone. The sketches and portraits I commissioned of some of my servants and guards—gone. My embroidery and cross-stitch supplies, my perfumes, my body creams—gone.

The King gave Parma a few cosmetics and necessities for the dressing table. They took everything else.

Gutted, I stand in the center of the room, my hands limp and empty. My heart is too ravaged for tears. Parma lingers by the dressing table, anxiously plucking strands of my hair out of the brush she used on me earlier.

One of the Vohrainians steps forward. The morning light from the three windows shines on his helmet's skeletal jaws. "Come. Now."

I step toward him, hollow and unsteady. When he grips my arms and brackets my wrists with manacles, I don't fight him. My wrists must also have been treated by the healer while I slept. They're no longer sore, and my skin is flawless. But if I'm forced to wear these cuffs too long, I have no doubt the pain and bleeding will return.

The guards escort me through familiar halls, while the bare shelves and empty drawers haunt my mind.

They're just things, Serylla. Objects, not people. You shouldn't be this deeply affected.

But I can't shake my devastation. My possessions had meaning to me, beyond their intrinsic value. In a kingdom where I was uncertain of my place and had little control over my future, my belongings represented the small zone of my influence, my choices. And those leather-bound notebooks represented years of my private musical compositions, my lyrics, my thoughts, and my emotions. They are treasures I can never recreate. I feel like I've suffered a violation of my soul.

The guards hurry me along, past faces I know—precious faces. Some of them turn away, flushed and tearful, overcome by the sight of me. Others meet my gaze with their heads held high. From somewhere behind us, a woman shouts, "The Queen is dead. Long live the Queen!"

One of the Vohrainians whirls around immediately and stalks back down the hall, hunting for the woman who shouted. I'm shoved forward, hustled down the steps into the great marble foyer.

When I'm brought out into the courtyard into the mild warmth of the spring morning, the stable-master is standing there, near the heads of four horses harnessed to a royal carriage. Two of the stable-master's hired boys stand with him—both of them gangly fellows, scarcely into their teen years. One boy's face is red, his eyes wet and despairing. The other's features are stiff with anger, and his gaze burns vengefully as he takes in my appearance. The stable-master puts one hand on the second boy's arm, a warning not to react, not to do anything foolish.

This entire kingdom was abused by my mother, sacrificed to her pride. They are as wounded and weary as I am. And yet they love me. I felt the love in Parma's touch while she braided my hair. I heard it in the defiant shout of the woman in the hall. I see it in the tears, the anger, and the sympathy of the stable-master and his boys.

My heart swells, and so does the music in my mind—a golden burst of notes.

I haven't heard music in my head since I was taken from Kyreagan's nest.

I suck in a swift breath of surprise, charmed by the miracle of the melody unfurling through my consciousness. In spite of poison and exhaustion, grief and terror, the music is still mine. Whatever they steal from me, they cannot take *this*.

The works I lost were pieces of me, but not the *whole* me. Strip everything away, and still *I remain*. I composed music on Ouroskelle, despite being a captive there. And I will keep making music here, if only in my heart.

"Up you go," barks one of the guards. I mount the carriage step, and the next second I'm shut inside, blinking in the gloom as I settle onto the seat.

The curtains over the windows are drawn nearly closed, admitting only a little sunlight. On the padded seat across from me, where my mother would usually sit, is the King of Vohrain, his knees and thighs spread wide, his flat, emotionless eyes fixed on me.

"You don't sit there," he says. "You sit on the floor. Between my feet."

Tightening my lips, I slide slowly off the bench onto the floor, debating whether I should try to catch him off guard and throttle him or something. But his neck is so thick, and he's so huge and strong—I dare not try any aggression without some kind of weapon.

I sit between his spread legs, silently thanking the Maker that he's not asking me to suck his dick.

"It's a short ride," he says. "We may as well put that pretty mouth to good use."

Fuck. I glance up, my face hot.

He chuckles. "Not like that, Spider. What a foul mind you have. I only meant that we would practice your lessons along the way. Repeat after me… You are worthless. You are foolish. You are alone."

Grasping my fragile hope, clutching my vengeance, clinging to the love of my people, I recite the lies.

And I fight against the part of me that wants to believe them.

9

KYREAGAN

Midway through trying to eat a meal with a fork, I transform, smashing the stool beneath me and part of the table. I rush for the exit, blasting out through the waterfall in a burst of fire and steam and savage wings.

It's been two days since we arrived at the rebels' cave and I'm still unable to perform convincingly as a natural-born human.

I land above the pool, tear a sapling out of the ground with my jaws, and fling it from the grassy edge of the bank. As it falls, I light it on fire and watch it burn on the way down.

"Impressive." It's Meridian, picking his way down the path toward me. The early morning sunlight glints on the gold embroidery of his eye-patch, and the rays turn his dark red hair to bloody fire.

I chuff out a frustrated breath and swerve my head away from him.

"You're doing well," he says.

"I'm not."

"You *are*. So well, in fact, that I think we should make our first excursion."

I whip my head back around and huff smoke at him. "I'm not ready for the palace."

"Not quite, but I've been talking with a few of the others. We're going to visit the market just outside the east gate of the city. Sort of a trial run, as it were. We'll be in disguise, and there won't be any dining, dancing, or court conversation to worry about. It'll be good practice for you and Hinarax, and we might pick up some information. At the very least we'll get an update on the state of things among the people. A few of my friends will wreak a little havoc while we're there, but they'll keep their distance so no one links us to them."

A little havoc sounds far more satisfying than the painstaking work I've been doing—cramming knowledge into my brain, trying to learn how to use fiddly little tools like forks, practicing the different types of bows and salutes that are appropriate in a court setting. I'd much rather learn about the rebellion—how humans use their small size and stealth to their advantage when faced with a greater foe. "You said you've been harassing the Vohrainians. How, exactly?"

"Like any other army, they have to receive supplies. Sometimes we intercept the carts and wagons, steal the goods, and give them to the people. Remember when Anzuli and the others left yesterday? They went to burn one of Vohrain's census stations."

"Do you have more allies, beyond these caves?"

He huffs a laugh and props his back against my shoulder while filling his pipe. "There are members of the resistance all over Elekstan. A good two dozen of them have been undercover as Vohrainian sympathizers for weeks, working on a special project for me. Did you know Rahzien established two weapons forges on Elekstan soil, long before he conquered this kingdom?"

"I heard something to that effect, once, but I was never told where they were."

"The most recent one is located in an old mine not far from here, between the Capital and Guilhorn, in the hills to the east. It runs on water power harnessed from a subterranean river. It's been in operation for a few months, harvesting Elekstan resources with a very specific purpose—to design more accurate guns for Vohrain's army."

"Some of my dragons were assigned to that area." I inhale the fragrant herbal smoke unspooling from Meridian's pipe. "I was told to have at least three of my clan on guard in that region both day and night, but they never told us why."

"Now you know." He blows a smoke ring toward the waterfall. "Did you also know that Vohrain is conscripting anyone with even the slightest magical ability? The few healers left in the land are now confined to the palace, forbidden from using their powers on anyone but the Vohrainian soldiers. Imagine being forced to heal the enemy."

"That would be infuriating," I reply.

"Indeed."

"Conscription, identity papers, census stations… Human life is far too complicated," I tell him.

Meridian chuckles. "No doubt. A lot of humans seem to enjoy adding conditions and regulations to their lives. Personally I prefer to live free of all that. But to dismantle a system, you sometimes have to conform to it, so you can get close enough to hit where it hurts. This morning some of our folk will be creating a controlled explosion to destroy the gallows at the center of the market. The gallows has stood there for ages, mostly inactive, but the Vohrainians have been making frequent use of it lately, executing anyone who openly rebels or refuses to show Rahzien the proper deference. Speaking of which—you and Hinarax must remember to bow and step aside for the Vohrainians. That is the one rule you *must* follow during our excursion."

"Very well." I'll hate it, but for Serylla's sake I would do anything. Bow to an enemy, eat with a fork, walk in boots... even wear a fucking cloak.

"You and Hinarax have about six hours of humanity left, yes?"

I bob my head in confirmation.

"Good! Then we'll set off as soon as we assemble your disguises. Oh, I forgot to ask—have you ever ridden a donkey?"

I stare at him blankly.

Meridian makes an apologetic face. "Of course you haven't. Well, you learn something new every day."

"Or a thousand new things every day," I mutter, following him toward the cave. As the path narrows, I shift back to human form.

Meridian casts a glance over his shoulder and does a double-take at my nude body. "Fuck, man—you can't be swinging that thing around in polite company, or even in unsavory company. You're a fine specimen, but not everyone is as comfortable with large dicks as I am."

"When I lost my temper and transformed, my clothes were shredded," I reply. "I will need new pants."

He sighs. "Do you think pants grow on trees?"

I stop walking, suddenly uncertain. "No... I don't think so. I believe you fabricate them somehow... though I've never given much thought to the process."

"God, no—it's a saying." He laughs. "Something that grows on a tree is common, easy to access. Pants are less common, less easy to access."

"I don't understand."

"Never mind. Wait here, and I'll fetch you some pants. Then we'll see about your disguise."

Apparently the most esteemed wig-maker in the region is part of Meridian's rebellion. The wig-maker, Galather, plies his trade in one of the upper caves, where light pours through a crack and provides ample illumination for his work. On pegs and hooks studding the rock wall, Galather has arranged a selection of false facial hair and wigs for the rebels to use when they perform their deeds of sabotage and sedition.

As Galather bundles my long locks into a tight knot in preparation for the placement of my blond wig and beard, he comments on the length and silkiness of my hair several times. He even asks if I'd be willing to cut it and gift some of it to him, but I decline. Serylla likes my hair. I'll keep it, for her.

Hinarax's locs prove too thick to conceal beneath a wig, so he wears something called a turban, in which a length of cloth is wound many times around the head, then pinned in place. With the addition of a false black beard, he looks so different I would never recognize him.

Clad in voluminous layers of coarse, thick, brown clothing, Hinarax and I follow Meridian and a handful of the other rebels along a narrow tunnel, a secondary exit from the cave system. Beyond the exit, a little way down the slope, lies a pen in which several donkeys and a few horses are grazing on the patchy grass.

Meridian opens the gate. The moment he steps inside, a tall dapple-gray mare trots over to greet him, nearly dislodging his hat with her slender nose. He's wearing a glass eye instead of his usual patch, probably so his appearance will be less memorable to those we meet in the market.

"I'll be riding Jester," he says, patting the mare's nose. "The rest of you will ride the donkeys. They'll save us precious time getting to the city." Using his walking stick for leverage, he bounds up and lands neatly on the horse's back, then gestures to me and Hinarax. "Kyreagan, you take that one—Hinarax, the one over there. Quickly now. Get your asses on the asses."

Aeris rolls her eyes. "He makes that joke every time." She conceals her knives in the folds of her clothing, adjusts her black wig, and hops onto a donkey.

I've never been astride any living thing—except Serylla, in a very different context. My long human legs make mounting easy, but my feet drag until Aeris points out two triangles of leather and metal, called stirrups. Once I've tucked my boots into the stirrups, riding turns out to be less uncomfortable than I thought. It's far preferable to walking in boots, and there's a pleasant rocking rhythm to the donkey's gait as we descend the sloping, forested path leading down from the mountain.

Serylla would enjoy this morning—the bright, fresh spring air. But thoughts of her lead my imagination into dark places, and my body heats with panicked fury. I can't let myself envision what might be happening to her—what she might have suffered in the few days since I lost her. If I visualize it, I will go mad, transform, and dismantle the capital of Elekstan with claws and with fire until I find her, or until Rahzien's forces kill me.

Despite their inaccuracy and frequent misfires, the Vohrainian guns are still formidable weapons. Each bullet is the size of a human eyeball, shot with a force capable of piercing armor or dragon scales. If Vohrain's battle against Elekstan had been fought mostly in open fields, Vohrain would have won easily. But Elekstan had the defensive advantage. Many of its cities possess high, thick walls fortified with asthore, a strong, lightweight material against which human catapults and battering rams have little effect. And Elekstan had airships—slow, clumsy, and fragile compared to dragons, but still a technology

Vohrain has yet to develop. Without my clan's help, Rahzien would have had to lay siege to multiple cities for months, maybe years. Our alliance shortened the war dramatically.

An exasperated cry from Hinarax dispels my reverie. "This creature doesn't like me," he complains.

In truth, his donkey does seem unhappy. It keeps bucking as if it's trying to throw him off.

"Normally I would think of this type of animal as lunch," mutters Hinarax. "Walk straight, donkey, or I'll dine on you before the day is out, I swear."

"Perhaps refrain from threatening it," I suggest.

"It can't understand me."

"But I think it senses your mood. Try breathing deeply and settling into the rhythm of the ride."

Hinarax shoots me a glare. "You look quite at ease there. They gave you the nice donkey."

"Actually Kyreagan's donkey is usually quite restive," Meridian says, grinning over his shoulder. "I gave you the docile one, Hinarax, out of the sheer goodness of my heart. I'm devastated that the two of you aren't getting along."

Hinarax grumbles under his breath.

I frown at Meridian. "You gave me a difficult donkey on purpose?"

Meridian laughs and faces forward again. "I knew you would either clash or cooperate. Two stubborn, grumpy asses."

Aeris, who is riding a few paces behind me, erupts in a peal of laughter, which startles Hinarax's mount. His donkey begins bucking wildly all over the path, and within moments Hinarax flies off and tumbles into the grass. The donkey bolts, springing across the mountainside like a goat. It vanishes within seconds.

Hinarax climbs to his feet, brushing dirt from his rear, while I cup my hand over my mouth to stifle my laughter. I hate myself for laughing while Serylla is in danger, but at the same time, I know if she were here, she'd be laughing too. She'd be grateful that I could enjoy a moment's relief from my worries.

Meridian is doubled over with laughter. He laughs so hard that his big hat falls off into the dirt. "Grab my hat for me, would you?" he says to Hinarax. "You can ride with me. Jester is strong enough to carry both of us."

Hinarax struggles to mount the horse, but he finally makes it into the saddle behind the rogue. I can't help noticing how snugly he and Meridian fit together, and it makes me miss Serylla even more. After I save her, maybe she and I can share a horse sometime.

Or perhaps she'll want nothing to do with me, since she was planning to leave anyway. She was all too ready to abandon me and our eggs.

Whatever happens between Serylla and I, at least I will have *them*. Our little ones, each carrying a part of her. Watching her birth those two eggs was the most beautiful and terrifying thing I've ever witnessed. Her courage, her strength, her beauty—fuck, I'm weeping. Not sobbing, but tears are rolling down my cheeks as we ride. At least most of the others are riding ahead; no one will notice—

"You alright, Prince Dragon?" It's Aeris. She has moved up to ride alongside me.

I clear my throat and swipe the back of my hand across my eyes. If I had a cloak now, it would come in handy for drying my tears.

"I already liked the Princess before the war," says Aeris quietly. "But after watching you do all this for her—she must be even more special than I thought."

Her tone is usually sharp and sardonic, and it's strange to hear her speak softly. It weakens, dissolves, and disarms me.

"She sat with me in my grief," I confess. "She should have hated me, and yet her heart was so full of empathy and compassion that she couldn't. She helped me find empathy, too. Bared her heart and her body to me. She birthed my children."

"Oh shit," breathes Aeris. "But… how?"

"The spell that changed me also enabled the synthesis of our reproductive cycles into something entirely new. From my seed, she laid two eggs. Their emergence did not harm her, but she was weary when Fortunix took her from me. I had almost forgotten him in my need to reclaim her." My voice hardens with new purpose. "When she is safe and Rahzien is dead, I must kill Fortunix, too."

"Sorry, I'm still stuck on 'seed' and 'egg-laying,'" gulps Aeris. "Fucking weird shit happens on your island, eh?"

"That's fair to say." I give her a half-smile.

She has many questions about Thelise's spell, and though I don't have all the answers, I do my best to give thorough replies. For once, I'm grateful for the human propensity for conversation, as it makes the time pass more quickly until the forest ends, and across the fields I see the outlying buildings and high walls of a city whose shape will be forever seared in my memory—the capital of Elekstan.

This is where I came when the memory of my sister's death was fresh and bleeding. This is where I first saw Serylla, standing atop that tower, gripping the giant crossbow, aiming it at me. She looked so tiny and fierce, with her pink skirts whipping around her and her bright golden hair streaming in the wind. Something linked us from that first look, a cord tied between her soul and mine, drawing me toward her even as she trained that arrow on my heart. The arrow itself may have missed, but I was doomed to love her from that moment.

We leave the donkeys in a trampled field studded with wooden posts—hitching posts, as Meridian calls them. One of the rebels stays behind to watch the animals, while three others, including Aeris, leave us and go their own way.

"Will they be punished if they're caught?" I ask Meridian.

"They won't be caught," he says cheerfully, adjusting his broad hat. "Come on, lads."

We wind through streets lined with human houses, built shoulder to shoulder in slightly crooked rows. It's like marching along a roofless tunnel, being channeled toward some sinister destination. Now and then a window or a door bangs open, or someone shouts in rebuke or greeting.

I'm not used to being this size, enduring the suddenness and volume of human life on this level. I prefer soaring above such buildings, knowing that I could demolish them and their owners within seconds. I don't like being small, without my scaly armor or my fire, attacked on every side by the voices and jostling shoulders of passersby, all hurrying in the same direction.

"Lots of neighborhoods like this," comments Meridian. "Folks who work in the city, but can't afford to live within the walls. It's quiet for a market day."

"Quiet?" I snort.

"There's such *life* here," Hinarax says. "Do you feel the energy? The intensity?"

"It's called 'the drive to survive after a wretched fucking war,'" says Meridian dryly. "Here we are. The Outer Market."

The street along which we're traveling empties into a broad space paved with lumpy cobblestones. During our alliance with Vohrain, I saw many streets and squares with such rocky surfaces. I like them. There's room to land, and the stone is familiar. Unfortunately this square is crowded with booths, tables, and tents, a bit like the market we visited on the coast, except on a much grander scale. If the tiny coastal market was a puddle, this one would be a lake.

At the far end of the market, across the colorful tops of the tents, beyond the pennants snapping in the brisk breeze, I spot the gates of the city.

"The gates are open." I point out, and Meridian nods.

"Open, yes, but there's a blockade and a checkpoint," he replies in a low voice. "No one enters without the proper identity papers and either a tradesperson's day pass, a residence permit, or foreign dignitary documents, properly sealed. We'll get there soon enough. Now let's do some shopping. Mind your disguises. Keep your wigs and beards on straight."

"No problem there." I wince, feeling the tug of the glue the wig-maker applied to keep my false beard in place. In human form, my hair doesn't seem to grow. I still have no stubble along my jaw, and the light dusting of hair across my chest never seems to thicken. Another strange effect of the spell Thelise cast—one that sets me apart from human males, who apparently must groom their hair if they wish to keep it under control. I've seen Meridian shaving his face meticulously, as well as trimming the hair of his chest and underarms. Odrash, on the other hand, is the hairiest man I've ever seen. His entire back is coated with dark hair, just like his chest and stomach. Hair even sprouts from his shoulders.

Human hair has always fascinated me. I used to find its placement extremely odd, but now, as I follow Meridian and Hinarax into the market, I'm fascinated by all its colors and textures, by the vast array of styles and ornaments. Hair seems to be an extension of a human's personality—part of their being, an expression of themselves. A way of blending in or being noticed.

Today, I'm dedicated to blending in. As I watch other men walking through the market, my own walk becomes easier, less studied. Voices swirl around me—the low mutters of hurried conversation, strident cries from sellers at their booths, peals of raucous laughter... And then, in the midst of it all, a tiny voice crying.

My attention snaps to the source—a young man with a bundle strapped to his chest. Not a bundle—a baby. As I watch, he absently pats the infant's back with one hand while correcting the trajectory of a second child, an older one who toddles at his side.

It strikes me like a bolt of lightning from the Mordvorren itself—that my children, once they hatch, will not only be dragons, but babies.

I can't take care of such miniscule humans alone. What if I accidentally hurt them when I'm in dragon form? According to Thelise, they won't shift into humans for the first time until they're six months old, but even with that delay, the thought of raising them myself is terrifying. I won't know what they need, or what instruction they require at different phases of life. Only with Serylla's help can I ever hope to navigate the unknown skies of their childhood.

My boot hits a jutting cobblestone and I nearly fall, my shoulder bumping against a broad back. The man turns around. He and his two companions wear uniforms of smoky blue, their faces concealed by metal helmets with skeletal jaws. I've seen those uniforms and those helmets many times.

"Watch it," snaps the Vohrainian soldier.

I glare into the eye-slits of his helmet. My first instinct is to grip him by the throat and hurl him against the nearest market booth, then smash his skull on the ground until he coughs up information about the Princess.

But Meridian tugs at my arm. "So sorry, milord," he says to the soldier. "Our apologies. Won't happen again."

"See that it doesn't." The three Vohrainians march on, while Meridian pulls me between a couple of booths and into an alley at the edge of the square.

"Watch yourself," he whispers sternly. "If they say you've done something wrong, confess it and apologize for it, immediately. Grovel if you must. There's no room for foolish pride here, not if you want this to end well. Do you understand?"

"Perfectly," I grit out.

"Good. We're going to stick to the fringes of the square and buy a few things. Stay close."

With firm taps of his staff, he ventures into the market again. Instead of walking ahead with Meridian, Hinarax slinks along near me, and though he doesn't speak, I can sense that he's brimming with a hundred questions. He stares with barely concealed delight at the goods spread along the tables, which to us seems like endless bounty, although Meridian mutters that "pickings are scarce today, nothing like post-war deprivation to make folks discontented."

Apparently he has a list of things he was asked to purchase for some of the other rebels, and he takes his time chatting up each vendor and poring over their goods. Sometimes he'll hold up an item and compliment it in great detail. "What a fine straight razor! And it folds so nicely!" or "These long matches are perfect for lighting a fire without burning one's fingers."

After he's done this several times, I realize that he's explaining the items to Hinarax and me, sating our curiosity without arousing suspicion. We're learning about common human items and their value, all while observing normal movements, greetings, and social behavior.

Gratitude surges in my heart. This man could have taken our treasure and left us in that cell, but he is helping us. True, he's getting something out of it—our help to defeat Rahzien—but that's a future benefit, one he might never enjoy if things go wrong. In the meantime he's being patient with us, teaching us. He's willing to wait until I find Serylla and get her to safety before we move against Vohrain. Thief and miscreant though he is, he's honorable.

Meridian guides us to the next booth. It's the most interesting one yet, stocked with bolts of cloth in every imaginable color and pattern. At the side of the booth stands a rack with ready-made clothing on it, including a pair of black leather pants. I run my fingertips along them, pleased by the supple softness of the leather. If the pants were thick or rigid, like the boots, I would hate them, but they feel both protective and pliant. The way they shine faintly in the light pleases me, too.

"You like those?" asks Meridian, grinning. "They look about your size. I'll buy them for you."

If he hadn't taken our treasure, I could have purchased them for myself. But I don't argue the point. "Yes, I want them."

Meridian argues goodheartedly with the vendor. Once they've settled on a price that satisfies them both, the vendor wraps the pants in thick paper and string before handing me the bundle.

Just as I tuck it under my arm as I've seen other humans do, a horn blares from the direction of the city gates. That single burst precedes a volley of triumphant, brassy notes. From our vantage point, all I can see is the top arch of the gateway—but I don't need an unobstructed view to know who's coming. I've heard that fanfare before, after each successful conquest of an Elekstan city.

My head whips toward Hinarax. His mouth is grim, his shoulders tense. He went to war with the clan. He knows that sound as well as I do.

"It's Rahzien," he breathes. "The King of Vohrain is coming."

"Stay calm," advises Meridian in a low tone. "We didn't expect this, but it was always a possibility. Observe only. Do nothing to draw attention to yourselves, understand?"

Hinarax nods, but my blood is suddenly awake, red-hot in my veins, and my body thrums with a desperate awareness.

"She's close by. I feel her. She's with him." My voice deepens to a growl.

"Are you sure?" asks Meridian. "How do you know?"

"I just know." I lunge forward, but Hinarax clutches my upper arm and speaks tersely in my ear. "Look, my Prince. See the Vohrainian soldiers there, and there, and over there—everywhere, scattered through the market. Many of them have guns. If you transform right here, snatch her up, and try to fly away, they will shoot both of you. Your wings will be blasted with holes, and she'll be killed by the bullets before you crash to the ground. Don't do it. Not like this."

I shake him off and forge ahead through the churning crowd. Many of the people seem to be trying to leave the market, but the Vohrainian soldiers have spread out along the fringes of the crowd, herding everyone together, preventing them from leaving the square. Whatever is about to happen, the King wants it to be a public spectacle, with an audience. Which does not bode well for Serylla if she's with him.

I've reached the center of the crowd, where Vohrainian soldiers have created a protective ring around a large wooden platform. At one side of the platform, narrow steps lead up to a walkway. Along the walkway are three trapdoors, with loops of rope hanging above each one.

The other two catch up to me and Meridian speaks in an undertone. "That's the gallows. The square chunk of stone on the platform is the chopping block, where they remove heads."

Ice solidifies in my chest, chilling my blood. This may not be the same square where Serylla's mother was beaten and executed, but it's similar. And it's also the spot Meridian's allies were planning to attack today.

I glance over at the rogue. The taut concern on his face does nothing to allay my fears.

"There wasn't an execution or a flogging planned—I checked," he says, low. "Not on market day. Never on market day."

"Does that rule still apply under this new regime?" Hinarax inquires anxiously.

"So far it has," Meridian mutters.

The half-hearted reassurance isn't enough. I grip Meridian's shoulder, leaning down so I can speak in his ear. "Tell me your people aren't going to do anything while Serylla is near this spot."

"I'm sure they won't," he says. "They'll notice what's going on... they'll wait." He swallows hard. "But if the King of Vohrain steps up there, they might see it as our chance to—you know."

He doesn't have to finish the sentence. If Rahzien mounts the platform and stands over the spot where the rebels planted their explosives, they will blow him up without hesitation, along with anyone nearby.

A carriage halts beside the platform. Vohrainian guards swarm around it, brandishing pikes, holding back the crowd.

Hinarax nudges my arm. "More on the rooftops," he says out of the side of his mouth.

Sure enough, helmeted figures draped in smoky blue cloaks perch among the chimneys and gables of the buildings around the square, guns in their hands. They're covering the area, watching for threats, ready to eliminate them.

The carriage door opens.

Rahzien exits first, his broad figure unfolding from the darkness within the carriage. He looks different than when I met him on the clifftop. He has trimmed his hair and beard very short, which fascinates me. It's as if the change of his hairstyle represents a change in how he wants to be perceived.

He wears a shining breastplate, and a lightweight cloak billows around him like sinister smoke. The effect is admittedly impressive.

Rahzien turns back to the carriage and snaps his fingers imperiously.

From the gloom within, Serylla emerges.

She's thinner and paler than when I last saw her, clad in a black garment so sheer that every curve of her body is visible.

Her hair is elaborately braided, and her face has been painted—her eyes, lips and cheeks tinted to exaggerate their color and shape. As if her natural beauty isn't breathtaking enough.

My throat swells tight as rage burns through my brain. Heat boils inside me—the fire of my dragon side, demanding to be unleashed. My mind races through scenario after scenario, but there are too many unknown factors here, too many dangers, and I can't concoct a plan that would ensure Serylla's survival. Either the rebels will set off the explosion and she'll die on that platform, or she'll die in the air, pelted with gunfire as I try to carry her away.

I must wait, and trust that the rebels will postpone their plan. I hope Rahzien only intends to humiliate Serylla, not kill her. If he threatens her life, I will transform instantly and do my best to protect her, no matter what happens to me.

Hinarax stands with his shoulder pressed against mine, letting me know with his body that he is here. He is with me. He's a decent warrior—not as good as Varex, but loyal and zealous. If necessary, he'll fight until we're both killed.

I've spent my life yielding to impulse, making choices in the heat of the moment. Swearing a bone-oath to my father, allying with Vohrain, concocting the plan to capture the women, snatching Serylla as she fell from the wall.

This time, I will be ready to act. But until the moment arrives, until I have no other choice, I will do something infinitely harder. I will *wait*. I will stand here, in this disguise, pretending to be human, while the King of Vohrain draws my Princess onto the platform with him.

At his direction, she kneels, facing the crowd, while Rahzien takes his place behind her.

He places one hand on Serylla's golden head, almost fondly, and my hatred for him doubles.

"Citizens of Elekstan," he calls out. "Behold—your beloved princess has returned."

10

SERYLLA

I'm on my knees with the King of Vohrain at my back, his hand heavy on the top of my head. Throughout the square stand my people, a variegated painting of countless whispering colors. So many faces, in shades from deepest black and golden tan to icy white. Eyes, green and brown and blue, trained on me.

Since I was a child, I have loved this city, these people. I've found friends in every town I've toured throughout my life, but the Capital holds my heart. It's huge, and yet I recognize at least three dozen faces to which I could put a name.

With their eyes and their expressions, my people sing me a voiceless melody of sorrow, sympathy, and vengeful anger. They are a silent symphony, heartstrings pulled tight, vibrating, on the verge of breaking after everything they've been through. My soul draws strength from them, as it did from Parma, from the woman in the hallway, from the stable hands in the courtyard.

I still can't forget the face of the girl I killed on the island, the one who tried to drown me. I'm sure there are people like her throughout Elekstan, whose rage is focused on me now that my mother is gone. But in this moment, all I sense from the crowd is sympathy.

"The dragons stole women from this city," Rahzien declares. "Some of you lost wives, daughters, sisters, friends, all of whom have been brutally raped and devoured by their dragon captors."

Someone in the crowd begins to wail, a heartbroken, keening sound.

"Because of this travesty, the dragons are no longer our allies," Rahzien continues. "I have taken measures to ensure that they will never again be a threat to you or any other humans. The only captive I was able to save from the dragons was your princess. However, she is not blameless. She and her mother refused to surrender to my forces, and their obstinance resulted in countless deaths. Rest assured, she will be punished for her part in this bloody, unnecessary war. I am teaching her the error of her ways. Teaching her to submit. To know when she's been beaten."

He's so cruelly skilled at this, at twisting the truth and transforming it into something ugly and hopeless. I only hope my people have the wisdom to see through his lies.

Rahzien's next words are quieter, directed only to me. "Repeat the words I have taught you, Spider. Speak them loudly, so everyone can hear."

"Please," I whisper. "Not in front of them."

His hand clamps on the top of my skull, his thick fingertips digging against bone. "Say it."

I clear my throat and manage the words, in a quavering voice. "I did not save my people, nor can I save myself."

"Louder," demands Rahzien.

"I did not save my people, nor can I save myself," I cry out. "I am worthless. I am foolish. I am alone. I have no value, and no one wants me."

Soft sobs and angry murmurs ripple among the people as Rahzien presses down on my head and commands, "And the other part. Repeat that as well, so there is no confusion about what you are."

"I am your pet," I say. "I do as I'm told. When I do as I'm told, I receive good things."

A swell of protest from the audience, and in the middle of it I discern something else—a *growl*.

A thrill jolts through my chest, and I scan the crowd with frenzied eagerness, hunting for a certain handsome face. But the people are surging, moving like a pot of water at full boil, and I can't see Kyreagan.

It couldn't have been him. Not after what Rahzien told me, about the poisoned prey of the Middenwold Isles. Kyreagan is languishing in a cave somewhere, or he's already dead. I must have imagined that feral, vengeful snarl.

"Silence!" bellows Rahzien, with such vehemence that I startle.

The crowd falls quiet instantly. Clearly they've heard that tone from him before, and like a pack of chastened dogs, they know better than to defy it.

"I hereby declare the former Crown Princess of Elekstan to be my first Conquered Consort," Rahzien continues. "As my empire expands, I expect that she will be joined by other scions of defeated royal houses. Like her, each one will be magically tethered to me. If they flee too far from my presence, they will die. And if I perish, so will they."

I can't help a faint gasp. He never mentioned that aspect of the poison—only the fact that if I run too far from him, I'll die. Is my life really linked to his? He could be lying about all of it—the death of the dragons, the poison in my veins, my death being tied to his own. I haven't seen any Royal Poisoner or heard of such a person. What if they don't exist?

There's no way to know if he's lying, unless I can test one of the claims he made. For now, his words seem to have had the desired effect on the crowd. They've stilled, stricken.

Though I'm not looking up at him, I can tell by his voice that Rahzien is grinning. "Please recognize this woman's new role by repeating aloud, 'Hail to the Conquered Consort.'"

To their credit, every person in the market square remains utterly silent.

"You see, this is the problem." Rahzien grasps a fistful of my hair and drags me with him as he walks a few steps along the platform. "The defiance. The rebellion. But I think I've devised a solution. You're familiar with the concept of a 'whipping boy,' yes? When royal children do something wrong, they do not suffer for it. Instead a young servant, a whipping boy, takes the punishment. I had a whipping boy when I was a child, and I propose we take the idea to a new level. From now on, your defiance toward me shall be directly reflected on the body of your former princess."

He yanks on my hair so savagely that I'm afraid he'll tear away a chunk of my scalp. A whimper escapes through my gritted teeth.

"Repeat after me," Rahzien commands. "Hail to the Conquered Consort."

Sullenly the crowd repeats the phrase.

This is what he does. He forces others to verbalize the reality he wants until they believe it to be true. He's diabolically manipulative.

"Now, on to more serious business," says Rahzien. "Yesterday a census station was destroyed by a group of ragged miscreants who believe themselves to be heroes. From now on, let it be known that any such action by foolish insurgents shall carry consequences, not just for them, but for the Conquered Consort as well." He bends, leaning over me from behind, and cups my chin with his hand. "Insurrection brings the penalty of death for its perpetrators, and will result in severe pain for our new whipping girl. Her first punishment will happen today, as a direct consequence for the destruction of the census station."

He steps back and snaps his fingers. Immediately two helmeted soldiers advance, closing cuffs around my wrists, each one linked to a separate chain. The soldiers attach the chains to posts on the platform, so that my arms are stretched wide as I kneel where Rahzien left me.

Booted feet thump on the boards. Then the crack of a whip, and fire splits open the flesh of my back. A scream tears from my throat. It feels as if someone slashed a knife across my shoulder blade and spine.

The whip snaps and strikes again. This time I manage not to scream, but I'm sobbing, hissing great broken breaths through my teeth, blinking back gushes of hot tears.

Another line of liquid fire across my back, and I cry out. Two more in quick succession—so much pain I can't breathe. My lungs seize up and all I can see is white-hot agony and the dark blur of the crowd.

"Just five lashes for now," says Rahzien's voice, distant and calm. "Let that be a warning to those who would rebel against their king. Kill me, and you kill her. Strike against any Vohrainian soldier or installation, defy any royal order, and she will be punished for it publicly. Fear not—I won't let your sweet princess die. But I can hurt and heal her, over and over again, until she begs for death."

If there are people in this city who hate me for my mother's sake, the King just showed them how to hurt me. As for the rest, Rahzien hampered their ability to fight back—gave them a moral dilemma over which to agonize. It's a clever strategy, and sickeningly cruel.

The guards unshackle my wrists, and I almost pitch face-forward onto the boards of the platform, but one of the men holds me up. As they drag me to my feet, I realize that the flimsy garment I'm wearing is glued to my back with blood.

"I won't keep you from your daily errands any longer," Rahzien says cheerfully to his captive audience. "Enjoy this fine afternoon."

He descends from the platform and returns to his carriage. I'm thrown into the carriage after him.

I lie crumpled on the floor, terrified to move because every tiny shift makes the damaged muscles of my back scream and twitch.

The carriage door closes, the driver shouts to the horses, and we rattle away from the square. I sob quietly on the floor, partly from agony and partly from anger.

"Is any of it true?" I manage through my tears. "Or are you lying to all of us?"

"Repeat your truth, Spider," is the only answer I receive.

When I'm silent, he says, "Repeat it, or I'll do worse than the whipping."

"I am your pet," I choke out. "I do as I'm told. When I do as I'm told, I receive good things."

"Like healing," he assures me. "You'll be healed as soon as we return to the palace. Tomorrow I have a treat planned for you—a dinner party and a dance with many of the nobles of Elekstan. It's by invitation only—an evening with the Conquered Consort. The invitations went out this morning, and I've already received many replies, which is encouraging. After our demonstration today, I'm confident everyone will behave themselves at the party. Unless, of course, I give them permission *not* to behave. I suspect most of them will be craving a taste of the ruined princess."

"But not you," I say faintly. "You don't want a taste?"

"Trust me, Spider, I plan to ravage that little cunt of yours, when the time is right. I like to fuck, and I fuck hard. But there are more tempting pleasures to be had from you at present."

"Like fucking with my mind."

He guffaws, a harsh sound that startles me like his shout back in the square. It's the most frightening thing about him—the way his cool intentionality explodes into violence without warning.

"Well said, Spider. Well said." He parts the carriage curtains and looks out the window, while I close my eyes and breathe through the flashes of pain.

Kyreagan has a temper, to be sure, but it's more of a grouchiness—a morosely simmering, occasionally flaming, never-truly-cruel sort of anger. I suspect once my dragon's grief abates and his world settles into something resembling normalcy, his anger will cool as well. Besides, even at his worst moments, Kyreagan never injured me, at least not on purpose. He was merciless during the war, and his heart might be a tumultuous place, but there's a vast ocean of tenderness in it for me.

I miss him so intensely that the pain of my wounds fades for a moment, and my memory replays the sound I heard in the square—the deep, rippling growl of a dragon.

Imagined or not, that sound gives me more hope than the loyalty of a thousand citizens.

11

KYREAGAN

Meridian and Hinarax are both hanging on me like desperate barnacles. As if they could really hold me back if I wanted to break free. In truth, three things prevent me from shifting to dragon form, killing Rahzien, and saving Serylla from the whip.

First, the knowledge that I might end up dooming us all.

Second, Rahzien's strange comment about his life being linked to hers, and about a magical tether that keeps her from running too far from him.

Third, my brother Varex's voice in my head, begging me to be cautious.

After Serylla is tossed into the carriage and driven away, Hinarax and Meridian relax their hold. I whirl away from the platform and stride through the crowd, shoving people aside if they don't move.

Walking in boots is easier when I'm angry. In fact, it's downright enjoyable. My rage appreciates the satisfying beat of the hard leather soles on the cobblestones. I keep going, not pausing until I reach the street corner. Then I stop, because I can't remember which way to go next.

Hinarax catches up, carrying my package and a few of our other purchases. Meridian is close behind, his face tense as he jams his walking stick against the street with every fierce step. He pauses, leaning on the stick, and wipes the back of his wrist across his sweating forehead.

We're alone on the street corner, for now, but I keep my voice low anyway. "Your people didn't blow up the gallows."

"No. But this king is worse than any of us realized. Perhaps they should have lit the fuse."

"Fuse?" I ask.

"A long string soaked in flammable liquid, leading from the explosives," Meridian explains. "We use a special type of hair developed by Wig-maker Galather. It's artificial hair made from rune-tree fibers, treated with a special dye. The fuse is so thin it's practically invisible, and once lit, the flame is difficult to put out. It moves fast, and there's no trace left behind."

"You must halt any subversive activities for the time being," I tell him. "You heard what Rahzien said, about Serylla being magically tethered to him, and her life being linked to his. Is such a thing possible?"

Meridian shrugs. "My knowledge of magic is limited. I know the basics—that spells siphon energy from the caster, and that each spell requires different natural ingredients and charms, as well as physical material from the intended target. And every spell must be written down. The more durable the material on which it is written, the stronger the spell. Most charms or curses can only be undone by the one who laid them."

"You know more about human magic than we do." Hinarax shudders. "Sorcery disturbs me. I much prefer the dragon style of magic—simple, innate, practical. You're born with one of a handful of possible gifts, and if you use your gift too much you must let it recharge, in a manner that best suits your ability. I have basic yellow fire, like Kyreagan's orange fire. We recharge best in the sun."

"It's a fascinating topic, mate," says Meridian, clasping Hinarax's shoulder. "But let's save further discussion for our return journey. At least we know that the Princess is in the city, most likely at the palace. He could be keeping her in his rooms, her royal suite, the dungeons, or any number of other rooms. The plan hasn't changed—we need access if we're going to get her out, and we need more information about how she's linked to him, and who performed the spell."

"Rahzien told me that the few sorcerers at his disposal are weak, useless for war," I say. "I doubt any of them would be capable of binding his life to Serylla's."

"Rahzien wouldn't necessarily have shared everything with you, even when you were his ally," Meridian points out. "If there's someone in his ranks with that kind of power, he might prefer keeping their identity a secret. Something else to investigate once we make it into the palace."

When we arrive at the hitching posts where we left our animals, Aeris and her companions are already there. She's tossing one of her knives, flipping and catching it with frenzied speed, anger flickering in her every movement.

"You saw that, Meri?" she says. "What the Vohrainian shitbag did to the Princess?"

"We saw," replies Meridian. "What we did *not* see is the gallows exploding into sawdust and splinters."

"I set the fuse, but I couldn't light it. Not after getting to know *him*." She points emphatically at me. "He's so stupidly in love with her. And you saw her up there. She's fucking *brave*, but that Vohrainian bastard is wearing her down. She'll break eventually. I've been there, Meri, you *know* I have, and we can't fucking let it happen. God!" She punches one of the hitching posts, and a donkey brays in protest. "Look, I designed that explosion to be tight and neat, to take out only the gallows and nothing else, no other casualties. If the Princess hadn't been up there, I would have done it. But when I saw her... I just couldn't."

"Aeris, love, come here." Meridian pulls her in, and she endures the hug, though she punches his chest lightly.

"I don't blame you," he says. "Not sure I could have done it myself. We'll save the gallows for another day and head home. Our dragon friends are running on borrowed time, and we need to be back at the cave before they shift again."

I don't speak to anyone on the ride back. I left Serylla with that cruel wretch, and even though I had no choice, I can't forgive myself.

By the time we reach the caves again, Hinarax and I have a little less than an hour before we revert to our dragon forms, which infuriates me. I never thought I'd be so desperate to stay human for as long as possible.

The fury, impatience, and self-loathing I feel cannot be contained, and the instant we're back in the main cavern, I seize Meridian's shoulder and pull him around to face me. I let my claws and horns emerge, glaring at him from my full height.

"Enough waiting," I tell him. "Finish the forged diplomatic papers tonight. Tomorrow we enter the city. I will play the role of the Southern prince, gain the King's confidence, and make him tell me more about his hold on the Princess. No more training, no more practice. You and Hinarax are both quick with your tongues—the two of you can make up excuses for any lapses in my behavior."

"We can tell them you're a little mad," says Hinarax.

I hook an eyebrow at him. "Why would the Southern King send a mad prince to negotiate with Rahzien?"

But Meridian is nodding, tapping his lips. "Actually, I can work with that. We can claim you had an accident aboard your ship and hit your head—you're suffering from memory lapses, momentary fits of dizziness. Sometimes you may need to go take a long rest. Ha! It's perfect!" He claps his hands. "Why didn't I think of it before?"

"So you agree, then?" asks Hinarax. "We can enter the city tomorrow?"

"We don't need his permission," I growl.

"But you *do* need the forged papers, and your costumes, and your fake retinue." Meridian smirks at me. "And yes, I agree that it's time to move. I despise the monarchy, but I recognize courage and spirit when I see it, and that Princess of yours has both. She's playing his tune right now, but I'll wager she's watching for a way to escape. In fact she might have already slipped free of him if it weren't for this magical tether between them."

"If this tether is real, it will be much harder to get her away from him." I fall heavily onto a wooden stool and prop my forearms on the table.

"See, now, that movement and posture were very human," Meridian praises me. "And to reward you both for your excellent work blending in today, I think we should introduce you to another human custom—a tonic for wounded hearts, sorrowful memories, and restless souls. Odrash, Kehanal, bring out the ale!"

Hinarax perches his butt on the table near me, propping one leg on another stool. His pose is easy, unrestrained. He's doing better at appearing natural in this form—he's more talented at it than I am.

"Ale!" he exclaims enthusiastically. "Did you hear, Ky? They're bringing out the ale! I can't wait to try it."

When I don't reply, he lowers his voice. "I want you to know, I will put on my best performance tomorrow. I'll do everything I can to help you save your life-mate."

"She's not my... that is, she..." I hesitate, then dig into the sore place in my heart. "She was going to leave me. If Fortunix hadn't stolen her, I would have taken her to the mainland myself and set her free."

"Oh." Hinarax puckers his full lips for a moment. "So you don't think she loves you."

"I'm not sure." I look down at my hands, their light brown color contrasting against the dark wood of the table. Sometimes, when my emotions are close to the surface, flecks of fire glimmer on my skin, or perhaps just beneath it. I lift my hand and flex the black claws jutting from my fingertips.

"Even if she hated me, I would save her," I say quietly. "Even if she had sworn to crack my ribs open and claw out my heart upon our next meeting, still I would traverse oceans and mountain ranges for her, fly through a forest of voratrice tongues, brave the Mordvorren itself if I could spare her from pain."

"Good god, you're charmingly pathetic." Meridian laughs and slams down a foaming tankard in front of me. Aeris sets another tankard down near Hinarax. "Drink up, boys. Drown your sorrows."

I stare morosely at the ale. "Shouldn't we practice more? I'm still shaky on the names of the other six Zairon princes—"

"No." Meridian props his stick against the edge of the table and hoists himself up to sit beside Hinarax. "Enough practice. Trust me—this is what you need. You, too, handsome. Bottoms up." He gives Hinarax a nudge and a wink.

"Bottoms up, indeed," murmurs Hinarax, and he fixes the other man with a bold, heated stare.

Meridian's cheekbones turn faintly pink, and he laughs again, but it's a breathless sound, one which he drowns by snatching another mug of ale from a fellow rebel's hand and taking three noisy gulps.

"Go on, Prince," urges Aeris, her dark eyes fixed on me. Hinarax is already draining his tankard, while the rebels cheer him on.

If ale can temporarily blur the image of Serylla's agonized face, I'll swallow a barrelful. If it can help me cope with the fact that I had to fucking *leave her there*, with Rahzien... by the Bones, I'll drink an ocean of liquor.

"It might sting at first," warns Aeris as I raise my tankard.

At the first gulp, heat sears my tongue and throat, burning all the way down to my belly. It's not exactly painful, but it's startling.

I take another swallow. Warmth spreads through my gut, not unlike the sensation of my liquid fire when I'm in dragon form.

"Drink is the best way to forget the things you can't change, until you get the chance to change them," says Meridian, trailing his fingertips along Hinarax's long locs. Hinarax licks the ale from his lips and faces the rogue, eye to eye. Energy pulses between them—the same energy I sensed between Thelise and Ashvelon. Hunger, need, and a wicked, reckless glee. The passionate quiver before the kiss.

I turn away and down the contents of my tankard. I'll be a dragon again within the hour, and until then I'd rather not think about love, or loss, or Serylla's pain, or my own.

"More," I demand, shoving the empty tankard at Aeris.

She frowns uncertainly. "Are you sure? The full effect won't hit you for a minute, so maybe you should—"

"Meridian says this drink can distract me."

"Yes..."

"More. Please, Aeris."

"Oh, very well." She pours me another drink. "Go slowly this time... and you've already swallowed it down. Well, then. I guess we'll see how fast a dragon shifter can get drunk."

When I hold the tankard toward her again, everything slants, and I waver.

"Really fast, then." Aeris chuckles, gripping my shoulder to keep me steady on my stool.

Time melts, turns liquid and slow. Warmth spreads through my chest and my limbs, and a pleasant haze floats through my brain. I still miss Serylla, but the pain of her absence is muted. I'm concerned about my clan, my eggs, everyone back on Ouroskelle—but the worry is softer. I'm not myself, and not being myself is a wondrous relief.

One of the rebels starts playing a fiddle, another a pipe. I've learned a few facts about instruments since we arrived here, because Meridian is addicted to music, and cannot present a lesson or invent a plan without a song playing in the background. He's dancing without his walking stick, upheld in the strong brown arms of Hinarax, and they're laughing, both of them, joking, as if nothing is wrong with the world as long as they are touching each other. I know that feeling. I miss that feeling.

When I turn back to Aeris, she's watching Hinarax and Meridian too, smiling a little.

"More ale," I say.

"I think you've had enough. When you can't stand properly, that's a sign to quit."

"I can stand." I haul myself to my feet.

"Yes, but can you dance?" She hops up, too, extending hands clad in ragged black gloves.

"I've never danced as a human. I don't know how."

"I'll teach you."

"On Ouroskelle, we do not dance except during mating season, for our intended partners," I say cautiously, thickly. "I'm not sure if I should dance with another female. I love the Princess. Her name is carved on my bones."

Aeris quirks a brow. "Intense. But among humans, a dance can just be a merry bit of exercise among friends. I'll teach you the basics, and then, when you get your princess back, you can dance with her."

She leads me away from the table, toward the flat, open space in the center of the cave where a dozen or so rebels are dancing. Hinarax and Meridian remain near the fringe of the group, caught up in each other, but Aeris and I join a merry circle. I feel like a fool, clumping along in my boots, but everyone else is stamping, clapping, and cheering so heartily that I forget my awkwardness and let the ale loosen my limbs. It's a dizzy whirl, a mad heat, and the harder I dance, the more distant my grief becomes. But it's there, crouched like a fenwolf in the shadows, ready to leap at my throat the moment I stop moving.

The song changes, from a jolly jig to a tune I know... one that paralyzes me, freezes me cold where I stand. The people around me begin to shout the words of the song, each phrase punctuated with laughter.

"I once had a wife who took my life..."

I'm struck sober in an instant, as if a giant clawed hand slid around my heart and squeezed until blood burst from the pierced muscle.

"Kyreagan?" Aeris's voice is distant, dulled.

At a measured pace, with perfectly even steps, I walk through the dancers to the mouth of the cave. Behind the waterfall I strip my body naked, and then I descend the narrow path until I come to a huge rock overlooking the pool. Sunlight glows on that rock, turning it warm and golden.

Seated there, with the rush of the waterfall in my head and the heat of the ale in my body, I break under the agony and uncertainty of it all. Whether I can save Serylla without beginning another war, whether I can rescue her before the King forces himself on her.

And if I can save her, what then? Would I really ask her to live in a cave on Ouroskelle? Or would I offer to change my own way of life, my culture, my existence, for the reward of having her by my side?

Tears feel different in human form—liquid on skin, not scales. The sounds I make are huge, harsh, and painful—great spasms of my lungs and chest. My nose tingles and clogs until I can't breathe through it, and still the tears flow.

I want my family. Sometimes Hinarax reminds me of Varex, but he isn't my brother, the one of our sibling trio who always knows what to say. If my family were here, Varex would sympathize and support me, while Vylar would poke my wing with hers and tell me to toughen up. Grimmaw would give me some obscure nugget of Dragonish wisdom in poetry form. My father would insist that I think of the clan first, not my own desires or needs.

And Mordessa—she would weep with me, then promise to help me find Serylla. Her soul was that beautiful—rich in kindness. I hate that I pulled her into my father's war, that her final acts involved the slaughter of humans. She deserved better.

My skin vibrates, the precursor to transformation. Hinarax comes running out from behind the waterfall, stripping hastily and yelling, "Fuck!"

The moment I turn into a dragon, the haze of the alcohol dissipates completely. Perched on the rock, I stretch my wings, lash my tail, and look over at Hinarax.

He shakes his scaled body and chuffs with frustration. "Fuck this. Meridian was about to kiss me."

"My condolences."

He lifts his head and neck, arches his wings. "You probably don't want to hear about it."

"I'm pleased you two are finding joy in each other. But your paths don't exactly align."

"Neither do yours and Serylla's."

I swivel my head toward him, baring my teeth, and he cringes back. "Apologies, my Prince."

"We should sleep," I tell him. "We can rest in the same cavern we used last time, as long as it's still empty. We'll have to be careful walking back through the main cave. Don't swing your tail this time."

"I won't."

"I'll ask Meridian when he wants to head for the city. We may need to switch forms briefly tomorrow to make sure we have enough human hours at the right time."

Hinarax hesitates, threads of smoke sifting from his nostrils. "What if we make a mistake, and betray ourselves to Rahzien? What if we're discovered?"

"Then you'll leave me, and you'll fly back to Ouroskelle and tell Varex what happened. If I die, tell him he is under no obligation to avenge me. I'll let him decide what's best for the clan."

"Leave you?" Hinarax snorts. "No chance of that. I'll fight for you and the Princess, and if our enemies are too strong, we'll perish together. We may not be good fighters in human form, but as dragons we can take down a lot of them before they manage to kill us."

"I swore I wouldn't harm any more of Elekstan's people," I reply. "Vohrainians are fair game, but we must be careful not to shed innocent blood. And that includes destroying buildings and crushing the people within them."

"That will complicate my fighting style," Hinarax admits. "I'll try, but no promises. The vow was yours, not mine."

"Fair enough."

As I speak, several birds fly up out of a tree not far away. I peer at them, hunting for any telltale glint of scarlet in their eyes, but I see none.

Hinarax tosses his head and chuffs out a few tongues of yellow flame. "Do you think Fortunix told Rahzien that we're able to transform into humans?"

"I doubt it. Fortunix is a clever old dragon, and greedier than any of us suspected, judging by the private hoard I found in his secret cave. I'm sure he was paid when he turned over Serylla. I think he'll hold the information about our shifter abilities and wait to see if he can benefit from it somehow. His greed, coupled with his shame over becoming the thing he hates, should keep him quiet."

"And like Thelise said—even if Rahzien knows, he has never seen our faces," Hinarax adds. "So he won't recognize us. There will be no reason for him to suspect we are anything but a moody Southern prince and his retinue."

I huff superheated air at him. "Moody?"

"If the boot fits." Hinarax chuckles.

"I can be charming."

"Be yourself. Meridian and I will be charming on your behalf." Hinarax readies his wings for the flight through the waterfall. "Though you could try being more optimistic. Kyteia says the best way to ensure the outcome you want is to envision it, over and over. Picture yourself succeeding, and you will."

I stare down at the pool below, at its rippling waters thrown into shadow by the setting sun, and for a moment I let myself picture it—the ideal outcome of all this, the ending I crave.

I imagine leading Serylla out of the palace, along the shadowed streets of the city, and through the gate. We'll run into the woods together, and once we're clear of the guards and the watchtowers, I'll switch to dragon form and we'll soar east, leaving Elekstan behind forever. But before we return to Ouroskelle and our eggs, I'll take her to some tiny coastal village, to a tavern or an inn. We'll sit together at a table, like two normal humans, and I'll order the one thing she has asked for, over and over, since the day I ruined her life.

A cup of hot tea.

12

SERYLLA

I'm healed by a short, plump, motherly-looking woman I've never seen before. She speaks only a few words to me, but they have a lilt that tells me she's Vohrainian. Everyone on this continent speaks the Eventongue, but people from different regions tend to have their own accents and turns of phrase. Hers is a northern manner of speech, with the voice rising at the ends of phrases and a slight nasal quality to the "o" sound.

Besides her accent, she wears a tiny silver ring through her septum, possibly indicative of Vohrainian nobility, or at the very least, royal favor.

"All done," she says cheerfully, patting my face as if her king didn't just have my back flayed in the public market. "You can sit up now."

I've been lying on my stomach, and at her words I gingerly push myself up. Not a twinge of pain. She did her work well.

I'm no longer in my own room. Perhaps that's a privilege I've lost, or perhaps the King doesn't want to keep me in the same place too long. Even though he claims not to be concerned about Kyreagan or any of the other dragons, he's still cautious.

Perhaps he fears that the rebels he mentioned might try to liberate me. God, I wish they would.

The motherly little woman smiles at me. She has round, rosy cheeks and fat fingers stained with something like paint. Perhaps she's an artist in her spare time. For a strange, fleeting moment I consider asking her for a hug. She looks like the type of person who would give excellent hugs.

But she is Vohrainian, and we are enemies. She's already turning away, leaving the small bedroom.

The instant her comforting form vanishes from the doorway, it's replaced by Rahzien's broad figure. I tense, conscious that I'm naked, and I drag a blanket from the bed across the front of my body.

Which Rahzien must I endure now? The bluff warrior with the boorish laugh? The indomitable king who announced my new status as "whipping girl" for the entire nation? Or the quiet, ruthless Rahzien who slices into my thoughts with all the incisive skill of an expert torturer?

He has changed his clothes. He's wearing loose, cream-colored pants and a satin-black tunic that falls to mid-thigh. Since he trimmed his red beard close to the jawline, I can see his mouth better—full lips with a cruel tilt. The royal ring glints between his nostrils as he pulls a chair close to the bed and sits down.

"I don't enjoy displays of that kind," he says. "Public executions, beatings, and the like. Sometimes I pretend to enjoy them, because it suits my goals. If people think you relish physical violence, they are less likely to provoke you."

I give him the coldest stare I can muster.

"I do enjoy violence, of a kind," he admits. "Broad strokes of merciless death, like the mowing down of lines upon lines of soldiers on a battlefield. There's something uniquely satisfying about watching the bodies fall. And watching the dragons slaughter your people—that was beautiful. The way the fire just—" he makes a sweeping motion, with a faraway look in his eyes. "Pure destruction. Brilliant. It's a shame I had to destroy the dragons. I tried to think of a way to keep them under my control, but they are wild, brutal creatures. I could never have been sure they wouldn't turn on me. Best to let them go out at the height of their glory, just after winning a great war."

I was determined not to speak to him, but I can't help releasing a huff of disgust at his words.

A jealous awareness flickers in his gaze—the understanding that he still hasn't broken me.

"I thought I had you, back there, in the Harlowes' dungeon." He leans forward, eyes narrowed. "And then again, in the market. But you're a slippery one. You're still fighting me, aren't you, Spider? Because you don't really believe it yet. You're starting to, though."

"Believe what?"

"That this is what you deserve."

My breath stops for a second. As if he choked me, without touching me.

"You know it, deep down. That your mother was as much a villain as you believe I am. That you carry the same seeds of darkness inside that soft, sweet body, because you watched her shove your people off the cliff of war into the maw of death, and you never tried to stop her."

"I didn't think I *could*," I falter. "I was afraid."

"No." His tone is suddenly thick, brusque, threatening. The burly warrior, instead of the thoughtful monarch. It's as if his personality is split in two, and he's switching back and forth depending on the effect he wants to elicit from me.

"No, it was more than fear," he growls. "You liked standing aside, surveying the carnage from the comfort of your daily routine. Aloof, in denial of your own responsibilities. Perhaps you even enjoyed watching your mother race to her own destruction and drag everyone else with her. Perhaps it was a kind of vengeance for you. Vengeance against her, against a role you didn't want and a title you despised."

"I didn't despise my role." I don't know if I'm trying to convince him or myself.

He stands abruptly, bends his great bulk over me, seizes my chin in his calloused hand. "Don't lie to me, Spider. You never wanted this, did you? Royal children who want the crown are always sure they could run the country better than their elders. They crave the throne, scheme for it, strive for influence. From what I've heard, you did none of that."

I'm shaking, clutching the blanket to my chest, my mind swirling with horrible uncertainty. "She wouldn't have let me do anything. She never—"

"Stop it!" he bellows, spit flying from his mouth and misting my face. "Stop fucking *lying* to yourself! Stop shifting the blame to your bitch-queen of a mother! You could have stopped her and surrendered to me. You should have stuck a knife in her heart to save hundreds, even thousands. You didn't. You're to blame for their deaths."

"But *you*—you attacked us," I choke out through a shuddering sob. "You crave conquest and power."

"Yes." His hand squeezes my face tighter. "Those are *my* motives. We're talking about yours. Your failure. The deaths on your conscience, the blood on your soul, the punishment you deserve."

He's right.

About all of it.

And I shatter.

It's a silent fracture, a soundless explosion of my heart into bloodied shards.

"I did not save my people," I whisper.

"It was your duty to save them. Your birthright." He's leaning close, his lips nearly brushing my cheek, his voice sinuous and dark. "You failed. Worse—you *chose* to fail, to do nothing. You condemned them. You would not let yourself see your true nature, or feel the guilt, but now you feel it. *Now you do*. No more shifting the blame. No more shutting your eyes to your own wickedness, your unworthiness. You see it now. You understand why I'm doing this to you, why you're suffering. Not only because I want to keep the people subservient, but also to bring justice upon you for your sins. A good king never has just one reason for anything he does. And thus my purpose for you is threefold. You are the whipping girl, the defeated princess, and—" he places his hand across my lower belly— "the womb for my firstborn."

I suck in my stomach, away from the heat of his hand, but he presses more firmly. The hand still clutching my face tenses for a second, and his eyes dart to my mouth.

I am limp and wretched inside, hollowed out and sore. And yet if he tried to kiss me, I think I could summon the strength to resist.

Maybe he knows that, and he doesn't want to give me a reason to rally, to fight back. He removes his hands from my face and body, withdraws, and leaves the room, closing the door. Leaves me empty and crushed under the weight of everything I failed to do.

I've grappled with this guilt before. I've had similar thoughts to the accusations he voiced just now, and I thought I had laid them to rest but perhaps I merely buried them, too afraid of their ponderous weight oppressing my soul.

I am worthless. I am foolish. I am alone. I have no value, and no one wants me.

I did not save my people, nor can I save myself...

Save myself...

If I *am* what the King says—if all those deaths lie at my door, I can either succumb and perish inside, existing as an empty shell until I crumble with age—or I can try to atone for my sins. And before I can help anyone in Elekstan, I must first free myself from the King of Vohrain.

He warned me that poison flows through my veins, that if I venture too far from him I will die. I should test the truth of that warning. If he lied about it, then maybe he was also lying about the poisoned prey and the death of the dragons.

If he lied, perhaps there is hope. And right now, I am in desperate need of hope.

I stare at the half-open door. This bedroom is one of the palace's guest suites, meant for an ambassador or a visiting dignitary. Some of these chambers have secret exits through which people could escape during an attack, or listening stations where my mother's spies could observe the occupants without their knowledge.

The maids know every bit of the palace, including its secret passages. And because I've worked closely with the palace staff, I know the location of each hidden door and secret panel. Including the concealed exit from this room.

Cautiously I slide off the bed and knot the blanket over one shoulder, so it will stay mostly in place while leaving my hands free. I'll be damned if I run away naked. I'll steal clothes as soon as I get the chance.

In this room, there's a pressure point on the bed frame that causes the headboard to slide over, revealing a small door halfway up the wall, a simple square cut into the plaster, on the same level as the mattress. It hasn't been used in ages, and I break three nails digging my fingers into the plaster, trying to pry it open. The quiet scrape of the headboard didn't alert the guards, and they don't enter at my low cry of pain, either. They think I'm trapped in here, with no way to escape.

When I finally manage to claw the secret door open, I crawl across the mattress into the dark space beyond and hop down onto the floor of the narrow corridor between the walls. There's a lever in here, intended to reset the door and the headboard, so I press it down. The plaster door is pushed shut as the headboard slides back into place, and I'm left in the dark.

At least there aren't any multilegged spider-mice skittering in this passage.

In the pitch blackness, I fumble along until I encounter a grate leaking thin threads of light—a listening post at the end of a hallway. Setting my eye to the grate, I peer at the carpeted corridor beyond and gain my bearings by the paintings on the walls.

I'm not sure how long I shuffle through the dusty gaps between the walls of my mother's palace. I used to stride these halls proudly, and now I crawl through dark cracks like a spider dressed in cobwebs, spinning schemes for my freedom.

The head housekeeper had the back passages cleaned once every month or two, so I've navigated this maze before, but always with a servant to guide me. We swept, dusted, and disposed of any pests that had crept into the corners. I don't encounter a soul this time—no servants or spies, and when I finally locate the door I've been looking for, I have to work up the courage to open it.

If I'm correct, this door leads into the servants' pantry, right near the palace kitchens. I might find allies here. Or I might find people who are too frightened of their new ruler to help me.

"Please," I whisper. "Please, please."

With my fingers on the door handle and my cheek pressed to the rough wood, I picture Kyreagan. It's his dragon face, so defined and vivid that I can see the orange mist of his breath and the gleam along the edges of each scale. I can see the sleek horns, the fiery golden eyes, the long jaws lined with razor teeth. This is the Kyreagan I need right now—the powerful dragon who claimed me as his, in every way one being can claim another.

"I can do this," I whisper to him, and in my mind he gives me that familiar dip of his great head, a nod of trust, of reassurance.

Clutching the handle, I push the door open.

The door is actually the back panel of a shelving unit stocked with spices, which swings aside heavily as I emerge. I push the spice rack back into place until it clicks, then move toward the outline of light I can see around the pantry door.

Footsteps pass outside, purposeful and quick. A servant moving from one task to another.

Barefoot and silent, I slip out of the pantry and look both ways along the hallway.

To my right, the receding back of a maid. To my left, a few doors, and then the archway leading into the enormous palace kitchens.

A door opens, and one of the kitchen maids, Ondette, steps out. She must sense a presence, because she looks toward me immediately. And freezes.

"Princess?" Her olive skin turns a shade paler.

"Ondette," I whisper. "I'm running away."

Her astonishment transforms instantly into fierce purpose. "Of course you are. Come with me."

I could sob with relief. I could throw myself into her arms and weep with gratitude, but there's no time. I hurry after her, up a narrow flight of stairs, along a hallway, into her room. She shuts the door behind us, yanks open her wardrobe, and pulls out a simple brown dress and a hooded cloak. "Put these on, quickly."

When I'm dressed, she takes my blond hair in both her hands and bundles it into a knot at the back of my head. She hands me her spare pair of shoes, the soft leather slippers she uses for night duty.

"But these are your only—" I start to whisper. She shakes her head sharply, one finger pressed to her lips, and gestures for me to put the shoes on. I obey, and then she pulls me out of the room and leads me back downstairs. "We'll go out the side door, where the pump is," she says under her breath. "You can wait there while I speak with Callim. He'll sneak you out by the offal gate."

The offal gate is a narrow exit from the palace grounds, through which the stable-boys transport not only the soiled straw from the stables, but also the refuse from the palace. It's the least carefully guarded of all the gates—though I'm sure a king as smart as Rahzien has someone posted there.

Ondette guides me past two scullery maids who are too involved in giggly gossip to notice us. When we emerge outside, into a small courtyard, she tucks me into a shadowed corner near the old water pump. "Wait here."

I grip her arm urgently. "Thank you."

Pain flickers on her face, and she presses her palm to my cheek for a moment. "Sweet girl. Of course."

Her kindness breaks my heart. I watch her hurrying across the yard, ducking through the archway that leads past the gardens to the stables.

I know she lost her sister in the war. Why doesn't she resent me? How can she agree to help me without pause, without question?

With my back pressed to the stone wall, I tilt my face up to the sunset sky. It's deep purple and pale blue, streaked with bright orange like Kyreagan's flames.

Whether my dragon is dead or alive, I will never stop thinking about him. He changed the very chemistry of my brain, altered the composition of my body. He was the spell that transformed me into something new, and I can't shift back into the person I was before.

Deep in my heart, I make a vow—a bone-oath of my own, that even if he's gone, I will remain *his* for the rest of my life. I'll see him everywhere—in the brightness of the sun, the flicker of firelight, the smoke from chimneys, the clouds of a thunderstorm, the blackness of night, the steam from a cup of tea. Sometimes it will hurt, and other times it will make me smile, like seeing the face of an old friend.

"Kyreagan." I breathe his name into the quiet evening air, sealing the promise. It suffuses my heart with a mystical peace, even though my pulse is racing with the fear that at any moment, my absence will be discovered and Rahzien's soldiers will drag me back to the room I left. If the King catches me, I'll be punished again—no doubt of it. I'm beginning to wish I'd stayed put, rather than risk the keen lash of his tongue, cleaving my heart into bloody slivers. I fear his words more than I fear physical violence from him.

Ondette returns with one of the stable-boys at her elbow—Callim, the one who glared with such fury at the Vohrainians as I was loaded into the carriage.

"Go with him," Ondette says, low. "He'll get you out of the palace. Then go to the *Snarling Hound* tavern on Rivenlee Road, near the south gate, and ask for Ambert. He can take you out of the city tomorrow." She squeezes my hand briefly. "Fortune follow you."

"Burn the blanket I left in your room," I tell her. "Let no one know you helped me."

She nods, and I hurry away with Callim.

He guides me behind a bristly hedgerow to the back of the stables, where sits a small cart half full of garbage and horse-shit. A donkey stands in the harness, flicking its ears to startle away the flies.

"It's the only way," mutters Callim, gesturing to the cart. "I'm sorry, Princess."

"I'm supposed to climb in there?" I ask.

He grimaces. "Yes."

"It's not a problem." I almost laugh. He has no idea that I've pissed in a dragon's nest, smeared myself in dragon-shit to conceal my scent from my captor, and pushed dragon eggs out of my vagina. I do what I must to survive.

While I stare anxiously up at the towers looming above us, Callim uses a shovel to create a hollow in the mess of garbage and offal. Then he lays a ragged piece of canvas in the hollow. I climb onto it, and he wraps me in the canvas from head to toe, leaving space for my mouth so I can breathe. At least I'm somewhat protected from the shit, though the stench makes my eyes water. I breathe shallowly through my teeth, praying that I won't vomit.

Callim shovels more filth on top of my canvas-wrapped body, then arranges half-rotted vegetables and lawn trimmings over my face, leaving a gap for air. With the gloom of evening and the stench of the cart, it's doubtful anyone would look closely enough to see the lower half of my face.

At a click of the boy's tongue, the donkey starts walking, and the cart trundles over the cobbles. I close my eyes and focus on breathing just enough to stay alive and conscious. *Don't throw up, don't throw up.*

It takes ages to reach the offal gate, but once we arrive, the guards let us pass without incident. A few gruff words, and we're rolling through, toward Murkmouth Square, where Callim is supposed to offload his cart into a larger one that will leave the city in the morning.

I lie still until the cart stops again. The shovel thunks into the manure beside me, and after removing a few scoops of garbage, Callim hisses, "Now."

I surge up, rotted vegetables and straw-studded clumps of manure rolling off me. I scramble out of the cart, keeping as low as I can, and run bent over under my cloak, toward the nearest alley. The stable-boy parked near the edge of Murkmouth Square, so it's not far.

In the darkness of the alley I pause and inhale great lungfuls of the comparatively fresh air while I mentally map out my route to the southern wall, to Rivenlee Road. If I take it slow and stick to less-traveled streets, it'll take me a couple hours, maybe a little longer. It would be so much faster on horseback, or by carriage. But I have no way to secure such transportation, so I set off on foot.

Shortly after I leave Murkmouth Square, two women pass me. One coughs and chokes at the lingering fumes of manure trailing from my cloak. It's just as well—my odor will encourage people to keep their distance and not ask questions. I pull my hood lower over my face and stick to the gloomy dark, avoiding the circles of light cast by the gaslamps along each street.

Vohrainian soldiers patrol the city in pairs or groups of four, so I make sure to give them a wide berth. Lucky for me, they seem more interested in harassing attractive women heading home from their day's work. They don't seem interested in hooded waifs who reek of the stables.

The foul stench from my clothing and my hands curdles my stomach until I have to stop in an alley and retch up bile. I don't dare leave my cloak behind, despite its smell, but I find a bucket beneath a drain pipe and rinse my hands and face in the rainwater before moving on.

During the next hour, my stomach pain worsens, as if I swallowed a bag of razor blades and they're twisting deeper into my gut. My head aches, too, like nails being hammered behind my eyes. I duck into another alley and vomit again, behind a rain barrel. Gasping, I cling to its edge, my back and chest slick with sweat.

After a few minutes I keep walking, refusing to believe what my body is telling me. If I truly am poisoned, and I can't go far from Rahzien without falling ill, it means he wasn't lying about having a skilled poisoner in his service. Not just any poisoner—one with magic, who can design the cruelest, most twisted types of poison. Which also means that what he told me about the death of the dragons is probably true as well... and I can't accept that.

So I stagger on, clinging to brick walls and storm shutters and window boxes to keep myself upright. Forcing one foot in front of the other.

Night has truly fallen now. I'm ignored by the guards. They probably think I'm one of the drunkards who haunt the city during the late hours.

I don't remember exactly where I am, or where I'm going. My head reels, and I barely manage to round the corner of the next building before I fall headlong into a puddle of brackish rainwater. My stomach clenches, and a raw retch breaks from my throat, echoing in the alley. I can taste blood on my tongue. Something warm trickles from my left ear.

Wings rustle and flap somewhere overhead, and for a moment my dizzy mind brightens with hope. But the creature that lands near me isn't a dragon, only a bird. A small hawk with a white-and-brown-flecked breast and glowing red eyes.

That's not possible. Birds' eyes don't glow red. I must be hallucinating.

The bird cocks its head and hops closer to my face. "Found you," it croaks.

Now I *know* I'm hallucinating. Birds can't talk.

"Found you, Spider," squawks the bird. "Found you."

Fuck...

With an enormous effort, I lift my head. "What did you say?"

"Found you, Spider. Found you. Your escape was too easy. You should have known I was watching. Lie still. Help is on the way."

13

KYREAGAN

"Announcing his Royal Highness, Prince Gildas, seventh son of Garjun, King of Zairos, brother to Crown Prince Bessian, Duke of Lantikesh, and Bravelyn, second son..."

Meridian drones on and on in a grandly pompous tone, both arms extended as if to encompass every courtier and guard standing in the throne room of the Elekstan palace. He's the only one of our group to have stepped over the threshold—Hinarax and I are waiting in the hallway with the other three, until Meridian finishes presenting us to the court and receives the King's nod to approach.

I keep my face expressionless, though inwardly I'm seething at the ridiculous length of human introductions. Dragons use few honorifics. If I were introduced in my dragon form, a herald might say, "Prince Kyreagan, son of the Bone-King Arzhaling, lord of Ouroskelle," and that would be more than sufficient. But this introduction seems interminable, and it's all I can do to maintain the mask of haughty indifference that Meridian instructed me to wear during all our interactions at the palace.

We got through the city gates easily enough. Apparently the documents Meridian presented were so perfectly forged no one thought to question them. The Southern prince was expected, after all, and highly anticipated as the first dignitary to visit Elekstan since its conquest. No one seems to have heard of the real prince's demise at the hands of the pirates; but Meri warned us news of that event could arrive at any time. We're supposed to confess to having some trouble with pirates, so that any further news will seem like a partially accurate report at best.

At this distance, standing just outside the doors of the throne room, I can barely see Rahzien on his throne, thanks to the large plumed hat Meridian is wearing. He claims it's the height of fashion for heralds in the Southern Kingdoms. I was spared from wearing such a monstrosity. Instead I'm clad in skin-tight pants, boots with curved toes, and a tunic made of something called essensilk, which I'm told is unique to Zairos. The essensilk feels unsettlingly fragile, but its slippery glide against my skin is pleasant. Almost as lovely as the sensation of Serylla's bare body against mine.

I'm haunted by a thread of awareness in my soul—the tug of proximity. She's somewhere nearby, but I can't be sure where, or how close. I want to run to her, scoop her up, and smash our way out through the palace walls before leaping into the bright air and flying away.

But I must not let myself yield to the impulse. I need to find out if there is some foul magic linking her to Rahzien. I won't risk her safety to soothe my own impatience.

As Meridian's introductory speech drags on, my stomach churns with nervous bile. I swear my very bones are itching so badly that I want to flay myself wide open with my claws, carve right down to my skeleton if it will assuage that crawling, creeping sensation. My heart rate climbs higher with every phrase from the rogue's mouth. If he doesn't stop talking, if I can't *move* soon, I will lose my fucking mind. My ribcage seems to have shrunk, compressing my lungs, squeezing my heart.

This feels like the fit I suffered right before I told Mordessa's fathers about her death. But I can't panic here, can't lose control. By the Bone-Builder, I wish I had Varex with me. He has a way of calming me by his very presence.

Meridian turns and waves me forward with a flourish of his gilded walking stick.

I stalk slowly into the throne room, trying to breathe steadily, to keep my face haughtily calm, to wash all traces of hate and vengeance from my gaze and replace them with faint, cool interest.

There he is. Rahzien, upon his throne. His thick ringed fingers tap the sides of a silver cup as he watches my progress down the scarlet strip of carpet toward the steps of the dais.

Each time I've met him, I've been a dragon. I've towered over him, more glorious and powerful than he will ever be. It's unutterably strange to approach him in my human form, to feel so naked, vulnerable, and exposed, even though I know he can't recognize me. I dispelled my horns and claws, my tongue isn't cloven, and I'm striding easily, as if I've walked on two legs all my life. In this form, my voice isn't as deep, nor do I pronounce words quite the same way through my human teeth, so he won't recognize my voice. There is no way Rahzien can know I'm the dragon prince who helped him win this palace.

As Thelise said, my face and form are the most effective disguise I could hope for.

Close behind me, on either side, I hear the steady footfalls of Hinarax and the slightly off-kilter steps of Meridian. Behind them, the booted feet of our three false guards.

I risk darting my eyes aside twice, once to the left and once to the right. I've never set foot in such a magnificent space as this, and I can't help marveling at the tall columns and elaborately decorated arches. The marble floors are so highly polished they shine like glassy water, mirroring the columns and making the hall appear twice as immense.

In addition to many helmeted Vohrainian guards, several other people stand here and there among the pillars. Even though Norril tried to instruct me on the different classes of society and the various ranks at court, I can't be sure whether those people are palace attendants or nobles.

My heart sinks as I realize Serylla is not in the room.

Meridian clears his throat lightly, the signal for me to take one more step and then halt. Coming to a stop, I bow in the manner of the Southern Kingdoms—one hand on my right hip, my left arm stretched out to the side. I repeat the words Meridian had me memorize.

"Health and glory be upon your house, great King. I come with greetings and congratulations from my father Garjun, King of Zairos and from my esteemed brothers, Bessian, Bravelyn, Victoran, Larrence, Trysteon, and Davrith."

"God's balls," chuckles Rahzien. "Quite a mouthful, those names. Welcome, Your Highness, and please carry my gratitude and respect to your honored father the King upon your return. His friendship means a great deal to me. I regret that I cannot offer you the same quality of food and entertainment that I usually have at my disposal in Vohrain."

"Any hospitality you can offer will be greatly appreciated," I reply. "Our journey has been harrowing. We encountered pirates during the voyage, and barely escaped being seized and scuttled. We placed our valuables in a skiff and sent it toward their ship, and they allowed us to leave with our lives while they collected the tribute. As such, we have brought few possessions, and I regret that I have no gift to offer Your Majesty at present. Rest assured, my father will make it right as soon as possible."

"Begging your Majesty's pardon," Meridian interjects with a bow. "His Highness would never mention it, out of deference to Your Majesty, but my lord prince endured a severe injury during our encounter with the pirates. They fired at us a few times before we yielded the treasure, and His Highness was struck in the head by—"

"By a cannonball," puts in Hinarax helpfully.

"Ha ha! No," says Meridian with a peal of forced laughter. "The Prince's esquire does enjoy a little joke from time to time. No, the Prince was struck by a piece of flying debris, a spindle from the broken railing of the ship. In fact both he and his esquire were hit by the same spindle—they were standing side by side, you see. Inseparable, these two. They've both suffered some pain, and a few lapses in memory, but they seem to be recovering. Though the Prince may need to take more rest than usual during our visit to your illustrious court."

"It sounds as if your journey has been harrowing indeed." Rahzien's eyes rove over me, and I have the sense that he's collecting details, like a dragon collects treasure.

"Never fear, the lack of a gift does not offend me," he continues. "Though truthfully I was hoping to claim the support of Zairos in a tangible way. No matter—we can discuss it when you are not so exhausted from traveling. Perhaps we can cheer your hearts this evening—I'm hosting a feast here in the palace, with dancing to follow. I've invited many of the Elekstan nobles to join the fun."

"My father will be pleased to hear that the Elekstan nobility are acclimating so swiftly to your rule," I say.

"The nobles are adjusting," replies Rahzien, with a broad smile that does not reach his eyes. "After tonight, I think they will be even more eager to embrace the future. The guests for this dinner are solely male, you see—an exclusive group. And I've arranged for a number of the finest pleasure escorts from the Capital and the surrounding cities to be our dance partners. My guests can enjoy a spirited dance and an equally spirited tryst afterward, if they so desire. And each man will also get the chance to taste a previously forbidden, but most delectable fruit."

"What kind of fruit?"

"You wouldn't ask me to give away the surprise, would you, Your Highness?" Rahzien smiles, and for a moment I spot the serpent beneath his leonine exterior. There's a duality to him—the brawling warrior and the slithering strategist.

"Of course not." I give him a curt nod. "I will be pleased to join you this evening. May I have your leave to bring my herald and my esquire? This one is rather amusing at parties." I gesture to Meridian.

"By all means," says Rahzien, with a generous wave of his hand. "My servants will show you to your quarters, where you may rest and refresh yourselves before the festivities. We will revel tonight, and do business tomorrow."

"Very well." I repeat the Southern bow, and the King rises to return it. It's a mark of honor, one I might appreciate if we were not mortal enemies.

Servants and guards come forward to escort us from the throne room. As we accompany them, the members of my "retinue" converse quietly in the Eventongue about the perils of our fictitious journey.

After traversing a reception room and a short hallway, we arrive at a staircase. With a cold blast of shock, I realize that neither Hinarax nor I have ever climbed steps.

When I glance back at Meridian, I know he's thinking the same thing. Steps are commonplace for humans—I'm sure it never entered his mind that dragons never use them.

"You're weary from your journey, my lord," he says to me. "Hold onto the banister as you go." And he grasps a long, slim piece of polished wood that follows the upward slant of the stairway.

Following his cue, I grip the banister and begin climbing the steps. It's simple enough, like stepping onto a rock, except I have to keep stepping upward at a uniform height and distance. Ahead of me, Meridian's breathing becomes labored, and I realize that with his injury, raising his right leg high enough for each step must be a difficult task, perhaps even painful. Yet he persists.

Reaching the second floor is a triumph, and I allow myself to absorb my surroundings, to picture Serylla running through these halls, first as a child, then as a young princess. I'm not as intrigued by the human lifestyle as Hinarax, but even I can barely refrain from commenting on the intricate crystalline lamps, the lush patterned carpets, and the paintings of somber people and cloudy landscapes. It's all so delicate, so easily destroyed. Why waste so much time on beautiful things that could be ruined in seconds?

But perhaps humans are fascinated with frail luxuries because they themselves are so delicate, so easily broken. I remember how Serylla's slender frame felt in my claws, the way the dainty bones shifted beneath her skin when I held her wrist. So brittle, so beautiful.

We're guided into a suite of large rooms, the biggest of which is mine, according to the servants, who abandon our group as soon as we're safely ensconced in our quarters. My chamber is sparsely furnished and nearly as big as my cave back on Ouroskelle. In fact, it's so large my dragon form could fit in here if I pinned my wings to my sides and curled my body around the bed. A dragon as bulky as Fortunix or Ashvelon wouldn't fit, but my form is sleeker than theirs.

Meridian enters behind me, leaning on his stick. "This room should work for your dragon form if we move aside the chairs and tables in the sitting area. Not sure what we'll do for Hinarax when he's a dragon. He could probably fit in the bathing room."

I glance sharply toward him, alarmed that he's speaking so openly, but he waves away my concern. "Oh, we can talk freely. The servants left. We're alone."

"What is the bathing room?" I ask.

"It's one of those places that reeks sickeningly of the luxurious privilege of the rich," he says. "Come with me."

The bathing room resembles a cave of pale green marble threaded with veins of black and gold. When Meridian wrenches a copper handle, hot water gushes into a huge, rectangular pool, also cut from marble. The *bathtub*, he calls it. He points out three smaller bowls with more handles and water pipes, each standing about waist height.

"These are sinks," explains Meridian. "I told you about them, remember?"

I have no recollection of such a thing, but Hinarax, who has appeared beside me, nods enthusiastically. "I remember."

"And is that also a sink?" I point to a low bowl-shaped object connected to more pipes.

"That's a toilet," says Meridian. "You sit on it or stand over it to relieve yourself, then you pull the chain when you're done, and everything goes away."

"Goes where?" Hinarax inquires.

"Through the pipes to an underground stream, which empties into a subterranean river," explains Meri. "It will be good to use a bathroom again, instead of the woods or a pit in the caves."

Hinarax approaches the toilet, takes out his cock, and points it at the bowl. "Like this?"

"Usually when you're alone," says Meridian with a wry laugh. "But yes."

Hinarax starts pissing, and I turn away to inspect one of the sinks. I'm fascinated by the way the water pours from the opening of the pipe and instantly drains away into a hole in the bottom of the sink. "This seems wasteful," I announce.

"It's running water," says Meridian. "No more wasteful than the flow of a stream or a river. And now, if you'll turn off the water, Kyreagan, and if Hinarax will put his dick away, we can settle in. I have a feeling tonight's 'delectable fruit' may be of interest to us."

"You think it's the Princess?" Hinarax asks, turning toward us with his cock still out.

"For god's sake—shake it, don't stand there dripping," Meridian says.

Hinarax shakes his dick over the toilet, tucks it into his pants, and buttons them up again.

"Now you flush it," Meridian prompts him. "Use the chain."

Hinarax tugs on the chain hanging near the toilet. There's a rushing, sucking, swirling sound, and the yellow water in the toilet disappears. Within seconds, clean water rushes in to replace it.

"By the Bone-Builder," breathes Hinarax in awe. "Are you sure this is not magic?"

"Far better. It's science."

I step forward, intrigued in spite of myself. "Do it again."

Hinarax pulls the chain, and we watch the water swirl away. The sound is most satisfying.

"Try it," says Hinarax, so I grip the chain and pull. Again there's the pleasant, rushing swirl of water draining away, before more water takes its place.

"And this will carry away shit as well?" I ask.

"Yes," Meridian replies. "Human-sized shit, not dragon-sized. God, we're going to have to figure that out, aren't we? Or perhaps you could just avoid shitting while in dragon form. You're flushing it *again*, Kyreagan? I think that's enough for now. Come, Hinarax, and I'll instruct you in the use of soap." He steers Hinarax toward the sinks.

"I already know about soap," I comment.

"Excellent. Thus far neither one of you seems to sweat or smell as heavily as most men do, but perhaps you should wash yourselves before the feast tonight. I suppose I shall have to teach you how to bathe."

"I've bathed before, with the Princess," I tell him. "I can do it myself."

Hinarax gives Meri a sly smile. "I have no idea how to bathe. I'm not even sure where I would start. Perhaps you could join me in the bath, and show me how it's done... to make sure I'm clean *everywhere.*"

Meridian tries to stifle a grin and fails. "Perhaps I could. It'll be a terrible imposition, of course, but such little sacrifices must be made in the interest of the greater good. Off you go, Kyreagan, and explore the rest of the rooms. Hinarax and I have bathing to do."

For the next hour I prowl the suite, trying to ignore the groans and sighs of pleasure from the bathing room as I familiarize myself with various objects. I've heard of some of the items, either through Serylla or the rebels. Others are strange to me. Fortunately Aeris accompanied our group, playing the role of a bodyguard, so I ask her the names and uses of several things, and she's good enough to answer patiently.

To my surprise, many of the items on the dressers and shelves of the suite are purely decorative. I'm especially fascinated by a porcelain figure of a dancing woman, whose gold-painted hair is frozen in a gleaming swirl.

"That's supposed to be a figure of the Princess," comments Aeris.

"Her nose isn't right," I peer at the small statue. "And her collarbones aren't so straight—there's a curve to them. Her belly swells a little more, just here." I point to the figure's lower stomach. "And her thighs are thicker. But her ankles are more delicate."

"You know her so well," Aeris says softly.

"I know the scent of her skin," I murmur. "I know the arch of her foot, the hollow of her hip, the texture of her hair. I know the smell of her fear and her lust, the curve of her lower lip, the shape of her navel, the strength of her thighs when they're pinned around my face..."

"I get the idea," Aeris says with a breathless chuckle. "Can you sense her at all? Hinarax said you can feel her when she's nearby."

"She's close enough for me to sense her, yes. But the link between us is a vague, distant awareness. I don't think she's on this floor of the palace."

"We'll find her," Aeris assures me. "We'll figure this out. And we got lucky with the size of these rooms. Instead of smuggling you out of the city when you need to change, you can simply rest here in dragon form tonight, after the ball. We can keep the servants out of the suite until late morning."

"I'm hoping we won't be here that long," I tell her. "If the Princess attends the ball, I'll find a way to speak with her. Once we know if she's truly linked to Rahzien, we can proceed with rescuing her and killing him."

"And if she doesn't appear tonight?"

"Then I'll leave the festivities early and walk the halls of the palace until I sense her or someone stops me. Whichever comes first."

"And…" Aeris hesitates so long I know what she plans to ask. "If she's truly linked to Rahzien? If she can't leave?"

"Then we must find some way to break the spell, unravel the bond, dissolve the link. Whatever it takes."

"I may have an idea where we would start with that." She lowers her voice. "I haven't told any of the others this, but… you're not the first dragon I've met."

"You encountered dragons during the war." I nod grimly.

"No, that was different. I'm saying I've met a dragon. She was badly wounded, and she's in the care of a sorcerer friend of mine—they're both in hiding, because he doesn't want to serve Vohrain with his magic, but—"

Heat flares through my body. I grip Aeris's shoulders. "What the fuck did you say?"

"My friend, he's hiding from the King—"

"No," I choke out. "The other thing… you said *she* is in your friend's care."

"Yes, the dragon."

"The dragon… is female?"

Aeris nods slowly. "I should have told you before, but I wasn't sure I could trust you, and then I thought it might be too much, on top of everything else. But yes… there's a female dragon here in Elekstan. One who survived the Supreme Sorcerer's curse."

14

SERYLLA

"There, there." The Vohrainian healer strokes my forehead with her soft palm. "Poor dove. Sweet thing. You'll be alright soon." She wipes my mouth and sets aside the bowl I just vomited into.

"I'll be alright because I'm back in close proximity to the King," I say faintly. "That's what you mean, isn't it?"

"Well, yes."

"He poisoned me. You know that, don't you?"

She nods sympathetically, hitching her embroidered shawl more closely around her shoulders. "Healers can't purge poison, lovey."

"I know." I draw in a deep breath and release it as a long sigh. I'm in yet another room—an even plainer one this time, intended for the servants of palace guests. It's a sign of the King's disapproval with my escape attempt, but I'm fortunate he didn't throw me in a cell. At least this bed is comfortable, though I would trade it for Kyreagan's nest in a heartbeat.

"Thank you for your help," I tell her. "Do you know how long the poison lasts? What if I get pregnant? Would it affect the baby? Who made the poison for the King?"

She darts an anxious glance at the bedroom door. "Your stomach should settle now. I'll have the kitchen make you some good chicken broth. Try to drink it all when it arrives, and then get some sleep. The King has quite the evening planned for you tomorrow."

After rinsing the vomit bowl in the bathing room, she hurries away. I don't blame her for being too nervous to answer my questions. Rahzien must be a terrible man to serve.

He wasn't lying about his access to magical poisons, or the link between us. And it follows, then, that he must have been telling the truth about the poisoning of the dragon clan.

Surely they'll find a way to survive. They have Thelise with them on Ouroskelle—maybe she can counteract the magical poison. Kyreagan won't die. *Can't* die.

Parma brings me the broth. She's sporting a large bruise on one cheekbone. "One of the guards," she whispers when I ask her about it. "I didn't bow to him."

"Fuck these bastards," I hiss under my breath.

"They say you tried to escape." She looks at me tentatively, biting her lip.

"I did. But I've been poisoned, and the farther I get from the King, the sicker I become. I nearly died tonight. Could you check on Callim and Ondette for me? Make sure they're alright, that no one saw them helping me."

She nods and picks up the soup tray. "Try to sleep, my lady."

"Not much chance of that."

But I do sleep, against my will and my worries. My body demands rest, and punishes me with nightmares in which I sprout wings and try to fly back to Kyreagan, only to be endlessly buffeted by a storm until I crash into the ocean and drown in the deep.

Morning crawls between the curtains, a drab gray light from an overcast sky. Parma assists me with a bath and dresses me in a silky white gown that splits in the front, just below my breasts, and flows open when I walk, revealing my body. The cups of the bodice are covered with crystalline gems and edged with lace, drawing attention to my cleavage. It's like the gown a bride might wear on her wedding night, and the undershorts I'm given to wear beneath it are equally silky and lacy, cupping my hips and thighs like a soft, sinister promise.

Parma helps me into the white lace stockings, ribbon garters, and high-heeled shoes I'm supposed to wear with the ensemble. She arranges my hair in loose golden waves, then adds a few silver bracelets.

"Just as the King commanded," she says quietly, as she tints my lashes, cheeks, and lips with cosmetics.

I submit to all of it. I don't want to make trouble for Parma, and I need to pick my battles with the King. I haven't seen him since the Vohrainian guards found me in the alley and brought me back to the palace, but I'm sure he'll have plenty to say about my attempted escape when we meet again.

"What about Callim and Ondette?" I whisper to Parma.

She shakes her head. "I couldn't find them last night. It was late... 'most everyone was in bed, Your Highness."

"Thank you for trying."

Knuckles rap sharply on the half-open door of the bedroom and a guard leans in. "The King demands your presence in the rear courtyard, Conquered Consort."

"'Conquered Consort' is such a mouthful," I say coolly, rising from the chair. "I'll take a 'Your Highness' instead. Or a 'Your Majesty.' Rolls off the tongue, don't you think?"

"You'll be less mouthy once you see what's waiting for you in the courtyard, bitch," he replies. "Move your ass."

Lifting my chin, I stalk past him with the haughtiest expression I can muster, one that would have pleased my mother immensely. But when we reach the rear courtyard, a tremor runs through my body, and all my strength drains out of me.

Callim and Ondette kneel beside the fish pond. The King stands before them, facing away from me. He's naked to the waist, his broad, muscular back thickly dotted with freckles. He's holding Ondette by the chin, speaking to her in low tones. Her teeth are bravely clenched, but there's terror in her eyes. Callim's head hangs low, despair in the slump of his shoulders, his defiance extinguished.

At the sound of my footsteps and the guard's, the King turns around. "Ah, Spider, here you are." His eyes widen as he takes in my outfit, and for a second he doesn't speak.

He has mentioned his appreciation for my body before, but this is the first time he has openly admired me. There's a hint of vulnerability in the admiration—a sliver of a crack in his stony gaze.

"Why am I here?" I speak as calmly as I can.

Rahzien clears his throat, his eyes still roving my body. "Surely you recognize these two servants? The ones who helped you leave the palace last night?"

I arch an eyebrow and shrug. "I've probably seen them around the palace before, but not recently."

"Leaving me *and* lying to me?" Rahzien frowns. "I thought we were past this kind of defiance, Spider. In fact, I'd planned to let you off easy at the dinner with the nobles tonight, allowing them nothing but a kiss or a squeeze—but perhaps I'll give one or two of them more liberties with your royal person."

I swallow and pinch my lips together.

"Tell me the truth, and I'll set boundaries for tonight," he says. "Keep lying, and forfeit my protection. Did these two servants help you escape? They have each sworn they never saw you."

"They're right," I say tightly. "They didn't help me. I escaped alone. I used a secret passage, stole clothes, and sneaked into the refuse cart without being seen by anyone."

Rahzien gazes flatly at me, but I'm beginning to read him better, and I can see a jealous kind of sorrow at the edges of those hard gray eyes. "I'm disappointed, Spider. Because of these two egregious sins, the lying and the leaving, I must punish you severely. I don't want to, do you understand? But you're forcing my hand. Tonight, you will share your bed with a man of my choosing. One of the nobles of Elekstan."

Oh... shit.

"But you want me for yourself," I falter.

"Yes. But you've proven that you're not worthy of me yet, and tonight is all about proving to the nobles of Elekstan that I can be generous to those who swear allegiance to Vohrain. I intend to bind the nobles to my will, and there's no better way than by getting them all to compete for a forbidden prize, a shameful pleasure. Don't worry, Spider—if the winner comes inside you, you'll be given a tonic to prevent pregnancy."

"Enough," gasps Ondette. "I confess. I took the Princess to my room, and I gave her my clothes and shoes."

Callim speaks up, his voice trembling. "And I hid her in the refuse cart and transported her beyond the palace walls."

Rahzien closes his eyes and smiles. "Honesty. How beautiful." Then he spins around, seizes Callim's head in both hands, and snaps his neck.

Ondette screams, but the sound is cut short as Rahzien grips her skull as well. The *crack* of her spine reverberates in my bones.

I sink down onto the steps, silent, my eyes bone-dry and wide with a horror too deep for tears.

He killed them both. Right in front of me.

Killed them. A moment ago they were breathing, speaking, warm and living—and now they lie limp, tumbled onto the cobblestones, their eyes empty.

Rahzien lifts Ondette gently, like a man might lift his bride, and drops her into the fish pond. The immediate frenzy of fins and silvery bodies makes me sick. My mother stocked that pond, not with pretty, harmless goldfish, but with vicious razorfins. And they probably haven't been fed in weeks.

Rahzien's bare back flexes as he picks up Callim and flings him into the pond, too, with a splash of glittering drops.

Then the King comes to me, where I sit motionless, devastated. He drops to one knee and tips my face up to his.

There's no admiration, no humor, no mercy in his gaze now, only an endless void.

"I value honest communication between us," he says. "It's something my family never had. I want you to understand how important it is to me."

I stare at him, incapable of feeling anything but shock.

"Now you understand what will happen if you try to run," he says quietly, almost comfortingly. "Not only to you, but to others. Have mercy on them, Spider. Don't make me do this again. Come on, now—repeat your lessons. These words are meant to guide you. Accept them, believe them, and we won't have to experience such unpleasantness again."

Hoarsely I begin to whisper the phrases. "I did not save my people, nor can I save myself."

"That's right, Spider," he murmurs, kissing my forehead with rough, warm lips. "Good girl."

I don't cry. Not even when I'm taken back to my room and left there for hours.

My mind is dull, hopeless, and hollow. Not a note of music anywhere in my soul. Even if someone came and filled the room with my favorite things, I wouldn't have the heart to touch any of them. They would give me no joy at all. I physically can't do anything except sit on the bed and gaze into nothing.

When evening approaches and Parma comes to my room to freshen my hair and makeup, I don't speak to her, because I can't form words. Nothing I could say has any meaning.

She brushes my hair, and plucks the loose strands free from the spines of the brush afterward.

Rahzien himself comes to fetch me for the feast. He's carrying two objects of silver filigree.

"This one is a mask." He fits it over the lower half of my face and locks it in place with a tiny key. "You'll be able to open your jaws enough to speak a little, and your lips are left exposed in case anyone wants to kiss you, but no one can put their cock in your mouth unless I give them the key."

I stare into the mirror, at the silver cage that entraps me from chin to cheekbones. A triangle of silver fits over my nose, and small silver teeth surround my lips, angling inward.

"Lift your foot, Spider. Now the other one." He slides the second contraption up my legs until it fits around my hips, over my undershorts. Rahzien latches the contraption shut, runs his finger beneath the top edge to make sure it's tight, and locks it with the same miniature key.

A triangle of silver filigree covers my pussy, while a thin band of silver runs between my legs and curves upward again between my ass cheeks, rejoining the belt at my lower back.

"This is a chastity belt. It works the same way as the mask, allowing limited access unless I gift someone the key," he says.

"Ingenious, isn't it? I'm glad it fits. I wasn't sure it would. It was made for someone else."

Maybe he wants me to ask who wore it first. I couldn't care less.

When I don't respond, he peers into my eyes. Whatever he sees there must please him, because he smiles. "Come, Spider. Our guests are beginning to arrive. I'll dine with them, and you'll join us afterward. In the meantime, you and the other women will rehearse your entrance."

He takes my hand as we walk the hallways of my home. My white dress parts in the front, flowing open, revealing the silver prison around my hips. I cast one sidelong look at Rahzien, clad in a gleaming white suit with a white satin half-cloak pinned to one shoulder. The key glistens on a silver chain around his throat.

I can't bring myself to care about what will happen to me tonight. None of it matters.

"You're my pet," murmurs Rahzien.

"I'm your pet," I repeat tonelessly. "I do as I'm told. When I do as I'm told, I receive good things."

"Excellent." He pauses, gesturing to a door. "I'll continue on to the banquet hall. You'll enter here and practice with the other girls. Be good. Don't make me come and chastise you."

"Yes, Master."

"The guest who pledges loyalty to me in the most tangible way will receive the key to these." He gestures to the belt and the mask. "You will entertain that guest sweetly in your bed, without screams, struggles or tears. Do anything he asks of you. If I hear that you've been anything less than docile, Parma will join your friends in the razorfish pool. Am I understood?"

"Yes, Master," I whisper.

As he turns away, I reach for him impulsively and grab his sleeve. "Please... choose someone kind."

He looks back at me, his face still as stone, his expression unreadable. Then he jerks his arm away and continues down the hall.

A servant in Vohrainian livery pulls open the door to the room he indicated. I recognize the servant, but I'm careful to avoid his gaze, to show no sign of friendliness or connection. I can't put anyone else in danger.

The room I step into is one I've visited many times, a space where the palace orchestra or visiting groups of musicians would prepare for a performance. I liked to slip in and watch them tune their instruments and practice warmups. Many times I thought about giving a piece of my music to the palace conductor and requesting that the orchestra perform it. But I knew the conductor would have to say yes, whether or not she thought the piece was truly good. She couldn't refuse a royal request. And I couldn't bear to have my music performed simply because of my title. It was too precious for that.

The familiar asynchronous sounds of instruments being tuned greets my ears, and I release a long breath, tension easing from my limbs. Some of the musicians are familiar, and they glance at me with expressions of surprise and alarm. "Princess," someone murmurs nearby, but none of them speak to me any further, probably because of the ten armed Vohrainian guards lining the walls of the room.

Beyond the musicians, in an open area, about twenty young women stand in three rows. They're practicing a series of dance moves under the guidance of a woman who looks familiar, though my weary mind can't place her immediately. I think she performed at court once or twice.

Every girl in the group is dressed like me, with a filmy gown that parts in the front, revealing their stomachs and lacy undershorts. They wear lace stockings, heels, and ribbon garters, too. But their outfits are all jewel-toned, rich red, vivid green, luxurious purple, royal blue. My white dress was designed to stand out among all those enticing colors. And I'm the only one wearing a chastity belt and a mask.

"Princess." The lead dancer turns and nods to me. "Please join us. You'll be in the center as we enter the ballroom. Don't worry, your moves are very simple."

She keeps her voice light and casual, but her hooded eyes barely conceal the heaviness of the emotion within. I can't tell if it's fear, sorrow, sympathy, anger, or all of those at once. I remember her now. Her name is Avrix, and she's a performer of fluid gender, sometimes appearing in her birth aspect as male, other times presenting as female. She likes her pronouns to match the gender she's manifesting at the moment. No matter how she chooses to appear on a given day, she's a magnificent dancer.

"Before we begin," she says, low, "I think you could use a hug." She looks at me, questioning, and my throat swells tight with tears as I nod.

Her arms fold around me, squeezing lightly, filling my nose with the scent of vanilla and sandalwood. Silk and hot skin and strength. I close my eyes and hitch a shaky breath, trying not to fracture. Trying not to cry.

"There." With a final firm squeeze, Avrix lets me go. "Let's do as the King commands. Make room for the Princess in the center, ladies. Hip, swish, step, belly swirl, arch the back, roll the shoulders, neck-whip, *face*. All together, one, two, three, and—"

15

Kyreagan

The dinner is interminable. I'm seated near the King—not directly next to him, thank the Bone-Builder—but near enough. According to our forged papers, Meridian and Hinarax have noble titles, so they're allowed to sit with me rather than dining at a secondary table or in the servants' quarters. Apparently it's quite common for human princes to have lords as their esquires or attendants.

The fork I must use is larger and heavier than the one I practiced with in the rebels' hideout. I take bites slowly, giving myself time to adjust to the difference. The food tastes delicious, but I can barely swallow it with the fucking King of Vohrain sitting at the end of the table, a mere four chairs away from me. I try not to picture myself transforming into a great black dragon, crashing into the center of the table, and ripping him in half with my jaws.

If I keep imagining my own transformation, it will happen, and then all will be lost. So I attempt to focus on Meridian's inane jabber. He's engaged in lively conversation with the Vohrainian lord across from him. There's a handful of

Vohrainian nobility mixed in with the Elekstan nobles, easily distinguished by their pierced septums, each featuring a gold or silver ring, some set with tiny gems. Rahzien is the only one with a scarlet gem in a gold ring.

Meridian and Norril never mentioned the possibility of other Vohrainian nobles being in the palace. But I suppose it makes sense that some of them would be part of Vohrain's army, and thus invited to such a feast. It's odd that Meridian is being so conversational with one of the enemy. He's so perfectly at ease, it's unsettling.

"My brother used to dabble in potions," he says cheerfully to the Vohrainian lord. "Usually with rather explosive results. Unintended, of course. Nearly blew himself up several times, truth be told. It's a fascinating art, but both potion-making and spellcasting are skills far beyond my talents. We have some sorcerers in Zairos, but probably none that would rival the ones you have in Vohrain."

"We have very few sorcerers in Vohrain," replies the lord.

"Oh." Meridian looks puzzled. "One of the servants mentioned a rumor about a magical link between the King and the conquered Princess, which sounds both sexy and fascinating. I just assumed—"

"Assumptions are for asses," says the lord caustically.

"Of course, of course. It must be an Elekstan sorcerer who cast the spell for him, then. I've heard that Elekstan's magic is astonishing! Perhaps that's why it took so long for His Royal Majesty to conquer them."

The lord bristles. "Vohrain excels in all things, and the conquest took place as planned, on schedule. We may not have many sorcerers in our land, but when it comes to subduing a wayward princess, all you need is one, as long as that one has a skillful hand and an eye for creative solutions."

"Of course, of course," says Meridian. "And it helps to have plenty of ingredients on hand, though they might be difficult to come by in a time of upheaval such as this."

"The King keeps his poisoner well supplied, even here," replies the lord. He seems as if he's about to say more, but the fish course arrives. Platters are set down at intervals along the table so the guests can enjoy the presentation of the huge, whole fish, each one boasting a pair of glossy black eyes and a jutting jaw set with long, curved teeth.

"Razorfish from the palace's own pool," says Rahzien. "Freshly fattened this morning." He grins as a servant carefully lays a flaky portion of fish on his plate.

I've never liked fish, though I've eaten them when game was scarce. I haven't learned the human method for dining upon fish, so when a servant attempts to give me a portion, I shake my head. "No."

"His Highness ate too much fish during our voyage," interjects Meridian with a chuckle. "He's weary of it."

"I'll take his portion and mine as well," offers Hinarax. When he's served, he shovels a large bite into his mouth and heartily chews both the flaky fish and the fine bones within. By contrast, everyone else at the table is deftly extracting the white flesh with tiny forks, leaving the bones on the plate.

The lord across the table frowns as Hinarax's teeth crunch the fish bones. I grip Hinarax's knee under the table by way of warning.

"Why is your esquire eating the razorfish bones, Prince?" asks a lord of Elekstan, from two seats down the table.

And then everyone is staring at us. The entire dinner party. Including Rahzien.

I glance at Meridian, who has choked on his wine and is coughing behind his hand. I can't tell if he's sincerely choking or if he's giving himself time to think of an excuse. Either way, I cannot allow this silence to drag out any longer.

I clear my throat. "That's how we eat fish in Zairos. It's recommended by the palace physician. Good for digestion."

"Doesn't it hurt?" inquires the Elekstan lord.

"Not at all. Perhaps our throats and stomachs are tougher than yours." I reach over with my fork, stab a large chunk of Hinarax's razorfish, and eat it. The slim bones snap between my teeth as I give the other dinner guests a savage grin. "Delicious," I manage through the gritty, spiny mouthful. I nudge Meridian. "Isn't this how we eat it in Zairos?"

"Oh… yes." Meridian lifts his fork, stares forlornly at the bone sticking out of the white flesh, then puts the bite into his mouth. "Just like home," he wheezes.

"Well then. A toast to the men of Zairos and their iron-clad throats," says Rahzien, lifting his cup. "May the women who entertain us tonight be blessed with such fortitude."

He laughs raucously, and so do most of the men at the table. I drink several swallows of wine to wash down the fish bones. Thankfully, once the toast is done, the attention of the group moves away from the three of us. Meridian makes a soft gagging sound once, but he seems to improve once the main course is served.

So far, so good. We have a little more information about the magic at the King's disposal, we know that the poisoner is here in the palace, and we avoided detection, if clumsily. I'm disappointed that Serylla hasn't yet made an appearance, but I suspect she will, after the meal. If not, I'll find some excuse to slip away and search the palace for her.

A palate cleanser is served, then another main course. When will this meal end? Dragons gulp their food quickly and move on, while to humans, eating seems to be a form of entertainment, not simply a means of survival.

Next comes the cheese course, during which I begin to suspect that I've passed into the afterlife, and the Bone-Builder has condemned me to an unending nightmarish banquet. But at last the servers present *dessert*, which according to Norril is usually the final course. I cast a wary eye over the fluffy confections of pink, lavender, and pale green on tiered white trays.

After sampling one of the desserts, Hinarax turns to look at me, his eyes wide and delighted. "You must try these."

To please him, I pop one of the fluffy things into my mouth. It tastes like Serylla, like flowers and sugar. I hate it, because I want *her*. I take another pastry, a green one this time.

I've barely swallowed it before Rahzien rises from the table, a broad smile on his bearded face. "And now, gentlemen, if you would join me in the ballroom, we've prepared some entertainment. I've invited a group of agreeable ladies to make themselves available to us this evening, both during the dance and in every way possible afterward. They've been well paid, so please enjoy them thoroughly. If you require privacy for such enjoyment, one of the servants can direct you to rooms prepared for that purpose. And there is a unique treasure tonight that only one of you will receive. If you wish to partake of that treasure, come speak with me about how you plan to support the Empire of Vohrain in the future. The most generous coffers and the best-laid plans will gain the ultimate prize."

A murmur of interest ripples around the table, though I notice some of the Elekstan nobles glancing at each other with concern or caution. How many attended this event because they wished to pacify their new ruler? How many came to the palace out of fear, not loyalty? More importantly, how many could be potential allies against Rahzien, in support of Serylla?

As the guests leave their chairs, Meridian edges closer to one of the Elekstan lords. "So may you rise," he says, in a cheerful undertone.

After a second, the other man responds quietly, "So may we all."

It's an innocuous interchange. To anyone overhearing them, the words could refer to everyone getting up from the table. But I've heard Meridian speak that phrase before, back in the seaside village where we first met him. And I've heard it a few times since then, among the rebels. If I'm correct about its significance, at least one of the noblemen in attendance tonight is a friend to the rebellion. I'm not sure what Meridian plans to do with that information, but the presence of another ally is reassuring.

Hinarax, Meridian, and I head into the ballroom with the other guests. The arched ceilings are cavernous, exquisitely decorated with ornate patterns. My grandfather would have loved this place, would have stored the beauty of it in his mind and reproduced it later on the walls of a cave.

In the highest arches of the ceiling, great glittering objects hang from gold chains. Each one looks as if the Bone-Builder gathered two armfuls of stars and formed them into a cluster of brilliant illumination.

"What exquisite chandeliers," Meridian says pointedly, by way of informing us, and Hinarax breathes the word reverently: "Chandeliers."

At the head of the room is a tiered platform, rising in broad steps to a gilded archway. Along the edges of the wide steps, musicians sit on stools, cradling their instruments.

As the last of the dinner guests file into the ballroom, servants close the three sets of double doors along the north wall. My skin crawls at the sensation of being trapped, boxed in with Rahzien and his guards. Vohrainian soldiers seem to be everywhere, next to each pillar, standing in every alcove, haunting each corner. For once, none of them are wearing helmets, perhaps to make the party seem more relaxed and inviting.

Music crashes against my ears. I flinch, because even though I'm used to the roars of dragons, this seems sharper, more threatening. I've never heard so many instruments playing together at once.

Thankfully the bold, brassy sound only lasts for a moment. Mist billows down the tiered platform, and from the archway at the top, a figure emerges.

Her appearance synchronizes with a fierce tug in the depths of my soul, the reawakening of the connection between me and my Princess.

She's dressed in white, her golden hair bouncing around her shoulders in loose, soft waves. A silver mask covers the lower half of her face, and she wears a silver cage around her hips. Her long legs are half-clad in lace, with ribbons around her thighs—a most pleasing effect, but I can't enjoy it because my heart feels hot and swollen—it's pounding right out of my chest. Blood thunders in my head.

As Serylla descends, more women emerge from the archway and file down the tiers of the platform on either side of her. They all pause, with her in the center, and after a breathless moment, the music swells, and they begin to dance.

I don't know how the male dragons and I appeared to our captives when we danced for them, whether we were comical, majestic, or a little of each. But the vision before me now is breathtaking. Long silky limbs, fluttering skirts, figures both voluptuous and slender, skin of varying shades—it's an exquisite storm of female beauty, and yet only one form holds my gaze.

There's a gentle pathos in the way Serylla dances, slow and graceful amid the bolder movements of the women around her. She's performing at the King's command, but her movements are listless, vague with despair. Her gaze floats somewhere in the distance, blank and sorrowful.

I drift toward her like a hatchling caught in a powerful stream of wind, like a victim sucked in a void orb. I should not approach her, not now, and yet I can't stop myself. Meridian grabs for me but his fingertips only brush my sleeve—I'm out of his reach.

Look at me, my heart begs. *Look at me, my love, look at me.* But her eyes remain distant, vacant. She doesn't look at anyone in the room.

The dancers assume a final pose as the song ends, and I turn away abruptly, sucking in a quick breath.

It's better that she didn't notice me. She'll see my face soon enough, but if she'd spotted me while she was dancing, she might not have been able to hide her reaction. What was I thinking, putting us both in danger like that? I'm a lovesick fool.

Rahzien smacks his hands together, slow and loud, and all the other guests follow his example.

"Applause," says Meridian quietly, moving in beside me. "Do it."

I imitate the repeated gesture until the King calls for silence. While he speaks, I keep my body turned slightly away from the platform, and I bend my head so my hair curtains the side of my face.

"Allow me to present Serylla Shanavris, former Crown Princess of Elekstan, my Conquered Consort," says Rahzien. "She is the unique treasure of which I spoke. Anyone may have a kiss and a dance with her this evening, but she will be entertaining one fortunate guest tonight. Impress me with your vows of loyalty and your gifts of allegiance, and the man who pleases me most shall receive this." He holds up a silver key, attached to a chain around his neck. "I don't have to tell you what it unlocks, or why." He chuckles darkly, a sound echoed by several men in the room. "I have the Consort's word that she will be docile and charming for whoever comes to her bed. And now, gentlemen—we have wine, women, music, and money—let us be merry!"

The musicians begin to play again, a brisk tune that reminds me of a deer bounding through a sunlit forest. I'm starting to understand Meridian's affinity for music. My clan enjoyed singing, poetic chants, and percussive music created with our feet and tails, but with the skill of human hands, so many more sounds are possible.

I glance cautiously toward the platform and glimpse Serylla descending the last step, holding the King's hand. "Fuck," I snarl under my breath, turning toward Hinarax. "Talk to me, talk to me right now, or I think I might kill him."

"Oh, um… chandeliers… intriguing, aren't they?" Hinarax says hastily. "So many candles, or are they lit by gas?"

I stare at him. "Gas?"

"Meridian was explaining gaslamps to me. It's new technology, but it shows promise. The gas burns, you see, and—"

Rage churns in my gut. "Why are you talking to me about *fire?*"

"Right, right! No fire… water. Think cooling thoughts… oceans, breezes, fountains, the waves of the ocean…"

"The ocean." I nod. "Deep, dark waters where you can plunge your enemies, so they will sink and never be found, and the sharks can clean their bones…"

Hinarax sighs. "I'm no good at this. Meridian?"

But Meridian is preoccupied, eyeing a table at the side of the room, where two men stand ready with parchments and feathers.

"Palace clerks," Meridian murmurs. "They're ready to take bids from the guests. It's an auction."

"What's an auction?" Hinarax whispers.

"Each man tells the King how much coin he's willing to donate to the royal coffers, or a number of servants or soldiers he'll contribute, or a piece of land he'll relinquish to the Crown. Not that any of it is truly theirs, now that they've been conquered, but he's letting them feel as if it is, confirming that if they transfer their loyalty to him, they'll be allowed to retain their titles and holdings. It looks as if each guest will be signing official pledge documents, which means their gifts of loyalty, money, and service cannot be retracted, even if they don't win a night with the Princess. It's all a game, really. A high-stakes gamble, with her body as the prize—and yet it's more than that, it's allegiance from them and clemency from him. Genius." Meridian glances at us and hastily amends, "Evil genius, of course."

"If you're done admiring our mutual enemy, perhaps we should look as if we're having a good time," I mutter.

Meridian cocks an eyebrow. "You first."

I try to summon a smile worthy of a human celebration, but before I can manage it, one of the dancers approaches us. "Evening, my lords. I'm Krissa. Would you care for some company?"

"No," I say.

"He means *thank you*, and *yes*," says Meridian cheerfully, tossing his gilded walking stick to his other hand and cupping the girl's waist. "Come here, love. Aren't you precious?"

Hinarax's usually cheerful features compress in a thunderous frown, but the girl doesn't seem to notice. She cozies up to Meridian with a simper and a flutter of her lashes. "Thank you, sir! I like coming to the palace. Me and my friend Taleya over there—we've come here a few times to serve His Majesty and the generals from Vohrain."

"Indeed?" Meridian waves Taleya over, and she hurries to join us, dimples popping into her plump cheeks.

"How cozy this is!" crows Meridian. "Now, my Prince, my lord…" he looks pointedly at Hinarax. "Let's be charming, and perhaps these lovely ladies may tell us their *darkest secrets*." He places special emphasis on the last two words, and Hinarax's frown smooths out as comprehension dawns. Meridian views everyone as a source of information, and these women are no exception.

"I've no time for dark secrets," I say. "I want to place a bid for the Princess."

Caution flares in the rogue's eyes. "Careful, my Prince. Remember, you lost everything in the pirates' attack."

"Then I'll bid with my father's treasure," I reply.

"I'd advise against that," Meridian begins, but Krissa gasps, "Pirates? How dreadful! You must tell us all about it."

"Yes, do," replies Taleya.

"Very well," Meridian says. "We'll dance, and I'll tell you a tale if you promise to tell me one afterward."

His voice and the giggles of the women fade as I move through the crowd. Much as I hate it, Meridian is right. I have nothing with which to barter. The seventh prince of Zairos is in no position to bid for a night with the Princess. Nor can I sign pledge documents, because my signature won't match the one Meridian forged on our papers. I'm a dragon. I can carve Dragonish symbols, but I haven't learned to write the Eventongue with these hands.

No matter which way I turn, obstacles seem to leap into my path. But there is one thing I can do tonight. I can reveal myself to the woman I love. Maybe knowing I'm here will soothe some of the wounded despair I saw in her eyes while she was dancing.

Rahzien himself has cleared the way for me to have a moment with Serylla. I simply need to claim what he promised to every man in this room.

A dance and a kiss with the Princess.

16

SERYLLA

I barely feel the touch of male hands at my waist, at my back. I'm dancing with men I've known most of my life—elder dukes, middle-aged counts, young lords. There are some notable absences—some of my mother's closest allies, who were probably executed unless they managed to flee the kingdom.

As I'm passed from man to man, I acknowledge distantly that they're being respectful, for the most part. No one has grabbed my breasts or my ass, or murmured lewd comments in my ear. The few kisses I've been given, through the aperture of the mask, were brief and polite. But the evening is young, and despite the outward deference the nobles have shown me, I know they're bidding on my body. Even now, as I dance with Lord Natley, I see Count Meddows in close conversation with Rahzien. After a moment, they both nod, and the Count heads for the clerks' table to make his pledge.

The Count is old enough to be my father—perhaps even my grandfather. I've known him since I was child—he and his family used to come to the palace on feast days. And yet there he is, bidding on me as if I'm livestock.

After signing a document at the clerks' table, he approaches Lord Natley and requests a dance. Lord Natley kisses me lightly on the mouth, then dances away with one of the escorts Rahzien hired.

"Count Meddows," I say stiffly.

"My dear." He lays a palm against my waist. "Forgive me, I've done my best."

"What do you mean?"

"I've wagered all I can. But I had to reserve a little to protect my household. Let us hope that it is enough for me to win you."

Anger rouses me from my lethargy for a moment. "What would your wife say to this?"

He looks confused, then says in a low, urgent tone, "Oh, I wouldn't *have* you in that way! No, no, my aim is to win the key so I can spare you from pain and humiliation, Princess. We could simply have a conversation in the room, and then I would leave."

"Oh, you sweet man," I gasp, relief turning me weak. "I was disappointed in you for a moment there."

He chuckles, but it's a taut, pained sound. "It's been a terrible time, Highness, but I should hope most of us haven't sunk that far. And if we have, we shall rise together." He says the last four words so quietly I can barely hear them beneath the lilting music.

He waits, as if he expects some response from me, but I only nod vaguely, unsure what he wants me to say.

"Kiss her or get off the pot, old man," says a caustic voice behind me. "Let us younger folks have a turn."

I close my eyes, clinging a little tighter to Count Meddows' hands. I know that voice. Zevin Harlowe.

As the Count and I spin through the next part of the dance, I see Zevin, clothed in velvet up to his chin to hide his scars. He's wearing a blond wig in a style that sweeps down over the scarred side of his face.

On either side of him are two other young lords. I recall their faces, dimly, but I don't know their names.

"The Count's dance isn't over yet," I say. "You'll have to wait."

"Oh, I've waited for you long enough." Zevin's pale eyes hold so much venomous anger that my blood chills. "I've wagered everything on tonight, you hear me? Everything. My dear old parents couldn't take much with them when they left, so I've got plenty to spend. You'll be mine."

Shit… he's probably right. In addition to their townhouse in the Capital and their mansion in the woods nearby, the Harlowes had bountiful farms in the west, as well as several vineyards. Zevin is reckless, impulsive, so when he says he bid everything for me, I have no doubt he means it.

Count Meddows' face falls. He too knows the value of the Harlowes' holdings. "Princess, I'm sorry."

Tears prickle in my eyes. "You tried," I whisper.

He bends closer. "I have only a few guards left, and they didn't accompany me tonight. And none of us were allowed to bring weapons into the city, or I would make a stand, I'd defend you myself…"

He's offering to fight for me. But he'd be slaughtered in a second.

"Enough citizens of this kingdom have died because of my family," I say hoarsely. "Don't add your blood to theirs. I'm not worth it."

"You are," he says. The song has ended, and I'm holding his hands—he's clinging to mine. "But I have others to protect. I'm sorry."

"Be at peace," I tell him, and then he's backing away, grief on his weathered face.

Zevin catches my wrist and jerks me around to face him, while his friends close in from either side. One of them tilts his pelvis forward, pushing against my hip so I can feel his erect cock through his pants.

Zevin cups both my breasts and squeezes so hard I gasp with pain.

"Not going to fight back?" he sneers. "I admit I had my doubts that His Majesty could tame you, but it seems he's done a thorough job of it. Look at this, boys." Zevin runs his hand between my legs, over the protective silver filigree. "A pretty cage for the royal pussy. We should see if we can smell her cunt through this thing. But I want my kiss first."

He clutches a handful of my hair, jerks my head back, and crushes his mouth to mine. It's a hard kiss, designed to hurt. I keep my teeth clenched despite the wet thrusting of his tongue against the seam of my mouth.

"Fuck you, Serylla—let me in." He pinches my nose shut and slams his mouth on mine again, waiting for me to run out of breath and open for him.

I try to pull away, but his friends grip my arms and shoulders, holding me in place.

Suddenly Zevin is yanked back by a tall figure with a swirling sheet of long black hair. The newcomer flings him several feet away, so violently that his flying body knocks down two other guests. The crowd gasps. The music falters, then fades.

The stranger's back is to me. All I can see is glossy black hair cascading over broad shoulders, and a powerful back that tapers down to a narrow waist and long legs.

"What's all this?" Rahzien looks up from his discussion with two of the nobles.

"He *assaulted* me!" screeches Zevin, pointing a shaking finger at the stranger as he picks himself up off the floor.

"Begging your pardon, sir—my lords." A pale red-haired man with a walking stick comes forward, bowing apologetically, first to Zevin and then to the room in general. "In our country of Zairos, publicly groping a royal concubine in that way would not be tolerated. Prince Gildas was simply defending the honor of your Royal Majesty and your Conquered Consort. No slight was intended."

Prince Gildas of Zairos? My mother considered marrying me off to one of those seven brothers, but then she and the King had some sort of falling out, and the deal fell through. Zairos is one of the countries I'd planned to approach once I left Kyreagan, to see if they'd be willing to help me reclaim my kingdom. But a royal's presence here means that the King of Zairos has validated Rahzien's claim to the Elekstan throne. And with that knowledge, I sink a little deeper into despair.

Rahzien's rolling laugh eases the tension in the room. "How honorable of you, Prince Gildas. I promised every man a dance and a kiss, so perhaps we should leave the rest of the Consort's charms to be enjoyed by the winner of our little game, eh, Lord Harlowe? Surely you can wait a bit longer." He winks at Zevin. "If you crave a woman so desperately, feel free to grope any of the other beauties as forcefully as you like. They are here to be used."

My gaze travels to one of the dancers standing near the King. Her brilliant smile never falters, and her eyes remain bright, but there's a rigidity to her stance for a second—a brittle hardness. The next second she's all sinuous curves as she slinks up to Zevin. He swats her away, his vicious gaze trained on me.

Rahzien turns his attention back to the tall, black-haired stranger. "As for you, Prince Gildas, while I respect your zeal for the honor of my court, I will not tolerate such violence. Enjoy your dance with the Princess, and then perhaps you should take your rest, in preparation for our conversations tomorrow. I am willing to make allowances for your weariness and your head injury—but only this once. Assault any of my people again, and you will pay for it… or your father will."

A beat of anxious silence. Then the King's face, which darkened grimly over the last few words, melts into one of his broad, disarming grins, and the guests chuckle with nervous relief.

"More wine!" calls Rahzien. "More music, more dancing!"

Zevin's friends hustle him off to the side of the room and ply him with wine, while the music starts up afresh and couples begin to whirl across the dance floor again.

Mouth dry, hands clenched, I wait for the stranger to face me and claim his dance. I liked how he threw Zevin across the room, but if he's a violent, angry person, that doesn't bode well for me.

He turns around.

And my world comes alive.

My chest thrills as I stare at him, trying to comprehend what I'm seeing. The handsome tanned features, the dark eyes, the crisp jaw, the straight, elegant nose...

It's Kyreagan.

He's right here. Right in front of me, dressed like a human, with no claws or horns to indicate otherwise.

Kyreagan is here.

Kyreagan came to save me. He isn't dead.

Thank the Maker, thank the Bone-Builder, thank whatever the fuck. *Thank you, thank you.*

He's alive. I want to cry and shriek and laugh and dance in circles and kiss his beautiful somber face until it softens into a smile just for me.

Kyreagan, Kyreagan, Kyreagan.

He's here. He *cares*. He looked for me, and he found me.

Fortunix didn't tell the King that dragons can take human form, so Rahzien has no idea that the man standing in front of me is the dragon prince. It's an effective disguise, but a fragile one that will dissolve if Kyreagan makes one mistake.

Shit, he's in so much danger.

"Shall we... dance?" His voice is strained, and his eyes scorch mine, fervent with pain and anger and need and joy.

"We shall." The two words are barely a breath. I can't say anything else or I'll cry, and I can't do that, because we're being watched. I need to stay calm and pretend he's a stranger.

Trembling, I touch him. I guide his hands to my shoulder and waist. A tight sigh of desperate relief bursts from his lips as his fingers settle on my body. Like he couldn't truly rest until he touched me again. I want to scream that I feel the same way. That I've been outside my skin, floating in some dreadful, dark place, and the heat of his palms is bringing me back. Securing me whole within myself.

I take the lead in the dance, because I have strength now. I think I would have found my courage on my own, eventually, but it's so much easier with him here. Why did I ever think I could leave him? We were broken when we came into each other's lives, so we fit our jagged edges together and healed as a new whole. The bones we share now are thicker and stronger than ever, and our scars match. Tearing us apart ruins us both.

As we dance, the crowd softens and blurs until there's only the music, swelling and sinking, swirling and soaring. Kyreagan stumbles a bit at first, but then he gives himself to the melody and to me, and we flow, like wings on the wind, like notes on a page.

They're watching us. I think I've kept my face stoic enough, and Kyreagan has, too, but our eyes—maybe our eyes have betrayed us. Maybe the bond knotted from his heart to mine is pulsing visibly in the air. Maybe the magnetic compulsion between us is tangible, tugging at everyone else like the inexorable currents of a whirlpool.

The music has stopped, so I bring us to a sudden halt, too. Everything I want to say piles onto my tongue—I can't speak any of it in this room. He's here, and yet we're still trapped.

He cups the side of my neck, and I shiver with delight at the heat of his strong fingers. "Is it true?" he whispers, his lips barely moving. "If we go now—"

I give him the tiniest nod. "I'll die."

Agony fills his eyes. "Then this is good night." He raises his voice to normal speaking volume. "I'll claim my kiss and retire to my room."

He leans in, heat pouring off him in angry waves. I can feel his entire body quaking with the effort of holding himself back. He touches his lips to mine and whispers, "Say the word and they all burn."

"Kill him, and you kill me," I breathe against his mouth. He growls low in his chest, a feral sound, and a fresh wave of heat surges from his body. Alarmed, I clutch the back of his neck to keep him close. "Promise you won't turn. You'll control yourself. Promise me."

A throat clears nearby, and a high male voice says, "Excuse me, Prince Gildas, I believe you've had more than your fair share of the Princess's time. I would like a turn."

For a second I'm sure all is lost, that Kyreagan will transform and incinerate half the room. Which would doubtless end with him being shot full of bullets and dying at my feet.

The vision terrifies me, and I hiss out, "Obey me," without really thinking.

Kyreagan straightens. His burning gaze never leaves mine. "Yes, Your Majesty."

He steps back, and another lord takes his place. As I dance with my new partner, as he whirls me around and around, I look for Kyreagan, tracing his retreat to the doors, his exit from the ballroom.

No, no, no. Come back...

But he can't. He needs to get away, before he does something stupid.

Did Rahzien notice anything between us? I glance at him, but he's immersed in a deep discussion with a cluster of nobles.

So far, so good.

Over the next hour I endure the attentions of more guests, parrying the awkward attempts at conversation by men who know me, and yet are bidding for the chance to fuck me. I whirl round and round in their arms, I submit to their kisses, and I wait for Rahzien to decide my fate.

The King alternates between conversations and dances until finally, with one of the dancers clinging to his arm, he moves to the clerks' table and pores over the sheets of paper for what seems like an age.

At last, apparently satisfied, he strides to the head of the room and mounts the first two tiers of the platform, signaling for the music to stop.

"My lords, thank you for joining me this evening. I am pleased by your enthusiasm, your generosity, and the high value you place upon my Conquered Consort. My servants will take her to her royal bedchamber, and one lucky man will join her there." He takes the chain with the key from around his neck and dangles it before the eyes of the men. "That generous, loyal, exceptional man... is Lord Zevin Harlowe."

Zevin roars his victory and leaps forward to claim his prize. Still grinning broadly, Rahzien grips his forearm as if to congratulate him—but he pulls Zevin close and leans down, speaking close to the young lord's ear with an expression so intense that I frown. What could the King be saying? Whatever it is, the words drain the triumphant color from Zevin's face.

The King lets him go, resuming the same effusive grin, and calls for celebratory drinks and a final dance while I'm ushered out of the ballroom by two guards and taken upstairs. Neither of them are wearing helmets, and none of the guards in the ballroom were either. Perhaps the omission was meant to humanize them, to put the Elekstan nobles at ease.

The corridor leading to my suite is empty, which doesn't surprise me; I know from long experience that most of the servants will be busy with the party, and the rest are probably in the servants' kitchen or common room. The ground floor of the palace was teeming with guards, and several were stationed near the main staircase, but since all the valuables have been removed from this part of the palace, there's no reason to place extra guards here. Undoubtedly Rahzien is living in my mother's rooms, which are on the opposite end of the palace, as far from me as she could get.

The absence of guards seems to trouble one of my escorts. "Is two of us enough to guard her chamber?" he asks his companion.

"Lord Harlowe will be coming up soon," replies the second guard. "He'll have his own men to keep watch."

"I suppose."

We're nearly to the main entrance of my suite when a figure rounds the corner at the far end of the hall. He's short, with wavy red hair, a pretty face, and a scar through the right side of his mouth. I recognize him as the man who intervened after Kyreagan's fight with Zevin. He's leaning heavily on a gilded walking stick, limping and wincing as he approaches us.

"Finally, someone to help me!" he exclaims, with a huge sigh of relief.

"What are you doing up here?" demands one of my guards.

"I think someone played a terrible trick on me. You see, I was supposed to meet a very lovely dancer for a little tryst, and I do believe she gave me false directions. It's terribly hurtful to be treated this way, and I'm so fucking tired… please, can you help me?"

"We have our orders," replies the guard. "You'll have to find someone else to assist you."

"At least give me directions." The red-haired man limps closer—he's just a few paces away. "I have no idea where the stairs are."

"You'll head down this hall—" The first guard turns, pointing back the way we came, and at that moment, the red-haired man's stance changes dramatically. The weariness drops from his body and the exasperation vanishes from his face. He swings the bulbous head of his walking stick and strikes the skull of my second guard with a vicious *thunk*. As the first guard turns back around, he takes the blunt force of the walking stick right in his face. Bone crunches, and he falls backward like a felled tree, his nose and cheekbones crushed into his face. Dead.

The red-haired man sets the butt of his staff to the throat of the other guard, the unconscious one. Then he takes a deep breath and bears down until there's a dull crack.

"Right, then." The stranger steps back and leans against the wall, breathing hard. "God, murder takes the shit out of me. Now I remember why I don't kill people more often. Give me just a moment."

Stunned, I watch while he inhales a few deep breaths. I consider fleeing, because I doubt he could catch me when he's in this state, but I don't think it's wise to underestimate him like the dead guards did. Besides, I'm curious, and the only way to get answers is to wait.

Once his breathing slows a bit, he whistles softly out of the scarred side of his mouth. Three black-clad people hurry around the corner, pick up the dead guards, and carry them away.

"Where are they taking those men?" I ask. "Who are you?"

"Trust me, love, we know how to dispose of bodies so they won't be found." He lifts the flap of his brocade jacket and uses the lining to polish a few dots of blood from the head of his staff. "And to answer your second question, we're friends. Well, not exactly *friends*, perhaps, but thereabouts. We got no love for Vohrain, anyway."

"You were with the Prince of Zairos. Earlier."

The man smirks. "Kyreagan. Yes."

Hearing Kyreagan's name in his mouth sends a jolt of delighted panic through my chest.

"Then you know about him?" I lower my voice. "What he is?"

"Fuck, love, who do you think taught him how to behave decently while in a palace? He was plain feral when I found him, wasn't he? And now look at him. Acting like a true gentleman."

"Where is he?" I step forward, my heart beating frantically. "I need to see him. There are things he should know—"

"Easy, Princess. I'm here to take you to him."

I take an eager step forward, and then I recall that Parma's life is on the line if I don't obey the King tonight. "If I'm not in that bedroom when Lord Harlowe arrives, the King will kill my maid, Parma. She's more than a maid—she's a friend. I have to be docile, he said, or she dies."

The red-haired man tilts his head, eyeing me soberly. "You were going to sacrifice your body for her life."

"Yes, and that's why I can't go with you. Harlowe will be here any minute." I wince, tapping the cage around my hips. "He has the key to this."

"Does he now?" The stranger purses his lips. "What's this then?"

With a flourish and a twinkle of silver, he produces the very same key Rahzien used to lock my belt and my mask.

I gasp. "How did you—"

"Magic. Not the spellcasting kind, but some might say this sort of magic is better." With a twirl of his hand, the key vanishes, then reappears again. "Lord Harlowe will be hunting for this key for quite some time, wondering where he dropped it. And I've arranged for him to be plied with strong drinks during his search—drinks with a little special powder in them—so eventually he will simply topple over. He'll be put in his carriage by an ally of mine, and when he wakes up, he won't remember a thing about what he did or didn't do tonight. So you can come with me, love, and rest assured that your maid will be in no danger. But we should go quickly."

I don't hesitate for another moment. True, I just saw this man murder two Vohrainians right in front of me, so I should probably be scared of him—but he's allied with Kyreagan, and right now that's enough.

We hurry along the next hall, and then the man pushes open a door to one of the standby rooms, where the maid on night duty could remain close by in case I needed her. It's a simple chamber, plainly furnished with a bed and a dresser. There's a small privy closet at the back.

In the center of the room stand two men. I don't even care about the other man—I leap for Kyreagan, throwing my arms around his neck, gripping him with all the force in my body.

"You," I sob out, kissing his cheek, his mouth, anywhere I can reach. "You came after me."

His fingers tangle in my hair as he tilts my face back to look at me. "Fuck yes, I did," he says fiercely. "When I found out Fortunix took you, I had no choice. How could I live, knowing you were in pain, knowing what Rahzien would do…" His gaze darkens. "Did he breed you by force?"

"No." I shake my head, but I can't repress the shudder that travels my skin. "It was almost… worse."

"Worse how?"

"I'll tell you sometime. I can't now." I hunch my shoulders against the echo of Rahzien's voice in my mind. "He told me you were dead. He said the same sorcerer who designed the poison that keeps me from running away created another kind of poison, too. They gave it to the flocks and herds on the Middenwold Isles—contaminated them, somehow. The poison is activated by dragon saliva, and he said every dragon who eats prey from the Isles will die."

"That can't be true." Kyreagan pulls back, his handsome face stricken with horror.

"I didn't believe him at first. But then I tried to escape, and I got so sick, Ky. I nearly died. If he was right about the poison inside my body, could he be right about the other poison, too? When you left the clan, were they safe and healthy? Had they eaten any prey from the Middenwold?"

The man behind him says, "Oh shit," in a faint, terrified voice. He's tall and gorgeous like Kyreagan, but with broader, softer features, brown skin, and long coppery locs.

"This is Hinarax," says Kyreagan. "He and I left Ouroskelle four or five hours after you were taken. When we departed, no hunting parties had yet gone to the Middenwold Isles. By now they must have hunted there, and eaten the prey…"

"We have to find out. We need to know," Hinarax interrupts, his voice breaking.

"Go," Kyreagan tells him. "Find the tallest tower of this palace and take off from there. It's dark—perhaps no one will see you. Either way, we must know what has happened."

"Wait." The red-haired man has been waiting by the closed door of the room, with his left ear pressed to the wood, listening for footsteps. But he comes forward now, his brows bent, his scarred lips pinched with worry. One of his eyes appears to be made of glass, but the other holds tumultuous emotion as he looks at Hinarax. "You'll come back? Because if I fucked a dragon that well, only to never see him again, it would be—"

"Tragic?" I offer.

He gives me a twisted, pained smile. "Exactly. The Princess understands."

"All too well," I murmur.

"I'll return when I can," says Hinarax. "In the meantime, Meridian—take care of my prince and his life-mate."

I look at Kyreagan, my eyebrows raised, and I silently form the word, *Life-mate?*

He glances away without replying. "Fly swiftly, brother."

"I will."

"I'll help you find your way to a tower," says Meridian. "Otherwise you'll be wandering the palace until morning. You two, wait here until I come back. Be good, and for fuck's sake, be *quiet*." He winks at Kyreagan and flips the silver key through the air. It lands perfectly centered on the feather pillow at the top of the bed.

With the other two gone, Kyreagan and I stare at each other. The uncertain fate of his clan hangs between us, an awkward weight in the air.

"I'm sorry," I murmur, taking his hand. "I wish I didn't have to tell you that, but I thought you'd want to know. You can leave if you need to. Go with them, find out if the clan is alright."

Pain flickers through his eyes. "If they aren't, there's nothing I can do to save them. But I have to believe they're alive. My clan is strong. If there's a way to survive, they'll find it. What concerns me more is the existence of this poisoner. Do you have any idea who it could be?"

I shake my head. "I haven't come into contact with many people. Rahzien has been keeping me isolated, moving me around. I rarely sleep in the same room twice. And I'm lucky to even have a bed. The first couple of days I spent in his power were torture. He keeps telling me things—making me say terrible things about myself…" I press a hand to my forehead. "Sometimes I believe him."

Kyreagan's gaze softens, and he takes my waist, pulling me closer. "You mean the things he had you repeat in the market, before you were flogged. Trust me, Serylla, they're not true."

"You were there?" I look up at him, startled. "Then the growl I heard—it really *was* you."

"Forgive me for leaving you there," he says earnestly. "I would have snatched you away, but after what he said about the two of you being linked, I didn't want to risk killing you while trying to save you. I want to get you out of this without causing any more harm to the people of Elekstan. They have suffered enough of my fire and destruction. But Vohrain—" his expression turns malevolent— "they will have to pay for this. And I think I will make one exception to my rule, and destroy that Elekstan lord who groped you tonight. I'll burn off both his hands."

"He is already scarred by dragon fire, body and mind," I say. "Though I think the damage to his soul started long ago, at the hands of his family. Speaking of family, did you leave our eggs by themselves?"

"Of course not! I left them in the care of Rothkuri and Everelle."

"The blue dragon and his girl?"

"Yes."

"Oh, that's good. I like them. What about your brother, and the others—are they—oh fuck—I was going to ask if they're alright, but we can't be sure."

"When I left, everyone was in decent health, except for one dragon and two women who drowned when their cave flooded. The rest were hungry, but alive. And there were eggs, Serylla. Eleven of them, with more on the way. Even if something happened to the rest of the clan, perhaps Hinarax and I can care for the eggs, and the hatchlings. Our species won't be entirely extinguished."

"It won't be just you and Hinarax." Tears pool in my eyes, and I can't stop my lips from trembling. "I'll be there to help."

Kyreagan tenses, his chest rising and falling with quick, harsh breaths. "You will?"

I nod, pinching my lips together. Two tears escape my eyes and trail down my cheeks. His hold on my waist tightens, and I sense the great power of him, the strength of this body and the raw, feral fire of his soul.

"I should have realized it sooner," I whisper. "Being here, enduring this… it made me realize what I want, what's important to me. And that's you, and those two beautiful fucking eggs we made together. Strange as it sounds, that's my family. I want to free my people from Vohrain if we can, if there's a way... but after that, all I want is you. And if it comes down to Elekstan or our family... I'm going to be selfish, and turn my back on everything else, and choose you."

Wait... he doesn't look happy. He looks conflicted. Oh fuck... did I read him wrong? Maybe all he needed was a carrier for his eggs and now he's done with me. Maybe he only came to save me out of a sense of responsibility or guilt, not because he loves me. Maybe I've been a fool.

"If you don't want me, just say so," I bite out.

"It's not that." He lets me go, turns away. "It's all of this. Everything in your society, the comforts you're used to having. I understand it more now, and I can see how living with me would be a miserable kind of deprivation."

"Oh god, is that all?" I release a soft laugh of relief. "I won't lie, I might appreciate a few extra comforts. We can talk about that after we get out of this mess. But I won't ask you to change your whole culture or way of life for me. We can compromise."

"Compromise." He mouths the word as if he doesn't quite like the taste of it.

"Yes, dragon. It's what people in relationships do... I think. I've witnessed a few functional ones, here and there."

"Perhaps we could arrange for water pipes and toilets somewhere on Ouroskelle," he says.

I blink. "Well, that's a huge concession to comfort, and I won't say no, but it would be a complex undertaking. One thing at a time. Speaking of toilets... I have been locked into this thing for hours, and I need to pee."

Stepping past him, I pluck the little silver key from the pillow and poke it at the keyhole, but from my angle, it's hard to see what I'm doing. The keyhole is inset between swirls of silver filigree. "Can you do it?"

Kyreagan takes the key and kneels in front of me. His black brows pull together as he peers at the hole. I can't resist sliding my fingers through the glossy ink of his hair while he wrestles with the key and finally manages to unlock the belt. With a sigh of relief I unlatch it, lower it down my legs, and step out. When I return from the privy, Kyreagan is inspecting the craftsmanship.

"It's a cruel device, but beautifully made," he says. "Let me remove the mask as well."

I stand still while he slips the key into a crevice of the mask and turns it with a soft click. With the flip of a latch, the mask opens, and he lifts it away from my face.

"There you are," he murmurs.

My breath turns light and quick, and my stomach flutters under the warm gaze of those dark eyes. Gently I trace my fingertips up his arm. "Kyreagan," I whisper. "How much time do you have left in human form?"

"Not long," he admits. "I'll need to be back in my room soon. There's enough space in there for me to exist in dragon form if I'm very still and I remain curled up in the same position. It will be unpleasant, but I can endure it. What's harder to endure is the knowledge that while I'm in that form, I'm useless. I can't look for the poisoner, or protect you from Rahzien."

"I can handle Rahzien, now that I know you're alive," I tell him. But the thought of being in the King's presence again makes my skin crawl, chills my very bones with a cringing sense of vulnerability. I don't want to have to face the King, to recite my "lessons," to be whipped in front of my people if any of them have dared to defy their conquerors. Any of that could happen tomorrow. Or Rahzien could decide to force himself on me. The idea of him thrusting into my body makes me want to vomit. I shudder, remembering the mouths on mine during the ball tonight, remembering the press of men's hands and the squeeze of their fingers. The dull, animal hunger in their eyes.

"I need you to do something for me before you change, Kyreagan." I look up at him desperately. "I know it's terrible to want this when we're in here, surrounded by enemies, when the fate of your clan is uncertain, but—"

He bends his beautiful face to mine, glides his silken lips against my cheek, and murmurs, in the deep voice I love, "You want me to fuck you."

"Yes," I breathe. "Please. As hard as you can. But we have to be quiet."

"I like making you loud."

A laugh wells up in my heart. "I know. But for now, we'll both have to be quick and quiet."

"Very well."

"One more thing," I say softly. "Just so we're both very clear on this point. You love me. And I love you back."

He wraps both arms around me, lifting me right off my feet as he carries me, not to the bed, but to the wall. He pins me there with his body, his hands bracketing my wrists. I'm engulfed by his heat, his scent, his strength—I'm breathless, helpless, and safe.

There's a soft, wicked glow in his eyes as he looks at me, an encompassing gaze as if he's memorizing my face. "From this day on, your only title is 'Queen,' and I am your captive. My place is wherever you are. My will, my future, and my body are yours."

17

KYREAGAN

I can't believe I have her here, between my arms, against my chest. Her heart is thumping even faster than mine. She tugs against my grip, so I release her wrists, and she begins fumbling eagerly with the buttons of my doublet.

"I'm not used to you wearing so many clothes." She vents a breathless laugh. "I need them *off*."

"I'll be no help with that," I say. "Meridian dressed me for the ball. I can handle some buttons, but not these tiny ones, or the pins."

"We don't have much time, so—" Her hands drop to the front of my pants, unfastening them and pushing them down my hips. My cock emerges, and she wraps greedy, silken fingers around it. I bite back a groan, remembering Meridian's caution, that we must be quiet.

"I need this inside me." A shaken whisper, her blue eyes on mine, pleading. "I need to feel you."

"Are you well enough, after birthing the eggs and enduring the whip?" I slide a palm over her belly. "Are you sure—"

"I'm sure. I've been healed since then. Kyreagan, please. I want this, before you have to go—please." Tears glitter in her eyes.

Her heart is a jewel, and I don't understand all the facets of her emotions in this moment, but she has told me what she needs, and it is both my duty and my pleasure to provide it.

"Here, by the wall?" I ask gently. "Or on the bed? I haven't used a bed yet... While we were with the rebels, I slept while I was in dragon form, so I could use my human hours for practice."

"The bed." She tugs her undershorts off, kicks them away, and lies down, adjusting the pillow beneath her head. "It's narrow, but comfortable." Her fragrance wafts from between her parted legs, and I inhale through my nose, reveling in the familiar sweetness.

With a focused thought, I return my tongue to its cloven form. Then I leap onto the bed with her and plunge my face between her thighs with a blissful sigh. She sucks in a breath and exhales a tiny sound of shocked pleasure.

I've missed this. The taste of her, the soft wet lips of her pussy that part easily for my tongue. I slide it so deep inside her that it strains at the root, and I wriggle the twin halves until she whimpers.

Pulling back, I reach up and cover her mouth lightly with my hand. "Hush, love."

She nods frantically and twists away from my palm to whisper, "I want you to come inside me. I need your cum to be there, instead of—"

She breaks off the sentence, but the pained quiver of her lips tells me the rest. She thought she was going to suffer the invasion of the young lord I attacked at the party. He won't be harming her tonight, thanks to Meridian; and she knows it, but she needs me to soothe that latent fear. She's affirming her choice, her power. Using me to feel secure again.

And I am all too happy to be used by the one I love.

Sitting up, I draw her body closer, then push her legs up and grasp my cock. I slide the tip over her clit, down her pussy, watching her breasts rise with her eager breath, delighting in the way her thighs tighten and her hips surge, as if she could pull me inside her by sheer force of will.

I'd like to go slowly. But my last hour as a human is expiring soon, and I'll need time to make it back to my room before I shift.

Still, I hold back for another moment, just to admire her arousal glistening on my cock head, to breathe in the earthy sweetness of her scent, to enjoy the way her legs look with the ribbons, the lace, and the elegant shoes. Her face is the loveliest part of her, like a pale flower blooming amid the swirl of her golden hair.

"Kyreagan." Her rosy mouth forms a pout with which I'm all too familiar, and it makes me smile. "If I'm your queen, you need to obey me, and fuck me now."

I reply in my deepest tones, "Yes, Your Majesty." And I slide into her.

She tilts her head back. "Yes, god." One of her hands clutches her pillow, the other reaches for me. I grasp her fingers with my right hand and use my left to hold one of her thighs up as I thrust into her. The gliding friction is just as mind-melting as I remember, and for a fervent second I thank the enchantress for granting me this body and all the pleasures that go with it.

"Harder," Serylla whispers. "Deeper."

My hips rock faster, my body slapping against hers. At the sound, her eyes fly open, and she glances nervously at the door.

I change positions and move forward to brace myself over her, while she curls her legs around me, pinning me inside her. We can be quieter like this, and the angle at which I'm grinding against her clit seems to please Serylla immensely.

She stares into my eyes, a desperate, glorious light shining in her gaze. Her plump lips are parted just enough to let soft little sobs of pleasure escape. They're getting shorter, quicker—she's about to come.

"Come inside me," she pants, her voice jerky from my powerful thrusts. "Mark me as yours. I belong to the dragon prince, and you'll keep me full of your cum so everyone knows it."

Those words thrill through the most primal depths of my soul, and I thrust deeper than ever. I come with a compulsive tremor, a pulsing heat pounding through my cock into her pussy. She comes immediately afterward, with a tiny squeal and a series of sharp, panting breaths. Her fingernails dig crescents into my arms, even through my shirt.

"Yes," she sobs softly. "Yes, yes. Oh my god… I needed that so badly. Oh god…" Her pussy squeezes me again, and more cum surges from my body into hers.

I nuzzle her cheek. "Mine."

She releases my arms, captures my face in both her hands. "You need to get me away from him, Kyreagan."

"I know. I will."

"I'll try to help. I'll try to figure out who the poisoner is."

"Meridian is working on that as well. One of the women at the party has been with the King multiple times, so Meridian plans to seduce her, to find out if she has heard or seen anything important."

"Seduce her? I thought he liked Hinarax." Serylla frowns.

"He does. But I don't believe they have pledged any sort of loyalty to each other."

"He killed two Vohrainians without hesitation, without regret," she says. "I can't decide if I should admire him for that, or be terrified."

"Perhaps a little of both. But so far, he has proved worthy of my trust."

She lifts her head and kisses me, then moves higher on the pillow until my cock slides out of her. I lean back on my heels and tuck my thumbs against the lips of her pussy, pinning them open so I can see my cum gleaming white inside her pink slit.

"Beautiful." I bend and place a kiss on her clit. She tastes so good I let my tongue swirl over the little peak of flesh, but Serylla pushes me away with a shaky laugh.

"I'd love more of this, but I should go to my room in case someone comes to look for me," she says. "And you have to hide in your chamber before you transform. Kyreagan, you're in so much danger, it terrifies me. Have you seen how many guns they have? More every day, it seems. They could take you down even in dragon form, couldn't they?"

"Not before I did some damage."

"Please be careful. Please control your temper."

"I watched a man grope you tonight, and I did not incinerate him," I say haughtily.

"And you deserve praise for that." She climbs onto her knees and pats my head. "Good dragon."

I give her a disapproving look, and she grins. The smile fades almost immediately, though, and she leaves the bed to pick up her undershorts.

"You make me so happy," she says in a sorrowful tone. "Your very presence is healing. I wish we didn't have to go. I wish we could stay here... or better yet, leave together."

"We'll find the poisoner, and we'll force them to undo what they've done to you," I say. "And after that, if they truly did kill the remaining dragons of my clan, I will carry them to Ouroskelle and feed them to a voratrice, so they will suffer the slowest, most agonizing death possible."

"The eggs will be hatching soon." Serylla's voice softens with longing. "I hope we can be there."

She steps close to help me refasten my pants, and when she's done I kiss her, a slow, savoring kiss that turns desperate, because I can't help it, because I can't let her go and yet I must. She kisses me back just as fiercely, her small tongue lashing through my mouth, her fingers pressed against my neck.

"We have to, Ky. We have to," she whispers against my mouth.

"Fuck." I kiss her again, a swift, hot brush of my lips. We break apart, and she hastily picks up the mask, the belt, and the key. She listens at the door for a moment, then glances at me and says, with a look of beautiful misery, "I love you."

And then she's gone.

I barely make it to the suite in time to strip off my clothes. My bones begin to buzz with the energy of Thelise's magic, and within seconds I transform into my dragon self. I nearly crunch the bedpost with my foreleg, but I manage to pull back and arrange my body in a semicircle, occupying the empty space around the bed. I don't understand why wealthy humans need such spacious bedrooms when their bodies are the same size as those of other humans. But at least their vanity works in my favor.

Aeris enters my room cautiously after the change. "Meridian isn't back yet," she says. "And where's Hinarax?"

Keeping my voice as quiet as I can, which is difficult in dragon form, I tell her about Serylla's warning and Hinarax's flight back to Ouroskelle. "As for Meridian, he should have returned here after taking Hinarax to the tower."

"Maybe he came across something of interest. An opportunity for spying or sabotage." She perches on the dresser, takes out two of her knives, and begins juggling them. I've come to understand that such activity soothes her.

"How was it?" Aeris asks. "Seeing your Princess again? Did you—" She waggles her eyebrows violently.

"Are you ill?" I peer at her. "What is happening to your face?"

She sighs. "God, you dragons… it's a signal. It means did you fuck her?"

"Then why not simply ask me? Why do this?" I attempt to move my brow ridges like she did.

Aeris snorts with laughter. "We humans like to talk with our faces or hands sometimes, instead of saying the actual words. Especially if we're trying to be… diplomatic."

I still don't understand, so I answer her question instead of delving into the idea of *talking with faces*. "Yes, I fucked her."

"Do you think that was wise? Or considerate? I mean, after what she's been through."

Offended, I scowl at her. "I wouldn't have done it if she'd been averse to the idea. She begged me."

"Did she?" Aeris chuckles. "Damn. And Meridian keeps gushing about his time with Hinarax, too. Dragon shifter dick must be good."

"At first I thought mine was far too small in human form," I confess. "But the Princess assures me it is above average for a human male."

"Congratulations." She chuckles again, but the smile doesn't reach her eyes this time.

"You want to ask me something else."

"So you *are* getting better at reading humans. I wanted to talk about the thing I told you before—about the female dragon who's hiding out with my sorcerer friend."

"The one who survived the Supreme Sorcerer's curse."

"That's the one. You haven't asked me about it again."

"I've been considering what it means."

"And wondering if you should believe me?" She catches one of the knives and jams it into the top of the dresser. When she yanks it out, the dark gloss of the wood is marred by a pale scar.

"Are you sure the dragon is female? It can be difficult to tell, for those unfamiliar with dragon anatomy."

"She said her name is Nyreza. My friend has been doing experiments with her blood. Apparently she's immune to magic. Entirely immune."

Nyreza, Saevel's sister. Suddenly it all makes sense. "Her fire never worked properly. I didn't want to bring her to war with us, but her mother and brother begged me to give her a chance. If she's immune to magic, that would explain why her innate magic was blocked."

"I've never heard of such immunity. But if it's true—what if my friend could use some of Nyreza's blood to make an antidote, something to counteract the magical poison in the Princess's veins?"

Hope brightens in my chest. "How fast could your friend produce it?"

"I'm not sure what he would need. It might require something from Serylla—a bit of her blood, tears, or spit— maybe strands of her hair or nail clippings. It's too dangerous for me to send him a written message from here, but I could take samples from Serylla and go to him in person. I hate to leave you and Meridian and the others, but I don't think there's another way. I don't trust anyone else with his location, and he wouldn't let anyone but me through his protective barriers, anyway."

"So you trust each other."

Aeris squirms a little. "He and I used to be married. It was a stupid, impulsive decision. Didn't work out. But we still care about each other. He has done things for me that no one else would."

"You'll get the samples from Serylla tonight, and leave now?"

"Or I could wait until Meridian gets back, and make sure he agrees with the plan."

"I thought he wasn't your leader."

She rolls her eyes. "He insists that he's not. But you've seen how our group works. What do you think?"

"Still, you don't need his permission for this, do you?" I lift my head higher. "The sooner we can free Serylla from Rahzien, the sooner we can kill him. Meridian promised to help me find and rescue her, and in return I promised to help you destroy Rahzien and drive out Vohrain. Our goals are inextricably intertwined."

Aeris lowers her voice. "Not everyone in this group believes we should wait to free Serylla before we take out Rahzien. We've never had this much access to him, and Odrash thinks we should take advantage of it, before we lose our chance. He likes Serylla, but he would consider her death to be an acceptable loss."

A growl reverberates in my chest. "Until the poison within Serylla is neutralized, I will defend Rahzien from any attempts on his life."

"But you can't do that while you're in dragon form," Aeris points out. "Look, I'll talk to Odrash again before I leave. I don't think he'll make a move without Meridian's blessing. But when I'm gone, watch the others, and be cautious. If Meridian starts joking more than usual, yet at the same time keeping his distance from you, it means he has made a hard decision, one he doesn't want to live with, but one he believes to be necessary. That's when you should worry."

She hops off the dresser and sheathes her knives. "I'll go get the samples from Serylla now, and leave the city tonight. I have my forged papers that identify me as part of Prince Gildas's retinue, so I should be able get back into the Capital, as long as the rest of you haven't blown your cover by then. I'll return as soon as I can, hopefully with good news."

"With the antidote," I reply.

"I'll do my best." She touches the door handle, then turns back to me. "Get some rest. I have a feeling tomorrow is going to be shitty for everyone."

18

SERYLLA

When the door to my room opens, I startle upright and scoot back against the headboard.

I thought Meridian had taken care of Zevin, that I'd be spared from entertaining the vengeful young lord tonight. My fingers wrap around the handle of the hairbrush under my pillow—the closest thing to a weapon I could find. Though I'm not sure I could bring myself to use it, after Rahzien's threat against Parma's life.

To my relief, the person who enters isn't Zevin, but a young woman dressed in black, with a lithe build, tawny skin, and curly hair. Candles still burn on my bureau, and their light flickers on the twin blades in her hands.

"I see they haven't replaced your guards yet," she says without introduction or explanation. "Have you thought of an excuse for their absence? Other than Meridian killing them, of course."

So she's with Meridian, the red-haired pickpocket. Which means she's also a friend to Kyreagan.

I lay down the hairbrush. "I'll come up with a plausible reason why they left. But I'm more concerned about someone finding the bodies."

"They won't be discovered for weeks. Give me your hand."

I narrow my eyes. "Why?"

"I'm going to find a sorcerer who's caring for a wounded female dragon who just so happens to be immune to magic."

There's far too much information in that sentence. "Wait… a female dragon survived?"

"Yes. And we have no time for further questions. Her blood might be the key to detaching you from Rahzien, but to find out, I have to take some of your blood, hair, and spit to my sorcerer friend."

"Isn't that dangerous for you?"

"Very dangerous. Hold this." She shoves a small glass tube into my left hand, then pricks my right forefinger with the tip of her knife and holds it above the open mouth of the tube, squeezing mercilessly. "I'm used to danger. Rather enjoy it, actually. Besides, he's a good man, your dragon prince."

"Yes, he is."

I watch my blood drip into the tube. When it's nearly full, she says, "Suck on that for a second," and produces a miniscule cork to seal the tube. Then she grabs my hairbrush and inspects it. "Strange, I thought there would be a few strands stuck in here. I suppose we'll have to do this another way." With an unceremonious yank, she pulls a lock of my hair taut and sets her blade against it.

"Wait!" I exclaim. "Do it from the underside, so Rahzien won't notice."

"Good thinking." She separates a lock from beneath the rest of my hair, near the base of my neck, and cuts it free. "Now, spit into this vial a few times."

When I grimace, she rolls her eyes. "Would you rather provide a piss sample?"

"No," I say firmly. "Give me a minute."

Seconds later, she seems satisfied that I've provided a decent sample. She stoppers the second vial, wraps everything carefully in a cloth, and tucks the bundle into the satchel at her side. "It's been a pleasure, Princess."

She's striding purposefully to the door, and yet I still have so many questions churning in my mind. I settle on the simplest of them all. "What's your name?"

"I'm Aeris. Be well, Princess." With a brisk nod, she's out of my bedroom, closing the door. I barely hear her footfalls on the carpet of the sitting room as she leaves.

I don't blow out the candles. Instead I stay sitting up for a long time, clutching the hairbrush, wondering if perhaps I dreamed her, and she was never really there at all.

Parma doesn't come to dress me in the morning.

I try not to panic about it. There's a pink day dress hanging in my empty closet, and a fresh corset and underwear lying on a cushioned stool by the full-length mirror, so I put them on. The mask and belt from last night are hidden under my bed now, and I wedged the key into a crevice behind one of my dresser drawers. Rahzien could have my rooms searched and find the items, but I don't want to make it easy for him to put me back in those demeaning contraptions.

I'm braiding my hair when Rahzien enters, looking ominous.

"Where are your guards?" he says tersely.

"When Zevin came to me last night, he yelled at them to leave, and finally they did," I say. "He had his own men stand guard while he was in my room."

His frown darkens. "Were you unpleasant to the young lord?"

"Not at all. After I left the ball, I waited a long time for him to visit me. When he finally arrived, he was very drunk. He said he had lost the key you gave him, and that he looked for it for hours before he finally found it. He barely managed to unlock my belt and mask, but he couldn't, um... perform. He stumbled out of my room, and I'm not sure where he went after that."

Rahzien lunges forward, grabs my arm, and wrenches me away from the dressing table, yanking me close to his body. His stony eyes glare into mine. "Are you lying to me?"

"No," I whisper.

"No *what*?"

"No, Master."

Rahzien's hand collars my throat just beneath my jaw, and his thumb strokes my chin. The fury and accusation vanishes from his eyes, replaced by an expression I like even less—a patronizing sort of intimacy.

"I had to frighten you a little just now, Spider, to be sure you were telling me the truth," he says, almost soothingly. "I did hear reports of Zevin wandering the halls last night, drunk out of his mind, yelling about a key. And I heard that one of the lords found him nearly unconscious and helped him into his carriage. I wanted to see if your story corroborated those reports."

I bow my head. "You own me. I wouldn't dare lie to you. Not when it could endanger people I care about."

"One thing's for certain—Zevin Harlowe has forfeited his time with you. He made an idiot of himself, after I chose him above all the others. What a fool he was, not to enjoy his prize. This charming, entrancing little prize..."

Someone taps on the half-open bedroom door. I use the distraction to extricate myself from Rahzien's hold and step back. He throws me an irritated look, then whirls to face the guard who just entered. "What?"

"Your Majesty, something you should know—one of the sentries on the east wall reported seeing a dragon."

Rahzien makes a scoffing sound. "Unlikely. Was the sentry drunk on duty? If so, have him killed."

"Begging Your Majesty's pardon, he seemed quite sober when he reported the incident. He said a dragon took off from the palace's highest tower and flew east."

"In broad daylight?" Rahzien says incredulously.

"No, Sire—the sighting occurred last night."

I can't see Rahzien's face, since he turned his back to me, but I note the way his whole body goes rigid, exuding a nearly tangible cloud of threat. The guard shrinks back a step.

"This sighting occurred *last night*?" Rahzien says in a terribly calm voice. "And I'm just being informed of it now?"

"Forgive me, Your Majesty—I was going to tell you sooner, but when I arrived at your chamber with the news, you were— with a couple of ladies. I didn't want to interrupt."

"And after the ladies and I finished our fun?" says Rahzien evenly. "Why did you not tell me then?"

"Sire, you were asleep. And I thought—"

"No." Rahzien cuts him off. "You didn't think. *Fuck* my life. Am I to be forever surrounded by fools? If anyone sees a dragon anywhere near this palace, this city—anywhere within our borders, the creature is to be shot on sight, and I'm to be informed immediately. I don't care if I'm sound asleep or balls deep in god's asshole, you tell me at once. I thought I'd made that clear to everyone, but it seems I shall have to emphasize it."

He strides toward the guard, who retreats again, babbling a plea for mercy right before Rahzien's hand grasps his throat and chokes off the words. Rahzien is bigger, stronger, fueled by rage.

He drags the soldier out of my chambers, then orders over his shoulder, "Spider! Come with me. Now."

I hurry out of my suite and follow the King down the hall. My stomach growls as we walk. I'm sure Rahzien hears it, but he doesn't comment. I haven't had anything to eat since lunch yesterday. He likes to keep me hungry and weak, less able to think clearly or fight him.

We head out of the palace into the main courtyard, where a contingent of Vohrainian guards is training, performing smooth, synchronized movements under the early morning sun. Together they take one step forward, draw the large, cumbersome guns from the holsters on their backs, aim as if to fire, then reseat the weapon and retreat a step. A commander stalks through the rows of soldiers, hands folded behind him as he calls out each maneuver and scrutinizes the troops.

Rahzien marches toward his soldiers and throws the unfortunate guard to the ground. He drags the man's helmet off, revealing a pale, terrified man with a shock of brown hair and a brass ring through his septum.

Rahzien steps behind him and kicks him in the back. The guard doubles over, wheezing.

The soldiers halt their maneuvers. Scores of skeletal silver helmets angle toward the King of Vohrain.

"This man withheld a report from me," Rahzien bellows. "He kept crucial information to himself for hours rather than telling me that a fucking dragon had been sighted near the palace. I'd given orders that any such sightings were to be reported to me at once. But this man thought he knew better."

The guard bows down, his face to the paving stones. He's sobbing; I can see his shoulders shaking.

"Perhaps I have not made it clear enough," Rahzien continues. "The dragons should all be dead by now. But if one or two of them survived, and they come within range of your weapons, you have my royal command to shoot them down, immediately. Am I understood?"

The soldiers stamp and strike a salute.

"And to ensure you do not forget, witness the fate of this one who has disappointed me so deeply." He clutches the man's hair, tugging his head back, and draws a short, wide blade from a sheath at his belt.

Then he glances back at me. I can see the idea dawning in his eyes, the cruel smile tugging at his mouth.

Oh, no. Fuck no.

"You've been yearning to spill Vohrainian blood, haven't you, Spider?" he says. "Now's your chance."

I shake my head, taking a step back.

Rahzien's expression freezes into something ice-cold and dreadful. "What are you, Spider?"

"I am your pet."

"That's right. Obey me, and kill this disobedient worm."

Last night, I would have let Zevin fuck me to spare Parma from death. But this is a line I cannot cross. And Rahzien intends to push me over it. I can see the determined fury in his eyes, the gleeful resolution to crush another part of my spirit.

He flips the dagger around, holds the hilt out to me. "Do it. Or suffer."

My eyes flick across the gleaming helmets, each with its own rictus grin. In the distance, across the courtyard, a few stable-hands and servants hurry about their chores. None of them look toward me.

Hinarax is probably nearing Ouroskelle by now. Kyreagan is hiding somewhere in dragon form, lying in wait until he can be human for a couple of hours. I have no idea where Meridian is, and even if he knew what was happening, he couldn't stop it.

No one can save me from the consequences of the choice I'm about to make.

Rahzien frowns at me, a keen awareness waking in his eyes. "You've changed since last night. Fuck, we were so close, Spider, so close to perfect submission, and now we must start all over again. I won't be as gentle this time, because I need you to learn your place. Kill this man, or you'll suffer worse than five lashes."

I draw a deep breath in. "I won't kill for you."

"You won't kill for me?" He chuckles, incredulous, and waves his hand toward the silent rows of soldiers. "Every man and woman in this group would kill for me, and so would countless other Vohrainians spread out across this city, this kingdom. They know their place, and their duty. Unflinching obedience to their king."

"I used to be afraid of defying a ruler," I reply, raising my voice so it carries across the courtyard. "I was afraid of my own mother, the Queen. She made terrible choices, and I did nothing to stop her. She made me complicit in her careless cruelty, and I stained my own hands with blood through my inaction. I promised myself I wouldn't stand by and witness the death of more innocent people. I'll be your pet, your whipping girl, your consort, but I won't be your executioner."

The Vohrainian soldiers are listening. I can sense that I've captured their interest by refusing to kill the guard.

Perhaps Rahzien senses their attention, as well. Perhaps that's why he turns to the disgraced guard and says, "Punish my consort for me, and I'll forgive you for your foolishness."

The guard looks up at me, his eyes swollen, his face crumpled, tear-streaked and drooling. He sniffs, scrubs the back of his wrist across his mouth and chin, and climbs to his feet, a panicked frenzy in his eyes.

I fully expect him to spare me, because I refused to kill him. So the punch comes as a shock—his fist crashing into my face. I stagger, and he hits me again, in the stomach this time. Then the face again, with greater force. The blow sends me reeling, and I collapse at the feet of a motionless Vohrainian soldier.

Sickened and dizzy, I lift myself and spit blood onto stone. A few of my teeth feel loose.

The disgraced guard stumbles toward me, and I barely have time to curl in on myself and shield my face with my arms before he's kicking me, over and over, his cries of effort and desperation ringing in my head. Pain explodes wherever he strikes, until my brain is a blur of oozing scarlet agony.

"Enough," says Rahzien.

Thank fuck, the worst is over. I suck in a breath that tastes like blood and relax my body.

The guard sees an opening. Rams his boot into my belly with such force I can't breathe.

I've never felt such horrific pain. As if something in my stomach burst and released a flood of nauseating agony.

I'm barely conscious. Dimly I hear Rahzien's roar of fury as he holds the disgraced guard above me, snarls, "You are forgiven," and slashes with the knife, drenching me with the lifeblood of the man I wouldn't kill.

Rahzien drags me upright, clasping me against his chest like he's comforting a lover. He murmurs into my ear, beneath my bloodied hair, "I told you I don't like this kind of violence. But you made it necessary."

He picks me up, and I can't help a weak cry. I think I'm dying. I think I'm broken, deep inside.

"I'll take you to the healer," Rahzien tells me. "But I need to make a stop first."

My eyes are swollen nearly shut as he carries me past the stables, into the garden, to the aerie where we kept my mother's hawks.

Rahzien sets me down on the straw-covered floor, and I lie motionless, suffering through each breath. I'm grateful Kyreagan isn't here. If he saw me like this, he might bite Rahzien's head clean off, and then—well, I'd be dead too.

"Your mother kept beautiful hawks here," Rahzien says. Through the blurred cracks of my swollen eyelids, I see him opening a cage, reaching for a bird with glowing red eyes. I think it's the same one that found me in the alley, after I tried to escape. He holds the bird gently, stroking its feathers with one thick-fingered, ring-laden hand. "When she saw she had lost the war, she could have set them free. Instead I found them dead. She broke their necks, one by one, rather than let me have them. I have to admit… I respected her for that."

He lifts the bird and speaks softly to it. "Open the mind, free the voice, understand the purpose. Fly to Ouroskelle, Isle of Dragons, and tell me if any of the dragons still live. I'm especially interested in the fate of the dragon princes, Kyreagan and Varex. Secure the mind, preserve the voice, retain the purpose."

The bird bobs its head and flies from his hand, circling upward and darting out through one of the skylights of the aerie.

"Activation and closure phrases," says Rahzien, turning back to me. "The sorcerer who created these talking birds for me died some time ago, but as long as I say the correct phrases to trigger the spellwork at the beginning and confirm my intent at the end, I can still use the birds."

He crouches and picks me up again. He's broader than Kyreagan, barrel-chested and packed with hard muscle. He smells all wrong to me—heavy cologne and leather. I cringe inwardly at the feeling of his arms around me, but another wave of pain washes over me and I nearly lose myself.

"Stay awake," Rahzien orders. "Eyes open, Spider."

The last lucid part of my mind understands that in this instance, he's right. I'm wobbling on the very brink of death, and if I want to survive this I need to stay conscious until we reach the healer.

My mind registers the steady beat of Rahzien's boots. Long hallways, gray ceilings. Then a change in temperature. A dry, dusty smell, like old books, and the crackle of a fire.

"Not here," says a woman's voice, low with caution and concern. "The room down the hall."

More booted footsteps, and then the hiss of water running into a tub. "I'm going to strip her and wash her first. I need to be able to see the damage before I heal her."

"I thought you could see inside the body," protests Rahzien.

"In a manner of speaking, but actual sight helps with the process. Stop fussing and hold her still."

My brows pull together, a faint effort at a frown, and I protest weakly, but Rahzien is already propping me upright while the healer cuts off the blood-soaked dress.

"Fuck," Rahzien mutters as it falls away and I'm left semi-conscious and naked in his arms.

I'm lowered into the tub and rinsed off quickly. At one point my lungs begin to rattle, and blood dribbles from the corner of my mouth. The healer makes an alarmed sound and directs Rahzien to pick me up again. His arms are huge and smooth against my slick wet skin.

My mind is a swirling blur, submerged beneath pain, and I can't seem to see anything, no matter how much I struggle to open my eyes. Are they open? I can't tell. I can barely breathe.

I'm draped on sheets... a bed. Rahzien's hands slip away, and my body relaxes a little, relieved at the absence of his touch.

"Look at these eyes of yours, all plump and pink and purple," croons the healer. "Like fat plums, eh, lovey? We'll take care of those in a moment. The worst of it's inside you, isn't it, dove? Something burst and bleeding, I can sense it." She clucks her tongue. "We'll have you healthy in no time, sweet thing."

Her fingers move across my stomach, and I moan.

"Oh, yes, I know it hurts, I know," she murmurs.

She keeps pressing, and the pain spikes in every place her fingers touch. I can't help a sharp cry at each poke.

"You can cry, dove. Go on—cry all you like, I don't mind," says the healer soothingly. "That's a good girl."

"Enough, Cathrain," says Rahzien in a tone of warning.

The healer chuckles, then a slow, seeping warmth suffuses my belly, and the pain begins to fade. Within moments, I can breathe more easily.

"I have a meeting with the fucking Prince of Zairos soon," says Rahzien. "Fix her. I'll send someone with a dress and underthings, and they can take her to her room when you're finished here."

"Of course, Your Majesty."

Rahzien bends down, brushes his lips against my forehead, and strides out of the room.

The Prince of Zairos? So Kyreagan has a meeting with Rahzien today. His pretense of tenderness angers me, but I'm distracted by the realization that Ky and Rahzien will be in the same room, conversing and bargaining.

As the healer does her work and my pain level decreases, my anxiety spikes. What if Kyreagan says or does something to make Rahzien suspicious? With the party and our tryst, the night was a short one—what if Ky didn't spend enough hours as a dragon to be able to hold his human form for the duration of the meeting?

While we were sequestered in his cave during the Mordvorren, we discovered that his sixteen hours as a dragon and eight as a human don't have to be sequential. Once he has spent two hours as a dragon, he can spend one as a human. Or four hours as a dragon, two hours as a human. But if Ky didn't parcel out his time correctly, he'll be compelled to transform before the meeting is over, and his ruse will be discovered.

"How fast can you fix me?" I ask. The words sound thick and strange through my puffy lips, and I taste blood when I talk.

"Patience, lovey," hums the woman. "I'm going as quick as I can. Takes energy, you see."

I want to tell her that I'm familiar with healers, though I may not understand all the facets of their magic. We had two healers in the palace. Their capabilities and energy levels differed, but they did good work. If Cathrain is Rahzien's favorite healer, she must be the best in Vohrain.

"Will you be alright?" I manage through my swollen mouth.

"Oh, sweet thing! No need to worry about me. I know my limits. These wounds are not difficult to manage, not at all." She prods my forearm. "Such colorful bruises here! Almost a pity to erase them. Green and yellow, purple and blue." Her voice has a mellow lilt, like a mother singing a child to sleep in the nursery. Not that my mother ever rocked me—I had the palace nurses for that. But I've watched Huli sing my little protégé Taren to sleep. In fact, I rocked him to sleep myself, many times. I miss the smell of his warm, wispy head, the faint lavender of his eyelids when he was truly exhausted, and the rosy, milky scent of him. Sweet baby. Parma said he and his family left the city. I hope they're safe.

I hope my own little ones are safe, too. Guilt swirls like black ink in my soul because I keep forgetting about them—too deeply invested in my relationship with Kyreagan, too preoccupied with his safety and mine. But I swear, if Kyreagan and I make it out of this, if we can disentangle my life from Rahzien's and break his hold on the people of Elekstan—then I will focus on my hatchlings, my babies. No matter what form they're in, I will love them with all my heart.

"Do you have children?" I ask impulsively.

"I had two." The healer's tone is warm, cheerful. "They didn't make it, poor things. But His Majesty, King Rahzien—he's like my son. I've been with him a long time, since he was a tiny tot. Got a keen mind, that one. People think he's just a big bear of a warrior, but he's clever beyond what most understand."

"He's cruel," I murmur.

"Only when he has to be. Some folk cause pain for the joy of it, but he always has a purpose." She touches one of my eyelids, and the puffiness gradually subsides. "It's a conviction we share. No death or pain without a greater purpose, dove."

"So you think he was justified in having one of his guards beat me until I nearly died?" I ask.

"I don't question his methods, just as he doesn't question mine," she replies. "He must have had a reason."

"But you're not like him." I try to catch her eye, but she's acting nervous again, avoiding my gaze. "You help people. You're kind. I think you could help me, if you wanted to. Tell me who the King's poisoner is. Please, Cathrain." I reach up and lightly grasp the wrist of the hand she's using to heal my left eye. "Please."

Anxiety flushes her round face. She's struggling, on the verge of yielding to my plea. Her embroidered shawl lies nearby—she must have removed it to avoid it being stained with my blood. She picks it up, wraps it around her shoulders, and ties a knot with fingers that tremble slightly. It's almost as if she's putting on a layer of armor. I wonder if the shawl's bright, embroidered flowers give her courage and cheer amid all the suffering she encounters in Rahzien's service.

"You don't agree with everything he's doing," I murmur. "I can see it. Sometimes people do the wrong thing, even though we love them… and then we have to take a stand. Apathy and inaction only lead to tragedy and guilt. I'm living proof of that. Don't stand by and let him hurt me like this, over and over. I can't take it, Cathrain."

"Hush, now. Let me heal this poor pretty mouth." She touches my swollen lips, pity welling in her eyes. Then she leans in and lowers her voice until it's barely a breath. "I'll tell you one thing. The King brought some nobles from Vohrain with him."

"You're saying the poisoner is one of them?"

"Look for the one who doesn't fit," she whispers. "Look for the one with the viper's eye."

19

KYREAGAN

I hate being still this long. For hours I've been coiled up in the bedroom, afraid to move my tail or wings an iota lest I smash something.

Meridian said he would come and fetch me shortly before our meeting with the King of Vohrain. I wish we could get out of it. Sitting with Rahzien at a table, talking about diplomatic affairs and alliances, feels both sickeningly familiar and incredibly dangerous, especially since my knowledge of Zairos is thin at best. But negotiating with the King is a vital part of my assumed identity. The meeting can't be avoided. I can only hope it won't last long, and that Meridian can run interference for me if I run out of things to say.

Perhaps it's best that Hinarax won't be there. Charming though he is, he can be careless, and his presence would double the risk of discovery.

The door to my chamber opens, and Meridian enters, flanked by Odrash and Kehanal. All three of them look displeased.

"Apparently Aeris left," says Meridian, in a tone sharp with weariness and frustration. "Do you know where she went?"

"She knows of a sorcerer who may be able to neutralize the poison in Serylla's body," I reply.

"She shouldn't have left without speaking to me first. We need her. If things go wrong today—"

"I'll do my best to protect you," I finish.

Meridian snorts. "One dragon against dozens of guns? You could cause some damage, but you wouldn't last long."

"When we first made this arrangement, you seemed to have more faith in me."

"That was before I saw how many guns they have. And they're manufacturing replacement gun barrels and a new kind of ammunition for better accuracy. I have plans in place to counteract that, but those plans are not yet ripe. I need more time."

"We believe Rahzien is going to turn Elekstan into a base of operations for his next conquest," says Odrash.

"What nation do you think he'll attack next?" I ask.

"Tekkesh, to the west."

Kehanal speaks up. "We have to kill him now, before he begins another campaign."

"He won't, not until Elekstan is stabilized," Meridian says. "Which could be a year or more, if he's counting on producing an heir with the Princess."

Odrash slams a palm onto the dresser next to him. "Doesn't matter. We need to act *now*. We've never gotten this close. We won't have access like this again. Every passing hour carries more risk of discovery, and then we'll be killed or imprisoned. The plan is falling apart, can't you see that? We smuggled two dragons into the palace, and they were supposed to help us take over—but now one is gone, and the other is practically useless."

Meridian turns slowly, with such force in the gaze of his one blue eye that Odrash moves back a step.

"We made a bargain," says Meridian grimly, "that we'd help the dragon save his princess in exchange for the treasure and for his assistance in bringing down Rahzien. The plan and the timeline may have changed, but the deal hasn't."

"Look, I like the Princess. I do," replies Odrash. "But she is one person. We need to take down Rahzien, and if her life is the price, I say it's tragic, but necessary."

My head lowers, snaking toward him on my long neck. "And where does that leave me?" I hiss, exhaling fiery breath in his face. "The Princess is the only reason I'm here, the only reason I don't gobble you up right now. Threaten her, and you threaten me. Killing the King destroys her. And if she dies, I will ensure that before I perish, I'll have the pleasure of seeing your body dance and shrivel in my flames."

"Now, now, there's no need for such talk." Meridian steps between Odrash and my smoking nostrils. "I see your point, Odrash, I do. And Kyreagan, you must understand that we're looking out for our people, our nation. You said yourself, you've done terrible things to ensure your clan's survival—"

"And it might all be for nothing," I snarl. "They might all be dead now. We made a mistake, trusting Vohrain, and we're paying for it. I have lost everything, do you understand? Everything. And by the Bone-Builder, I refuse to lose the one thing I have left. Serylla is all that matters to me. As long as there is hope of saving her, you will not touch the King."

"We'll wait." Meridian nods to me, then gives the other two rebels a firm look. "Won't we, boys? We'll wait another day or so, and see if we can't disentangle the Princess from the King, yes? And then we'll revisit the matter."

Grudgingly they agree and shuffle out of my chamber. The moment they leave, Meridian's shoulders slump with exhaustion, and he limps past my wingtip, over to a chair. He sinks into it with a groaning sigh.

"Where were you?" I ask. "After you saw Hinarax off, where did you go?"

"Well... he and I had a short farewell interlude." Meridian clears his throat. "And then I went to entertain two of the escorts from the party. I gave them all the pleasure and wine they could want. *My* tongue loosened *their* tongues, you might say." He laughs tonelessly. "One of them has serviced the King several times, including twice during his stay at a mansion outside the city walls. Apparently he kept the Princess there for a while, before bringing her into the city."

"Any hints about the identity of the poisoner?"

"I'm getting to that. I asked her about people who seemed close to the King, and she named a few. The young lord to whom Rahzien gave the key—Zevin Harlowe. Two of the Vohrainian lords, Straussan and Occria. And she said he had more than one visit from the Princess's maid, Parma."

"But Parma and Zevin are Elekstan citizens," I muse. "So they couldn't be the Royal Poisoner."

"Unless..." Meridian chews the scarred part of his lower lip. "Unless the King didn't have a Royal Poisoner until the invasion of Elekstan. We've been thinking the poisoner is Vohrainian, but we have no instances of him using poisons like these until he came to this kingdom."

"You're saying the poisoner might be from Elekstan? A traitor?"

"I'm saying we can't rule it out. We know Rahzien was actively establishing himself within Elekstan long before he actually conquered it. Anything is possible." Wincing, Meridian reaches down to massage his calf with both hands. "Fuck this leg of mine."

On impulse, I swerve my muzzle toward him and exhale heat onto his leg.

He sits back and stretches his leg out farther. "Fuck, that feels good."

"You've been on your feet too long."

"I do what I have to do," he says grimly. "I won't be pitied or coddled."

"Certainly not. I wouldn't know how to coddle a human, anyway."

He chuckles. "True."

For several minutes he enjoys the heat of my breath, and then he says, "You should revert to human form and prepare for the meeting. I'll coach you on a few topics that might arise."

"Have you had any sleep?"

"I said no coddling. I'll sleep when I'm dead." With a stiff groan he hoists himself to his feet with the help of the walking stick. "Let's talk about the primary natural resources of Zairos."

Less than an hour later, Meridian and Kehanal lead the way from our suite while I follow more slowly, trying to mark the route in my mind and familiarize myself better with the layout of the palace. I'm wearing different boots today, and I'm finding it difficult to adjust to the way they feel. I don't understand why all human footwear can't be exactly the same.

I'm looking down, glowering at the white leather boots encasing my feet and half my legs, when I sense it. The pull in my chest, the surge of awareness.

Serylla is close by.

We're crossing an intersection of hallways—one going straight ahead, a staircase ascending to the right, and a corridor branching off to the left. Meridian and Kehanal continue ahead, but I hesitate, eyeing the left-hand corridor. It appears to be a shortcut from one wing of the palace to another, with tall windows on both sides. Between the windows are recesses flanked by thick, midnight-blue curtains. Some of the alcoves contain paintings of flowers or landscapes, while others appear to be missing the works of art which once hung there. Only empty hooks remain.

A stocky servant is ambling down the corridor toward me, and right behind him is Serylla, walking with her head down and a small frown on her pretty face.

Then she looks up. Straight at me, where I've paused mid-step.

The servant passes by me with a half-bow and continues on, his eyes fixed on a paper in his hands—some sort of list.

Serylla follows him with slow, measured steps, her gaze flitting up to mine. She's so close, and I'm immobilized by her nearness, her soft scent, her breath, the shine of her yellow hair.

Meridian and Kehanal have continued on, oblivious to the fact that I'm no longer behind them.

Serylla is almost past me now, and I reach out, just a little, until the backs of my fingers brush hers when she walks by.

I'm holding my breath. Didn't realize it until now. I start to exhale—but then a small hand seizes mine, and Serylla tows me into the shortcut passage and shoves me into one of the curtained alcoves. My back thuds against the wall.

She yanks the curtains into place behind us, leaving only a sliver of light leaking through.

Her body collides with mine, her hands finding my face, pulling it down to hers as she rises on tiptoe. Her kiss sears my mouth, the same frantic urgency that throbs in my own heart. I gather her to my chest like an armful of the most precious treasure.

"I had to risk it," she whispers shakily in the dark. "I couldn't let you just walk by... after the morning I've had..."

I recognize the twinge of pain in her voice. This is more than the distress of last night—this is something new. "What happened? Did Zevin Harlowe come to your room?"

"No, no… whatever your friend Meridian arranged, it worked. He was too drunk to show up, and he has left the palace, probably angrier and more embarrassed than ever. No, this morning was about Rahzien."

"What did the bastard do?" I ask in a growling whisper. "I swear, Serylla, when this is over I'm going to bite off his limbs one at a time and roast them in front of him—"

Serylla presses harder against me and clamps slender fingers over my mouth.

Someone is approaching our hiding spot.

For once, my dragon hearing failed me, or perhaps I was too immersed in visions of revenge—I didn't hear the voices until this moment. They sound faintly muffled, like helmeted Vohrainian guards.

"We need to hurry and catch up," says one of the men. "If anything happens to the Conquered Consort on the way to her room—"

"What's going to happen?" drawls a second man. "She's with a servant, and it's not far. Besides, it's not like the King would care if she were hurt. You saw what he had Skonn do to her. I thought he'd killed her for sure."

"At least she gets a healer to fix her up, good as new," mutters the first man. "I wish the healers for the troops were as good as Lady Cathrain."

The voices fade, and I pry Serylla's fingers from my mouth, rage mounting high in my chest. "You were beaten?"

"It doesn't matter now."

"The fuck it doesn't."

"The healer fixed me," she whispers harshly. "I'm fine. Now kiss me."

Repressing a snarl, I take her mouth, my lips crushing hers.

"Yes," she gasps. "Harder."

I pick her up, my hands clasping her rear, and I turn us around so she's the one being pressed to the wall. She wraps both legs around my waist, grinding her pussy against me through the clothing between us, rubbing urgently against the rigid hardness between my legs.

"I need to get to a meeting," I murmur, devouring her cheeks and lips with fierce kisses.

"This isn't the time or place for fucking," she agrees breathlessly, wrenching at the fastenings of my pants. Her fingers are small, hot, and frantic, digging my cock out of my clothing.

I shove her skirts up her thighs, but her underwear is in my way, so I summon my claws and rip through them. I stuff the lacy remnants in my pocket, and the claws vanish again at a thought from me.

"How did you do that?" she whispers. "And why don't you have your horns in this form? I forgot to ask last night—"

"Questions later." I duck my head and trail my tongue up the warm, silken column of her throat. "Fuck now."

20

SERYLLA

Kyreagan looks more handsome than ever, in a dark blue suit with a ruffled collar that frames the deep V of his tanned chest. Foamy lace falls from his cuffs, and his sleek black hair is tied with a blue ribbon. When I spotted him in the hallway, it was as if my primal feminine self took over—leaped from some ancient, instinctive part of my soul and claimed control of my body and mind. I *had* to touch him. Had to feel him, to remind myself that despite how close I came to death, I'm *here*, I'm alive, and so is he. My body has learned to equate him with security, with wholeness, with home, and I need him now, with a ferocious hunger that won't be denied over such paltry objections as *reason* and *caution*.

This morning I was beaten almost to death by the man I wouldn't kill. Rows of soldiers watched him pummel me, without so much as twitching a finger in my defense. I wanted to scream for mercy, and it was all I could do not to resort to abject pleading. But the worst part of it was the helplessness I felt, the utter lack of choice.

Right now, Kyreagan is my choice. I choose boldness. I choose pleasure. I choose his skin, and his hair, and his soft dark eyes and his sweet, hot mouth.

This alcove once housed an ancestor's portrait, which has since been removed and probably destroyed by the Vohrainians. The curtains concealing us could be yanked back at any second, dooming us both. I know it distantly, grudgingly, and I don't care. I only care that I'm helplessly wet for him, that his bare, warm cock is slipping against my soaked pussy, that his hands are in my hair and my legs are locked around him, my ankles pressed against his firm ass.

Kyreagan moves one hand down, swirls his thumb over my clit. It's so exquisitely sensitive that I almost whine aloud, but he kisses me hard, drowning the sound with his tongue.

One of my arms is wrapped around his neck, but my other hand dives between us, my fingers curling around his cock, guiding its thick, smooth hardness into my pussy. Kyreagan tenses as he enters me, joins me, his huge length gliding deep, filling me whole.

This is how he and I were always meant to be, frenzied and panting and out of our minds, fucking desperately, reason blurred by reckless passion.

"Make me come," I pant against Kyreagan's ear. "Make me come, dragon. I need to come."

He growls low in his throat, and his beautiful body surges with power as he obeys my command, as he fucks me furiously. He finds the angle we had last night, where his body rubs my clit just right with each thrust. The slick pumping of his long cock, the strength of his arms, the hectic danger of what we're doing—all of it drives my body to screaming heights of ecstasy, and I break with a hoarse little shriek.

I muffle my cries against Kyreagan's mouth, and I keep kissing him while he comes inside me. My brain is screaming *fuck, fuck, fuck,* but I'm nearly silent as we convulse together, as he bucks his hips into me for a last deep thrust, giving me every drop of cum.

"We have to go," I gasp. "You *need* to go. Your meeting."

"Yes. Shit... yes." He pulls out of me, his chest heaving. But I lace my arms around his neck for one more second and whisper to him, "Your cum will be dripping down my thighs when I walk away from here."

"By the Bone-Builder," he breathes. "Now I won't be able to stop thinking about it."

"Be careful, be smart, be safe. Now go."

He's getting better at straightening his clothes quickly. As he does so, he whispers, "Meridian found out that Parma visited the King while you were being kept in the Harlowe mansion."

"What does that mean? I never saw her there. Why would she—"

"I don't know what it means, but we have to think about the possibility that the Royal Poisoner is from Elekstan."

"That's not possible." I frown. "Parma has no magic. She never met the King before the invasion of the Capital. And she would never—"

"I'm not saying she's involved. Only that she was with the King for unknown reasons. Just be careful, Serylla."

"But I spoke with Rahzien's healer. She says the poisoner is one of the lords. The one who doesn't fit in, the one with the viper's eye, she said."

"Interesting." His dark brows bend. "I will see what I can observe during my meeting with Rahzien. Meridian said there will be Vohrainian lords present. Until we know more, trust no one."

"Except you."

"That goes without saying, my Queen." His lips find mine in the dark, the spiced heat of his breath making me weak and needy again.

"Go, before I decide to keep you here," I tell him.

With a soft laugh, he disappears through the curtains.

I slump against the wall of the alcove, feeling the sore, delicious warmth of the orgasm between my legs, and the drip of his cum along my inner thigh. I came hard, but I'm nowhere near satisfied, physically or emotionally. My body and my heart crave him more than I ever imagined needing anyone.

But I can't have him like I want to. Not yet.

My dragon is gone.

And he has my damp underwear in his pocket.

21

KYREAGAN

I get lost trying to catch up with Meridian and Kehanal. Thankfully they noticed my absence and Kehanal finds me before I wander too far.

"Where did you go?" he asks.

"Exploring," I say vaguely, tugging at the hem of my vest.

"Well, come on. We're late."

When we were allies, Rahzien and I always met out in the open air. Today we're meeting in a huge room, its walls painted a deep charcoal, almost black. Bronze tasseled curtains frame the windows along the north wall, and the opposite wall is plastered with dozens of maps, all different sizes. My gaze lingers on those maps, with their promise of distant lands my clan has never heard of. Dragons can only fly so far without rest, and our oral histories only deal with the nearest continent and its denizens. Humans, with their ships, have journeyed farther than is possible for us, across unknown seas to new continents.

Varex lit up at the thought of incorporating human skills and crafting into our way of life, and Hinarax enjoys human fashions, foods, and entertainment. But as I survey that wall of maps, I realize something about myself—that my interests are broader than a quiet life in a cave on Ouroskelle. That I would like to travel, to explore.

Perhaps meeting Serylla stimulated my taste for adventure and discovery. I've certainly never felt such a wild, sweeping excitement before... as if I might have a life after this nightmare. As if Serylla and I might live to see brilliant, wonderful things together. We could bring the little ones along, undertake a voyage by ship, pause at islands along the way. In dragon form, I could fly above the ship for a full day without tiring, then land for a rest. It could work.

"Your Highness." Meridian clears his throat.

His voice breaks the enchantment of the maps, and when I turn, I see that everyone is seated, looking at me expectantly. Half a dozen human males, seated around the table, watching me. Expecting me to behave as one of them, when I'm far more at home soaring over mountain peaks and whirling in the bright air, high above the earth.

Yes, this is a nightmare. And what makes it worse is that I must speak civilly to the wretch who just hours ago had my darling beaten within an inch of her life. I'm furious at him, and furious at myself for knowing nothing of the incident until it was over.

For a moment, I entertain the thought of transforming into my true shape and blasting them all with avenging fire.

No, not yet. The time will come. Have patience. I hear the admonitions in my brother's voice. My brother, who might be dying from a sinister poison because of the wicked king at the head of the table—the King whose eyes are beginning to narrow with displeasure at my behavior.

I must be strong enough for this. For Serylla's sake.

"My apologies." I walk to the chair Meridian is holding out for me, and I seat myself as smoothly as I can. "My head is aching today."

"We'll make this quick then," says Rahzien.

"I would be grateful, Your Majesty. My esquire is also feeling poorly and remained in our chambers, so by your leave, my herald will attend me today. I trust him in all things, and so does my royal father."

"Does he indeed?" Rahzien lifts his reddish brows. "I'd heard that the King of Zairos is a cautious man."

"His trust is not easily gained, it's true," I reply. "But my herald has saved not only my life, but the life of the Crown Prince, my eldest brother."

Rahzien nods. "Understood. Your herald is welcome to a seat at your side."

"Thank you, Your Majesty." Meridian bows and sits to my left, propping his walking stick against the table. With a respectful bow, Kehanal withdraws and leaves the room.

"Allow me to introduce some of the lords of Vohrain, my comrades in arms throughout these long weeks of war." Rahzien tells me the name, rank, and home city of each man at the table. I've met a few of them before, during the course of my clan's dealings with Vohrain. But two of them are new to me, including a young, dark-haired man whose right eye is brown while the other is bright green. The green eye has a vertical slitted pupil.

The one who doesn't fit in, the one with the viper's eye. That's what the healer told Serylla. Is this the Royal Poisoner? Rahzien calls him Lord Jaskar, but doesn't say where he's from.

"Now that we're all friends—" Rahzien claps his hands, and servants approach with trays of silver goblets. "Let's drink to the healthy alliance of my empire with your father's kingdom."

It's a calculated move on his part. Celebrating the alliance before we've settled on terms. Comparing his "empire" to my supposed kingdom—a hint of his dominance, a subtle threat. Varex would be better equipped for a diplomatic comeback, whereas all I can do is nod and drink. In reality I have no kingdom, no army, and no resources, so any alliance we forge today is nothing but lies. A fantasy to lull Rahzien into believing his empire has been recognized by at least one nation.

I drain all the liquor in the goblet, despite the warning nudge of Meridian's boot against mine. He's too late to stop me from drinking, but his nudge does remind me of the words he told me to say.

Setting down the goblet, I address Rahzien. "You mentioned gifts, certain things you would appreciate receiving from my father."

"Straight to the point." Rahzien chuckles. "Very well, young prince, we'll speak plainly. I have certain ambitions for my life and my future empire. An early understanding between myself and your family could ensure that Zairos remains an ally of mine, one which enjoys the certain benefits and protections in exchange for…support."

"What kind of support?"

"What are you prepared to offer?"

Before we left our chambers, Meridian advised me to let the King do most of the talking, to force him to delve into specifics so I won't have to, so I counter, "A great king such as yourself must be aware of the type of resources we can offer. Perhaps you could tell me what piques your interest."

Rahzien leans forward, his gaze keen. "Is your father so ready to pay tribute to another ruler?"

"Tribute?" I frown. "What would you do with the bones of another nation's dead?"

A confused silence falls, and the lords glance at each other. Rahzien picks up his goblet and sips, watching me over the rim.

"Your Highness, he is speaking of monetary tribute," Meridian says aside to me. "Tribute of land, resources, soldiers, technology, and workers."

Shit.

I fucked this up. As a dragon, the tribute I'm most familiar with is bone-tribute, the sacred gift of a bone from a deceased dragon.

"I've been reading about the habits of dragons," I say. "I heard you were allied with them, so I thought I should be somewhat familiar with the beasts. Just this morning I was reading a passage about their morbid custom of bone-tribute. The concept was fresh in my mind, so I misunderstood your meaning. My brain, as you know, is a bit muddled of late."

Rahzien quirks an eyebrow. "Are you quite sure you're feeling up to this discussion, Prince?"

"If my lord could have some water," Meridian interposes.

Rahzien gestures to a servant, who hurries to pour a glassful from a pitcher.

I drink a few swallows. "Let's discuss the tribute, then," I continue, in what I hope is a cool, confident tone. "We have the mines of Arnat. Perhaps you would be interested in refined ore?"

The men around the table seem to accept my explanation; they move forward in the discussion without further inquiry. But as they argue back and forth about the benefits of different resources, I sense Rahzien's eyes on my face. When I glance in his direction, he smiles. A broad, friendly, open grin.

I've never distrusted a smile more.

After the tribute debacle, Meridian enters the conversation several times, usually to steer a direct question away from me or to prod at any conflict he can sense among the Vohrainian lords. At long last, we settle on a yearly amount of tribute to be given to Rahzien, in exchange for friendly relations between Zairos and Vohrain. Essentially, Zairos will be paying Vohrain not to conquer them…at least for a few years. We rise from the table with the understanding that I will be writing to my father, the King of Zairos, to gain his blessing upon the agreement.

The other lords rise and begin to drift out of the room, deep in earnest conversation with each other. Lord Jaskar, with the viper's eye, lurks at the fringes of the group, addressing no one. I'm about to head toward him and strike up a conversation when Rahzien claps a huge hand on my shoulder.

It's the closest I've been to him. The first time he has ever touched me. The same hand clasping my shoulder has touched Serylla—cupped her chin, seized her hair... I grit my teeth, fighting to keep flames from quivering visibly beneath my skin.

"Well done, young prince," Rahzien says jovially. "You're a credit to your kingdom."

I'm not sure why he keeps calling me "young prince." He can't be more than a few years older than I am. Perhaps this, too, is a way of putting down others, unsettling them. Asserting his dominance, once again.

"Thank you, Your Majesty." The heat from the liquor burns in my brain, making it difficult to keep my tone and expression under control.

Rahzien peers at me. "You seem distressed."

"Not at all. It's only the pain in my head."

"Right. Your head injury. How did it happen again?"

The wine blends with my suppressed fire and churns through my gut, a roiling inferno so fierce I can barely think. "A banister was blown apart by cannon fire." *Is that the right word? Banister?* "And a piece of it struck me."

"Struck your esquire, too," says Rahzien sympathetically, still looking deep into my eyes. "You said he's feeling unwell."

"Yes."

"I'd be happy to send my healer, Lady Cathrain, to look at you both. In fact, I must insist on it."

"I'd hate to disturb my esquire while he's resting," I object.

"Of course, of course. Then we'll have her take a look at you. Sometimes if the injury is too old, she can't help, but there's no harm in asking, is there?"

"I... suppose not." I want to glance in Meridian's direction to see how he feels about this turn of events, but I suspect that breaking eye contact with Rahzien and looking to my "herald" for approval would only raise suspicion.

"There's a parlor adjoining this meeting room," says Rahzien. "I'll call for the healer, and she'll come to you there. Meanwhile if you need anything—tea, water, more wine—let one of the servants know, and they'll fetch it."

He ushers Meridian and me into a shadowed parlor clad in furnishings of dark green and deep purple, then closes the door. The only light comes from a gap between the velvety cloths draping the windows.

Oddly enough I feel rather at home in the space. It's peacefully gloomy, and the rich colors remind me of a shady forest or a quiet cave. Still, the way Rahzien shut us in here is odd.

"Why do I feel as if we've been imprisoned?" I mutter.

"Because we have." Meridian throws himself onto a long piece of furniture—a sofa, I think, or perhaps a couch. Too many terms, too many new objects, all swimming around in my head.

"I wonder if the healer will be able to tell what you are," Meridian muses, his frown deepening. "I suppose we'll know soon enough. Can't be helped now. If we refuse the healer's attention it will look much too suspicious. We've bared our asses, and must endure the paddle."

"What makes me fucking furious is that I've lost the chance to question that lord, the one with the viper's eye," I mumble.

"Viper's eye?" Meridian quirks a brow, so I tell him, in low tones, what Serylla said to me in the alcove.

"So that's where you went." He smirks. "Never fear, Prince. When we're done here, I can put some feelers out among the guards and servants, find out who he is and how we can discover more about him. Leave it to me."

I choose a chair and sit down, but it's far softer than I expected, and I sink into it deeply and suddenly.

Meridian smirks at me. "Comfortable?"

I speak low, even though we're alone. "This chair is like a voratrice throat. Sucks you right in."

"I don't know what that is."

"Perhaps you'll visit Ouroskelle sometime and find out." I sigh, yielding to the plush cushioned depths of the chair. "I fucked this up, didn't I?"

Meridian pries the lids of his right eye open and adjusts the glass orb in the socket. He blinks a few times, then focuses on me.

"Yes, you fucked up," he says in an undertone. "But I don't think Rahzien suspects the truth. How could he? I would have thought it impossible had I not seen it with my own eyes. If anything, he'll suspect you, Prince Gildas, of hiding your true intentions—perhaps being a spy your father sent, with no true intentions of creating an alliance."

"And how do you think he'd react to that?"

Meridian shrugs. "Who knows the mind of a king?"

"You seem to understand the behavior of all kinds of humans."

"Why, thank you. It's part of being an excellent thief, pickpocket, and con artist. Understanding your mark. Knowing how they'll react to distractions or stimuli. Anticipating wants and needs. All part of the game."

"And Hinarax?" I ask the question in spite of myself, out of a protective impulse. "Is he part of your game?"

The rogue's cocky smile fades. "That's between him and me."

"I'm his prince," I reply. "His well-being is my responsibility."

Meridian puckers his lips and looks away. I expect him to argue the point or ignore me, but he says, "Hinarax and I have enjoyed our trysts, our dances, and our conversations. I hope to see him again. If I don't, life goes on." Something hard and bitter edges his light tone. "I've parted ways with plenty of people I cared for. Few relationships last, and the ones that do, change. They morph into something unrecognizable. When that happens, it's best to move on."

"What about accepting the change?" I ask. "Adapting and making the best of the new reality?"

"With life events, maybe. But I'm talking about people. When people change, you'd best cut the cords and start over elsewhere. Otherwise you're asking for pain. Me, I never stay in one place or with one group very long. The people I'm with now, I haven't known for more than a few months—some for mere weeks or days. I trust them to a point—not beyond it. And I'm always ready to cut ties and strike out alone at a moment's notice. Travel light, stay flexible. Keep your wits about you. That's how to survive as a human. If people don't know where your heart is, they can't stab it. No roots, no ruin."

I don't reply at once, and when I do, I speak in slow, measured tones, heavy with the weight of my words. "On Ouroskelle, we believe in bones. The bones of our ancestors built our island, and the bones of our loved ones continue to build it to this day. The exchange of bone-tribute after a dragon's death, and the laying of their bones upon the fields—those are meaningful rituals for us. They connect our lives to all that is past, and make us a part of all that will come. We are creatures of the air, yes... but land, home, family, and stability are important to us."

Meridian watches me in the half-light, the thin fingers of his right hand playing over the head of his staff.

"Every dragon I know has changed." I look down at my hands, my human fingers. Short nails, not claws. "We've been altered externally, of course, but who we *are* is changing as well. I believe that if my clan survived the war, the loss of our females, and the great transformation, we can survive anything, even Rahzien's poison. The evolution of our minds and hearts will not tear us apart. We will not flee from each other. We are family, a bond that is bone-deep, unchanging, even after our spirits ascend."

The rebel leader looks away, his scarred mouth twitching, and not with humor this time. "Fuck, that's beautiful," he mutters hoarsely. "But for someone like me, that sort of family isn't in the cards, mate."

"You never know. I never thought I would be sitting here, in a palace parlor, talking to a man like you."

"A thief?"

"A friend."

He shifts in his seat, as if the word makes him uncomfortable. Truth be told, I'm not so comfortable with it myself, but the respect and warmth I feel for him can be described in no other way.

The door opens, admitting a plump, pleasant-looking woman with rosy cheeks and bright eyes that crinkle at the corners when she smiles. The garment around her shoulders is decorated with colorful flowers, much like the blooming trees around the hot springs on Ouroskelle. She wears a dark brown dress, and a woven bag hangs at her hip, its strap crossing her body.

"I'm Lady Cathrain. Knocked your head, have you?" she says cheerfully. "Let's have a look, then. No, no, don't get up, boys. Stay comfortable. I'll just check the Prince's pate."

Her fingertips sink into my hair and press against my skull in various places. "I don't feel any surface fractures. Let's go a bit deeper."

"There's really no need." I begin to rise, but she clucks her tongue and pushes against my shoulder. "Now, now, be a good prince. Hold still."

Her fingers travel the entire surface of my skull, including my temples, the tender spots beneath my ears, and the corners of my lower jaw. Barely breathing, I wait for her to speak.

"Too much tension," she says at last. "That's the only thing physically wrong with you." She takes her hands from my hair. "Brain injuries can be tricky things, difficult for healers to detect. And it's always possible that you're suffering from a sickness you picked up during your voyage. Let's see if I missed anything."

Lady Cathrain picks up my hand and pricks the tip of my index finger with a tiny tubular needle. Blood blooms from the spot, and the little tube fills with a few scarlet drops. She holds it up to a ray of light from the window.

"The color of your blood looks good. Open up, there's a good lad." She sets the tube aside and taps my lips with a small, flat stick.

I glance sidelong at Meridian. He doesn't look happy, but he nods, so I open my mouth. The healer presses the stick down on my tongue, then sweeps it along the inside of my cheeks.

"Well, Your Highness, you seem to be in excellent health," she says. "Any lingering memory issues or pain should clear up in a couple of days. But you'll receive the best of care as long as you're visiting us. The servants can bring whatever you need, and they know where to find me if your symptoms grow worse." Her eyes fix on mine, warm and earnest, and she says, more quietly, "If you're in any trouble, please know that I keep an open mind and an open door to all those who need mending."

With a polite curtsy, she gathers her things and bustles out of the room.

"Well, that's over," mutters Meridian, swinging his legs off the sofa. "Went better than I expected, honestly."

I'm hardly listening, because the healer's words gave me an idea. "Can we order anything we want from the palace kitchens?"

"I suppose so. That's what the servants said when they showed us our suite."

"Could I order something to be sent to a different room? One that isn't mine?"

"You could try." He shrugs.

I heave myself out of the deep chair. "Soon I'll need to switch forms for another few hours, but before that, there's something I want to do."

22

SERYLLA

After my tryst with Kyreagan, I don't return to my bedroom immediately. The chance to wander the palace without guards or servants is too good an opportunity to miss. So I take less-traveled paths down to the first floor, on the west side of the palace, and I follow the corridor that leads to the conservatory.

About halfway down that hall is a pair of enameled double doors leading to the music room. They're never locked, so I slip inside, into cool gray gloom that smells faintly of rosin and horsehair and paper. The floor is a glossy chessboard of marble tiles, and gray statues stand between the cabinets that house the palace's finest instruments.

My mother didn't care much about music unless it was glorifying her or stirring up Elekstan's soldiers into a victorious frenzy. This collection of instruments began with her father, my grandfather—a man I never met. I added a few pieces here and there, like the case of Oxian flutes in the cabinet across the room.

Though I can pick out simple tunes on most instruments, I'm an expert at none of them, except perhaps the piano. I can play any instrument flawlessly in my mind, though, and I can hear exactly how its unique sound would fit into a composition.

Slowly I pace from cabinets to shelves to drawers, experiencing a soft thrill every time I see an instrument lying unharmed in its usual resting place. Even the big leather cases at the far end of the room still contain their instruments. Nothing in this space has been damaged or moved, and the knowledge heals me a little inside.

A limited supply of sheet music resides on the shelves of the music room, but none of my own compositions are among them. I was always very private about my music. Didn't like sharing it. Maybe I was insecure—afraid of my mother's mockery. Maybe I was reluctant to draw more attention to myself. Or maybe I was simply terrified that none of my music was any good.

My fingers travel the brassy curve of a huge, bell-like tuba, and I press its keys gently before closing the case and latching it. My ears are hungry for music, and my fingers itch to play the piano in the center of the room, but I can't risk being overheard. So I open a shallow drawer and take a pipe from its velvet bed. This pipe is a whispernaught, with a soft, muted sound. Just the thing.

I tuck myself into the shadows behind a large cabinet and sit cross-legged on the floor. Fitting the pipe to my lips, I begin to play nothing in particular... any combination of notes that comes to mind.

It takes a few false starts, but then my brain unlocks and I slip into the creative flow I've missed so much. Notes trickle from the pipe like glittering water through a pebbled stream-bed, like translucent rays of yellow light lancing between green leaves, softening into a golden glow.

The song turns plaintive, because I miss Kyreagan and I'm worried about him. He's sitting somewhere in the palace right now, having a meeting with Rahzien. *Don't say anything foolish,* the pipe murmurs. *Be careful, be careful, be careful.*

I play for an hour, judging by the tall clock in the corner. It's a gorgeous timepiece, ornately carved, with a gilded pendulum. Someone has kept it wound and dusted despite all the upheaval in the palace. Probably Berthew, the palace timekeeper. He's a frail, hunched, gentle old man who creeps quietly through the halls and rooms, tending the clocks. I hope he's still alive.

Laying down the pipe, I go to the doors of the music room and poke my head into the hallway. If something had gone dreadfully wrong in Kyreagan's meeting, there would be roaring and screaming, not to mention gunfire and flames. But there's no yelling, no smell of smoke, no rumbling or crashing sounds. All is quiet.

Closing the door, I return to the pipe and use a thin rod and a soft rag to clean out the condensation caused by my breath. Once it's dry, I tuck it away reverently in its case.

Has Rahzien realized I'm gone yet? After the meeting with Kyreagan, did he go to my room, only to realize I'm not there?

I can't flee far from Rahzien, but perhaps I'll slip into the spy passages within the walls and hide from him. To do that, I'll have to find an entry point into the passage network, and the closest one I know of is two corridors over from where I am.

Cautiously I open the music room doors again and look down the hall.

Three guards are just rounding the corner. Fuck.

"There!" one of them shouts, and they sprint toward me.

My first instinct is to run. But they're between me and the nearest access point to the passages, so it's not as if I can really escape. I'm in enough trouble for slipping away from my escort; I don't need to make it worse by fleeing from the guards.

I stand calmly where I am until the guards reach me. They hustle me upstairs and back to my suite, where Rahzien is sitting in an overstuffed chair, drumming his fingers on the armrest. His face darkens when I'm dragged in and thrown at his feet.

"Leave us," he snaps at the guards, and they hurry into the hall, closing the door behind them.

"I told them you would be in one of three places," he says coolly. "The kennels, the gardens, or the music room. Accessing the kennels would require cooperation from the servants, and you wouldn't want to put any of them at risk by bringing them to my attention. The gardens, though beautiful and refreshing, would feel too exposed. So I suggested they check the music room first. Was I right?"

He's so perceptive. It makes him more dangerous, not only to me, but to Kyreagan.

I remain on my knees, my eyes fixed on the rug. "Yes, Master. I was in the music room. Forgive me—I love music."

"I know," he says quietly, cupping my chin and lifting my face. "That's why I had my soldiers destroy your study. To relieve you of distractions and to help you focus on what's important. Anything I take from you is for your own good, Spider. To help you accept your future. Clinging to the past only harms you."

"So I can't have music? Or my notebooks?"

He pats my cheek and leans back with a sigh. "Eventually, perhaps. But such things are only a complication your mind doesn't need. They confuse your true purpose."

"Being a whipping girl?"

"For now. But when I put a baby in you, everything will change And that needs to happen soon. Once my position in Elekstan is stable, I'll be able to secure the allies and resources I need for my next endeavor."

"Isn't the Prince of Zairos your ally?" I say softly, innocently.

"I'm not sure." He rubs a hand over his short red beard. "He's an odd fellow, that one, and he's hiding something. I think his father sent him to spy on me, not to bargain in good faith. Either that, or he's not who he claims to be. The arrangement he proposed today was a ridiculous one, and included the mines of Arnat, which I happen to know are now empty. So either Gildas is trying to cheat me, or he doesn't know about the mine's true condition, which would mean he's no prince of Zairos."

"Maybe he's simply not very good at diplomacy," I venture.

"Oh, he is. King Garjun's seventh son is well-known for his diplomatic skill. Yet during this visit he has behaved like an arrogant ass, a volatile drunkard, and a buffoon." He leans forward again, lowering his voice to a confiding tone. "I've decided I'll have him assassinated tonight."

Alarm flames through my whole body, setting my nerves afire. I clear my throat and try to appear calm. "Won't that cause a war with Zairos?"

"Not if I blame the assassination on the Elekstan rebels. I think we have a couple of the little weasels in the city as we speak, so when I unearth them, I can hang them publicly as the murderers of Prince Gildas. If the man really is the prince, enacting justice on his assassins will mollify his father. And if King Garjun won't be pacified by justice, so be it. I'm already craving another war." He rubs both of his broad hands together, his thick rings clinking.

I stare at the floor again, afraid that if I meet Rahzien's eyes, my gaze will betray the tumult in my mind. Rahzien doesn't know Ky is a dragon, which is a good thing—but he's planning to have Ky assassinated anyway. This is such a mess. How do I fix it? How do I warn Ky?

Rahzien chuckles. "You look so downcast, Spider. Perhaps you fear that I'll punish you for going to the music room?"

"Yes, Master," I murmur.

"Look at me, Spider."

After taking a second to compose myself, I lift my head. It's easy to let tears spill over and roll down my cheeks.

Rahzien watches me with the cold gray eyes of a shark, but this time there's a quiver of warmth in his gaze.

"I do love it when a pretty woman cries," he murmurs. "There's nothing quite so arousing in all the world."

You're sick, I snarl inwardly, but I keep my eyes sorrowful, and I let my lips tremble.

"I can be merciful," Rahzien says quietly. "But only to a point. You'll remain in this room for the rest of the day. You'll repeat your lessons to me five times, right now. And you will never go anywhere in the palace again without my permission. Am I understood?"

"Yes, Master."

He shifts his position, spreading his legs. He wants me to see the shape of his solid cock, thick and hard under his pants. He wants me to know what he could do to me, anytime he likes.

"Repeat your lessons," he orders. "Five times each."

I begin the recitation, nervously eyeing Rahzien's hand, which is on his thigh, perilously close to that obvious hardness. "I am your pet..." He's getting noticeably harder as I kneel there, as I voice each demeaning phrase about myself. And when I say, "no one wants me," for the fifth time, his cock jerks beneath the material, and his fingers twitch as if he's aching to touch it.

But he doesn't say a word, not until I've finished speaking. Then he gets up stiffly, adjusts his pants, and walks to the door that leads out into the hallway. "I'm going to lunch, then for a ride. I'll take care of the prince later this afternoon. This evening, you'll join me for a private dinner, after which we can discuss when you might feel ready to come to my bed."

Incredulous and furious, I get to my feet. "Wait."

Fuck, I said that too sharply.

Rahzien turns around with predatory slowness, his face a stony mask.

I clench my hands, my voice unsteady. "It's just that—you gave Lord Harlowe permission to rape me, and you ordered that guard to beat me... but you won't rape or beat me yourself. It's as if you think you're a better man for not performing those despicable acts with your own hands. But you're not. You might be worse."

"A better man," he says, with an easy calm that terrifies me. "There is no such thing. No morals, no right or wrong. Only the weak claim such principles, because they fear the strong."

"And you believe I'm weak."

He laughs softly. "You are... pliable. Instead of breaking when I crush you, you bend, like a reed, and you spring up straight again once I remove the pressure. I thought you might have the prideful stubbornness of your mother, but you have something more interesting—an unexpected resilience."

"Don't talk about my mother," I seethe.

The corner of his mouth curves. "You were so meek and submissive a moment ago. And now, this defiance. You know you'll have to pay for it. Must I put you back in that cell at the Harlowes' mansion? I'm sure Zevin wouldn't mind having you as a guest. He sent me a message today, begging for another chance with you. Says he can't remember what happened last night. Perhaps I should let him try again, after all."

Fear crawls up my throat, twisting together with the anger until I feel sick. "Please... not him."

"Don't worry, Spider. I've already sent someone to deal with him. He delivered his holdings and possessions to me, and that's all I wanted from him. He was a dead man from the moment he signed that pledge. Do you really think I could let him live once he'd had you?"

I stare, disbelieving, trying to make sense of the fact that Zevin is dead, or soon will be. Hard as I try, I can't bring myself to be sorry.

"I warned him," Rahzien continues. "I told him that if he wasn't careful with you, he'd regret it. Rest assured that when you join me in bed, I'll make sure you come until you can't manage another orgasm."

I retreat farther from him, and he shakes his head with a short laugh. "You'll agree eventually."

"I won't agree. Never."

A spark of jealous irritation flickers in his eyes. "Is it the dragon? Kyreagan? How does he have such a hold on you? If he wasn't already dead, I'd ask him."

"You don't know for sure the dragons are dead," I counter recklessly. "That's why you sent the bird. To see if the poison worked."

"It worked." His voice is harsher now, like he's steeling himself against doubt. "Her poisons never fail."

Her poisons.

So the poisoner is a woman.

A memory flashes through my mind… Parma taking strands of hair from my brush.

If curative spells require samples from the target, perhaps magical poisons do as well.

It's unthinkable, and yet… Parma was so quiet when she came into my service. So reserved. Seemingly shy. Maybe there was a reason for that. Maybe she was hiding secrets.

No… that can't be right. I *know* her. She cares about me. She would never—

Would she?

Rahzien is flushed, still aroused and possibly angry at himself for hinting at the poisoner's identity. "Forget the private dinner," he says. "You don't deserve it. No meals for you today." He turns on his heel and marches out of my suite.

No food, again. And I'm starving.

I drop into a chair, my strength sapped by the moment of defiance. Somehow I have to escape this room and warn

Kyreagan that Rahzien plans to kill him. I don't know if I can physically summon the energy. If only I had something in my stomach...

Irritated conversation from beyond the door attracts my attention. I don't hear Rahzien's voice, but someone is arguing outside my room. I venture to the door and open it.

Vela, a servant from the kitchens, stands in the hall with a tray, her face flushed as she confronts the two Vohrainian guards flanking the entrance to my room. "Begging your pardon, but I have my orders," she says.

Neither guard is helmeted today. It feels strange, seeing the bare faces of the conquerors. They look so... normal. One of them leans forward, his nose wrinkled as he peers at the tray. "The King said the Conquered Consort isn't allowed any meals."

Vela looks from the guard to me. Perhaps she sees the hunger in my eyes, because she says, "Respectfully, milord, this isn't a meal. It's tea. And it was ordered by Prince Gildas of Zairos, as a courtesy to the Conquered Consort, a thanks for the dance they shared last night. None of us want to be responsible for a diplomatic incident, nor should we disturb the King with such a small matter. Please allow me to make the delivery."

Kyreagan sent me tea. Delighted warmth spreads through my chest as I imagine him ordering it. Fuck, I love him.

The guard looks at his companion, who shrugs. "His Majesty said no lunch or dinner. Never said she couldn't have tea."

"Oh, very well. Proceed."

Vela enters and sets the tray on the table. "A selection of our finest teas, with the Prince's compliments." In an undertone she adds, "And some things from the cook, to accompany the tea."

She nods toward a small covered dish, then backs out of the sitting room and closes the door.

Snatching the lid from the dish, I discover a toothsome selection of tiny cakes and frosted cookies. Greedily I stuff my mouth with them, devouring each crumb as fast as I can, lest the guards think better of their decision and try to take the food away.

Once the sweets are safely in my stomach, I lift one of the tiny teapots and inhale the fragrant steam from its spout. "Fennel and apple," I murmur. The second miniature teapot is black tea with bergamot orange—I recognize its sharp, bitter smell. That one's good for restoring energy, so I pour the contents of the fat-bellied little pot into a cup, blow on it to cool the surface, and drink it down.

I'm on my third cup of tea—chamomile and honeybush—when a plan forms in my mind. A way that I can leave my suite and locate Kyreagan, so I can warn him about the King.

The study door and the sitting room door are both guarded, and the secret passage in my closet has been bricked up. But all I have to do is get the guards to leave—and Kyreagan unknowingly handed me the perfect strategy.

First I go through my study to the secondary exit from my chambers. When I open the door, the guard who's standing there startles violently and chokes on some liquid that he was drinking from a small flask. He wheezes so horribly that I pat him firmly on the back, as if I'm trying to help.

"I'm sorry I surprised you," I say. "God, are you alright? I was only going to ask if you could go quietly to one of the maids and ask for some supplies for me. My bleeding cycle just started. Oh, and see if the healer has a tonic for the cramps. It's not something she can heal, of course, but I need some relief." I press one hand to my lower belly. "I know you're not a servant, but they've cut all the bells to my room, so I can't ring for one. I won't tell His Majesty about the drinking if you'll just do this for me. Please."

Still wheezing, he nods and hurries away down the hall.

For once, a man's discomfort with the topic of monthly bleeding has worked in my favor.

I could slip out this door, but the sightlines from this spot and the main doors of the suite intersect at the corridor I need to take, the only route the wing where diplomats and foreign dignitaries are usually housed. When I saw Kyreagan earlier, he was coming from that direction. Which means I have to get rid of not only this guard, but the other two as well.

Ducking back into my suite, I cut through my bedroom to the sitting room. Then I push over the table holding the tray. I wince a bit as the tea things clatter and tumble to the rug, spilling the rest of the tea. With a sharp scream, I crumple to the floor, holding my belly.

One of the guards opens the door and leans in.

"Help me," I gasp. "Oh god... I think Prince Gildas has poisoned me. I need someone—anyone—please, you have to do something!"

The first guard rushes in and drops to one knee beside me, but he seems unsure what to do next.

"I'll fetch the healer," shouts the second guard, and races away.

"Idiot!" the first guard exclaims. "Healers can't counteract poison!"

"You're right, they can't," I gasp. "But we have a palace physician—not a healer, but someone who made tonics. If he's still around, he might know what to do. And if he's gone, at least he might have some antidotes in his medicine cabinets. Oh fuck... fuck, this hurts. I think I'm dying!" My voice rises to a shriek. "The King needs me to give him an heir! You have to save me!"

"Right," gasps the guard. "I'll be back as fast as I can." He leaps up and charges out the door.

All the commotion might have attracted the attention of more servants and soldiers, so I only wait a few seconds before slipping out the unguarded door in the hallway. I take the corridor toward the diplomatic wing.

Cautiously I peer around the next corner and spot two Vohrainians headed my way. Shit. My mind races, recalling all the hiding spots from my childhood, all the hidden passages and spy holes. I retreat partway down the hall and duck into a large linen closet.

As well as shelves stocked with fresh sheets, there are two laundry chutes in this closet. One is real and leads to the laundry room. The other is fake—a secret entrance to the passages between the walls. If I remember correctly, the right-hand chute is the fake.

Fumbling in the darkness, finding my way purely by touch and memory, I lift the cover of the left chute and lean in as far as I dare. There's a faint warmth wafting up, along with the acrid tang of body odor. Definitely the real laundry chute. Closing that one, I carefully ease myself into the other chute, and after a short slide down, my bare feet land on dry, dusty boards.

There's an odd sense of glee and security that comes with being in the walls again, knowing secret paths of which the invaders are completely ignorant. The escape route leading from my closet was self-contained, so even though he discovered it, Rahzien can't know about the rest of the secret passages. And even if his men found the hole I used during my first escape attempt, there's no way they could have thoroughly explored all the hidden corridors and nooks in this huge old building. They'll have no idea where to look for me.

I take a moment to recall the layout of the passages and plot a circuitous route to my destination. From this point, I should head straight for a dozen or so paces. There will be a ladder, and then I'll have to wiggle through a crawlspace above a hallway, after which I'll end up in the network of spy-holes and passages dedicated to the diplomatic wing. My mother's spies were always very busy in that area, and the servants stayed busy as well, ensuring that the hinges of secret entrances were well-oiled and silent, and that the floors were padded and reinforced so they wouldn't squeak and betray the presence of a listener.

I have to hurry. Rahzien said he would carry out the assassination later today, but he might decide to do it earlier. I've got to get to Ky before he does.

23
KYREAGAN

I've been in dragon form for an hour when I hear someone knock at the outer door of the suite. I'm in my bedroom with the door closed, but I forgot to lock it, because locks are a pesky human concept. If someone enters the sitting room of the suite, they could walk right into my chamber and see me as a dragon.

Grumbling, I shift back to human form and grab my clothes from the bed. I only have time to pull on the pants before someone raps on the bedroom door.

"Prince Gildas." Meridian's voice. "You have a visitor. She insists on seeing you immediately."

A fluttering sensation passes through my chest, the sudden hope that against all reason, the visitor might be Serylla.

Quickly I snatch my shirt and put it on, leaving it unbuttoned. I yank open the door and step into the next room.

Our guest isn't Serylla, but a mild-looking girl with brown hair and the eyes of a frightened doe.

"I am Parma," she says with a small curtsy. "I am the maid to the Princess... the Conquered Consort."

Caution tightens my nerves. Even though Serylla insists that her maid couldn't be the poisoner, I can't rule out any suspects. Not after what Fortunix did to my clan. There are bruises on Parma's face and arms, which could mean she's being forced to design poisons for Rahzien, even if at heart she's still loyal to Serylla.

"The Princess sent you this." Parma holds out a small box. "She said I was to deliver it directly to you."

"Why would the Conquered Consort send a gift to the Prince of Zairos?" I ask.

"That's not my place to speculate, Your Highness. Please enjoy your gift." She curtsies and makes a quick escape into the hallway.

Meridian closes the door behind her. "That was odd."

I flick the tiny latch on the box and open it. Inside, on red velvet, lies a beautiful golden bracelet. It's among the most marvelously crafted pieces of jewelry I've ever seen, with flat, close-fitting links and a glossy luster. I pick it up, admiring the way the light plays on the gold.

"It's incredible," I murmur.

"The perfect gift for a dragon." Meridian approaches, tilting his head to admire the bracelet. "Your Princess has excellent taste. I'll put it on for you, if you like."

As he's fastening the bracelet around my wrist, someone else knocks at the door of the suite. Without waiting for a reply, a Vohrainian guard enters, accompanied by a young male servant.

"An herbal tonic for the Prince," says the servant, holding out an engraved goblet. "To aid your recovery and give you strength. A gift from the healer, Lady Cathrain."

"So many gifts for the Prince, and none for me." Meridian pouts, sauntering up to the servant. "You'll bring me something, won't you? I could use a drink. Maybe a fine, rich rum."

I sip the tonic, grimacing at its sour smell and bitter flavor. "Something is wrong with this."

"Does it taste like asshole?" Meridian inquires. "Not a fine, plump, clean asshole, but a crusty, unwashed asshole?"

"I suppose, yes."

"Then it's perfectly fine. Every herbal tonic I've ever taken has tasted like ass. You don't have to drink it."

"The healer requested that he drink it all," the servant pipes up.

I take another swallow, but Meridian snatches the goblet out of my hand. "Lady Cathrain said he was quite healthy. We appreciate her concern, but the tonic is not needed." He dumps the rest into a nearby vase.

"The healer will be most offended when I tell her what you have done," the servant declares haughtily.

"So don't tell her, there's a good fellow," replies Meridian. "I'll give you a kiss if you promise not to say a word."

The servant blushes deeply and beats a hasty retreat. Meridian closes the door behind him and runs a hand through his hair, cursing under his breath. "Before all these interruptions, I was coming to speak with you, Ky. I've sent Kehanal and Odrash out of the city on an important errand."

"Of course," I growl. "That's perfectly reasonable. It won't look suspicious at all that Prince Gildas's entire royal retinue has disappeared. First Hinarax and Aeris, and now Odrash and Kehanal."

"Couldn't be helped, mate. I needed two messengers to make this happen. Take heart! You still have me, and I'm worth at least a dozen men." He flashes me an ingratiating smile. When I glare at him, he winces. "No? Come on, you must admit I'm worth at least six."

"Two and a half. Maybe." My mouth twitches in a half-smile in spite of myself.

"There's the smile." Meridian slaps my shoulder. "Trust me, if this plan of mine comes to fruition, our enemies will take *themselves* out of the fight. We'll barely have to lift a finger—or a claw. Now you best head back into your room and be a dragon a while longer."

"Delightful," I mutter. "More hours I must spend squeezed into a room where I must be careful not to dislodge the curtains or splinter the delicate human furniture."

But as I'm walking toward the bedroom, I hear an odd tapping sound, not from the suite door, but from the wall. With a frown, I pause, half-certain that I'm going mad.

"Do you hear that?" I ask Meridian.

"I do." Gripping his walking stick, he moves closer to the source of the sound—a painting of a somber-looking gentleman and his pack of hunting dogs. The tapping sound is unmistakably coming from behind it.

"Open the painting," says a muffled voice—a voice that makes my heart jump. "The image of the six-petaled flower on the frame, and the sunburst on the opposite side. Push both of them together."

"Serylla?" I exclaim.

Meridian sets his stick against the wall and deftly presses the spots she described. With a sharp click, the painting pops slightly outward, and Meridian swings it open like a door. Behind it, in a dim, narrow passage, stands Serylla, looking rather dusty and hollow-eyed, but smiling all the same.

I reach for her, and she bounds out of the passage and into my arms. "Thank you," she whispers. "Thank you for the tea. I needed it so much."

"I've owed you that tea for a while." I kiss her forehead.

Meridian clears his throat. "Not that this isn't adorable and romantic, but Princess... why are you here? You really shouldn't be."

"You're in danger," she says. "Not just you, as Kyreagan, but you as Prince Gildas. Rahzien told me he's going to have you assassinated. In fact, he made it sound as if he'd come here and do it himself."

"Why? Has he discovered what I am?"

"He doesn't know you're a dragon, but he's very suspicious. He thinks you're a spy. Please, you need to leave."

"Not without you."

She shakes her head, fondness and frustration mingling in her tone. "But you can't take me with you, not yet. And I won't let you stay here and die, Kyreagan."

A reckless fury rolls through my chest. "If Rahzien comes here for a fight, he'll get one. Maybe I can't kill him, but I can at least damage him."

"And then what will his soldiers do to you? We keep going in circles, Ky—the same problems with no solution. But you're out of time. You came here for me, and I know you'll come back, but right now, you *have* to go. You have to turn into a dragon and fly away from here."

"No." The word comes out in my deepest growl.

Serylla's fingers tighten on my arms, and her eyes blaze into mine. "Stop it, Kyreagan. You *have* to go. I absolutely refuse to watch you die. Don't you understand—if I know you're alive somewhere, I can bear anything. But your death would break me. It would destroy me completely."

"And leaving *you* here alone would destroy *me*!" I burst out.

She narrows her eyes at my vehemence, but I'm beyond reason now. The bare thought of abandoning my mate again is revolting. It's against my nature. How do I make her understand?

Taking a deep breath, I collect both her hands in mine and try to speak calmly. "I restrained myself when I saw you being whipped, when I watched others dancing with you, touching you. When Lord Harlowe won that key, I sent Meridian to save you because I knew he was a better fighter than I am. I let him carry out the plan because I couldn't save you myself, and Serylla, it's killing me that I can't save you. A dragon isn't supposed to assume a false identity and lurk in corners when his mate is in peril. He incinerates the threat, devours the enemy. I've been holding back every day, for you, but you cannot ask me to do this. I will not leave you here, with him."

Her face is white, her eyes brimming with tears. "I understand how you feel. But you staying here is unutterably selfish, when I've told you I can't survive if you're dead."

"If I may," interjects Meridian. "Might I request that the two of you take my life into account while you're making plans?"

I blink at him. For a moment, I truly forgot he existed. "Fuck... of course."

"The only way to save Meridian and the others is for you to leave," Serylla urges. "Leave now, before—"

The door to the suite bursts open with a violence that kills the words on Serylla's tongue, and Rahzien strides into the room.

He looks at Serylla, no one else. His voice is low, his eyes like gray ice. "You ran straight to him, as I knew you would. Thank you, Spider, for providing the final proof I needed."

"What do you mean?" she falters.

"I told you a falsehood about my plan to assassinate Prince Gildas, a man you supposedly had never met before yesterday. I gave the guards orders that if you attempted an escape, they should go along with it and permit you to leave. How else do you think you got away so easily? Do you think yourself so very clever, or do you assume all Vohrainians are fools?"

"Fuck..." whispers Serylla, her eyes wide with horror.

"Fuck, indeed. When you risked everything to come here and warn this man, my suspicions were confirmed." Rahzien's gaze swerves to mine. "Allow me to welcome you properly, Kyreagan, Prince of Dragons, heir to the Bone-King."

Vohrainian soldiers file into the room around him and take up positions along the walls, each one holding a gun.

Serylla's eyes dart from Rahzien to the open portrait, then back to me. Despair floods her gaze.

I'm already holding her hands. There's no use denying the intimacy between us, no point in lies or pretense. Lightly I stroke the backs of her hands with my thumbs, a reassuring caress. She lifts her chin and gives me a brave little nod.

Rahzien paces in a slow half-circle, like a predator circling his next meal. "There was something strange about you from the moment you walked into my court as Prince Gildas. Something familiar, though I couldn't place it. I brushed it off at first, but then you danced with her at the ball, and you had such an obvious connection. At first I thought it was a case of instant attraction, but my instinct told me you two had a prior history. And then there was that report of a dragon taking off from one of the palace towers—and the notable absence of your esquire afterward."

Meridian grabs his staff, but the moment he does, three guns are aimed toward him. Rahzien chuckles. "Put the weapon down, boy. And tell your allies in the other room to come quietly, if they'd like you to live."

"I am not at all sorry to report that they've left the premises," Meridian says.

Rahzien jerks his head to one of the guards, who heads into the other bedroom to confirm the claim.

"As I was saying," continues Rahzien. "Prince Gildas and my Spider had a connection. And she seemed ridiculously obsessed with the dragon who captured her." He looks at Serylla. "Honestly, your affinity for an actual *beast* is your least attractive quality." His gaze snaps back to me, gleaming with triumph and challenge. "Then you mentioned bone-tribute, and that clinched it for me. I didn't know how you managed to gain human form, but I knew who you were."

"Then you should be afraid," I say evenly.

"I'm not. For so many reasons—among which is the link between Serylla and me. You can't kill me without killing her." Rahzien smiles. "But by all means, if you'd like to blow the place apart and scorch some of my men, take your true form, right now. I won't lie—I'm curious to see how your transformation works. It's a power I'd be very interested in exploring. So many possibilities."

There's relief in the knowledge that I don't have to hold back anymore, that my only option is to shift, to kill as many Vohrainians as I can without destroying Rahzien, and then escape with Meridian and the Princess. Taking Serylla out of the city would kill her, but maybe I could carry her to another part of the Capital, give her some distance from Rahzien. She could go into hiding, keep out of his grasp until we can counteract the poison.

"Go on, then," Rahzien taunts me. "Take dragon form, and do your worst, or yield the Princess to me."

I murmur to Serylla, "Stand back, but be ready."

She nods, stepping away from me into the hidden passage. She waits there, just inside the entrance, watching me. Everyone in the room is watching me, and the silence is like the heavy quiet before a clap of thunder.

Turning my focus inward, I trigger the change.

And… nothing happens.

Frowning, I try again. My horns reappear, and so do my claws, but I'm still human.

This isn't right. I should have many more hours left as a dragon. I should be able to change.

"Having difficulties?" asks Rahzien blandly.

With a strained groan, I fight for transformation. I can feel my other form, just beyond my reach, but I can't access it. Flecks of fire quiver beneath my skin, and sparks flicker in the air when I breathe, but no matter how fiercely I struggle to shift, I can't.

"A little advice." Rahzien saunters toward me and smooths the fabric of my open shirt. "When you're residing in the same palace as a powerful poisoner, you might want to be more careful what you touch or consume."

Meridian groans. "The bracelet... or the tonic..."

"Both, actually," says Rahzien. "We couldn't be sure you would accept the drink without suspicion, so we prepared the gift as well." He points to the gold bracelet on my wrist. "The poison absorbs through the skin. So you were doomed either way, and doubly doomed because you're such a trusting fool."

When he pats my face, I ball my fist like Norril showed me and let it fly. Rahzien moves to dodge but I'm too quick—I manage to punch him in the eye.

He staggers, grunts, and returns the blow with interest, two punches in quick succession, his fist smashing into my mouth, then my nose.

Claws out, I lunge at him with a snarl, but the guards move closer, raising their weapons higher as one of them shouts, "Stay where you are, beast!"

Rahzien steps back, wiping at a trickle of blood from a cut on his cheekbone. "I'd control that temper if I were you, dragon."

Again I try to transform, lines of fire cracking beneath my skin, a harsh roar erupting from my throat. But I can't do it. My ability to shift has been blocked.

I turn to Serylla, who stands wide-eyed and silent in the passage. "Run."

She shakes her head frantically.

"Serylla," I grit out. "Go."

"Spider." Rahzien's voice is heavy with power, with warning. "Come to me. You are my pet. You do as you're told. When you do as you're told, you receive good things."

My beautiful queen casts him a vulnerable, frightened look and shudders. I don't know everything he has done to her, how he gained even a little sway over her mind—but right now I need her to trust me, to see herself the way I see her.

"You possess no power over her," I tell Rahzien, though I never take my eyes off Serylla. "She was never truly in your control, and you did not break her. Nothing can, because she always survives." I keep looking at my mate, piercing her gaze with all the admiration and love in my soul. "She has the heart of a dragon."

There it is. The spark in her blue eyes—her spirit, her courage.

"I fucking love you," she says, low and tender. And then she's gone, disappearing into the passage.

Rahzien vents a sound of explosive frustration. "You three—go after her."

A few guards head for the passage, but Meridian presses something on the painting's frame, and it begins to swing shut, slowly and ponderously. As the guards rush past him, he sticks out his right foot, and one of them trips, careening against another guard. Before they can right themselves, the painting snaps into place, and the guards begin to fumble around the frame, trying to open it.

"Use your guns on the damn thing," orders Rahzien. "Blast the painting, rip it open, get through! I want her caught and brought to me immediately."

The guards open fire on the painting. I've heard Vohrainian guns before, but never this close. It's excruciating to my sensitive ears. My skull rings with the aftershocks of the volley as I watch the guards.struggle to wedge their armored bodies through the ruined portrait and hurry after Serylla in single file.

"Such a ruckus," comments a pleasant voice behind Rahzien. Lady Cathrain, the healer, in the same dark brown dress, but without her flowered shawl.

"You're here at last," says Rahzien. "It seems your solution worked."

"Of course it did." She beams at him. "When have I failed you?"

"Not yet." He gives her a fond half-smile.

Meridian and I realize the truth at the same moment. I can see it in his eyes, the same shock, the same dread.

"It's you," I growl at Lady Cathrain. "You're the poisoner."

"I'm a healer first," she says, with a kind smile. "And I never use my abilities to kill humans. My goal is to protect and preserve human life."

"But you tied Serylla's life to his."

"To protect my Lord and King. To preserve them both in harmony," she says. "Linking them this way diminished the likelihood of violence and death. It made everyone more thoughtful and careful with their actions."

Meridian gives a derisive snort. "Delusional."

"You slaughtered my clan." There's a stinging sensation behind my eyes, a gathering of tears that I can't stop. "You designed a poison to destroy us."

"Because you're not human. You are instruments of death and destruction," she says gently. "You're capable of killing great masses of people with one stream of fire. As His Majesty says, you're too dangerous to exist."

"She's a woman of principles," Rahzien says, squeezing her arm affectionately. "A guiding star to her King. Most healers can look inside the body and spot anything that isn't as it should be, so when she checked you after our meeting, she confirmed my theory about your nature, that you were a dragon in a man's shape."

"Your body bears markers of a deep physical spell," says Cathrain. "Not something I can undo—it's much too powerful. But since we came to the palace, I've been studying the supplies and spellbooks the Supreme Sorcerer left behind. He ascribed to the Jaanan school of magic, which uses eclipse gems and genestree sapstones as binding agents for the most powerful spells. The only other Elekstan sorcerer I've heard of who could turn one species into another is his daughter Thelise, and since she would have learned the basics of her craft from her father, I assumed she would likely have used the same binding agents. All I had to do was block the latent residual influence of the eclipse gems, which controls the timing of your shift, and there we are!" She gives me a beatific smile.

"So you trapped me in this form." I consider throwing another punch or two, but when I catch Meridian's eye, he shakes his head slightly and nods to the guns trained on my chest and his.

"Yes, you'll remain in this form, unable to change," says Lady Cathrain pleasantly. "As time passes, your body will suffer from my interference with Thelise's spell. The longer you remain in human form, the weaker you will become, until you eventually die. You may have escaped the death that your fellow dragons suffered, but fate knows your race's time is at an end."

"You ascribe your own motives to the cosmic forces of the world," I growl. "The hubris of it is beyond belief."

For the first time, the healer's face turns stiff and unpleasant. "I am a humble woman, not a prideful one."

"Lie to yourself all you want," I reply. "You are more of a monster than any dragon."

"Enough," Rahzien cuts in. "Take them to the dungeons. And have a selection of torture instruments sent to the dragon's cell. I have questions for him that he may be reluctant to answer."

I'm trying to maintain my courage, but I can feel it receding. Since the moment I arrived here, I had the confidence of knowing that my dragon form was only a thought away, that if things grew too perilous, I could summon it. Even if I perished, I would die in a blaze of glorious flame.

But now I'm bound in this weak, unprotected form. I don't have my size, my spikes, my scales, or my fire. I am limited to malleable flesh and thin skin. I am far too easy to slice and bruise. As a human, pain is sharper, more dangerous, nearer to the bones. My organs and my lifeblood are dangerously accessible.

As the Vohrainians close in, Meridian snatches up his stick again, presses the button to extrude the spikes from its head, and strikes the gun from the hands of the nearest soldier. He follows up with a ringing blow to the soldier's helmet, but then he's overwhelmed, restrained. His hands are yanked behind his back and bound tightly.

"Do you carry rope around with you all the time?" he says hoarsely to the soldier tying him up. "Seems odd. Where do you keep it? That satchel there? Is it your rope satchel? Do all of you Vohrainians carry a handy piece of rope, or is this man the designated rope carrier? Is it because he—"

"Shut up." The guard smacks the side of Meridian's face so hard his glass eye pops out of its socket and rolls across the floor.

"Now look what you've done." Meridian spits blood. "My best glass eye. It'll be all scratched up now, and it wasn't cheap. Not easy to match such a beautiful eye as this one." He winks his one blue eye. "I hope you plan to reimburse me."

Rahzien actually chuckles at the remark, but Cathrain only prims up her mouth. "I have a few things to tend to," she says. "May I collect samples from the shifter, once he's restrained?"

"Of course," replies Rahzien.

Cathrain nods and leaves the room. Perhaps she thinks that if she doesn't witness the violence, she need not feel guilty about it.

Inspired by Meridian's resistance, I don't go quietly. I manage to slash deep across the throat of one guard and the wrist of another. My height and my claws keep the Vohrainians at bay for a moment, but they're all trained warriors, and I'm borne down to the ground under the weight of them, under a flurry of blows and kicks. Rahzien lets them beat on me for several minutes before bellowing, "Enough! Take him below."

I'm dragged to my feet, my clothing in tatters and my body throbbing with pain. But I manage to slur, "Fuck you," at Rahzien through a mouthful of blood as I'm hauled out of the room.

24

SERYLLA

This is worse than I could ever have imagined. Worse than losing my city, my friends, and my mother to the invading forces of Vohrain. Worse than being snatched up by a dragon whom I thought was going to ravage me with his giant cock. Worse than weathering the Mordvorren and birthing a pair of dragon eggs.

I've been through a huge mountain of traumatic shit that I've barely had a spare moment to deal with, and yet I've never been so afraid as I am while I scuttle through the back passages of the palace like a rat.

This time, I slide through cramped spaces that I'm not even sure are actual passages, drag myself around tight corners, climb rickety ladders in the dark. I don't stop moving, not even when I can no longer hear the Vohrainian soldiers behind me. I just keep going up, and up, behind the hot bricks of chimneys and through cobwebbed spaces that the servants haven't cleaned in years.

I encounter more than one actual rat. But they're normal rats, which feels like a relief after the spider-mice, so I grit my teeth, let them pass, and move on.

My lungs are tight and my throat itches from all the dust. At last I run out of places to go and I stop moving, wedged in some pitch-black crevice in the bowels of my ancestral home, trying not to think about the size of the spiders that probably live in this space.

I'm hidden. Safe for the moment. But Kyreagan has been captured.

What if they kill him?

I should have stayed. Should have died with him. But he told me to go—commanded and begged me with those passionate dark eyes of his. I don't think Rahzien will finish Ky off yet—not until he has me back in his power. Rahzien loves the delicate agony of unraveling a mind, and he won't be able to pass up the chance to torture both Ky and me emotionally. He'll want to dismantle us in the most painful way. Which means I have a little time—a very small window of time, in which to figure out what to do.

They poisoned me, and they poisoned Ky. Rahzien knows the truth about the Prince of Gildas and his retinue, and if he has already notified the gate guards, Aeris might be arrested when she tries to get back into the city. Which means I can't count on her for an antidote.

I need to find the poisoner myself and force them to give me an antidote for Kyreagan. I'll resort to torture if I have to—my mother made me watch a few torture sessions when I was about fourteen, so I know how it's done.

First, I need information, which means I'll have to approach some of the servants. Rahzien killed the last two servants who helped me, and I'm sure the word of that tragedy has spread to the others. They'll be rightfully terrified, reluctant to aid me. They might even turn me in. But I have to risk it. I won't be the useless princess who stands by while everything she loves is destroyed. I did that once. Never again.

There are so many people I love in this palace, so many I care about in this city. And yet Kyreagan's life is worth more to me than any of theirs. Maybe that makes me cruel and selfish—maybe it's my mother's blood in my veins, but it's true. I would go to terrible lengths if I thought it would save him. He is mine. He has made me stronger, *better*. And he made me what I always wanted to be, even when I was rocking the servants' infants while they worked. He made me a mother.

Enough hiding in the dark—I need to save the father of my babies.

I pick my way back through the dusty crawlspaces, doing my best to remember the route I took earlier. I have to move slowly, carefully, lest a beam or board creak too loudly and give away my position. Fortunately for me, a few creaks and bumps are normal in an old building of this size.

Occasionally I hear the murmur of voices and I pause until they fade. At last, after what feels like interminable hours of fumbling and squirming through the dark, I see thin streams of light coming up from the floor, and when I crawl over to the grate, I can see down into a hallway.

I can't see much, but I recognize the pattern of that carpet. I'm in the oldest part of the palace, a mostly unused wing where antiquities and relics are kept. The Supreme Sorcerer's study was in this area, since he liked to work far from others, without being disturbed.

The Supreme Sorcerer was a gaunt, silent man with sallow skin and thick black hair, streaked with gray. High cheekbones jutted above the beard that cloaked his jaw, and full lips were visible beneath his mustache. I suppose he might have been attractive, though I only ever saw him as distantly dreadful. I've wondered occasionally if he and my mother shared more than a mutual interest in magic and power—if they were ever intimate. The thought makes me shudder.

I only entered his study once, in my mother's company. A huge dragon skull hung over his desk, and the shelves were full of books, bones, dried herbs, lumpy things in jars, and several animal skulls. I couldn't get out of there quickly enough.

Urgency thrums through my veins as a fresh realization explodes in my mind.

If I can think of one place in this palace where Rahzien's poisoner might want to spend their time, it would be the Supreme Sorcerer's study. I wish it had occurred to me earlier— I could have suggested that Ky and his allies check there for clues as to the poisoner's identity, though it might have been difficult for them to gain access to that wing without arousing suspicion. Perhaps it's just as well that I only thought of it now. I can head there alone and investigate.

After a few wrong turns, I manage to locate the nearest exit from the passages, and I emerge through the back of a wardrobe in one of the old bedrooms. The wardrobe doors creak loudly, and I have to fight my way out through the dust-sheet that's been draped over it. The whole chamber looks like a tomb, each piece of furniture shrouded in pale sheets. A little light slips in around the edges of the drapes, and after the darkness of the passages, it's an immense relief.

My clothing is a smudged, shredded mess, my hair a wild tangle. If I do encounter anyone, I'll probably look like some wretched waif, mistakenly buried, who had to dig herself out of her own grave.

Before leaving the room, I shove aside the sheets and ease each drawer open, hunting for anything I could use as a weapon. Lucky for me, a faded cloth case in the dressing table contains a single pearl-handled letter opener, sharp enough to pierce skin and flesh if I put enough effort into the blow.

Perfect.

At the door, clutching my new weapon, I hesitate, struggling with my fear of moving out into the hall, where I could be seen and recaptured.

"This is it, Serylla," I whisper into the somber silence. "This is where you shake off Rahzien's influence. Set aside all guilt, grief, and fear. Do what must be done. Save Kyreagan. Save yourself."

Right now, Kyreagan is either being tortured, or torturing himself for not being able to rescue me in some beautiful, dramatic way. I hope someday he will understand that he *did* save me, just by leaving everything and coming after me. At the moment I needed him most, the moment I was on the verge of fracturing beyond repair—there he was. Against wisdom, against self-preservation, he relinquished his role, his clan, and his offspring... and he became human in a deeper way, a more dramatic incarnation, for me.

And if I have to, I will become a monster for him.

I slip out of the bedroom and glide along the gloomy, deserted hallway. A few of Rahzien's men probably patrol here from time to time, but for now, I don't see anyone.

There it is—the entrance to the lair of the Supreme Sorcerer. A towering ebony door engraved with dragons, tentacled men, half-human serpents, and creatures that I now recognize as voratrix. It's a dreadful irony that the Supreme Sorcerer would have his door decorated with dragons, when his final act in life was to doom them to extinction.

Holding the letter opener in my right hand, I press the huge bronze handle of the door with my left hand, and I push inward. Firelight flares into the hallway, and my breath catches.

Shit.

I wait, but no one exclaims at my presence, and there's no sound from within.

Slowly I push the door wider, slip through the aperture, and close it quietly as I look around.

Someone has definitely been using this room. The fireplace has been recently fed. A bit odd, since it's springtime and sunny outside, but then again, the room does feel chilly. I remember it feeling cold during my last visit as well. A side effect, perhaps, of some spell gone awry.

Despite the firelight, the room is as morose and forbidding as ever. Unlit lanterns on long chains hang from a domed ceiling painted with yellow constellations on a deep blue background. Heavy, dark bookshelves stretch all the way up to the point where the ceiling starts to curve. Two ponderous tables stand in the center of the room, with an area of flat, slate-gray tile between them—the spot where the Supreme Sorcerer would draw the circles and symbols for his magic. Beside the fireplace is an oven with a flat top, and on the hearth rest two unlit dyre-stones.

The sight of them pierces my heart like a dagger. Kyreagan and I spent so many days in his cave during the Mordvorren, with dyre-stones as our only light. We cooked meals over them together. He traced Dragonish symbols on my bare skin in their warm glow.

How dare the Supreme Sorcerer have dyre-stones here? Where did he get them? What was his connection to the dragons, to the voratrix, to Ouroskelle?

I'm striding toward the dyre-stones when I see it. Slung over the big leather chair, its fringe trailing on the floor. Its bright, embroidered flowers contrast starkly with brown leather, the dark bookshelves, and the array of smoky amber jars on the table.

The shawl of the healer. Lady Cathrain.

I approach it skittishly, as if it's a living thing that might leap out and bite me. Directly in front of the chair on which it lies is a polished wooden tray, and on that tray are vials of blood, locks of hair, and nail clippings arranged in neat rows, with tiny labels beneath them. I spot an extremely long, shiny black hair, and I know whose it is even before I read the cramped script on the label: *The Dragon Prince.*

Near it lies a scrap of blood-soaked cloth marked *Serylla.* It's part of the dress Cathrain had to cut off me after the beating.

Fury snakes through my belly up into my chest, where it swells hot and molten.

She had the nerve to be kind to me. To pretend she was helping me solve the mystery of my poisoner, when all along it was *her.* And I even suspected Parma, my sweet maid, if only for a moment.

Surging through my anger is a golden wave of triumph, because *I figured it out.* I found her, Rahzien's royal poisoner.

I almost pick up the shawl and fling it into the fire. But I can't touch anything, can't leave any sign that I entered this room. And I need to find a good hiding spot, because if my guess is correct, she'll be back soon. Now that they've captured Kyreagan, she'll probably want more samples from him. He's an oddity to her, a creature worthy of study, so she'll bring the samples here to catalog and store them.

The enormity of what she's done to me, to Kyreagan, to the dragons—it rivals the Supreme Sorcerer's wickedness. I can barely grasp the idea that the rest of the dragons might be dead, and I can't even imagine how Kyreagan must feel. Surely they can't *all* be gone. It would be impossible to ensure that every single one of them would consume prey from the Middenwold Isles. Maybe Rahzien plans to send hunters to the island to ensure that any survivors are destroyed. It's what I'd expect from him. He's not one to leave anything to chance, or to leave a job half done. If the rebels hadn't been irritating him so effectively and the people hadn't proven to be so resistant to his rule, maybe he would have already sent men to Ouroskelle to finish off the clan.

Whatever the truth may be, I still need this woman. I have to make her set me free of Rahzien and unlock Ky's dragon form again.

I choose a dark corner between two bookshelves where I can stand comfortably yet be all but invisible in the shadows until I decide to dart out. My palms are sweating, so I switch the letter opener to my other hand, and wipe my right palm carefully before grasping the weapon again. Much as I'd like to use the long chopping knife lying on one of the tables, the healer might notice its absence the moment she enters. I can't give her any warning.

I need to take her by surprise.

Tilting my head back against the wall, clutching the slim pearl-handled blade, I wait. And while I wait, I compose a ballad of vengeance in my mind.

25

KYREAGAN

I'm on my knees in a stone cell, breathing through blood and bruises. My wrists are shackled to chains hanging from the ceiling, and two more chains are wrapped around my body for good measure. A few moments ago, some of Rahzien's men held me still while the healer Cathrain drew some of my blood, took a shaving of my skin, and chopped off a lock of my hair. She's still there when Rahzien arrives, and she doesn't leave immediately—she withdraws into the hallway and stands there quietly, watching.

Rahzien walks right up to me and punches me in the side. At the last moment I twist slightly and his knuckle rams into the chain around my body. He swears harshly, and I'm grimly satisfied that I managed to injure him, even though I cannot touch the fire I possess, or do anything except wrench my arms vainly against the chains.

Rahzien inspects the knuckles of his right hand, sucks the blood from a cut, and releases a sour laugh. "Well played."

"This is not a game," I reply.

"Tell me about the spell the Supreme Sorcerer's daughter performed. How did she do it? Is she still on Ouroskelle?"

"I wasn't present for the spell. And I've been absent from Ouroskelle for days—how am I supposed to know where she is?"

"Where was she when you last saw her? What does she look like? What supplies did she have available when she performed the spell?"

I clench my teeth and stare him down, defiant. No matter how simple or seemingly harmless his questions might be, I refuse to give him anything.

"You'll talk," Rahzien says. "You think you're in pain now, but we've only just begun. You and Serylla and I will have some very interesting times together before you die. And you'll be dying as a human. No little dragon spirit wafting up to the stars, no dragon bones laid upon the fields of Ouroskelle, no 'bone-tribute.'" He says the phrase with such scorn that I growl and yank at my chains again.

"Dragons have such a primitive belief system," Rahzien muses. "What do you call your god—the 'Bone-Builder?' Fuck, that's a juvenile term if I ever heard one. You're a swarm of pathetic animals, blinking wide-eyed at the stars, revering each other's bleached skeletons after death, clinging to your bits of bone."

He snorts and turns away, running his fingers along a selection of silver tools on a small table nearby. "But the way you kill—the magnificent slaughter—*that* I can respect." He picks up one of the sharp implements, then sets it down. "I don't usually torture prisoners myself. But for you, I'll make an exception. Perhaps I'll cut off your nose, your lips, your eyelids. That face isn't truly yours, anyway. It was produced by magic."

Fuck... I'm not familiar with human methods of torture... I didn't expect him to mutilate me. I like my face, and Serylla seems to favor it, as well. My resolve weakens, and I begin to wonder if telling him a few facts about Thelise would be so terrible.

"Ah, you don't like that idea." Rahzien bends, looking into my eyes. "You like being handsome, don't you, beast? Do you think Serylla will want you once I've sliced all the best bits off your face? You know, I told her once that I'd have a butt plug carved from your bones, that I'd put it in her ass when I fuck her, so you could be there in spirit. What do you think of that idea?"

In his malicious eagerness, he's gotten close. Too close.

"Careful, my lord," exclaims the healer—but I'm already swinging my head, whipping the sharp tips of my horns across Rahzien's face. He staggers back, blood streaming from his torn cheek and lip.

"Fuck you!" he sputters through the blood.

Cathrain sighs and enters the cell. She presses her hand to the wound for a few minutes, a look of concentration on her face. Then she pulls a cloth from the woven bag at her side and tenderly wipes the scarlet stains from his cheek and mouth. At the sight of the seamless flesh beneath, she nods with satisfaction. Rahzien is as whole as if I'd never touched him at all. Too bad.

The King holds out his hand, as if expecting her to repair his knuckles, but she raises her eyebrows and shakes her head. "Keep that one, as a reminder to be careful," she says. "I'm going to my study. I have a few ideas I want to try. I'm not to be disturbed, so try not to get your stomach slashed open by those horns, Your Majesty."

"Very well," Rahzien mutters.

I watch her depart, wondering why he allows her such freedom of speech with him. Even during the war, I saw him strike men full in the face or send them to the whipping post for failing to give him the respect he craves. But Lady Cathrain seems to be the exception.

Rahzien plucks a tiny, glittering knife from the table and tests the point against his thumb. "I prefer giving good things over dealing out punishment," he says, in a quiet, toneless voice. "It's not in my nature to be cruel, no matter what you may think of me."

"You can't fool me." I chuckle darkly. "Killer recognizes killer. You may believe yourself to be more evolved, but your desire to expand your territory is as primal an instinct as any other."

"This isn't just about gaining land and kingdoms." His voice is tense, earnest. "I could never make you understand— you, who possess the mind and manners of a beast. But even a beast should be able to answer a few simple questions."

"I don't know how Thelise transformed us," I tell him.

He runs the tip of the knife along the inside of my arm. "Perhaps instead you could tell me the location of your clan's hoard."

Laughter snags in my throat. "That is a secret I will never betray, no matter what you do to me. There are things far more dangerous than treasure hidden in that place—things my ancestors were given to protect."

"I wonder..." Rahzien taps his lips with the knife. "Is guarding this secret worth watching Serylla suffer untold horrors? If I slit open your princess's belly and unspooled her intestines in front of you, would you tell me what I want to know? If I cracked open her skull and showed you the glistening coils of her brain while she screamed for mercy, would you yield? I think you would."

He's right. I could not bear watching her suffer like that. I would give in, even if relinquishing the secret doomed the world.

"My father would have paid you a nation's ransom from our hoard, in exchange for the Middenwold Isles," I grit out. "You could have had a fortune from us, yet when he offered that price, you would not accept."

"Because I didn't want coins and baubles. I wanted fire. I needed your help with the war," says Rahzien. "And I knew, even then, that once I had destroyed all living dragons, I could retake the Middenwold Isles, and claim your entire hoard as mine."

"And *there* is the flaw in your plan," I say. "With no dragons left, you'd have no one to tell you the hoard's location."

"I planned to persuade Fortunix to tell me. But if neither you nor he will disclose the secret, there are plenty of buccaneers, mutineers, and mercenaries who, for the promise of a hefty share, will scour Ouroskelle and the surrounding islands until they find it."

"It's impossible to find, unless you're a dragon."

"All the more reason for me to extract the information from you." He adjusts the angle of the blade against my forearm, but before he can begin cutting into me, a Vohrainian soldier appears, carrying a brown-and-white hawk on his arm. The hawk's eyes gleam an unnatural red.

"Your Majesty," says the soldier. "Apologies if this is a bad time—but the bird has returned from Ouroskelle."

"About fucking time," snarls Rahzien. "Go on, bird. Open the memory, unlock the message."

The bird cocks its head, then croaks, in an odd, stilted cadence, "All dragons dead."

"All of them?" says Rahzien. "Did you check all the caves?"

"Dead bones in caves," says the bird. "All dragons dead."

No.

I wouldn't let myself believe it, or truly imagine it. Not until now.

All dragons dead. Dead bones in caves.

Tears spill from my eyes, tracing down my cheeks.

Varex... my brother...

But where is Hinarax? He should have returned by now, with news of the clan's demise. Unless he tried to save some of them. Or perhaps some accident took him down. Perhaps a fenwolf killed him in human form, perhaps he fell to his death…

"Was there no bronze dragon?" I ask hoarsely. "Or a black dragon with void magic? What about the eggs?"

My children, my children…

The bird's feathers ruffle for a moment and it repeats, "All dragons dead."

Rahzien's birds do not possess independent thought. They repeat simple messages, report basic concepts. Perhaps the bird does not understand what I'm asking. Surely some eggs must have survived, even if the primes and elders are gone.

There's no chance of Varex and my clan coming to help us—no hope at all, unless Serylla finds some cure for my poison and hers. But by then, I'll probably be mutilated, and unless I receive healing quickly afterward, the disfigurement will be permanent.

Not that my fucking face matters when the last of my kind have perished. I can't even grasp it. Can't comprehend a loss so massive, not when I've barely come to terms with the death of all the female dragons. Between my roaring grief and my helpless fury, I feel as if I'm ripping apart inside, bones cracking, tendons splitting, organs bursting into tears and blood.

"I wonder if the sorceress is still alive," Rahzien says. "Bird, did you see women on the island?"

The hawk only stares at him.

"Fuck," Rahzien mutters. "He can't answer because that's not one of the things I told him to look for. Fuck…" He turns back to me. "All the dragons, dead. And it must hurt all the more because you know it's your fault. The alliance your father made, the one you upheld… in the end, that's what killed them."

"Liar," I hiss. "You did all of this. You made a deal with Fortunix. You spread the disease that diminished our food supply, you forced us into the war, and then you turned on us like the traitorous monster you are. Without your greed for land and power, and your love for manipulation and deception, countless humans and dragons would still be alive today. Hear me now, Rahzien... you will suffer for what you have done to this world."

Rahzien's eyes go cold as the sunless stone in the heart of a mountain. "Are you threatening me? On your knees, in chains?"

"The threat isn't mine to make," I tell him. "It's a belief I hold, that the wretchedness you have dealt to others will visit you in turn. The wrong I've done has come back to torture me, and your fate will be the same—a violent end, in fear and blood."

"Perhaps." Rahzien nods. "But no matter what happens to me, I'll always have the satisfaction of knowing I ended the entire race of dragons. I'll always have the joy of this memory— the look on your face, right now. Devastation, despair. Oh, and I'll have the memory of coming inside your princess, too. One day soon, she will bear my children."

I give him a savage, broken smile. "She already bore mine."

It's a foolish, vindictive remark, one that I knew would anger him.

Rahzien's eyes narrow with icy fury. "I'm going to send my soldiers to collect any dragon eggs on Ouroskelle. I'll have them crushed and tossed into the sea. But I think I'll save one of yours, to be raised by my hand. They will call me 'Father' and obey me alone. It will be easy to break their spirit. I'll enjoy it. They will live in torment, knowing they are the last of their kind."

A wretched groan lurches from my chest. I hate letting him know how deeply his words affect me, but I can't help it. My heart is too full of grief and pain. It cannot be silent.

As the King leaves my cell, the soldier carrying the bird says quietly, "Your Majesty, General Varka requested your presence. The new gun barrels and ammunition have been delivered from the facility at the Risling Mines."

"Good. He'll have to manage without my presence, though—I have more pressing business to deal with. Tell Varka to have all troops in the city bring their weapons to the palace courtyard to have the old barrels swapped out. They need to turn in their old ammunition as well, in favor of the new. I want it done by dawn."

"By dawn?" quavers the soldier. "I'm not sure—"

"The new gun barrels are the same size," snaps Rahzien. "They were designed to fit in the same spot, with the same mechanism to secure them. The old barrels simply need to be unclamped, removed, and replaced."

"There's a bit of soldering to be done for each," ventures the soldier.

"Then let it be done. The sun has not yet set—you have all evening and all night. Get fires going, call in all the blacksmiths of the city, summon the troops, and make it so. Am I understood? I want everyone using the new ammunition by morning. Begone. Put that bird away, and tell General Varka it will be his head if it's not done."

The soldier hurries off.

"At last, some good news," says Rahzien. "Perhaps we'll string up your one-eyed friend in the market square tomorrow and show off our new precision bullets. Take out his ankles first, then his kneecaps, then his dick, and so on, right up to his one good eye. A lesson for the people, and a warning to the rebels. Perhaps I'll wait until then to cut up your face—make a show of it in the square. The princess and her people should watch your undoing."

"But you haven't found her yet, have you?"

A wave of irritation crosses the King's face. "She's a sneaky little spider. But no one can hide from me for long."

After locking the door of my cell, he stalks away.

My delight at Serylla's evasion of the King fades quickly, giving way to the pain in my body, the ache in my knees from kneeling on the stone, and the deeper agony of my heart. Yet in spite of the grief, I'm eerily at peace, knowing that so many dragons' spirits have gone before me, that they await me among the stars. Despite Rahzien's cruel words, I still believe my soul will ascend to join them, even though I've been trapped in this form.

It's almost a relief, having everything out in the open. Not having to feign another identity or suppress my thoughts and instincts so harshly. I yield to the quiet of the moment, the reprieve before the next terrible chapter of my life unfolds.

Some dragons believe that the Bone-Builder still surveys the world from a vantage point among the stars and orchestrates our experiences for some greater purpose. I believed that too, until our clan followed me into war and half of them died. Until a bird told me that the remaining dragons are nothing but bones now... bones in caves, bones upon the mountains.

Any deity who could have stopped such a tragedy, yet allowed it to unfold, isn't worthy of my respect. So I must believe that the Bone-Builder no longer exists, or has no knowledge of what is happening to my species. The alternative would be too painful.

Better to believe in someone who's here, who cares. Who might have a chance of doing something about my predicament and hers. Serylla isn't only my intended life-mate, queen of my heart—she's my goddess now. Whether I die or not, I know she'll have tried everything possible to save me. That's who she is—the brilliant, brave girl who aimed a crossbow at the leader of a dragon army. That's the woman who took me inside herself, knowing what being pregnant by me would mean for her. Birthing those eggs was possibly her bravest act. Or perhaps her bravest moment was facing a ballroom full of men who were competing for her body. Or enduring the lash in the marketplace. Or coming to warn me that my life was in danger.

She's the bravest creature I know.

My musings are interrupted when Meridian limps into view outside my cell, holding the bars for support since the soldiers took away his cane.

It takes me a minute to realize that they locked him up, just like they did me, and yet he's walking free. He's pale and bruised, but he gives me a weary smile.

"You escaped already," I say, a grin pulling at my injured lips. "Why does that not surprise me?"

"You'd think they'd take more precautions with their prized captives. Security in this place is pathetic, really." He takes a stud from his earlobe. When he pulls on it, the stud extends into a tiny sliver of metal, a lock-picking tool. "I'll get you out of here, but we have to move quickly. Remember the plan I told you about? It has nearly come to fruition. About damn time, too. But I need to give the final word so my people are ready to act, and then—"

Rhythmic footsteps echo somewhere in the distance, and Meridian glances in that direction anxiously. "Fuck, we might have to fight our way out."

"No. Just go. Follow through with your plan, get the word to your people."

"Kyreagan—"

"There's no time," I hiss at him.

"Fuck," he mutters. "I'll be back for you, I swear."

"I know."

He hurries away, not a moment too soon. Seconds later, a helmeted Vohrainian soldier appears and takes up a guard position next to my cell. Judging by the shape of the person, I think it's a woman. The soldier keeps turning to glance at me.

"What?" I say. "You've never seen a dragon shifter before?"

The guard's skeletal helmet leers blankly at me for several seconds before she turns back around.

Guarding a prisoner must be a tedious job. Almost as tedious as—

I smirk, my pain and grief receding for a moment.

And I begin to sing. "I once had a wife who took my life..."

26

SERYLLA

I don't have to wait long for the healer.

When she enters the study, she's humming a soft, contented little tune. Everything is going exactly as she hoped it would—I can hear the satisfaction in her voice, see it in the energy of her body as she sets down her woven bag and pulls out a few items, including what looks like a vial of blood. She puts the items on the tray and settles herself into the big leather chair.

I wait while she arranges the shawl around her shoulders, until she has selected a scrap of paper and she's carefully inking letters onto it. Probably a label for Kyreagan's blood.

Speaking of blood... I may not know much about the human body's inner workings, but I do know where the important blood vessels are.

Silently I step forward, seize a fistful of her hair, and poke the letter opener against the sensitive place on her throat where the blood pumps close to the surface.

"Be still," I warn her. "Don't scream."

"Princess," she breathes, in a tone of both delight and alarm. "Aren't you a clever little thing?"

"I'm a dangerous little thing," I retort. "I want an antidote, a cure for both me and Kyreagan. Right now."

"You must understand, I don't harm humans," she says. "I am first and foremost a healer, a mender of damage. That's why I wouldn't let Rahzien use my skills against Elekstan during the war."

"So you'll kill animals or dragons, just not humans."

"Exactly."

"And what about binding my life to Rahzien's? Keeping me from escaping, ensuring that if he dies, I will too?"

"That was also for the greater good. The sooner Elekstan bows to him, the fewer people he'll have to kill to secure their loyalty." Her voice warms, turning almost tender. "Besides, you're good for him. Maybe you don't realize it yet, but he likes you. Cares about you. With your influence, he could be a better man."

"Making him a better man isn't my responsibility. It's his." I dig the point of the letter opener a bit deeper, until a drop of scarlet blood beads on her skin. "Rahzien thinks he's perfect, transcendent, all-deserving. But he's a filthy murderer, a psychopath. Enough about him—give me the cure for the poison you put inside me. Or tell me when it will wear off."

"It won't," she says. "The ingredients were bound with perdura root and the spell was carved in petrified wood. Now Kyreagan's poison—that's a different story. I had to concoct it quickly, so it should wear off in about a week. He'll be dead by then, though. Without the ability to shift into his natural birth form, the energy sustaining his human form will dissipate, and his organs will shut down. He'll basically begin to dissolve from the inside—at least, that's what I suspect. I'm rather interested in how it will manifest."

"You're sick." I tighten my grip on her hair.

Cathrain laughs, a twinge of pain in the sound. "Not at all. I have a healthy curiosity about the human form and its potential.

Imagine it—having the power to perceive the inner workings of the human body. Imagine being able to sew veins back together, knit broken bones, and close open wounds, purely with your own magical energy. Then think of all the ways that the application of subtle, complex magical poisons can be used to alter the body's responses to certain stimuli and conditions. I've been a healer and a poisoner for decades, but only in the past few years have I given myself the freedom to conduct more experiments, to truly explore the potential of my gift—ahh!" She cries out as I cut her beneath the chin, a shallow, vindictive swipe of the letter opener.

"Shut up," I tell her. "Not another word unless it's about curing me and Kyreagan. Where do you keep antidotes?"

"I never make antidotes." Her voice is shaky with dread now.

"I don't believe that."

"I never use poisons without thinking it over carefully first and confirming my own intent," she says. "Which means I never regret it, and I never need to undo it."

"You're saying you can't fix me? Or Kyreagan?"

"I don't have antidotes."

"Can you make some?"

"I told you—I've never concocted any such thing. Learning how would take days… I would need supplies I don't have—special ingredients—"

I ram the letter opener into her round shoulder, right through the embroidered shawl. Then I yank the weapon out of her flesh and set it to her throat again while she whimpers with pain.

I should feel worse about what I'm doing. But after everything I've endured, this tastes like redemption, a keen rush of power through my veins.

"I'm not letting you leave this room for ingredients or anything else," I say. "There's plenty of magical shit here. Use what you've got, and make something that will counteract either Kyreagan's poison or mine—preferably both. Understand?"

She nods.

"Good. No false moves, or I really will kill you. I've been here too long—I want to get home."

I pause for a second, stunned because just then, when I said *home*, I meant Ouroskelle.

"Fix Kyreagan first," I tell Cathrain.

"Of course. I'll need a few things from that shelf." She points.

Reluctantly I back up, allowing her to rise from the chair. As she does, I lunge across the table and grab the large knife I noticed earlier. Having the knife in one hand and the letter opener in the other gives me an increased sense of security.

I follow her to the bookshelf she indicated, and I supervise while she examines the spines of several tomes, looking for the right title.

"Ah, here it is." She pulls out a large, heavy-looking volume.

Then she swings around and slams the book into the side of my face.

I'm stunned, thrown off balance, reeling and blinking while blood coats my tongue.

Cathrain lunges for the door. I leap after her in a mad, unseeing rage, throwing myself at her, both of us crashing against the door and then sliding to the floor in a tangle of blades and flesh and fabric. Her fingernails rake my face, perilously close to my eye.

I stab without thinking, a self-preserving impulse. The blade sinks into her body with a satisfying thump, and something inside me—snaps.

The next second I'm sobbing, screeching, stabbing, tears scorching my cheeks, breaths lurching raggedly through my lungs as the knife flies up and down, over and over.

She's everything I hate. I detest people who play with living things like disposable toys. People who ruin lives from a distance. People who believe themselves immune, who consider their aims loftier than others. People like my mother, like Rahzien. Cruel, cruel, wretched people.

I punctuate every thought with a blow.

And when it's too late, I realize what I've done.

I scramble backward from the lumpy, blood-stained mound that was Lady Cathrain. The knife drops from my shaking hand. I don't know where the letter opener is.

Fuck... I killed her.

She said she couldn't cure us anyway, but what if she was lying? What if she could have? And I ruined everything, I wrecked our chances, I messed this up...

Kyreagan will die now. Because of me. Because I couldn't control my own rage and pain.

I tuck my knees up to my chin and hold my head in my hands, rocking slightly as I wheeze out terrified breaths.

I am worthless. I am foolish. I am alone.

I have no value, and no one wants me.

Something inhales... heavy, low, rasping. I suck in my sobs and listen, every nerve galvanized with terror.

There it is again—a rattling, labored intake of breath. From the lumpy form of the royal poisoner.

She rises slowly, jerkily, one limb after another, and then her spine yanks up the rest of her body, and she's standing upright.

I snatch the knife, scramble to my feet, and retreat farther, holding the blade toward her.

She cracks her neck, spits blood, then dabs at her wet lips with the corner of her shawl. "Another little trick of mine—one not every healer possesses. I can heal myself."

"I guess I'll have to kill you more thoroughly next time," I gasp. "At least now you know that when I threaten you, I mean it. Make a cure for Kyreagan, and I'll let you go. Otherwise, you won't leave this room alive."

She looks absolutely furious, but there's fear in her eyes, too, and it strengthens me. She glances sidelong at the bell cord near the door, but I snap, "Don't do it! Step away from the door. Now." And she obeys.

I suck in a shaky breath, trying to ignore the pain in my jaw and cheekbone where she struck me with the book. Then I step to the door, pleased to find two large bolts that I slide into place. Thank god the Supreme Sorcerer liked his privacy.

With the door bolted, I turn back to my captive. "Now, Cathrain, unless you want to be stabbed again, I suggest you get to work."

With my knife as encouragement, the poisoner works all night. No one disturbs us. Rahzien probably assumes that she's busy working with the samples she took from Kyreagan. Which she is… but not in the way he'd expect.

She told me Ky's cure would be the simplest. She simply has to counteract the blocking agent she included in the poison, which she claims is the powdered essence of a sun-blessed opal, the antithesis of the eclipse gem Thelise used in her transformative spell.

"Eclipse gem shavings or black diamond dust would be the easiest way to counteract sun-blessed opal," she says conversationally as she chips bits off a twisted-looking brown root with her fingernail. "But since I don't have any of that, I'll have to try a work-around. As I told you, I haven't done this before. I know the theory of it, but I'm not generally a by-the-book sort of poisoner. There's an intuitive element to the process, much like with healing. I connect with the essence of the person I intend to poison, and based on my sense of their being and physicality, I decide which elements and ingredients would be most effective."

"What other ingredients did you choose for Kyreagan?"

"You can see it all written down, right there." She nods to the book again. "Flip it open to the page where the ribbon is—that's right. He's my most recent spell. I wrote all the ingredients at the top of the page, and the incantation below. Every spell must be written down and read aloud, you see. Crafted with the hand, interpreted with the eyes, and activated with the mouth—it's the principle of trifold intent. The words are spoken over the completed poison, and then it can be used as needed."

I glance at the list she indicated, darting my eyes back to her every couple of seconds. I refuse to be caught off guard again.

"What I'm doing now is trying to counteract the inhibitor—the sun-blessed opal—with a combination of wretchroot, onyx granules, and dried oxshade flowers," she says. "Essentially I am poisoning the poison I gave him. Not so easy. At least I have a larger sample of his blood this time. That should help."

"Why didn't Thelise have to take samples from all the dragons when she enchanted them?" I ask.

"Because she cast a wide-ranging transformative charm. To encompass the whole dragon race in her spell, she would only need something from one member of the species, not all. If you want to target an individual, the wording of the spell is different, the ingredients are different, and it takes far less energy. But you still need fluids, hair, or a piece of flesh from your target. Hand me that brown packet, the one with the flower printed on it."

I pass her the packet with my left hand, keeping the knife ready in my right.

"The poison I created for the Middenwold Isles was a brilliant bit of work, I must say," she continues, inspecting the contents of the packet. "I used earth from the Isles and some hair from each species, along with a scale shed by a dragon during the war. It's written on paper, not bound with any long-lasting ingredients, so its effects will wear off in a month or so."

"But the poison you made for me… is permanent," I say.

"As I said, your spell is carved into a lovely piece of petrified wood, meant to last for a lifetime, and the poison in your veins contains perdura root to keep your body from eradicating it. I would need an extremely rare and powerful counteragent to negate what I've done to you. There's nothing strong enough in this study, this palace, or this city."

An extremely rare and powerful counteragent. Like the blood of a female dragon who's immune to magic. Which means Aeris and her sorcerer friend are truly my last hope.

"I'm making the antidote for your dragon because it's practically useless," the poisoner continues mildly. "You'll never get it to him without being caught, and even if you do and he's able to shift, he won't touch Rahzien as long as you two are linked. If Kyreagan manages to leave the city with his life, the only things waiting for him on Ouroskelle are the bones of his dead clan."

"You don't know that."

"Oh, but I do. My poisons always work exactly as intended." She smiles placidly.

Her face infuriates me so much, it's all I can do not to stab her again.

"You said you wouldn't kill humans, but the dragons are human now, too," I point out. "If your poison worked, you've broken your own rule. And you've also caused the death of the captured women on the island, who might not survive without their dragons."

"The dragons aren't human at all. They're anomalies. Abominations. Hybrid creatures..." But a troubled expression shadows her face. "Partly human," she mutters. "I wonder if... no, that wouldn't make a difference. It shouldn't."

Frowning, she mixes some bits of root and black granules into an oily suspension in a small glass bottle, then adds a pinch of dust from a brown packet and stirs until the liquid turns blue. "Rip the page with your dragon's spell out of the book," she says. "We're almost done."

I do as she requests, and she burns the spell for Kyreagan in a bowl. Using a funnel, she drains ash from the destroyed spell into the glass bottle, stoppers it, and hands it to me.

"There you are. This will let your shifter turn himself into a dragon again. Not that it will do him much good."

She's smiling pleasantly, but there's something in her eyes—a festering concern.

"How do I know this won't kill him as soon as he takes it?" I ask.

"You can't know, dearie. You'll have to trust me."

"If this fails, I'll kill you," I tell her. "I make you that solemn promise. If you're responsible for Kyreagan's death in any way, either by the poison already in his body or this concoction, I'll kill you, no matter how many years I have to wait. If he dies, and I'm trapped with Rahzien, you and I are going to be part of the King's inner circle for a very long time, which means we'll be close to each other, and I'll have plenty of chances to end you for good. I won't give you a chance to heal next time. I'll cut off your head and burn it, do you understand?"

"Such violence in one so young!" The poisoner lays a plump hand over her chest. "Although I suppose it's not surprising, since your mother was such a warmongering bitch."

"She was." I release a short, caustic laugh. "And the daughter of that warmongering bitch is waiting for your promise, that this vial will do what you say it will."

"It will, I swear." The veneer of her calm cracks, and beneath it I see something surging—something more than irritation. It's impatience, or alarm. Fear, but not fear of me. This isn't about my threats, or my violent attack on her earlier. This is fear of something *else*, fear so great she can barely sit still.

Mentally I rehearse the most recent bits of our conversation. When did she start to look unsettled in a different way?

It was shortly after I said, *The dragons are human now, too.*

After which she muttered, *Partly human… I wonder if… no, that wouldn't make a difference. It shouldn't.*

I don't think she was feeling guilty, pondering any transgression of her personal morality. She was realizing something significant. Something that changes the game.

"I've done all I can for you." Cathrain rises from her chair, her fingers clutching nervously at her skirts. "Now keep your promise, and let me go."

"You're afraid it didn't work," I say slowly.

"I just told you, it *will* work." She scoffs a little, beginning to sidle toward the door.

"Not this." I tuck the bottle of Kyreagan's curative into a pocket of my dress. "I'm talking about the poisoning of the flocks. The demise of the dragons. You designed and delivered the poison a while ago, didn't you? The poison was fed to the flocks of the Middenwold at the end of the war, immediately after Vohrain's victory, I would guess. Which means the poison you designed was based on dragon physiology—pure dragon, nothing else in the mix."

Cathrain whirls and makes a dive for the bell. But I catch her and drag her to the floor, her nails scraping the wall just short of the cord.

"The poison wasn't designed for creatures that are part human," I gasp, struggling to pin her down. "You didn't know they'd be shifters. And now you're afraid it didn't work. You're desperate to warn Rahzien that the dragons might not be quite as dead as he expects them to be."

"Get off me," she screeches, clawing at my face. "Get off, bitch!"

She's a stocky woman with strength of her own, but I am a desperate creature of bones and pain and passion. I force her onto her back, my knees pinning her arms, my knife's edge pressing into the flesh of her throat.

She swallows, her eyes hollow with deathly terror. "I made you the antidote. You promised to spare me."

"I did promise that. But I can't let you warn Rahzien." My voice grates between clenched teeth. It's a hard voice, a cold, merciless voice.

It doesn't sound like me.

It sounds like my mother.

I have needed my mother countless times in my life. The void of her absence was usually filled by others… the same people who are being crushed and cowed by the wicked ruler this woman serves. To protect them, to give them a future, I need to be a queen of blades and betrayal, someone who could break a promise like a twig if her goals changed. I need to be a queen like my mother. Just for a little while.

So I carve open my soul, a deeper chasm than I've ever revealed to Rahzien or to Kyreagan, and I let my mother in.

When it's over, the poisoner's skull sits among the flames in the fireplace.

I threw up twice during the process, and that, plus the stench of burnt human flesh, makes the study reek of violence and wretchedness.

My skin is filmed with a cold, panicked sweat. Did I do the right thing? Should I have kept her alive longer? But I couldn't risk it—she and I have been unaccounted for all night, and they'll discover us before long. If I'd let her live, she would have warned Rahzien that the dragons might have survived the poison.

Of course, he'll get that report from his fucking messenger bird anyway, if it survives the trip to Ouroskelle. But if the dragons *are* alive, I'm guessing they'd recognize one of Rahzien's messenger birds and destroy it. They'll know something's wrong, and maybe they'll come to save us. I can't let Rahzien prepare for that. Our only chance is for the dragons to take him by surprise.

Either way, Cathrain was too dangerous a weapon in the King's hands. Maybe she used to have the best intentions, but then she began to do Rahzien's dirty work and rationalize it to herself. She was on the path to committing far worse atrocities.

And I murdered her. Twice.

I scrub my wrist across my damp forehead and let out a dry sob. I need to *leave*. It's over, and I promise, I *promise* I will never do anything like this again.

Get up, Serylla, get up. Get out of here, away from the body, the skull, and the smell...

Shakily I climb to my feet and undo the bolts on the door. I lean against the polished wood, cool and faintly sticky beneath my cheek. I slip my fingers into the pocket of my dress and touch the small bottle, the antidote for Kyreagan.

Someone knocks on the door and I jump back.

"Cathrain?" booms a voice.

Fuck. It's Rahzien.

There's nowhere to run, and if I hide, he'll find me. I can't let him see what Cathrain was doing, can't let him guess what she made for me before I killed her.

I sweep my arm across the table, sending everything to the floor in a jumbling crash. I empty a few of the shelves, too, knocking their contents off, crash after beautiful crash. There's relief in the wanton destruction, a channel for the self-condemnation gnawing at my heart.

Rahzien charges in as I'm throwing a glass orb to the floor.

"The fuck?" he exclaims. "Spider, what are you doing in here? I've been looking for you all night..." His gaze drops to the headless body in the corner of the room. Then snaps to the skull in the fireplace.

I watch his stony self-possession shatter into a thousand pieces. No plan, no purpose—just raw panic, naked grief. Yes... *grief*. He cared about her.

"You—" The flames dance in his eyes and glint on the royal ring through his septum. Both his fists curl so tight his knuckles crack, and his body tenses as if he's about to pounce, to pummel me into a bloody mess.

I've never seen him like this, so out of control.

He manages another word through those clenched teeth. "Why?"

"She refused to fix me, or cure Kyreagan." A half-truth. More than he deserves.

Rahzien's gaze ravages me, because it mirrors the grief and rage I've felt so often because of him. It's an exquisitely painful vengeance.

"You said you wouldn't kill for me," he rasps. "But you'll kill for *him*."

For Kyreagan. Yes, I did this for him, for his clan, for my people, not just for myself. And therein lies my absolution, the relief of my guilt. Much as I might hate what I did, and dream about it in hideous nightmares for the rest of my life, it was the right choice.

My voice is utterly calm when I say, "Do what you want with me. You can't ever use Cathrain to bind, control, or hurt anyone, ever again."

Rahzien grabs my chin so fast that I gasp. His thick fingers dig into my cheeks.

"Fuck you, Spider," he hisses. "Ever since *he* showed up, you've been different. Without him, you and I—we could have—"

I push his hand away and glare defiantly at him. "Stop acting like you care about me, like I could have cared about you. Whatever you pretend, Kyreagan is the better man—has *always* been the better man, even when he was a dragon. He and I will always be part of each other, even if you kill us both. And you hate it, don't you? You hate that you can't touch either of us, not really, not where it counts."

"Shut up." He's panting, shaking with rage.

Reckless, I laugh. "I should really thank you. See, before Fortunix took me, I wasn't sure about my path, or how I felt. But you helped me realize who I needed, who I adored, and then when Kyreagan came to save me, I knew he felt the same way. You brought us closer together."

"Stop."

"I would *die* for him." My tone is vicious, biting, razors in my smile, tears in my eyes. "And I'd live for him, too. If he dies, I'm still his. I'll never be yours, no matter what you make me say in the dark or before the crowds… no matter what you make me do—"

"Stop," Rahzien chokes out, breathing hard. "Stop talking, for fuck's sake, or I'll—"

Violently he collars my throat with his hand. Shoves me back against the bookshelves so hard that several objects rain down around us. He collides with me, brute force and raging heat. His mouth slams onto mine, rough lips and a thrashing tongue that pushes inside before I can stop him. I scream a protest into his mouth, but he only kisses me harder. His hips ram against mine, his erection grinding into my lower belly.

I twist and writhe, but he's a huge, bearded warrior-king, and both my knife and my letter opener are on the floor, out of reach. I jab my thumb at his eye, but he grabs my wrist and slams it against a shelf with such force that I scream again.

The impact and my second scream shake him out of his wild trance. He pulls back, steps away. Leaves me shrinking against the shelves.

"Guards!" he roars, never taking his eyes from me. Two soldiers rush in at once. "Get her out of here, before I—" He bites his lip, his glare hot as fire. "Take her to her room. Have Parma clean her up and change her into the new white dress— Parma will know the one. And my little Spider needs a crown— I'll bring that to her myself. We leave for the market square in an hour."

I've never been so happy to have two Vohrainian guards on either side of me, hustling me through the palace corridors. It's better than staying in that horrible room, with the *smell*, with the twisted King who devoured my mouth seconds after he found out I killed his beloved poisoner.

Even as we turn the corner into the next hallway, I can hear him roaring like an animal somewhere behind us. Bellowing like a wounded creature, raging against his pain, howling with fury at his own loss of control.

He's more deeply damaged than I imagined.

"He's mad about more than just her," mutters one of my escorts to the other one. "I heard Kotha saying the one-eyed rebel got out of his cell. Killed his guard, plus a few more. No one knows where he went. He just disappeared. Escaped."

"Shit," replies the other guard.

We descend a flight of steps, turn a few more corners. I think I have a few tiny shards of glass in my feet—the pain keeps stabbing deeper with every step.

We're nearing my suite when I notice someone lounging at the entrance to one of the servants' stairways. There's a cap pulled low over his ragged black hair. His face is streaked with ash, and he wears a sullen expression. He's leaning on an iron poker, as if he just came from tending a fireplace.

Something in his stance is familiar—the cap tilted over his left eye, the way he leans on the poker to take weight off his right leg.

It's Meridian. He's wearing a wig, but it's unmistakably him.

Possibly he plans to attack the guards as we go by. But I need him to do something else for me.

We're almost upon him now. My right arm is fully locked in one guard's grip, and the other guard is holding my left shoulder. Without moving my upper arm, I manage to slip my left hand into the pocket of my dress. Meridian is a pickpocket, a trickster. He'll notice the movement.

I shift my left hand around behind me, and I hold the antidote bottle in my curled fingers.

"I wish I could see Kyreagan, one last time," I say loudly, plaintively. "I'd like to give him something to remember me by."

"Quiet," orders one of the guards. He and his companion breeze past the servant with the poker as if he isn't there. At the same moment I feel a breath of air, a whisper of quick, clever fingertips, and the bottle I was holding is gone.

Meridian took it. And if he was listening, he'll know who that vial is for. There's no time to explain its contents, or to warn Kyreagan that the liquid might do more harm than good. I have to believe that it will work, that Cathrain's warped morals led her to uphold her end of the bargain.

When we reach my suite, the guards accompany me into the bedroom. This time they don't leave when Parma arrives.

"I'm sorry, Your Highness," she exclaims tearfully when she enters my room. "The King told me to give Prince Gildas the bracelet on your behalf. I knew it was odd, but I was terrified to defy him. And I didn't understand what was going on until Vela overheard some talk about poisons, and about a dragon who can look like a man—"

"No more talking," barks one of the guards. "The King wants her cleaned up and put into the new white dress. He said you'd know which one."

Parma nods and hurries to start a bath for me. While it's running, she plucks the bits of glass out of my bleeding feet. The guards insist we leave the door open while I bathe, so we make it quick, and afterward she brings me the dress. It's similar to the one I wore the night of the ball, except the material is thicker and softer, and the skirt is so long in the back that it trails behind me when I walk.

Parma is blotting the water from my hair when Rahzien walks into my room, dressed in fresh clothing and a white cloak.

I stiffen immediately, and so does Parma.

"Does it make you feel powerful when you enter a room and the women cringe?" I say caustically.

"Enjoy your defiance while you can," he replies. "You're about to regret all of it. Did you think you could run from me, murder my poisoner, and speak to me disrespectfully, without being punished? You're going to bleed and scream before Kyreagan and all your people. And you're going to watch me cut his face to pieces. We'll see if you still want to kiss him when he doesn't have a nose. Or lips."

Icy horror curls along my spine.

Parma is weeping openly, and Rahzien glances at her. "Put more cosmetics on the Consort's face. She looks like death." He turns back to me. "No bold words now, eh, Spider?"

"I'll love him no matter what you do to him," I reply, gripping my chair to hide how violently my hands are shaking. "But I'm asking you not to torture him. Please. He's dying anyway… please, just take out your anger on me."

"How noble of you." He speaks coolly, his perfect calm restored. But I've seen through the cracks. I know there's a volcano under the hardened rock of his face. "Honorable as your intentions may be, Spider, we're past all bargains now. Unless you'll agree to give me full access to your body and your enthusiastic consent anytime I want to enjoy myself."

"That would be false consent," I reply. "And that isn't what you want, is it?"

Not a twitch of his beard or a tremor of his stone-cold features. He pulls a black velvet bag from behind his back and hands it to Parma. "Put this crown on her head."

"Her hair isn't dry, my lord—"

"Do as I say."

Trembling, Parma eases the crown out of the velvet bag, and I fight to keep my face from betraying any emotion.

It's the crown I received on my sixteenth birthday. It's meant to sit directly above the brow, sweeping back in silver swirls to cup the sides of the wearer's head. It's just pliant enough to ensure a snug fit. Parma settles it into place and presses it tight against my temples. She runs her fingers through my wet hair, arranging the strands.

"More cosmetics," says Rahzien. "And earrings. Big ones."

I cast him a look, but his face is unreadable.

At last he seems satisfied with Parma's work, and he extends his hand to me. "Come, Spider. My heralds are calling the people together. We'll meet them in the Outer Market. And then we'll see how prettily you can scream."

27

KYREAGAN

I'm getting weaker. My body craves the shift to my birth form, but still I'm prevented. An aching shudder passes through me now and then, accompanied by painful contractions of my back muscles, where my wings would be.

I'm suffering through another spasm when three helmeted Vohrainians come to the door of my cell. One of them unlocks it, then comes in to detach the chains from my body and wrists. Briefly I consider trying to fight, but I can't summon the strength.

They drag me along the corridor, through a side door, into a small courtyard. A cart with barred windows sits there, and I'm shoved inside onto the straw-covered floor. I force myself partly upright, leaning back against the wall. There's a wooden bench across one end of the cart, but I don't bother pulling myself onto it.

"I'll ride with him and make sure he doesn't try anything," says one of the Vohrainians.

"Look at him," scoffs another. "He's in no shape to flee."

"Still, better to be careful," replies the first. "He's the King's prize captive."

"As you wish."

The first soldier climbs into the cart with me, and the door is shut. Within seconds, we're rattling across cobblestones.

"Where are we going?" I ask.

"The Outer Market." The soldier's voice has changed, and I recognize its merry, sardonic lilt. Hope threads through my soul.

"Meridian," I whisper.

He takes off his helmet and tosses back his shock of dark red hair. His eye gleams bright blue, triumphant. "I have something for you. A gift from Serylla." He holds up a glass bottle of blue liquid.

My heart sinks. "They caught her."

"Yes, but she obtained this first."

"What is it?"

"If I had to guess, she forced the healer—excuse me, the *poisoner*—to concoct it. It may be an antidote that allows you to shift, or it may cause instant death. It's your choice whether or not you want to risk it."

"What have I got to lose?"

"Exactly my thoughts. You could take it now, and break out of this cart, but I suspect it would be best to wait. I believe the King wants to bring you and Serylla together at the market, and chastise you publicly before the people. You should take this right before you leave the cart... or perhaps wait until you have eyes on Serylla. If you hold the vial just right, no one will see that you have it. Just like the street magicians do. Watch."

He teaches me a few ways to conceal the small bottle in my hand, and during the ride to the market, I practice them over and over.

"If they're getting ready to chain your arms, you'll have to drink it quickly," Meridian says. "Once the change happens, I'll help you protect Serylla."

I tip my head back against the wall of the cart and groan. "I still can't take her far from Rahzien. And the Vohrainians' guns are still a threat."

Meridian grins. "I wouldn't worry too much about the guns. Not today."

"What does that mean?" I ask. "What did your people do?"

But he sets a finger against his scarred lips, then replaces his helmet. The cart is slowing, rattling to a halt. We've arrived at the market square.

I palm the bottle like he showed me. Despite the spasming muscles in my back, the weakness of my limbs, and the brutal handling of the soldiers who drag me from the cart, I manage to maintain my hold on it. As I mount the steps to the gallows platform, Meridian stays on my left side.

Serylla is already there, dressed in white, with a silver crown on her brow. She's standing between two posts, her arms stretched upward in a V, pulled taut by chains. Defiance and terror shine in her eyes, and she has never looked more glorious.

It's a gray morning, clouds thickening overhead with the promise of an afternoon storm. The crowd filling the square is silent and somber, corralled by the forces of their conquerors, unwilling witnesses to whatever Rahzien has planned. Wind tosses the pale skirts of Serylla's dress, winnows through her hair, swirls in reckless eddies between her and me. It brings me her fragrance—and not only hers.

I lift my face to the wind, inhaling through my nose, trying to distill the separate scents. Grease from the food stalls, herbs from the market, the odor of warm bodies from the humans in the square, smoke from chimneys, the acrid stench of piss from the gutters, earth and leaves from the windowboxes of the townhouses… and beyond all of that, distant yet unmistakable, dozens of familiar scents, wild as the sky, keen as the wind.

The varied scents of the male dragons I've known my whole life. My brothers. My clan. They're here, circling above the thick clouds, waiting.

They aren't dead. The bird was lying. But Rahzien's birds do not lie, which means someone gave the bird a false message. Someone who used to loiter around the Vohrainian troops during the war, making friends with them, learning secrets from careless mouths.

Someone I underestimated.

"Well done, Hinarax," I whisper.

Rahzien stands beside Serylla, a white cloak billowing around him, a gold circlet on his head. "Put the dragon in the stocks," he orders.

Meridian moves in between me and Rahzien, grabbing my shoulder. "Come on, dragon scum," he snarls. "Time to move."

I take the hint, and the moment of cover he provides. I pretend to stumble, falling to one knee, my long hair shielding my actions as I tug out the tiny stopper with my teeth and swallow the contents of the bottle.

"Get him up," Rahzien orders, his thumb stroking the shining blade of a long knife. "In the stocks, now."

Another convulsion is beginning, drawing together the muscles of my back—only this time it's accompanied by the familiar buzzing awareness, the vibration that's the precursor to every shift.

"Move back," I mutter to Meridian.

The rogue backs away, each halting step taking him closer to Serylla. If Rahzien weren't staring at me, Meridian's limp might raise his suspicions, but he's fully occupied with scowling in my direction, as if he could flay the skin off my face with his eyes alone.

Glancing from him to Serylla, I smile.

Wicked delight leaps into her eyes, and she flashes me an answering grin so beautiful that I laugh aloud, a mad, wild sound that makes Rahzien's eyes widen. The laughter transforms into a mighty roar as my body expands, unfurls, explodes into the form my ancestors gave me.

My wings whip outward, knocking a few Vohrainian soldiers off the platform. I clamp one screaming soldier between my jaws and shake him back and forth before flinging him across the square. His body smacks into a building and slides into a crumpled heap.

Screams rise from the crowd, and above it all I hear Rahzien bellowing, "Shoot him! Shoot him!"

A spattering of small explosions break out across the rooftops and throughout the square—strange sounds, not the usual crisp *bang* of a bullet firing. Two bullets rip through my wings, but it's nowhere near as many as I expected.

And then I see a Vohrainian fall from a rooftop, his body streaming flames. As more of the soldiers fire, their guns explode in their hands, blowing limbs to pieces, setting bodies ablaze. One after another they ignite, until the troops who were slow to fire realize what's happening and drop their weapons.

Meridian has picked the lock on one of Serylla's chains, and the moment her hand is free, he claps the shackle onto Rahzien's wrist and clicks it shut.

Rahzien slashes at him with the knife, but Meridian is too quick. He dodges back and makes quick work of Serylla's second chain. "Go to Ky!" Meridian yells, and Serylla runs to me, leaping from my foreleg to my back. Meridian begins casting aside pieces of his Vohrainian armor, revealing the light tunic he wears beneath.

I roar again, the cry I used during the war to summon my clan.

They descend from the clouds like a whirling storm, wings spread and jaws wide. Dozens of dragons, whole and alive. My family.

At the head of the swarm is a dragon with gleaming bronze scales. I'd expected my brother to lead them, but Hinarax is a welcome sight all the same.

"Do not kill Rahzien, or the people of Elekstan!" I call to the dragons. "Only the soldiers of Vohrain!"

Hinarax lands on the platform beside me and lowers his neck so Meridian can climb astride it. When he lifts his head again, Meridian raises a fist and cries, in a voice that pierces the tumult, "So may we rise!"

From the crowd, dozens of voices reply, "So may we all!" And weapons appear, pulled from beneath cloaks or drawn from boots.

The mood shifts, from pure panic to fresh purpose, as the people of Elekstan realize this is not a slaughter, but a revolution. A rebellion against the conquerors. And this time, the dragons are on their side.

My role in this is protective—to defend both Serylla and the wretch Rahzien. By protecting him, I keep her alive. So I let Hinarax and Meridian lead the fight, while I use my wings, my tail, and my blasts of fire to shield Serylla and the King from any incoming attacks.

Between the damage done by the sabotaged guns, and the uprising of the rebels in the crowd, the market square is quickly cleared of Vohrainian soldiers, and the dragons move into the city to eradicate more of them. As they fly over the gate, I hear more shots, more explosions. More screams as the weapons of the Vohrainian soldiers burst into fiery shrapnel in their hands and become the instruments of their demise.

Odrash and Kehanal run up onto the stage to unchain Rahzien from the post. They shackle his wrists and ankles, and add an iron collar around his neck for good measure.

"The guns," I ask Kehanal. "What's wrong with them?"

"Our people infiltrated the manufacturing facility for the new ammunition," he explains. "They introduced imperceptible veins of explosives into most of the new batches of bullets. And Meridian bribed the facility's inspector with the treasure you gave him, so that he'd falsify the test reports and our sabotage would go unnoticed until the right moment. I imagine that inspector is far from here by now, off to the Southern Kingdoms to enjoy his new riches."

"You think yourselves so clever," Rahzien bites out. "I have soldiers stationed all over this kingdom. Your little rebellion has no chance of succeeding."

"But we have you," growls Odrash. "And within a few hours, most of the high-ranking officials in your army will be dead or captured. Without their king and their leaders, your soldiers will surrender. And if they don't—well, we have *dragons*."

I lower my head so I can look Rahzien in the face, and I'm pleased to find a glimmer of fear in his eyes. "Wasn't it you, Rahzien, who gave the order for the new ammunition to be distributed to all troops as quickly as possible? Even if not every outpost received it, the odds have been tipped in our favor. It may be a long fight, but the outcome is certain. You have already lost."

"And yet I've won." Rahzien's teeth glint through his red beard, a savage smile. "Because you can't kill me."

I bring my muzzle close to his face and bare both rows of my sharp teeth. "Not *yet*."

28

SERYLLA

Two of Kyreagan's rebel friends, Odrash and Kehanal, drive Rahzien toward the palace in the prisoner's cart, while Kyreagan and I glide over them, flying just above the peaks of the rowhouses and tenement buildings. I don't like that we're the only escort available for such a high-value prisoner, but the other dragons and fighters are needed elsewhere. Kyreagan will have to serve as backup if anything goes wrong on the ground.

His wings have two small bullet holes, and although the wounds don't prevent him from flying, I can sense the extra bit of drag, the slight struggle to stay on course and keep up his speed.

I keep my eyes trained below, on the chaos in the streets as the people realize what's happening and either shut themselves up in their homes and shops, or grab weapons and join the fight. The rebels drive groups of two or three Vohrainian soldiers from narrow streets into wider avenues where the dragons can finish them off.

"Their helmets and uniforms make them easy targets," I comment to Kyreagan.

"So they do," he rumbles. "Are you well?"

"Yes. Although I feel as if we should be doing more to help."

"You've done enough. I feel better with you safely on my back, out of the fray. It's bad enough that I have to keep you near *him*."

I wince, glancing down at the prisoner's cart, which has turned left into an alley to avoid a burning wagon and a knot of people fighting. As the cart proceeds down the alley, a cluster of five Vohrainians emerge from a building.

It seems as though they will bypass the cart at first, but something stops them. I'll bet my ass Rahzien heard them outside and yelled to get their attention.

The Vohrainians converge on the cart and begin attacking Odrash and Kehanal.

"Kyreagan!" I exclaim.

"I see them." He dives, then pulls up again, growling in frustration. "The street is too narrow for me to land."

"Shit." I lean farther to the side, watching the two rebels battle the guards. "They're outmatched, Ky. What do we do?"

But before Kyreagan can answer, a black-clad figure races out of the shadows and leaps into the fray. Even though we're high above the group, I spot the glitter of knives as the newcomer barrels through the cluster of Vohrainian soldiers, slashing, twirling, leaping. The soldiers fall, one by one, cut down before they realize what's happening.

"Who is that?" I exclaim.

Kyreagan replies, with a rumble of satisfaction. "I think that's Aeris."

"The woman who came to my room and took samples?"

"The very same."

"So she's back. Do you think she has a cure for me?"

"If she does, I plan to incinerate Rahzien the moment you're free."

I shift uneasily on his back. I want Rahzien dead—I do. He treated me horribly, and he was the driving force behind Lady Cathrain. If she deserved death, he deserves it more. I'm not sure I have it in me to end another life, but if Kyreagan is offering, who am I to deny him that pleasure?

"You're quiet." Kyreagan's deep voice penetrates my thoughts. "Do you not wish him dead, Serylla? Or have you softened toward him?"

"No," I reply. "I haven't softened. He deserves death, of course. It's just—there's been so much death, and..."

My throat tightens suddenly, and I can't speak. I keep seeing flashes of myself in the Sorcerer's study—the way I sawed through Cathrain's throat, hacked at her spine, wrenched at her skull until it ripped free—

"Ky, I'm going to throw up."

He swerves aside and lands on the flat roof of a tenement building. I slide off his back and bend over, a dry retch breaking from my throat. Though I gag several more times, nothing comes up, and after a few seconds I sit down, dizzy and faint. My breath is shallow, panicked, and my heart is racing.

The great black dragon looms behind me, a silent, steady presence.

"How do you cope with it?" I ask him. "The deaths you've caused?"

He's quiet for a moment, the subtle slump of his wings the only change in his stance. "You killed her, didn't you? The Poisoner?"

"I had to. Or I thought I had to. Or... I wanted to. And I thought I'd settled the matter within myself but..." My voice trails off.

"Whatever your motives were, the thing is done. You cannot change it. Nor can I bring back everyone I scorched to ashes during the war."

"She's not the only one I've killed," I confess. "Back on Ouroskelle, one of the other women tried to murder me. I killed her instead."

"I know."

My eyebrows rise. "You *know*?"

"One of the other dragons found her body. While we were preparing to weather the Mordvorren, he told me she'd been killed, and he mentioned where he found her. It was along the same brook where you and I kissed for the first time, except we were downstream from that spot. *You* steered us downstream. So yes—I knew."

"You never asked me about it. You could have, while we were waiting out the Mordvorren. Did you not care?"

"I knew you weren't the kind of woman to take a life recklessly. I trusted that you had a good reason."

"You should have asked me."

"Perhaps. Or maybe you should have told me. Did you fear I would think less of you? I, who have slain hundreds?"

"It's different when you're face to face with someone. When it's personal, and it's blood and flesh, and you're looking into their eyes when they..." My voice trails off, and I press my fingertips to my forehead. "I didn't want you to think I was capable of that."

"Serylla." His voice is darkly tender, and his muzzle bumps my shoulder lightly. "I think you're capable of surviving. Of protecting the ones you care for. I think you're capable of any number of magnificent and terrible things. Each of us carries a fire that can warm or wound. From now on we choose together, you and I. We decide which is the right way to wield that fire."

The battle rages on in the city below us. Dragons wheel overhead or dive between buildings. Explosions shatter the air and men scream immediately afterward. The streets echo with the hollow beat of mighty wings and the cries of the rebels and the citizens as they take back their city.

Kyreagan should be with his clan, helping to win the day. Instead he's perched on a rooftop, cherishing me with his words, with that rich, velvety voice of his.

I rise and take his sleek muzzle in both my hands. "I love you, you know."

He blinks inky lashes over his yellow eyes. "I know. And we'll talk more of this matter, if you like, but now we should follow Rahzien. If the distance between you grows too wide, you may start to feel ill."

When we reach the palace courtyard, I'm astonished to find most of the Vohrainians already corralled in one area, guarded by the stable-master, his boys, and one of the dragons. Many of the Vohrainian soldiers have lost arms or hands—I doubt most of them will make it through the day without healing. The lucky ones look traumatized by the turn of events, and terrified of the scarlet dragon who prowls the periphery of the group, snarling intermittently and exhaling plumes of smoke.

A section of one palace tower is on fire, but one of the dragons is jetting sparkling streams of water onto the flames. This dragon has different coloring than Rothkuri, and I'm glad, because that means Rothkuri is still on Ouroskelle, watching over our eggs. Have they hatched already? Will the hatchlings believe that Rothkuri and Everelle are their parents? Will they even want me and Kyreagan when we return? What if they despise me, like I despised my mother? What if they injure me with their teeth, fire, or claws, without meaning to? After all, I'm their weak, fragile human mother…

"Your Majesty!" It's Myron, the head cook of the palace kitchens. He and several of the other cooks and maids cross the courtyard, armed with butcher knives, frying pans, and fireplace pokers. It takes me a moment to realize that when they say "Your Majesty," they're talking to me.

Kyreagan stretches his long neck to its full height and gazes down upon them. They stop short, cautious about approaching him.

I climb down from his back and run to Myron. It's been so long since I was folded in his embrace and he smells the same, like cooking grease and baked bread and sage. I bury my face in his ample shoulder and hold on.

"Ay, there, don't cry," he whispers. "You did well. I only wish we'd had the courage to rise up sooner. Could've spared you the pain."

"No, you couldn't have," I tell him. "I'm glad you didn't. You would have been killed."

A shout erupts behind me, and I turn to see the prison cart rolling into the courtyard. Aeris stands atop it, her legs wide apart, knives in both hands.

More servants emerge from the palace, gathering around the cart as it halts. When Odrash yanks open the door and pulls Rahzien out, the crowd of servants bursts into a unified chorus of anger.

"Kill him now!" yells someone.

"Don't touch him!" bellows Myron. "His life is bound to the Queen's!"

At his shout, the crowd settles somewhat, and someone yells, "Let's search the palace! Find every last Vohrainian!" And they all rush back inside.

Odrash and Kehanal flank Rahzien, weapons ready in case anyone else has revenge on their mind. Aeris stalks over to me, and I instantly feel smaller in her presence. She's such a skillful warrior—so sure of herself and her movements.

"Did you get the cure for Serylla?" Kyreagan asks.

"In a manner of speaking." Aeris gives me a look full of sympathy. "My sorcerer friend did his best, but he doesn't think the potion he made can sever the life bond between you and Rahzien. A poison like this is beyond his skill to undo entirely. He said it would require the magic of the person who created it. They would have to take the original written spell and destroy it with their own hand—"

"That's no longer possible," I say quietly.

"I see." Aeris eyes me for a moment, then continues. "Well, at the very least, this should negate what he called the proximity link,' which means you can travel as far from Rahzien as you like."

Kyreagan gives a feral growl. "So I can't kill the bastard?"

"Not if you want to be sure Serylla remains alive," Aeris replies.

A blast of wind rushes through the courtyard, and Hinarax descends, with Meridian on his back. The rebel climbs down gingerly, holding his bloodied left arm close to his chest.

"Stray bullet—the non-explosive kind," he explains, leaning against Hinarax's scaly shoulder for support. "Fucking bad luck."

"We'll find one of the healers Rahzien conscripted into his service," I tell him. "They'll fix you right up."

"You have my thanks." Meridian gives me a grateful nod. "Well met, Aeris! Nice of you to join us. I assume you were successful."

"Partly." Aeris takes a vial from her satchel and hands it to me. "She'll be free to leave Rahzien and go where she likes, but in all probability if he dies, she will too."

"Well, that's a fucking shame," Meridian says. "I was looking forward to watching the Prince here toast His Anal Majesty into a crispy little nugget. Eh, Odrash? Wouldn't that have been fun?" He spits in Rahzien's direction.

Rahzien doesn't flinch. Doesn't react. His face is entirely blank, completely neutral. He has shut down again, withdrawn all emotion and sealed it within himself. Who taught him to do that, I wonder? A parent, a mentor? Who made him this icy ruler, this brawling warrior, this fiend so ravenous for conquest?

If I want to live, so must he. And perhaps, if he lives, he can change. Maybe he can learn to be different—to be better.

"Make him kneel," I tell Odrash and Kehanal.

They glance to Meridian for confirmation, and when he nods, they push Rahzien to his knees.

I walk over to him and grip his bearded chin, forcing his face up. "Look at me."

His eyes meet mine. Dead eyes, blank as stone.

"I need you to repeat something," I say softly. "And if you don't, Odrash will cut out your tongue. You don't need your tongue to live, after all."

It's a threat I'm not sure I'd carry out, but I steel my gaze, because I need him to believe it.

His lips tighten, but he doesn't respond.

"Say these words aloud," I tell him, and he repeats after me, in a slow, even tone.

"I am a man who does what is right. When I do what is right, I earn my place in the world. I have done great harm to others, and great harm to myself. From this day on, I will be worthy. I will be wise. I have value, and I can be redeemed."

The courtyard is deathly quiet as Rahzien speaks the words.

I don't have him say it again. I know he'll remember every phrase, as long as he lives.

29

KYREAGAN

I have never been so proud of Serylla, and I've never felt less worthy of her than when she looks down at the defeated king and gives him those words of mercy.

I hate him. I'd sooner bite off his head than allow him a chance to change. But with that option taken from me, I will have to endure his existence.

"We'll have to imprison him somewhere," I say.

Hinarax arches his neck proudly. "I know just the place."

I dip my head in assent. "Then we should leave immediately. I want him out of Elekstan. The remainder of his forces will be more likely to yield once he is gone."

"Now wait a goddamn second, dragon," says the burly man Serylla hugged. "Our Princess—our *Queen*—has had a hell of a day, and before you take her anywhere else, she'll be eating a good, hearty meal."

"God yes," exclaims Serylla. "Please cook me something, Myron! I've been half-starved for weeks."

"You're a cook?" I ask the man.

He looks up at me, swallowing nervously. I suppose he's never been this close to a dragon. But his voice is strong when he replies, "Yes, I'm a cook."

"Very well. I shall bring you with us to Ouroskelle. You will cook for my Queen, and for the women there."

The man's jaw drops, but Serylla hurries to say, "He's joking, Myron. Of course he's joking, aren't you, Kyreagan?"

She glares at me intently until I chuff out smoke and say grudgingly, "Of course. It was a joke."

Serylla keeps an eye on me as she uncorks the vial Aeris gave her and downs the contents. "How am I supposed to know if it worked?"

"You could test it," says Rahzien abruptly. "Cut off my head, see if hers falls off too. That's your preferred form of execution, isn't it, Spider? How appropriate that your mother died the same way."

"He's baiting you," says Meridian coolly. "Ignore him. In fact, does anyone have a gag? I have one, but it's a ball gag and it's my favorite, so I'd rather not waste it on the likes of him."

A couple of the servants produce strips of cloth for gagging Rahzien, a process which Serylla watches with satisfaction before the servants hustle her off to be fed. Meridian is escorted inside to rest until he can be tended by a healer. Odrash, Kehanal, and Aeris enter the palace as well, to assist with the final sweep of all the rooms to root out any remaining Vohrainian soldiers.

Meanwhile, Hinarax and I withdraw to the edge of the courtyard opposite the prisoners, where we can speak without being overheard.

"Thank you for bringing the clan," I say quietly. "Your arrival was perfectly timed."

"That was no accident," he replies. "We reached the area last night and went to the rebels' caves first, where I spoke to Norril. He said a plan was in the works for disabling many of the

Vohrainians' guns, and that we must wait for the next morning before attacking, to give the soldiers time to switch to the new ammunition."

"How did the clan fare in our absence? As Serylla and I were flying over the city, I noticed many of our brothers seemed to falter in flight, and their fire streams were thinner than usual."

"That's why I couldn't return sooner," Hinarax replies. "When I arrived on Ouroskelle, I found the clan suffering the lingering effects of the poison. A hunting party had gone to the Middenwold Isles shortly after you and I left, and they brought back plenty of prey for everyone. All the dragons consumed the meat. When they began to sicken, Thelise tested some of their blood and discovered it was magically toxic, full of a poison designed to be lethal for dragonkind. Because we were part human, we didn't die."

"She saved us," I murmur. "If Thelise hadn't enchanted us like she did, we'd have been wiped out entirely."

"Ironic, isn't it?" Hinarax replies. "It's enough to make one believe in Fate, I swear. Most of the dragons were able to shift into human form and avoid the worst of the symptoms, but when they had to switch back to dragon form, they became very ill. When I arrived, many of them were weak from lack of food. The women did their best to care for each dragon, but sometimes it was beyond their ability. So I had to spend time finding enough food for everyone and seeing them through the last of the sickness. As soon as enough of us were able to travel, we came to help."

"What of Ashvelon?" I ask. "I haven't seen him among the others. Did he stay behind?"

"He and Thelise came with us, but she said she had a 'separate mission,' something along the coast. I have no idea what she meant by that. But they promised to join us as soon as they can."

"Perhaps we'll meet them on the way back. As soon as Serylla is ready, I intend to take Rahzien elsewhere. You said you had a location in mind?"

Hinarax chuckles. "The Ashmount."

"The Ashmount... of course! It's perfect."

"I know."

I chuckle. "And your little trick—teaching Rahzien's bird that message and sending him back with false information—that was brilliant. It put him off his guard."

"Gave us the benefit of surprise." Hinarax flares his wings. "I wish I could have seen his face when we burst out of the sky!"

"I saw it. He was as astonished as if he'd sprouted a tail himself."

"Glorious." Hinarax swivels his head around to look at Rahzien, who kneels on the cobblestones in chains, with the gag in his mouth. "Strange, isn't it, that we helped him conquer this place, and then helped to free it from his rule?"

"Beyond strange," I admit. "And it's all because of the women we took. I thought we would change them, yet they have changed us, in more ways than we can even understand. The entire course of our future and theirs has been altered."

Hinarax hums his agreement, deep in his throat.

"And you?" I eye him sidelong. "You and the rogue?"

He tosses his head, glances away. "Our story is unfolding."

"Fair enough." I hesitate, then add gruffly, "I wish you joy with him. I think you're a match."

"Perhaps we are." He looks far more serious than usual. "Time will tell."

I arch my wings and toss my head. "While I take Rahzien to his new home, perhaps you could remain with Meridian and oversee the clan while we help Elekstan drive out their conquerors, as we promised?"

Hinarax's eyes glow brighter. "If my prince trusts me with such a great task."

"You've been by my side for all of this. I would trust you with anything. Well... perhaps not *anything*, but most things. Some things... a few things..."

He laughs. "I'll take it."

I want to ask him about Varex. My brother's absence is notable, and it worries me. He wasn't himself when I left Ouroskelle. But there's a strange dread in my heart when I start to speak of him, a reluctance to know the truth. If something is wrong with Varex, I'm not sure I can bear to hear it now. I'll wait until Serylla and I are back on Ouroskelle, until we've seen our eggs. Then I can seek out my brother and make sure he's well.

"What shall we do with the other Vohrainians?" Hinarax asks. "Burn them?"

"Perhaps." I survey the shivering, bloodied group of soldiers in the courtyard. "Or perhaps carry them over the border and drop them into Vohrain. Not from too high, of course."

"Fly low and drop them." Hinarax nods. "Understood."

I'm glad I didn't suggest burning the prisoners alive, because an hour later, two Elekstan healers show up, claiming they have orders from the Princess to heal the captives. They are rather reluctant purveyors of her mercy, and they claim they can't regenerate the hands or arms lost to exploding weapons. But they staunch the wounds and seal the residual limbs with smooth skin.

Shortly afterward, Serylla emerges from the palace wearing the same white dress and silver crown, with two satchels slung around her body. She walks up to me and pats my shoulder, a sign that she wants to climb on my back. Without a word passing between us, I understand that she is done with all of this. She's weary, she's emotionally exhausted, and it's time for me to take her home.

I say a brief farewell to Hinarax and Meridian, with the assurance that I'll return tomorrow or the next day. With Serylla on my back and Rahzien in my claws, I soar away from the palace. The stormclouds above the Capital are growing darker and heavier, and I want to be gone from here before the winds rise and the rain falls. My first priority is Serylla, and my second is our common enemy. I need to put Rahzien somewhere he can't do harm, and then I need to take my life-mate to our cave, where she can rest and recover from her ordeal.

We're nearing the coastline when I spot Ashvelon's bulk and his serpentine neck in the distance. I swerve in his direction, and within seconds I can make out Thelise, clinging to his back.

They change directions and fly alongside us.

"Are you alright?" Thelise calls to Serylla.

"I will be," she answers.

"Catch!" Thelise flings a small object through the air. By the shift of Serylla's body astride my neck, I assume she caught it.

"What's in this?" she yells back to Thelise.

"I figured you could use a drink. Where are you headed with *him*?" She points to Rahzien. "Going to drop him in the sea?"

"We can't," Serylla replies. "My life is bound to his."

"Oh fuck." Thelise cups a hand over her mouth, then says, "We'll come with you. I need to hear this."

30

SERYLLA

Rahzien's new prison turns out to be a formerly volcanic island a couple hours' flight east of Ouroskelle—a place the dragons call the Ashmount. It's a wasteland of huge spiked rocks, so oddly shaped that I imagine they might once have been the ribs of some titanic, arcane dragon, now heavily cloaked in layers of hardened lava. Dark flowers cluster in hollows, each ashen bloom emitting wisps of pale blue light.

"Ash-roses," Thelise calls to me as our dragons soar over the barren landscape. "They are a sign that the volcano beneath this island has spent itself, and is at peace. We need not fear it."

At the center of the island, on a rocky peak, stands an ancient stone fortress. Both dragons land on a lower parapet, a broad ledge rimmed with deteriorating stones, like broken teeth.

After Thelise dismounts, Ashvelon transforms into his human self. I don't want to stare because he's naked, but I'm terribly curious about his appearance, so I sneak a glance while he's putting on the clothes she brought for him.

Ashvelon is slim and tall, with a pale, boyishly pretty face, light blue eyes, and wavy blond hair down to his shoulders. Even though he's twenty-five years older than Kyreagan, his human form looks around the same age.

Kyreagan is watching him too, yellow eyes narrowed. He doesn't say anything, and I can't tell what he's thinking.

"You should shift," I tell him, unslinging the bags I brought. Back at the palace I packed one bag with some food and a change of clothes each for Kyreagan and me. The other bag contains more food and a few necessities for Rahzien's survival.

Thelise doesn't look away when Kyreagan shifts. She takes in every inch of him, then winks at me as if to say, *You're welcome.*

Kyreagan has barely pulled up his pants when Rahzien moves, quick as a wildcat. He charges Kyreagan, head down, barreling into Ky's gut and knocking him over. Rahzien stomps his boot at the dragon prince's face, but Ky rolls just in time. With a shout, Ashvelon leaps onto the King's back, locks both arms around his throat, and squeezes. Rahzien crashes backward into the wall, smashing Ashvelon's body against the stone.

Seething with anger, Kyreagan scrambles up, ready to join the fight, and I'm lunging forward too—but Thelise beats us both. She's in front of Rahzien before we can blink, her fingers splayed clawlike over his heart, crackles of violet lightning dancing along her palm.

"Enough," she says.

Rahzien snarls a laugh. "You can't kill me without killing Serylla."

"Oh, I don't need to kill you. I know how to put a beast down for a while." Her fingers flex, and Rahzien's face goes rigid. He topples sideways, limbs locked in place, and he hits the floor with a resounding thud.

"You alright, pet?" asks Thelise

Ashvelon peels himself away from the wall and wheezes, "Never better."

"Poor thing." She ruffles his hair with her fingers. "I'll give you a treat later. Time to dispose of the garbage, dragons. I assume you want him in the tower?"

Clearly Kyreagan and Ashvelon haven't thought about it beyond *put the bad king in the ancient human fortress*, but after a glance at each other, they nod sagely, as if that was their plan all along.

"Good boys." She snaps her fingers toward the stairs. "Off you go."

While Ky and Ashvelon drag Rahzien's body up an interminably long circular stairway, Thelise and I follow at a slower pace. I'm slightly unsteady during the climb to the top, possibly from weariness… or perhaps I took one too many sips from the flask Thelise tossed me.

Rahzien remains open-eyed and rigid, even when he's hauled into the tower room and tossed onto a wooden cot. It's a bare space, with a stone floor cloaked by a ragged bit of moldering carpet. There's no fireplace, and no furniture except the cot. A few rusted weapons lean against the wall, but Ashvelon picks them up and tosses them out the window.

"Tomorrow we'll bring him a dyre-stone for warmth and light," Kyreagan says. "We don't have the keys to his shackles, so he'll have to remain chained, at least for now."

"As long as he can reach his mouth to eat and his ass to wipe, that's fine." Thelise picks up a pair of wooden buckets and holds them out. "How perfect! One to catch rainwater, and the other for shit. All the luxuries the asshole deserves."

I can't help giggling, which seems to please Thelise greatly. She sets down the buckets and takes my hand. "Alright, my friend, tell me about this life-link between you and the King."

At first I'm hopeful that she'll be able to free me completely from my bond with Rahzien. But after I explain everything to her, she shakes her head with an apologetic grimace.

"I'm afraid I can't sever it, either," she says. "Proximity spells are easy to break. Life-links, not so much. Some magic simply cannot be undone, or it can only be unraveled in specific ways. There's no way around this, unfortunately, so we must keep him here. The good news is that his condition won't affect you in any other way. If he breaks a bone, you'll be fine. If he's ill, you won't feel it."

"So we don't have to keep him comfortable," Kyreagan says darkly. "We just have to keep him alive."

"Yes... except he might grow tired of this existence and leap from the tower, killing both Serylla and himself," Thelise muses. She plucks a few red-gold hairs from Rahzien's head, then plops down on the floor and opens her satchel. "Give me some time and space, while I devise an appropriate spell to prevent that."

Kyreagan and I leave her and Ashvelon in Rahzien's new quarters, and we head downstairs to one of the shabby, musty rooms. We stand together in the archway that leads onto the parapet, looking out over the dark, rocky landscape.

"I didn't expect a volcanic island to be so cold." I suppress a shiver.

"The volcano is dead," says Kyreagan. "No warmth left, or we would not risk leaving Rahzien here."

"I know." I rub my arms, conscious that I'm still in the white dress Rahzien ordered me to wear today. "Back at the palace, I took the time to pack but not to change. Silly of me. I intended to put on something else, but then I got to talking with Parma, and I forgot."

"Your mind is tired," Kyreagan consoles me. Then, stiffly, as if he's forcing himself to ask the question and pretending to care: "How is Parma?"

"She'll be fine, now that she's free of Rahzien." I squirm a little, remembering the awkward conversation between me and my former maid. "I offered to find her a new position, or bring her to Ouroskelle, but she didn't seem to want any help at all. I think she's done with life as a maid—and possibly done with me, at least for a while. I don't blame her. I'm now part of some of the worst memories of her life. She needs time, and space. I told her to take anything she wanted from the palace and just go. Start a new life. I hope she does."

I shiver again. Kyreagan starts to put his arm around me, then hesitates. "Come with me. I want to show you something."

He leads me outside onto the parapet, where he hands me his clothes and shifts into dragon form. We take off from there and glide over the forests of spiked rocks and plains of black stone, until Kyreagan seems satisfied with our location.

"Stand here, on this ridge," he tells me.

I stay put, rubbing my chilled arms as he prowls down the slope to the bottom of the valley, where the ancient lava flow hardened in ripples of ebony rock.

Under the overcast sky, with his black scales and spikes, Kyreagan blends into the landscape almost perfectly. His yellow eyes blink at me to make sure I'm watching. Then he faces the length of the valley, and a river of fire pours from his jaws. The heat is so intense I can feel waves of it from where I stand.

Kyreagan roars, flames shooting from his mouth, and the black rock beneath his feet begins to glow amber. With another burst of his magic, the rocks themselves seem to melt, and rivulets of orange lava trickle through the dark ground.

The texture of the slow, oozing lava fascinates me. It swells, rich and thick and molten, and along the bright glowing edges it holds intense color, deep purple or blue, before it fades to chalky black again.

Kyreagan shifts to human form and stands there, beautiful and naked and powerful, his black hair flowing behind him and his horns glimmering with traces of his fiery magic. He's motionless, glorious, surveying the flaming destruction he wrought.

I can't bear being this far from him, not after everything. I need to be touching him so I'll know he's real, that all of this is real, that I'm not feverish and hallucinating deep in some infested dungeon, waiting for Rahzien to come and give me a drink of water laced with poison....

I can feel myself going deeper into my head, into a dangerous and frightening place, so I halt that course of thought, and I pick my way cautiously down into the valley, avoiding any fiery spots or trickles of lava, until I reach my dragon prince.

"I told you to stay on the ridge," he says, with a half-smile.

"You knew I wouldn't listen. At least not for long. When do I ever do as I'm told?" Forcing a smile, I hand over his clothes. He pull the pants on and fastens them, but before he gets the shirt all the way on, I stop him. My palm presses to his skin... his hot, smooth, perfect skin. He's still bruised and scraped in a few places, and there's a seam of dried blood on the right side of his lower lip, but he's whole. He's safe.

My fingers glide over his chest.

"You're beautiful," I whisper. "And you looked like a king just now. Not the Bone-King, maybe, but a king nonetheless. And a king needs a crown."

I remove the silver band from my hair and exert a little pressure, bending it ever so slightly wider so it will fit Kyreagan. I set it above his brow, with the silver swirls arching back beyond his temples.

"It suits you," I say softly. "Better than it ever did me. Ky, I don't want to take my mother's place. I can't think of anything I want *less* than ruling Elekstan, honestly. The people are free of Rahzien, and I'm happy to let Meridian and the rebels take it from here. Let them set up a government of their choosing, or none at all."

"So you'd rather not be a queen?" His face is sober, his gaze uncertain.

"No. But I don't mind being the life-mate of a king." I slide my left hand around the back of his neck, delighting in the silken flow of his hair beneath my fingers. "As long as that king is part human, part dragon, and completely, obsessively, ridiculously in love with me."

"I think I know someone like that," he murmurs. His claws disappear, and one of his hands glides along my arm, while the other presses warmly against my waist. "But living with me on Ouroskelle won't be easy. Our clan is new to being shifters, and our way of life will have to change accordingly. Things may be difficult and confusing for a while. The work of discovering ourselves and raising the next generation will not be easy."

"All the more reason for me to be there and help you. I've never been afraid of hard work."

"Though when I first captured you, you wanted me to believe otherwise." His dark eyes sparkle, and he attempts to mimic my voice. "'Dragon, bring me soap, and a towel, and a cup of fucking *tea*!'"

His shrill fake voice is too much. I'm laughing so hard I have to let go of him, and I double over, holding my stomach, wheezing with laughter. He laughs too, a deep, rich sound that's so contagious I can't stop until there are tears in my eyes and my sides hurt.

"Oh god," I gasp finally, gripping his arm for support as I stand upright again. "That felt so good."

"So fucking good," repeats Kyreagan. Amber sparks glitter hotly in his dark eyes, and my heart flutters at the warmth, the deep affection, the desire in his gaze.

The fire in the valley has died out, and the molten rocks are cooling again, though an orange glow still mingles with the blue mist from the ash-roses. Kyreagan spewed an incredible amount of fire across the landscape, and he did it after burning several Vohrainians in the market square, too.

"How do you feel?" I ask. "You once told me that if you use too much fire, it takes a while for you to recharge. Do you feel—empty?"

"Not at all," he replies. "It was satisfying. I'd been saving it up for Rahzien, so I needed somewhere to put it. And ever since you and I started fucking, my magic has been stronger."

"Then it's true. Being active during mating season strengthens a dragon's magic. Do you think Fortunix's magic has lessened, since he spent the season alone?"

"Most likely." Kyreagan's expression darkens. "I'd rather not hear his name again, Serylla."

"Of course. Though I do wonder where he went."

"I'm sure he'll appear again, at the worst of times," grumbles Kyreagan. "Perhaps I'll hunt him down someday and make him pay for his part in all this."

"But not now. Not anytime soon." I rub his chest through the open shirt. "Let's go back to the fortress. Maybe Thelise has finished whatever she's doing, and we can go home. I'm getting ridiculously excited about seeing the eggs. Is that strange?"

"Not at all." He kisses my forehead. "I'm excited, too. They should be nearly ready to hatch, if they haven't already."

"I can't wait to meet them! Although that means we'll be having less sex."

"Why?" Kyreagan asks innocently.

I quirk an eyebrow at him. "Because we can't have sex in front of our children."

"During the mating heat, quarter-century dragons often see their parents mating with other dragons," he counters. "At least, that's what I've been told. And parents see their children mating as well. It's a joyful experience."

"Eww, no. No, no *no*." I wrinkle my nose. "For one thing, quarter-century dragons are primes at that point—adults, not hatchlings. And even then, I think it's gross. You're a human as well as a dragon now, Ky. Trust me—having sex in front of little ones would be deeply disturbing for everyone. Just think about it."

At first I think he's going to argue the point with me—but realization dawns slowly on his face, and his eyes widen.

"You're right," he says hoarsely. "That would be wrong."

"Yes. When we want to fuck, we'll have to find some privacy. Maybe a nearby cave or something…"

"I have an idea," he interjects, his eyes alight.

"Maybe ask me about it first, before you do it?" I wince at him playfully. "Just to be safe."

"Of course. We'll discuss it at home."

I half expect him to strip off his clothes *again* and fly me back to the fortress, but he holds out his hand. "Walk back with me?"

I slip my hand in his, palm to palm. A slow heat thrums between us as we make our way up the valley, toward the mountainous peak where the fortress stands.

Kyreagan's thumb circles across the back of my hand, rubbing gently. I don't know why that tender, tiny caress turns my skin ultrasensitive in that spot and sets every nerve in my body alight, but I can't seem to think of anything but the slow stroking of that strong male thumb.

Then he twists his hand slightly and traces the tip of his thumb across the heated center of my palm.

A thrill races right up my arm and into my body, then straight down to my clit.

When I look up, he's watching me with a sultry smile.

"Meridian taught me that," he says. "He called it a seduction move."

"Remind me to thank him. Not that it takes much for you to seduce me." I reach up and pull his face down to mine.

The kiss is molten lava, surging through both of us. I'm glowing at every point where our bodies press, incandescent and softening between my legs.

Kyreagan slides the straps of my dress off my shoulders, then pushes my neckline down until he can cup my bare breast in his hand.

"We're out in the open," I rasp against the heated silk of his mouth.

"Doesn't matter to me," he replies, wrapping his hand firmly around the back of my skull and opening his mouth wide to accept my tongue.

I kiss him deeply, lavishly, barely aware that he's scraping my dress upward along my thighs until his strong fingers cup my pussy over my wet panties.

"I love this tender little cunt," he murmurs, tracing the shape of my pussy lips through the damp fabric.

Deftly he tugs the material aside and sinks two fingers into me, while my mind goes hazy and desperate and blissful. I forget where we are… I forget everything except riding his hand. I cling to his neck, both arms wrapped tight around him while he plays with me. He had plenty of practice while we rode out the great storm, the Mordvorren, and he hasn't forgotten the skills he learned—grinding the heel of his hand against my clit, or caressing the tiny nub with his thumb while his fingers are buried inside.

"Come for me," he urges softly as I whimper against his shoulder. His lips graze my cheekbone. "Come in my hand, my darling, my queen, my life-mate. Come all over my fingers."

And I do. I come helplessly, with frantic little cries of bliss, and he cups me hard, humming with pleasure as my pussy spasms against his hand.

Kyreagan gathers me closer, his wet fingers slick against my shoulder. His cock is thick and hard under his pants, so when my breathing is back to normal, I drop to my knees, only to find that kneeling is especially painful on lumpy lava rock.

"Ow," I exclaim. "Give me your shirt. And your pants. You don't need them anyway—after this you're flying me back to the fortress."

"Maybe I shouldn't bother with clothes at all," he says with a wry smile. "I should be naked for you, always. Easier for shifting, too."

"When we're alone, yes. Always be naked. But humans shouldn't walk around naked in front of other couples, or in front of their offspring," I tell him firmly. I accept the clothes he hands me and fold them to form a cushion for my knees. "This will work, I think. I might still have bruises, but they'll be the good kind."

He sucks in a shuddering breath when I take him in my mouth. I run him deep into my throat, relishing the hot, salty flavor of his skin. He tastes like mellow sunshine, rich and smooth. Gently I cup his balls, and he moans, taking my head in both his hands. His claws have emerged, and they scrape lightly against my scalp.

He doesn't last long, sweet dragon. He's still so new to all this, so deeply affected by the most casual swirl of my tongue, the lightest sucking sensation. He comes with a cry that's lighter, younger, more broken than any sound I've heard from him. I let his cock pump everything down my throat. I love feeling his balls twitch and tighten against my palm.

Cautiously, carefully so as not to trigger my gag reflex, I ease him out of my mouth and throat. I can taste the salty, viscous creaminess of him on my tongue.

When I look up, his head is thrown back, his strong brown throat exposed, his chest heaving. When I move his hands from my head and rise, he staggers a little, unsteady with pleasure, his muscles still taut from the orgasm. It's one of the most dramatic and gorgeous scenes I've ever witnessed—him, standing naked and flushed in the center of the blackened landscape, with great stone ribs curving up behind him and the orange mist of his dissipating fire mingling with the blue light from the ash-roses. I wish the palace painter could see what I'm seeing, and capture it forever. The dragon prince, powerful and helpless, the moment after rapture.

But this moment will never be memorialized for anyone else. It is mine alone. Mine to cherish.

He wavers again, and when I steady him, he opens his eyes and grins, with a self-deprecating chuckle.

"Come on, dragon," I say, patting his face. "Shift, and give me a ride back. And next time we have a private moment, I want your dragon tongue again."

His eyes light up. "Of course. Whatever you like."

When we reach the fortress, Kyreagan barely has time to dress himself again before Ashvelon and Thelise come to find us.

"It's done," Thelise says, with a weary smile. "I made Rahzien impervious. He can't harm himself or be harmed. Ash carved the spell in stone, so it will last your entire lifetime, Serylla. You won't have to fear death because of him."

"Wait." I grip her arm. "Not that I'm not grateful, but… am I understanding this correctly? You made our worst enemy unkillable?"

"To protect you," she says haughtily. "You're welcome."

"Fuck, Thelise."

"It was the only way!"

"Was it, though?" I wince. "What if Fortunix comes and saves him, carries him back to his kingdom?"

"Why would Fortunix do that? I should think he'd be happy that his dealings with the bastard are over."

"I don't know," I muse. "Kyreagan, what do you think?"

"I don't like it," Kyreagan says.

Thelise rolls her eyes. "Of course you don't, you big pessimistic grouch. But trust me—it was the best choice. Have I ever steered you wrong before? Don't answer that—let me rephrase—don't my plans always work out for the best?"

"For now," I say, and Kyreagan mutters, "That remains to be seen."

Thelise whirls to face Ashvelon, who's in human form, running a hand through his wavy blond hair. "Ash, my plans always work out wonderfully."

He clears his throat. "Is that a question, my darling?"

"It's a fucking statement."

"In that case, absolutely. You're always right."

"Like I said." She turns up her nose. "Now, let's go home. I need a drink."

"You and Serylla will ride on my back," Kyreagan says. "Ashvelon, you should remain here until I send someone to replace you. From now on, each dragon in the clan shall take a turn guarding this island for a few days at a time. We'll set up a rotation. That way, Rahzien can't devise a way to leave, and if anyone comes to fetch him, we'll know. And we can keep an eye on his health, provide him with supplies."

"Of course, my Prince," says Ashvelon.

Thelise looks unhappy, but she doesn't protest Kyreagan's arrangement. She kisses Ashvelon and whispers something in his ear that makes him flush bright red. After I retrieve my bag, she follows me to Kyreagan's side, and we mount one at a time, finding places to sit between his spikes.

With the extra weight, the flight to Ouroskelle is a struggle for Kyreagan. The air currents aren't as favorable, and I can hear the wind whistling through one of the holes in his wings. But he manages somehow, and at last we drop off Thelise in Ashvelon's cave. It's so dark and chilly that I urge Kyreagan to light a dyrestone for her, which he does.

"You'll be alright?" I ask her.

"Of course! I'm worn out from the spell, anyway. Won't take me long to fall asleep. Enjoy your night, you two."

She waves us off with a cheerful smile, but when we're aloft and I look back, I see her standing alone in the great cave, silhouetted against the orange glow of the dyre-stone, shoulders slumped and head bowed.

"You should send someone to take Ashvelon's place tomorrow," I tell Kyreagan. "She shouldn't be by herself too long."

"Hasn't she lived alone most of her life?" he asks.

"That's why she needs him."

He rumbles in agreement. "I'll send someone in the morning."

We glide through the night, a silent shadow between the mountains, and then Kyreagan pounds his huge wings in one last effort to lift us higher, higher, until we reach the ledge of his cave.

My heart nearly stops at the sight of a dragon curled in the cave entrance, but then the dragon lifts his slender neck and I recognize the flared ears and jaw spikes of Rothkuri.

He startles up, bowing his head. "My Prince! You've returned! Then the rescue was successful? Where are the others?"

"They're disposing of the remaining Vohrainian soldiers. Carrying them across the border and dropping them into their own land," Kyreagan says dryly. "Serylla and I had some other garbage to dispose of. But we're back now, and we're exhausted. It was a most unpleasant experience."

"The clan will want to hear all about it," says Rothkuri.

"Tomorrow." Kyreagan's voice is strained, weary. "I should speak with Varex before I sleep, though. Is he in his cave?"

Rothkuri averts his gaze. "I'm not sure. I'm sure he will be pleased to see you tomorrow. Let me wake Everelle, and we'll return to our cave."

He prowls over to the huge nest, where his plump mate lies on her side, one arm beneath her head. Nestled against her large, soft belly are two pale eggs. Our eggs are nestled in the grass not far away.

Rothkuri wakes Everelle by licking her rosy cheek, and she smiles up at him with such adoring joy that I want to squeal with happiness for the two of them. She tucks their eggs into a sling bag stuffed with grass, which she wears across the front of her body, then she mounts Rothkuri's neck.

"Such a clever idea, that bag," I tell her.

"I'll make you one, if you like."

"I would love that. Thank you for watching over our eggs."

"We are in your debt," says Kyreagan, bowing his head.

"No debt," Rothkuri replies. "We were pleased to do it."

Once they disappear into the night, Kyreagan and I move to the nest. He noses the eggs and I lay my palm against each of them.

And for a moment we don't speak. We are simply grateful.

Then Kyreagan lies down, circling the eggs with his body, and I lean against his belly. I nibble a little food from my bag and sip from my water flask, but I've been awake for far too long, and my eyes are drifting shut on their own. So I give in, and sink into sleep.

31

KYREAGAN

I dream that I'm flying over Ouroskelle in the dead of night, through starlit space. Holes begin to pop through my wings, one after another, until I'm soaring with only the skeletal frame and the tattered remnants of my wings. Then my body desiccates and I'm only a spirit, a ghostly serpent slithering upward through the icy air, with the ashes of my destroyed body falling around me. I was a warrior once, and now I am alone, undone, nothing but wind and ash.

The stars race across the black night, condensing together to form a long, crooked line of glowing white. A seam in the sky itself, a scar, a glaring flaw…

The glow intensifies, and then the sky splits with a resounding *crack*—

Crack. Crack.

I blink, still caught in the clinging darkness of the dream. The sun is high already, morning light streaming into the cave.

The cave, my cave, *our* cave… we're home. No longer trapped in that terrible palace. We defeated Rahzien, and he's been confined. Serylla is free—*Serylla*—

I lift my head, staring around frantically, searching for her because she isn't beside me, she's…

She's kneeling in the nest across from me, staring at the two eggs that lie between us. When she lifts her eyes to mine, my heart nearly stops. There's so much joy shining in her gaze.

"I let you sleep," she says softly, "but I'm glad you woke up just now. They've been moving around for a while, and look!" She points to the blue-marbled egg.

There's a long crack in the shell, with two more cracks branching out from the central one.

I can barely draw my next breath. My heart is pounding.

This is what I was made for. What I've been working toward. The result of the desperate, primal frenzy Serylla and I experienced together in this cave. She made this possible—the beautiful, precious woman who gave herself to me.

I can't speak any word but her name. "Serylla…"

"I know." She smiles, her blue eyes sparkling with tears.

The cracks in the blue egg spread a little farther, as if the hatchling inside is cautiously probing the limits of the shell, uncertain about coming out.

Then the purple egg shatters so suddenly that Serylla leaps back with a squeal.

In the center of the broken pieces of shell sits a plump lavender blob. It wriggles, then uncurls, revealing two sets of small horns, a ridged spine, and a thick, stubby tail. The hatchling has the tiny jaw spikes all infant dragons possess. As they reach maturity, males grow extra spikes, sharper and more defined. This hatchling has the broad, soft nose and the ridged fold around the neck that mark her as a young female—the gender she chose while inside the egg.

My daughter opens enormous violet eyes and looks straight at me. She's so tiny. So beautiful. So perfect.

"Fuck," I breathe.

"Don't curse in front of the babies," Serylla exclaims with a breathless laugh.

The tiny dragon whirls around with an eager speed that reminds me so much of Vylar my heart nearly bursts. She bounds into Serylla's lap and snuggles there, her damp little wings drooping and her gaze focused adoringly on Serylla's face.

And Serylla bursts into tears. She gathers the little dragon up in her arms, sobbing while the hatchling licks her face.

"Fuck," I say again, because I'm crying too, great steaming tears rolling off the end of my snout. "Sorry—I'll stop saying *fuck...*"

Serylla laughs through her tears, still cuddling our daughter. "She's so precious, Kyreagan! But her wings... are they alright?"

"They'll dry and expand soon," I assure her, lowering my nose to greet the hatchling.

"How does it work for dragons, with naming babies?" Serylla asks in a quavering voice. "Can we name them now? Or is there a ritual of some kind—"

Before I can reply, a big piece of shell pops up from the top of the blue egg. The piece of shell rises slowly, perched on tiny horns, until a pair of blue eyes peek over the jagged edge of the egg. The second hatchling surveys all of us warily before sinking back inside. The top piece of shell fits neatly back in place on the egg, and all is still.

I stare at the egg, then at Serylla. She covers her mouth with her hand, stifling a giggle. "I think we've been deemed insufficient as a family," she says.

"So it would seem." I peer at the blue egg and breathe on it lightly. It doesn't move.

The tiny girl dragon hops off Serylla's lap and stalks over to the blue egg. She chirps at it.

Nothing.

So she butts it hard with her little horns.

The egg rolls over and our second hatchling tumbles out. This one has pronounced brow ridges and a sharper snout, indicating his chosen gender as male.

He squalls indignantly at being dumped out of the egg, and he scrambles to get back inside. His sister circles him with rebuking chirps, and when he tries to pull the big piece of eggshell back over the hole and seal himself in, she grabs it in her tiny jaws and chomps it into fragments.

"Oh god." Serylla looks up at me, alarm and amusement in her gaze. "Are they fighting already?"

"They are." I lower my nose to our daughter and nudge her away from her brother. She tumbles over in a roly-poly ball of spotted lavender skin.

"No scales yet," comments Serylla.

"Those will grow in soon." I stare down at the girl hatchling, who has pounced on my forepaw and is now gnawing one of my claws with her stubby teeth. "See if you can coax him out, Serylla. His wings need air."

Serylla scoots over to the blue egg and begins speaking in low, soft tones. "We've been looking forward to meeting you, little one. Won't you come out and stretch those pretty wings? I promise it's safe. Your father and I won't let anything happen to you." She meets my eyes again, her gaze warm and reassuring. "We're in this together for good, he and I. We've been through so much to be with you, and we won't let you down, I swear."

She keeps talking for a long time, but our son remains in his egg past noon. With great trepidation, I leave my little family alone for a short time so I can check on the clan. It's a quick flight, less than an hour, and I'm tortured by panic the whole time. When I return, my heart floods with inexpressible relief at seeing Serylla, our daughter, and the blue egg still in the nest. It might be years before I can leave them alone for any length of time without fearing they'll be stolen from me.

"He still won't come out," Serylla says. "Is this normal?"

"I don't think so." I prowl over to the nest and nudge the egg a little.

"Of course nothing is 'normal' anymore," she muses. "We're certainly not a normal dragon family."

"No, we are not."

"Does it bother you?" she asks uncertainly. "That I'm not the big, beautiful dragon life-mate you were supposed to have?"

Before answering, I shift into my human form. I snatch a blanket to wrap around myself before climbing into the nest and crawling over to kiss Serylla's rosy mouth.

"You *are* the beautiful life-mate I was supposed to have," I murmur against her lips.

She clasps her hands behind my neck and pulls me in for a deeper kiss. And when we break apart, there he is. Our son, sitting on his hind legs with his forepaws together, surveying us gravely.

"Oh," Serylla whispers, as if she's afraid she might startle him. "He came out!"

The hatchling's brow ridges contract, and he prowls a little closer, cautiously, nostrils flaring. His sister starts to bound toward him in exuberant greeting, but I catch her in both hands and hold her back. She's a surprisingly strong little creature, and the spines along her back dig painfully against my chest, but lucky for me, neither the spines nor her claws are very sharp yet.

"We'll have to have lessons on how to behave around humans," I say.

At the deep sound of my voice, she stops thrashing and goes still. I begin to hum softly, and she relaxes in my arms.

I lift my gaze to Serylla, eager for her to see the effect of my voice on our daughter, but she's entirely enchanted, because the little blue dragon is crawling onto her lap. He's tentative about it, but after a moment he flops down and closes his eyes.

At first I think he has fallen asleep, but then he opens one eye just a crack to look at me, before shutting it again.

I chuckle, and the girl dragon chirps with delight.

"About feeding them," Serylla says, wrinkling her nose. "Didn't you tell me that dragons chew the food for their young and then—"

"I'll do that part," I assure her.

"Thank you."

"And as for naming them... there will be a formal presentation to the clan at some point, and a visit to the hot springs when they're three months old... but we can name them whatever you like, whenever you like." My voice trembles a little, fragile with emotion. "I want to thank you for this, Serylla."

"Ky." She shakes her head. "All of this, with you, with them—it's an adventure beyond what I dreamed of. I would have been bargained away, sold into an arranged marriage by my mother, trapped in some distant palace with people who didn't care about me. Instead I have a whole new family—the dragons, the girls—and I have these two adorable, squishable babies, and I have *you*. And you, just *you*, would be enough, without everything else."

I move closer to her, until we're side by side, because I need to feel her. I need to have the smooth skin of her arm against mine, to feel wisps of her hair against my shoulder. When she tips her face up, I kiss her tenderly on the forehead.

We sit there, she and I, with our arms and hearts full of the life we created together. The new generation. The promise that dragons will continue to exist in this world.

"They'll sleep soon," I tell Serylla. "Hatchlings spend most of their time sleeping or eating for the first few months."

"Oh thank goodness," she breathes. "I'm still so tired."

"So am I."

She strokes my hair with a sympathetic murmur. "Too tired to think of names?"

"Not at all. What did you have in mind?"

"I thought we could call this one Violet," she says. "It suits her coloring, and it sounds a little like Vylar."

I clear my throat, willing the tears not to rise. "Yes."

"Good. And him—I'd like to name him Callim. After the stable-boy who tried to help me escape, and lost his life. I know neither of them sound particularly dragon-like, so we can change them if you—"

"They are good names. Those are their names."

"Good." She glances at the lavender hatchling in my arms. "I think she's asleep."

"So she is." I ease Violet onto the grass and climb out of the nest. "I should get dressed."

"Clothes are an important part of being human." Serylla gives me a saucy wink. "And after you're dressed, dragon, I shall relax here while you prepare something for me. You'll find everything you need in that bag, hopefully intact. I wrapped it as well as I could."

"And what am I preparing for you, my Queen?" I ask.

Her smile widens. "A proper cup of tea."

32

SERYLLA

ONE MONTH LATER

I stand in the hallway outside the ballroom, waiting for Kyreagan. Instead of a skimpy white dress and a silver cage around my hips, I'm wearing a voluminous golden gown and delicate lace gloves. Parma, who recently opened a dress shop in a nearby town, returned just for tonight, as a special favor to me, to do my makeup and style my hair into a towering mass of golden curls, studded with sparkling pins. She seems happy, and I'm glad of it.

I'm wearing my favorite necklace, reclaimed from the palace treasury where Rahzien had stowed it. By Meridian's directive, most of the jewels and fine things in the palace will be given to the people now, but I'm being allowed to keep some of my possessions. Tomorrow my bed and a few chests of personal items will be transported by dragonflight to one of two new chambers Kyreagan has carved at the back of his cave. One of the rooms contains a small nest just the right size for the hatchlings, and the other room is for me and Kyreagan, so we can have some privacy when he's in human form. Odrash has promised to come over to Ouroskelle soon and install doors on both chambers.

Kyreagan's original nest remains in the main area of the cave, since he does most of his sleeping in dragon form. Most nights, he drapes himself on the nest and I curl against his warm belly. The hatchlings nestle in with us, calmed by the great, slow breathing of their powerful father. They usually beg me to sing them to sleep, and I always oblige. Sometimes I share songs I've learned over the years, and sometimes I craft new songs during the day, just to please my darlings.

Tonight, our children are with Rothkuri and Everelle and their little ones, while Kyreagan and I celebrate the confirmation of all members of Elekstan's new democratic government. Meridian was asked to be one of the regional representatives, but he declined the role. He's more interested in adventuring with Hinarax. They set off for their journey southward tomorrow. Now that Elekstan is at peace, I'm sure the two of them will find a new cause to champion together.

For my part, I'm looking forward to sharing a bed with Kyreagan after the gala—at least for a few hours. He's been in dragon form all day, saving up his time so he can attend the event with me and visit my room afterward.

And there he is, rounding the corner and striding toward me, looking perfectly at ease in a pair of tall, shiny black boots. He's wearing a suit of deep purple tonight, with a loose, silky black tie at his throat, and a black vest. His long hair is tied back, and he wears the silver crown I gave him.

There's a sinuous grace to his walk now, a feral elegance that makes me tingle with delight. I can't stop thinking about how much I'd like to seize him by that tie, shove him into an alcove, and—

"By the Bone-Builder, you look like you plan to devour me alive," he says with a half-smile. He scoops up my hand, bows, and kisses my fingertips.

"Stop it," I whisper. "Stop making me want to fuck you."

He grins, a flash of teeth that's so very *dragon* my breath catches. "What about you, in this?" He gestures to the extremely low neckline of my golden gown.

"Oh, this?" I exhale, then inhale dramatically so my breasts swell above the edge of the bodice.

His gaze intensifies. "Fuck... do that again."

I breathe deeply, and he steps forward, bending to nestle his face in my cleavage. My nipples go instantly hard, and a glowing heat swells in my pussy.

We're not alone. There are a few guards stationed along this hall, a cluster of guests near the end, and hired servers coming and going. Plus the doors to the ballroom stand open, offering a glimpse of the colorful crowd beyond. Anyone who glances this way will see a tall, handsome dragon shifter with his face buried in the former princess's chest.

"Kyreagan!" I hiss, smacking his shoulder with my fan. "For god's sake, behave yourself."

His forked tongue slips out, a wet caress over the mound of one breast. Then he straightens with a deep hum of satisfaction. "I'm ready now."

I give the ballroom doors a sidelong glance. "Maybe we could be a little late... We could go somewhere first, enjoy ourselves..."

"No. I have a surprise for you, and it can't wait." He offers me his arm awkwardly. He may have mastered walking and kissing ladies' hands, but not all the formalities come easily to him. It doesn't bother me one bit. In fact, I find it endearing.

I take his arm, and we enter the ballroom together. Excited voices greet us, full of joy and admiration. We're not the only saviors of the land, but Kyreagan's role and mine have been loudly proclaimed throughout Elekstan.

Not everyone was so forgiving, of course. Many in Elekstan still rightfully resent the dragons for the slaughter they wrought during the war. That's why Kyreagan and Hinarax are the only representatives of their race in attendance tonight. But Kyreagan and I have learned that talking will not change the minds of those who hate us for past wrongs. All we can do, from this point on, is to show them how we have changed, and let them make their own decisions.

The crowd here tonight is favorable to us. They recognize the sacrifices we made, the pain we endured for love, and the work we've done since the day we defeated Rahzien. They're friends and allies, so I smile widely and greet them warmly, individually. There are no more palace servants—only employees of the new Capital House, who will be retained to help run the palace in its altered capacity as a government building and a house of refuge for those displaced by the war.

Kyreagan tows me along through the crowd, barely letting me speak two sentences to everyone who craves my attention. I'm starting to get peeved about it when he draws us both to a halt, right in front of the tiered platform where the orchestra plays.

The musicians are all present, in their usual spots, smiling at me. I recognize most of them—one or two are missing. I hope it's because they fled the city, not because they've perished in the war and robbed this kingdom of their incredible talent.

Silence falls over the crowd as Kyreagan and I stand before the orchestra, as the guests gather around us, facing the players. The conductor waits with both hands folded over her baton.

Then Kyreagan nods. She turns to the musicians, lifting her baton, and they begin to play.

It takes me a moment to recognize the rich strains of melody, the slow thump of the beat, the swelling and soaring of the strings, and the liquid notes of the flute dancing through it all.

This is *my* music. One of my grandest compositions, the kind that should only be played with a full orchestra. One of the pieces I never had the courage to give to the palace orchestra for performance.

It's one of the symphonies the Vohrainians cleared out of my study. I thought it was gone forever.

Each musician plays with a passion that makes me want to cry, and the effect is astounding, exquisite—a stunning blend of melody, sounds that existed only in my mind brought into brilliant existence. I clutch Kyreagan's arm as the music rolls and thunders, crescendos into a dazzling euphoria of sound, and then softens again, trickling away into delicate notes.

It's over, and the room is perfectly silent. Enchanted, or horrified?

Then applause shatters the stillness, and I look up at Kyreagan with tear-filled eyes. I can't speak.

He pulls his arm from mine, only to take my face in both his hands and kiss me in front of them all. The guests cheer louder, roaring their approval, but the noise moves to the background of my mind, and everything I see and feel is Kyreagan. His long, warm fingers on my cheeks. The soft skin of his lips pressing against mine. The flick of his wet tongue into my mouth. The heat of his breath.

He eases out of the kiss and looks into my eyes, smiling.

"How did you find the music?" I gasp. "I thought it was all gone!"

"Two of the servants found it in the palace cellar. Most of it had been burned, and some of the notebooks had been stored near a leaking pipe and suffered water damage, but they were able to salvage a dozen pieces. We didn't tell you because I wanted this to be a surprise." His smile fades as he notices the tears slipping down my cheeks. "I hope it was a pleasant one."

"Very pleasant," I choke out, leaning against his chest while his arms fold around me. "I never thought I would have the chance to hear my music played aloud, like that. I was always too nervous to make it happen. If I'd known it would sound that beautiful, I'd have done it sooner."

"It's brilliant, Serylla." His thumb strokes my cheek.

I give him a tight hug and then pull back. "There's just a few tweaks I'd like to make to the sheet music—"

"Not now!" Meridian appears beside us, with Hinarax in tow. "Right now, it's time to dance, eat, and drink, because we fucking deserve it."

Much as I'd like to get my hands on the music and make the changes, I push the urge aside, because Meridian is right—we deserve this. I dance with him, and Hinarax, and Kyreagan, and my former bodyguard Norril, until my feet are sore and my heart is full. And then I snatch a bottle of wine from a tray, grab Kyreagan's hand, and lead him out of the ballroom, through the palace, to the suite that once was mine.

The moment the bedroom door closes, I kick off my shoes and start pulling pins out of my hair.

"I'm having you properly," I tell him. "Completely naked, in a bed, among clean sheets. Take off your goddamn clothes this instant."

"Yes, Your Majesty," he rumbles, in a voice so dragonesque that a tantalizing thrill dances through my stomach, right down to my clit.

In moments I'm in my bare skin, warm and soft and aching for him, and he comes to me in that sleek, tall body I love so much. The long, thick cock he once thought was "too small" swings heavily between his strong thighs, and I catch it in my hand, running my finger along the hot, silken length until he groans. I have a dragon helpless in my palm, prey to my lightest touch, and I love it.

Gently I pat the tip of his cock with one finger, and then I place that fingertip, wet with his arousal, on my clit. He watches me smooth his precum over that spot and tease myself with his wetness.

"I need you," is all he says, but it's a deep, hoarse, desperate plea straight from his soul. I can't help thinking of the mating heat, when he beat himself against the cave walls to keep himself from fucking me in dragon form. There's something wildly arousing about a need so raw and primal.

Taking his hand, I draw him toward the bed. I turn down the covers, exposing the smooth sheets.

"Come on." I climb onto the bed and beckon to him. "You'll like this, I promise."

He climbs into bed clumsily. He seems uncertain how to sit, and he keeps frowning at the pillows.

"I know you're used to spending your sleeping hours in dragon form," I say. "But this is how humans do it. Lie down." I push against his broad shoulders until he lies back on the bed. "God, Ky… relax. You're so tight everywhere." I smooth my palm over the hardened mounds of his abdominal muscles.

"That's because I'm about to come," he says raggedly. "You realize I haven't seen you fully naked since we went to the hot springs two weeks after our return to Ouroskelle. And the last time we fucked was four days ago, in the woods, while the little ones were off in the meadow, chasing that rabbit—"

"I remember." I blush, recalling how urgently we rutted against the tree, how fast I came for him. Just like our tryst in the portrait gallery.

Kyreagan's dark eyes are tormented, his black brows bent, his jaw hard as if he's in pain. I bite my lip to hide a smile as I slide my palm down his abdomen.

"Just the sight of me naked does this to you?" I ask softly.

"Serylla," he growls in warning.

I cup my breast with one hand, squeezing lightly, and he gives a shattered groan.

"Look at your big cock, dripping for me," I croon, tracing one finger up the side. His length bounces heavily, a compulsive jerk of need, and more precum emerges from the tiny slit of his cock head.

I lean forward and scoop up the glistening liquid with my tongue.

With a roar of reckless need, Kyreagan lunges up. Seizes me by the shoulders, flings me back onto the bed. He gropes my breasts until they're pink and peaked, while I gasp with hectic delight, and then he takes most of my right breast into his mouth. With a faint squeal I arch off the bed, blissfully stricken by the suction of his lips.

He releases my breast, and I whimper as the cool air hits its wet, swollen, sensitive surface. Kyreagan bathes my other nipple delicately with his tongue, teasing it mercilessly while his hand softly squeezes the fullness of the underside. I can't stop the shrill gasps I'm making, can't stop my hips from bucking upward, seeking him, craving friction and fullness.

He slides down my body, hands caressing my sides, his kisses searing the flat of my belly. Lower, until his lips whisper over my mound and down to my clit—almost kissing where I need him but not quite…

"Ky," I shriek breathlessly. "Ky, please!"

He growls low in his chest, scoops his arms under my thighs, gathers me close and plunges his face into my pussy.

"Ky," I gasp out. "Ky, Ky, yes… god, yes…"

Nuzzling deeper, he plays along my spasming slit with his cloven tongue. I'm going out of my mind— "Horns," I beg him. "I need your horns, Ky."

They appear in an instant, and I grip them both, anchoring myself while he savors me. I'm climbing to the brink—nearly about to crash into dizzying bliss, my eyes rolling back—

"I love you," he growls, right against my clit, and I break with a sharp scream, with a twisting, dazzling, mind-searing intensity I've never felt before, ever.

Kyreagan suckles me, soothes me, brings me down from the peak with the firm pressure of his mouth and slow swipes of his tongue.

I relinquish my grip on his horns and let my arms fall limply aside.

But he's not done with me.

"Turn over, Serylla," he commands. "Ass up."

"Would you..." I purse my lips, wondering what he'll think of my request— "Would you call me 'captive' again? And tell me wicked things, and be rough with me—"

I've barely finished speaking when he flips me over and crushes his whole long body against my backside, pressing me into the mattress. I tremble at the heat and force of him.

His lips graze my ear, hot breath warming my cheek as he speaks, low and menacing. "Little captive. No one can save you from me."

"No one," I breathe, delighted. Maybe something is wrong with me for liking this game, but I can only play it with him because I feel so completely safe, so wholly loved.

"I'm going to breed you, little one." Kyreagan whispers harshly against my cheek. "You feel my cock, right there? I'm going to enter you, and I'm going to fuck you, and I won't pull out when I come. I'm going to come inside you. Empty everything I have into that hot little womb. Do you understand? Do you feel me sliding in?"

"Yes," I gasp, a shudder of ecstasy trembling through my body as his cock pushes into my hole.

His weight shifts. "Lift that fucking ass, captive."

"Yes, dragon." I raise my rear, and he settles in behind me, shifting forward until he bottoms out in my pussy.

He fucks me loudly, sloppily, violently, and neither of us care about the wet, lecherous sounds we make. He comes after only a few thrusts, but he keeps pumping, half-hard, squeezing every bit of cum into my body, forcing me closer to a climax. I come a second time, my body helpless to his unrelenting rhythm. The second orgasm is a wave of twinkling light, washing upward from my clit through my whole body.

I go weak on the bed, gasping softly while he settles his weight on top of me. My eyes drift closed, every muscle assuaged and relaxed by the heaviness of him, the security of his presence.

My darling. My dragon.

"I love you," I breathe into the quiet, into the slow huff of his breath as he recovers from the exertion.

He kisses the curve of my ear, then the back of my shoulder. Eases off me, but leaves one arm slung over my back, his fingers brushing along the skin of my upper arm.

"I'm happier than I've ever been," I whisper.

His voice is low, soft. "I'm happier than I thought possible, after…"

"Yes," I murmur, rolling over to face him. "After what you lost. What we both suffered."

"It still hurts," he says quietly. "But less now."

I collect his hand and kiss each finger with all the tenderness in my soul. Then I sit up, draw the sheets and blankets over us, and curl against him, holding him close, listening to the beat of his wild, beautiful heart.

"This is so fucking comfortable," he whispers at last.

I giggle. "What did I tell you? Beds are amazing."

We have sex once more before he has to leave. It's a warm summer night, so he spends it out in the garden. From my window, I can see the black, spiked bulk of his dragon form sprawled across the lawn. The gardeners won't be happy about the way he's smushing the grass, but it's only for one night.

The next day I say a proper goodbye to as many people as I can manage to see. It's goodbye for now, not forever, but I'm not sure when I'll be able to return to the Capital for a visit. There's much to do on Ouroskelle. Thankfully, the poison in the Middenwold flocks has dissipated, so there's plenty of food for the dragons. And the new minister of agriculture has put forth a proposal for some of the farmers to clear extra pastureland and supply additional food for the dragons when they need it—at a fair price determined by a third party. I'm not sure how much treasure the dragons have in their "clan hoard," but it's apparently a significant sum.

On the way back to Ouroskelle, I cast a glance to my right, past Kyreagan's huge black wing, to where two other dragons are flying with my chests of clothes. Beyond them are two more dragons, holding ropes attached to a large net with my bed inside it. The mattress, pillows, and bedding have been wrapped tightly with cords so they won't be dislodged during the flight. It's comical to watch the dragons carrying it all, and I feel a little guilty that I'll have a fancy bed while the other women on the island have makeshift bed frames and thin mattresses stuffed with grass. But Kyreagan insisted, and as one of the Princes of Ouroskelle, his word is law.

Despite the twinge of guilt, secretly I'm thrilled that I'll have a comfortable place to sleep whenever I want it. The bed is so huge that the hatchlings can sleep in it too, once they reach the six-month mark and shift for the first time. Kyreagan has already started work on digging deeper into the rocky ledge of his cave, creating an inset area, a deep balcony of sorts, with a protective wall to keep our babies from tumbling off the cliff when they're in human form.

Kyreagan has been working so hard, clawing and blasting into the rock to create the extra rooms and the balcony. The little ones know better than to get in the way while he's working, but whenever he takes a break, they're under his wings and feet immediately, vying for his attention. I love the way he noses tenderly at them with his great dragon's snout, the way he tumbles them over gently with his paw while they giggle and snort tiny bursts of smoke. Violet has already started emitting sparks when she's excited.

I'm still so new to being a mother. Sometimes I have trouble grasping the fact that the two adorable, energetic balls of wings and claws and teeth belong to me—that they came from me. They're talking a little, though it's mostly limited phrases in Dragonish, with some Eventongue words mixed in, thanks to Everelle's supervision during their incubation. But they were left alone in the silence more often than is normal for hatchlings, since the clan was ill from the poison for days. Their speech is somewhat delayed.

"They've been through so much, your people," I say to Kyreagan as we fly.

"So have yours," he replies.

"After so much pain and grief, do you really think they can heal?"

A rumble of reassurance rolls through his body into mine. "If you and I can find healing, surely they can. New life will make it easier. Do you know if Saevel and Nirada's eggs have hatched yet?"

"I spoke with her before we left yesterday… they're still waiting. They're a little nervous about the one that's glowing."

"With good reason. I've never heard of such a thing."

"At least Saevel knows that his sister survived the Supreme Sorcerer's curse," I say. "When Nyreza is fully healed, she can return to Ouroskelle."

"She would be welcomed back as a miracle among dragons," Kyreagan answers. "But I'm not sure she's in any hurry to return. I'm afraid we did not always treat her fairly. I myself overlooked her on many occasions. And we avoided bringing her on hunts because her coloring was so—unusual. It scared off the prey."

"You'll have a chance to make it up to her," I assure him. "Ah, there it is! Ouroskelle. We're almost home."

33

KYREAGAN

When we arrive at our cave, we let the other dragons land first and set their cargo down inside, while Serylla and I circle the peak of the mountain. Once we move everything into place, I will fetch the hatchlings from Rothkuri and Everelle's cave, and we'll be together again, all four of us.

I once thought spawning hatchlings would be the height of my joy, but my love for the girl on my back surpasses what I could feel for any other living thing. Still, becoming the father of two such adorable, intriguing little creatures has been the second greatest happiness of my life.

As Serylla and I glide lazily in the sunlit sky, preparing to enter our cave, a black tempest streaks up from the valley, shooting past us, high into the arch of the heavens.

I'd know my brother's shape anywhere, no matter how fast he's flying.

A dark void orb pulses from Varex's jaws, rocketing upward before fizzling and imploding on itself. Immediately afterward, a shudder runs through my brother from nose to tail, and for a second, every one of his spikes and scales glow red and yellow along the edges, as if they've been dipped in lava. My blood chills at the sight.

"That was beautiful, and terrifying," says Serylla. "Is that normal for him?"

"No," I growl.

"Is he sick?"

"I'm not sure. He's been keeping his distance for weeks, and I've allowed it—but I'm done giving him space. He hasn't been himself since the Mordvorren."

With fierce, determined wingbeats, I climb higher. Serylla's legs tense and tighten around the base of my neck. She's used to being on my back, and she knows I'll catch her if she falls, but being this high up is still frightening for her.

"The air is too thin," she gasps. "Lower, Kyreagan."

"Of course." I dive down immediately, then roar for Varex's attention. His head swivels toward us, and reluctantly he begins to descend.

He and I land on the mountaintop, facing each other.

"You saw that," Varex mutters.

"Yes, what the fuck?"

"What he means to say," Serylla interjects sweetly, "is that he cares about you very much. We both do. And we're worried. If you're in some kind of trouble, you need to tell us. Please."

Varex chuffs softly. "Your concern is appreciated, brother—and little sister." He dips his head to Serylla. "As much as I hate to admit it, I think you're right. I can't handle this on my own any longer."

"Handle what?" Serylla asks.

"Speak your mind," I urge him. "Did the poison affect you differently? Are you ill?"

"Nothing like that." Varex's long tongue glides along his jaws, and then he says slowly, "As you know… I have void magic."

"We're all familiar with it," I say dryly, and Serylla kicks her heel against my shoulder.

Varex doesn't seem to notice. "I once told Vylar that it felt as if there was a great void *inside* me, and that I had to keep tight control of it if I didn't want it to swallow me whole. If it becomes too much for me, I can squeeze pieces off the void—encapsulate bubbles of it—"

"Your void orbs, yes." I frown, concerned by his tone. He has never opened up to me before about how his magic feels—the fact that it frightens him. "What are you saying?"

He eyes me warily. "You're going to yell at me when I tell you."

"Maybe. I'll yell louder if you make me wait for the answer."

"Very well." He grimaces. "You know the Mordvorren lasted a long time."

"I was there."

"Right. For some of us, the food supply dwindled painfully low. Jessiva and I ran out of food two days before the end. And I'd seen the amount the others had stocked in their caves. I knew we were all going to starve if the storm didn't stop. By the time it quit on its own, we might be too weak to hunt or forage. I was desperate to save us, and I had an idea—a stupid fucking idea, more stupid than I realized at the time, and now I don't know what's going to happen to me—"

"Varex," I say, as calmly as I can manage. "What did you do?"

Varex takes a deep breath.

Looks me right in the eyes.

"I swallowed the Mordvorren."

The next book in the Merciless Dragons series is *Storm of Blood and Shadow*, Varex and Jessiva's story. Future books will follow the adventures of the other dragons and their partners, some of whom you met in this book. I can't wait to share their love stories with you!

Sign up for my newsletter through my website to receive a freebie!

MORE BOOKS BY REBECCA F. KENNEY

The WICKED DARLINGS Fae retellings series
A Court of Sugar and Spice
A Court of Hearts and Hunger
A City of Emeralds and Envy
A Prison of Ink and Ice

A Hunt So Wild and Cruel
A Heart So Cold and Wicked

The DARK RULERS adult fantasy romance series
Bride to the Fiend Prince
Captive of the Pirate King
Prize of the Warlord
The Warlord's Treasure
Healer to the Ash King
Pawn of the Cruel Princess
Jailer to the Death God
Slayer of the Pirate Lord

The BELOVED VILLAINS series
The Sea Witch (Little Mermaid retelling with male Sea Witch)
The Maleficent Faerie (Sleeping Beauty retelling with male Maleficent)
The Nameless Trickster (Rumpelstiltskin retelling)

THE VAMPIRES WILL SAVE YOU trilogy
The Vampires Will Save You
The Chimera Will Claim You
The Monster Will Rescue You

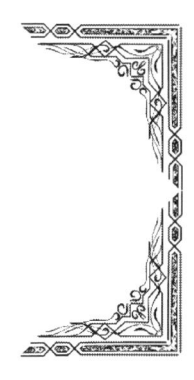

The MERCILESS DRAGONS series
Serpents of Sky and Flame
Warriors of Wind and Ash
Storm of Blood and Shadow

The GILDED MONSTERS classic retellings series
Beautiful Villain (retelling of "The Great Gatsby")
Charming Devil (retelling of "The Picture of Dorian Gray")
Ruthless Devotion (retelling of "Wuthering Heights")

The IMMORTAL WARRIORS adult fantasy romance series
Jack Frost
The Gargoyle Prince
Wendy, Darling (Neverland Fae Book 1)
Captain Pan (Neverland Fae Book 2)
Hades: God of the Dead
Apollo: God of the Sun

Related Content: *The Horseman of Sleepy Hollow*

The INFERNAL CONTESTS demon romance books
Interior Design for Demons
Infernal Trials for Humans

The SAVAGE SEAS books
The Teeth in the Tide
The Demons in the Deep

Made in the USA
Columbia, SC
29 September 2024

42565249R00211